CYBORG PROTECTORS

VOLUME 1

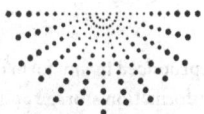

ALYSE ANDERS

Copyright © 2020 by Alyse Anders

ISBN: 978-1-7770382-7-4

All rights reserved.

No part of this book may be reproduced in any form or by any electronic or mechanical means, including information storage and retrieval systems, without written permission from the author, except for the use of brief quotations in a book review.

First edition: September 2020

Consumed by the Cyborg

ISBN: 978-0-9937319-9-0

Copyright January 2020, Alyse Anders

Mated to the Cyborg

ISBN: 978-1-7770382-0-5

Copyright February 2020, Alyse Anders

Saved by the Cyborg

ISBN: 978-1-7770382-1-2

Copyright March 2020, Alyse Anders

Healed by the Cyborg

ISBN: 978-1-7770382-2-9

Copyright April 2020, Alyse Anders

Cover Art by Amanda @ Razzle Dazzle Designs

CONTENTS

Consumed by the Cyborg   1

Mated to the Cyborg   95

Saved by the Cyborg   183

Healed by the Cyborg   277

Acknowledgments   369
About the Author   371

CONSUMED BY THE CYBORG

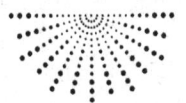

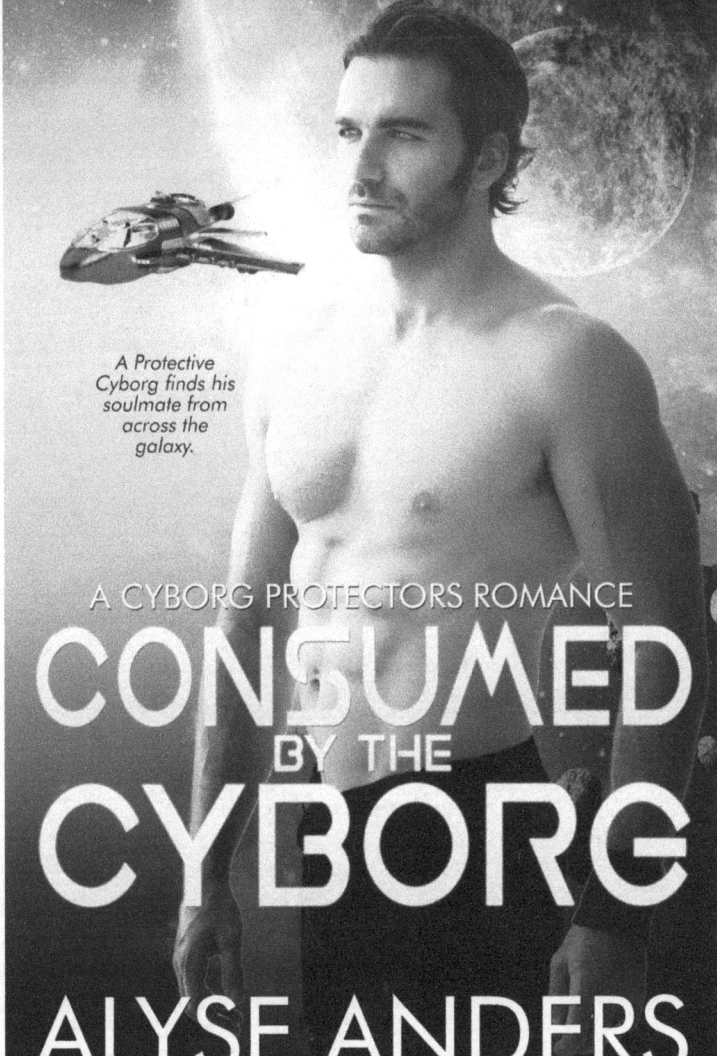

THE WAR

The Sholle came without warning.

Their planet long ago stripped of resources, they search the universe for resource-rich worlds to strip bare, leaving a wake of destruction behind them. Their ships attacked in waves – first small, then ever increasing, until their victims are worn down, unable to resist the inevitable.

Zarlan was the next planet in line, marked for attack.

The Grus sent an army forward to protect their people, evacuating their civilians up to Grus Prime, the space station that orbited Zarlan. The battle was hard-fought, but despite their will to win, the odds were stacked against them.

Until a lone scientist discovered a new weapon, their last hope to save their world.

A cybernetic matrix was implanted into the brain of the dead Grus soldiers – The Fallen – bringing them back to life. Their bodies were cybernetically enhanced, their emotions stripped, leaving them as the perfect killing machines.

The Sholle quickly became the hunted.

The Fallen destroyed the remnants of the Sholle, capturing who they could, killing those who wouldn't surrender, and driving the rest from their solar system. The Grus were the first race to lead such a defeat over the Sholle, their survival legendary. Joy reigned across Zarlan and Grus Prime, even as their world was left damaged. The deeper fracture came between the now split people – Grus and Fallen.

The Grus high council refused to let these walking weapons reintegrate back with the Grus, terrified of their abilities and enhancements. They were instead given Zarlan to live upon while the Grus would remain orbiting on Grus Prime. Regions were divided, leaders appointed, and the new state of the world was created.

And there they stayed; a people divided for fifty years. The Grus and the Fallen. The living and the re-born.

That was until a ship appeared far away in the night sky…

CHAPTER ONE

Rykal stepped onto the shuttle that would take him directly to the Grus Prime station, ignoring the warry looks of the flight crew. Cyborgs rarely left Zarlan, let alone spent any time on the station with the Grus. The memories of war and sacrifices made were too much for either side to handle with simple casual mingling. But Rykal was the designated leader of the cyborgs, and if something needed addressing with the Grus, then it fell on his shoulders to leave the planet and coordinate their handling with the Grus.

Normally.

Today he wasn't being summoned by Aidric, the high council, or anyone else. As far as he knew, no one was even aware he would be arriving. Rykal had a personal problem, something so minor that Aidric would no doubt call him foolish, but if Rykal didn't get a solution there was a strong possibility he'd murder someone. The last time a cyborg went on a killing spree, the Sholle were chased from the planet and out of their solar system.

The pilot and co-pilot kept casting glances back his way and talking softly between themselves. Rykal knew there wasn't an official request for his presence on file, but they still had to do as he told them if they wanted to stay on Aidric's good side. Rykal recognized the pilot, but the co-pilot was new, young, probably hadn't even been born until after the war. No doubt he thought of Rykal and all cyborgs as murderous ghouls who couldn't be trusted.

Boo.

"Please secure yourself, sir." The pilot called back, his voice somewhat familiar. "We'll be pushing off momentarily."

Rykal nodded but didn't move to comply. It didn't matter if he was injured; he couldn't be hurt from something as simple as a shuttle accident. His cybernetic implants and regenerative functions made that next to impossible.

Then again, maybe there *was* something wrong with them and that was why the itching in the back of his brain was getting worse. Why he'd become so fixated on a sector in space that he couldn't see beyond it. Aidric would know, and if he didn't, then at the very least, Rykal would make the bastard do *something* to fix it.

The lights on the shuttle dimmed, which made the transition from the planet's atmosphere to the inky blackness of space easier for the Grus pilots. The engines roared to life as the shuttle's fission reactors turned on, rattling the ship for a moment before the stabilizers kicked in and pushed them free of the ground and straight up into the sky. The shuttle pitched and rolled as the high atmospheric winds slammed against them, sending the small crew off to secure themselves with their restraints. The co-pilot cast a wary glance Rykal's way, no doubt terrified that he'd get hurt and the young man would be to blame.

These young Grus didn't understand the basics of what it was like to live life as an enhanced. His cybernetics evened everything out for him – no changes in vision, no equilibrium imbalances, no hunger, little pain. While he hadn't been manufactured in a factory, there were times when he felt that he might as well have been. The man he'd been before the war with the Sholle was dead, and all that remained was this odd mishmash of circuits and tendons, metal, and skin.

He might as well be dead.

"Business on the station, sir?"

Noting the young co-pilot's half-smiling face, Rykel quickly reviewed the facial recognition files in his memory storage. The man was barely old enough to have completed the training program, and there was no way he'd experienced any trauma beyond what he'd see in a simulator. Rykal had no patience for a child. He said nothing, merely leveled a hard glance on the co-pilot.

The young man's face paled as he snapped around to stare at the controls.

The pilot snorted and muttered a soft *that will teach you*.

Gods, Rykal felt like an asshole, but there was no point in pretending to be nice when he was the farthest thing *from* nice.

Not to mention the itch in the back of his brain was driving him insane.

Growling, he did his best to distract himself and instead focused on his internal systems. Maybe he needed to run another diagnostic, or he'd missed an errant bug that was causing him problems. Code flickered through his consciousness, the numbers and commands that ruled his life, that made him the leader of the Fallen. The thing that saved him, even as it killed who he'd once been.

Nothing was out of the ordinary. Every line of code was the same as it had been since he'd last run a diagnostic. And yet, that bloody itch was still there, growing more prominent the higher the shuttle rose into the sky. A rising crescendo of noise and vibrations, until the roar of the engines died away as the shuttle rattled and thrust its way past the planet's atmosphere and slipped into the silence of space.

Rykal got to his feet and stared out the port window. Normally, he'd look, taking stock of the large and small satellites that whizzed past, noting any changes in their velocity or trajectory. But not today. He leaned closer to the shuttle window and stared at the spot in space that had drawn his attention for days now. He'd used every method possible on the planet to see if there was something present, something that was coming closer to their home, but nothing was able to pierce through the planet's storm clouds on the southern hemisphere. That was where he knew something was coming, though Rykal couldn't figure out why or *how* he'd become aware of this presence.

There was a chance his cybernetics were finally malfunctioning, which would put Aidric in the uncomfortable position of having to permanently deactivate him.

Unfortunate for them both.

"We're only ten minutes from the station." The pilot didn't look at Rykal as he spoke, focused on the shuttle controls. "Who would you like me to inform of your arrival?"

"Commander Aidric." Rykal could hear the bitterness in his voice, but there was no way he could hide it. Not today.

The pilots shared a glance that Rykal ignored. He turned his attention from the spot in space and instead took stock of the station that he'd once called home, long ago. The bioluminescent black metal exterior panels gave the station a prophetic look and feel, giving the hull an imposing personality that Rykal despised. The energy shield was visible to him, the power cycling shimmer of the barrier registering as a blip in his field of vision. That had been one of the few things that had saved the station when the Sholle had attacked, sending their planet into chaos. Rykal watched as the pilots communicated with the station, and after receiving the code, the shield flickered off, allowing them to pass through harmlessly.

It had been months since he'd given in to the urge to return to the Grus Prime. Ghosts of his past lived there that often left him angry for the course his life had taken. He'd been a soldier working his way through his mandatory service, hoping one day to return back to Zarlan's surface where he could live out his days building a family. He'd been on Grus Prime when the Sholle attacked them, killing untold thousands of Grus before they'd been able to launch a counter attack.

These days Rykal would take shuttle trips into space to fly around the sector, ensuring that their enemies were well and truly gone. It was all he'd normally need to settle the restlessness that occasionally built inside him. But not this time.

Rykal took his seat once more, knowing once the shuttle landed, things would get out of hand until he was able to speak with Aidric alone. As he grew closer to the docking bay and his cybernetics slipped into range of the station's systems, his internal protocols kicked in.

Attention cyborg. You are now approaching Grus Prime Station. You are prohibited from connecting your systems to the central mainframe. Failure to comply will result in immediate decommission. Acknowledge.

He blinked slowly, waiting for the last possible moment to send his communication. *Affirmative.*

The station sent an additional flurry of commands, demands, and requirements, all of which Rykal let wash past him with little notice. The bloody itching was stronger up here and seemed to be growing more prominent with each passing moment he spent in space. Gods, what was wrong with him?

The station's tractor beam caught the shuttle and would take care of the rest of the landing procedures. The crew kept their faces forward, their hands resting on the command console. At least the young pilot knew that much. The shuttled lurched as the tractor beam dropped it to the floor with a thud. Rykal set his hands on his legs, palms up and opened, and waited.

The shuttle doors slid open, allowing a flurry of security personnel to rush inside, blasters up, and shouting commands at him. Rykal didn't move, said nothing, thankful that his cybernetics were able to regulate the volume, making their cries little more than a buzzing.

When the chaos subsided, he turned to look at the closest security officer. "Take me to, Aidric."

"On your feet." The Grus officer sneered at him and kept his blaster trained on Rykal's face.

Rykal wouldn't let the hate in the officer's voice demean or degrade him. With pride, he rose to his feet, taking pleasure in the way the six fully armed officers stepped backward to keep their distance from him. They *should* be afraid. Their weapons and body armor would do nothing to stop him if he wanted to tear them apart. Not that they needed to know that bit of information; it was best to leave them with their illusions.

"Thank you for the transportation." He nodded to the pilots but kept his tone cold.

The security officers surrounded him as they made their way through the station toward wherever Aidric had indicated their meeting would occur. It had been over a year since their last face-to-face conversation, and nearly a decade since they'd last spoken of anything beyond the security of his people or the station. They'd been close once, inseparable for many years, and Rykal couldn't help but wonder if Aidric wished things had turned out differently. A lot had happened between those days and now – fifty years, an entire war, and the bloody fallout later – most of which had destroyed their relationship.

The hallways that they were leading him down had been cleared of personnel, giving the station an abandoned feeling. The data washed over him as they moved, allowing him to store the details for later analysis. He recognized the corridor as one that led to a secure conference room where Aidric often held his interrogations. Not a complete surprise, even if the lack of trust was another barb added to the wounds Aidric had inflicted on him.

The door slid open as they approached, and the security

guards slipped to the side, with one stepping behind Rykal. "Inside – wait for the Commander."

It took every ounce of his resolve to not turn around and punch the man. Rykal did as he was told and waited for the doors to lock behind him before he allowed himself a moment to ease the tension from his muscles. The room was sterile – white walls, black stone flooring, and brown utility furniture – the least hospitable place on the station. Typical.

Rykal could have sat, but there was no point because he knew Aidric was watching him. The moment he'd let his guard down, the commander would arrive, and the mood would change yet again. No, it was better to keep his barriers firmly in place. Thankfully, it was only a matter of minutes before the doors slid open once again, revealing the square jaw grimace and steely-eyed glare of Aidric.

Aidric's green eyes narrowed on Rykal the moment he entered. His pale green skin starkly contrasted against his grey uniform, making him appear as detached from his surroundings as Rykal knew him to be. Aidric was almost as cold and reserved as any of the Fallen on the planet below; his intellect only rivaled by his need for control. Rykal didn't move, didn't back down from the silent posturing, the inevitable dance for dominance they'd undergo whenever they came face-to-face.

"Hello, big brother." Aidric had a way of announcing their familial relationship in such a way that it sounded like a curse rather than a greeting. Perhaps to him, it was.

Rykal waited for his cybernetics to regulate the rush of adrenaline that surged through his body. "Aidric." The door was closed, leaving the two of them with a bit of privacy. No doubt, they were being monitored somehow, but Rykal cared not. "I have a problem."

"What do you want me to do about it?"

Ah, there was the hate Rykal had come to love and cherish.

"There's a problem with my code. *Another* flaw. Seeing as you're the one who created it, you must be the one who can fix it."

Aidric lifted his chin and stared directly into Rykal's eyes. *That got his attention.* "What's wrong? Have you started attacking your kind? Running rampant and causing upheaval wherever you go?"

"No." Rage curled in his chest, threatening to explode out. "Why would you ask that?"

"It's happened with your kind before." Aidric held his gaze, making the statement even more painful. "A defect with no solution but to deactivate the cyborg."

"Would you enjoy doing that to me?" Rykal took a breath as his code frantically worked to keep his rage in check. "The Fallen are the same as you."

"You were once, but not any longer."

They stared at one another, and for a moment Rykal believed Aidric would send him back to the shuttle and the planet below without even listening to his problem, no longer caring about him or the fallout of what Aidric's meddling had transformed him into. Finally, Aidric pointed to the chair closest to him. "Sit, and I'll take a look at you."

Gods, things would never be the same between them ever again. He looked to where Aidric indicated, a spot close to the computer console where he'd be able to run diagnostics. It didn't matter that Rykal knew this was the best and only way to handle things, now faced with the prospect of having his insides inspected, it was difficult to make himself move. Checking the cybernetic code wasn't as simple as plugging a cable into the back of his head and running a scan; Rykal had to mentally release the security protocols that prevented someone from hacking into his command center and using him as a weapon without consent. He was allowing Aidric access to his very essence, exposing his thoughts and emotions.

"I promise to only review the relevant codebases. I have no

interest in meddling where I'm not wanted." Aidric's back was to him, but his tone had softened. "Sit."

The itching in the back of his mind was still there and getting stronger by the second. *Best to get this over with.* The sooner he had Aidric look at the code and figure out what was wrong, the sooner he'd be able to get back to his life on Zarlan. Opening the fastening of his shirt, he pulled it off, leaving his body exposed and cybernetics accessible.

He hated this, being reduced to little more than his component parts rather than the sum of who he was as a man. To the Grus, he wasn't anything other than a weapon; something to be feared or controlled. The other cyborgs who'd been condemned to spend the rest of their lives on the remnants of their planet either took pride in their augmentations, or were constantly comparing who was the strongest, smartest, most cunning. Those who thought they were lacking would continue to augment until there was little left of who they'd once been.

Aidric tilted Rykal's head forward and connected the data cable to the port in the back of Rykal's neck. "What are your symptoms?"

Gods, this was going to sound ridiculous. "I have a constant itching in the back of my brain."

Aidric paused briefly but continued connecting Rykal to the computer. "What else?"

The normal urge to argue evaporated as worry shifted up to the surface of his consciousness. "There's a sector in space that keeps drawing my attention. I don't know why, but I believe there's something approaching."

That got his brother's attention. "What sector?" Aidric moved to stand directly in front of him. "Why didn't you notify us of an impending attack?"

"Because I couldn't detect anything from the planet. As far as I could see on the scans, there's nothing there. But I know, *know* that there's something on approach. This means there's either something wrong with my programming or someone is coming through with stealth technology we haven't encountered before now."

"And you decided you were the problem and not the sensors." Aidric turned to the console and began his scans. "This will take a moment to sift through the code and check for irregularities."

The moment the station's computer connected with Rykal's matrix, the normal chatter of code that would buzz in his mind jumped to a roar.

Systems...analyzing...reviewed...testing...analyzing...

Emotional control check...analyzing...reviewed...testing...analyzing...

Error...analyzing...expected outcome...testing...analyzing...

THE ITCHING in his brain continued to grow. "Have you found anything?"

"No. But your code has expanded greatly since our last scan of your matrix." Aidric's eyes reviewed the lines of code nearly as quickly as they whizzed past Rykal's mind. "It's surprising how much data you've collected."

"It's been fifty years. Of course I've collected more data." It felt like a lifetime had passed since the day he'd faced the Sholle on the battlefield, giving everything of himself in order to keep his people safe.

Anger bubbled up as the code scans increased in speed, and the itching increased. He found it difficult to sit still, wanting nothing more than to get up, to move, to slam his fist into and through the closest wall to ease whatever this insanity was building up inside him.

"Rykal?"

Gods, all he'd ever wanted was to do his duty, find a mate to settle down with and live his life. He'd never wanted to be a leader, let alone a leader of a new, manufactured race of cyborgs. Why the hells had he been the one to die that day, to have his brother turn him into a machine that could kill with the slightest touch.

"Rykal, look at me."

He grabbed his head in his hands and squeezed hard, digging his nails into his flesh – didn't matter, he'd heal himself, nothing mattered – until he bled.

"Rykal!"

His gaze snapped over to look at Aidric, now squatted in front of him with his hand on a blaster. "There's something coming."

Aidric nodded. "I believe you." Those simple words were more than enough to ease the panic that threatened to blow past his emotional controls. Rykal relaxed further when Aidric shifted his hand from the blaster butt to his thigh, squeezing him gently. "I'm going to disconnect you, and we'll go to station control. We'll run the scans to see what's out there."

He nodded. "Okay."

"Don't move. This will hurt."

Rykal gasped as Aidric pulled the cable free from his port, turning his stomach and sending a jolt of pain through his normally tightly controlled body. "Gods!"

"This isn't right. All the scans came back normal." Aidric helped him to his feet, even handing him his shirt, though Rykal didn't put it back on. "We better get to control in case what your system is picking up on is a prelude to war."

This wasn't like the Sholle attacks. Rykal couldn't pinpoint their communications or determine their plan of attack from their data streams. It felt different, strange, and unsettling in a way that he'd only experienced once before; back when he'd first been cybernetically enhanced. He stumbled when he tried to take a step, forcing Aidric to grab his arm for support.

"Let go!" He jerked his arm, which sent him stumbling again.

Aidric stepped away immediately. "You fool. I was trying to help."

"I've had enough of your *help* to last a lifetime." He fought to regain control of his body. "Let's get to control so we can determine what in the hells is going on so I can return to my home."

The light in Aidric's eyes dimmed. "Fine. Follow me. If you try anything while you're outside of this room, you'll be shot, and disabled immediately."

I'd like to see you try. "Understood."

The moment they stepped out into the corridor, Aidric pressed the communicator badge on his wrist. "Station command alert. We're under attack."

CHAPTER TWO

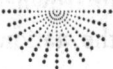

Every muscle in Rykal's body ached to do *something*, *anything* to relieve the rampant urge to run. Instead, he stood still, focused on an invisible point off in the distance of space that revealed nothing. "I'm telling you, that's where you can find whatever it is. The closer it gets, the more I'm aware of its presence."

Aidric glanced over at him from behind where the officer behind the system's scanners sat. "We've checked the sensors three times now, and they're showing nothing at all in that sector. And put your shirt on."

Rykal growled and continued to ignore the request.

Every time he came up to station Grus Prime, the urge to rebel, to fight the enemy was nearly more than he could handle. The war was long over, and he'd been reduced to little more than a diplomat, a living shuttle of information between the planet and the Grus on the rare occasions when that was necessary. But now another potential threat was here, and despite them not being able to detect it yet, Rykal knew it was something *fundamental*, something that would change their lives forever.

All he needed to do was convince the others that he wasn't losing his mind. "Check again."

Aidric stared at him hard but gave no outward indication of annoyance. "Scan sector three point seven again. Check all sectors surrounding it as well. If we don't see something this time, I authorize a shuttle to go out and visually scan the area."

"Yes, sir." The technician frowned at his screen but wasn't foolish enough to disobey the station commander. Aidric might be little more than an administrator now, but no one would forget what he'd done to stop the Sholle when they'd threatened their homes. Even those too young to have been alive during the war knew Aidric's name and his role in their success in driving off the enemy, and treated him with reverence.

The cold station air rolled across Rykal's skin, helping to ease the tension building inside him. It had the unfortunate side effect of putting his cybernetics on full display of the Grus on the command deck. Rykal knew what he looked like – a manufactured monstrosity – but he also knew each and every one of the Grus here would run behind him for protection if they fell under attack.

The temptation to connect himself to the station's mainframe and help enhance and direct the search was almost more than he could handle. It would mean his death, but it might just be worth it if that meant they were able to finally see what he knew to be out there in space. "Let me into the system."

The gasp of surprise around the command deck was loud enough to be heard over the alert claxon that continued to blast over the intercom. Aidric straightened and faced him. "Why would I ever allow that?"

"Because I know exactly where whatever it is, can be located. I can feel the spot in the back of my brain. You'll take forever to locate it this way, and by then it could be too late."

Aidric pulled his blaster from his holster but left it by his side. "Come here."

Rykal complied, ignoring everyone but his brother as he moved to stand beside the technician and the console. "It's the fastest way to ensure everyone is safe."

Despite how he and the other cyborgs were treated, the Grus were still theirs to protect and keep safe. Even when Aidric lifted the blaster to Rykal's head, he knew this was the only way.

Aidric's hand was steady, as was his gaze. "Do it. But if you attempt anything but direct the mainframe sensors to the location of the enemy, I'll shoot."

Rykal nodded even as he grabbed the data cable and slid it into the connection port in his arm. "I'd expect nothing less."

He slipped into the code and waited for the station's computer to recognize his presence.

Alert! Alert! Unauthorized cyborg infiltration!

"I NEED YOUR APPROVAL." His eyes were open, but he could no longer see Aidric or anyone else around him – only the code.

"Computer, cyborg entry authorized. Commander Aidric zero-beta-nine-nine."

Authorization granted.

DESPITE THE APPROVAL, Rykal could feel the computer's AI keeping a close eye on where he was going. *If you want to watch, fine with me. Keep up if you can.*

I plan to.

. . .

Ignoring the AI's presence as best he could, Rykal took control of the station's scanner. It only took him three microns to redirect the scanners to the exact spot in space he knew there was a presence. "Scanning."

Aidric's breath washed across his neck. "Have you found anything?"

"No, wait. *Yes*." The ship was so small it would have been easy for the most experienced technician to have missed. "Bringing it up on the screen now."

His vision returned to his eyes as he removed the data cable, and stepped away from the computer console so he could finally see the presence that had been driving him insane for days now. The ship was small – either a cargo ship or one that couldn't have contained more than the smallest of crews – and the slate grey ship's walls hardly stood out from the inky blackness of space.

"Sir, I don't recognize the ship's registration, markings, or even their metallic composition." The technician slid back into the spot that Rykal had abandoned. "If they're here to attack us, then they have technology we've never encountered. There doesn't appear to be any weapons or even shields. Of any kind." The young man looked back at Aidric, frowning. "I don't know how they survived out there."

Rykal did. Somehow, he knew that it was a ship out there, populated with people. They'd slipped through space like a ghost, hiding in the radiation blind spots as they silently sailed past. He could *feel* the people on board, was somehow aware of their presence as they drew closer.

He knew *she* was there.

"Bring them here." He turned to the technician. "Grab them in the tractor beam and pull them in. Now!"

His heartbeat had doubled, and the muscles in his chest tightened. She was out there all alone and unprotected, and he'd be fucking damned if he wouldn't get her and pull her to him, back to safety. He looked down at the crew, but none of them were jumping to do what he'd said. "Why aren't you getting them? They're in danger."

The technician looked over at Aidric, who still had his blaster drawn and pointed at Rykal. "Sir?"

No, he wasn't going to let some inexperienced Grus boy be the reason she got away from him, not when she was this close. With a low growl, he pushed the technician away, sending him crashing to the floor as he leaned over the computer console. "I'll do it myself." The high-pitched whine of the blaster charging up didn't force slow him down, but when Aidric pressed it to the back of Rykal's head, he stopped. "What are you doing?"

"Stopping you from breaking the law and potentially forcing me to kill you in front of my crew." Aidric leaned the blaster muzzle against his matrix hard. "Back away from the computer."

Rykal gripped the edge of the console, his cybernetically enhanced strength cracking and denting the metal. "You have to get them, bring them to safety."

"Who? Who's out there, and what do they want?"

"I..." He blinked rapidly, unable to clear his mind of the overwhelming rush of desire and need. "I don't know. But they're hurt. They need us, and I...we have to get them."

Aidric stepped in close, adding a hand to Rykal's shoulder. "Brother, you need to stand down. Let me take care of this, to find out who is out there and what they want. They could be using your cybernetics against you to grant them access to this station, to hurt us."

Gods, there was no way to explain it to Aidric without sounding as though his programming had been infected with some sort of virus. Rykal knew that she was out there, and she was *his*. If he had to back down so she could be brought to him, then so be it. He could be patient; he could wait until her arrival. He swallowed and nodded. "Hurry."

As quickly as the tension on the command deck started, everything eased when Aidric put his blaster back in its holster and Rykal took three paces away from the now damaged console. Rykal could only watch as Aidric snapped commands at his crew, sending them scurrying to action.

"Rey, send out a shuttle to get a short range tractor beam on that ship. Gunny, get a security detail down to the docking bay and ready to board the ship the moment its been cleared of the possibility of explosives and bioagents. Notify medical that we may have wounded people of unknown planetary origins coming their way. Move people!"

Watching Aidric snap to action, it was easy to see why they'd eventually won the war over the Sholle. With his strategic mind maneuvering the troops from above, while Rykal and his kind destroyed the Sholle on the planet, they'd become an unstoppable force.

It didn't take long for the shuttle to launch and reach the sector of Rykal's fixation. They watched as the tractor beam secured the ship and jerked it out of its original path and toward the station. Rather than feel relief knowing that she was finally on her way to him, panic set in. He could feel her emotions, practically hear her words in his head. No, no, no this wasn't right. Someone was after them and she had to try and keep her people safe. How had they been spotted? They had no weapons to protect themselves. *Oh Gods, would everyone be okay?*

Pain and fear cut through his head, making it nearly impossible to keep himself calm. Rykal pressed his hands to his ears, trying to block out the sudden onslaught of noise filling his head.

"What's wrong? Are you under attack?" Aidric again, closer once more. The concern in his voice was so unlike him. "Do I need to blow this ship up?"

"No!" Rykal roared, jumping to his feet and shoving Aidric away as he ran for the docking bay. He needed to be there when she arrived. She needed to know that he was here and that he'd keep her safe.

The station's claxon screamed once again as Rykal raced through the corridors. Security guards yelled at him, but he didn't hesitate, shoving them aside with the sweep of his arm, sending them crashing to the ground as he ran. Nothing mattered except her, getting to her and making sure she was safe.

The docking bay doors were sealed shut, but he could feel the ship approaching. It wouldn't be long now before she'd be here, and he could wrap her in his arms. No one would hurt her ever again. He was so focused on her that he nearly missed the sound of multiple blasters powering up behind him.

"Rykal?" Aidric's voice. "What are you doing?"

"The ship's almost here. She needs to know that no one's going to hurt her."

"You can't make that promise. We don't know who they are or what their intentions might be. I need to know that you're in control of yourself. That you're not going to go mad and kill us all if we need to take this crew into custody."

Gods, the mere thought of someone other than him touching her sent a wave of rage through his body. "No one go near her. She's mine."

Another chorus of blasters powering up. "I need to know that you're not going to hurt us." Aidric again, sounding far too condescending for his own good. "Are you going to hurt us?"

He'd never harmed a Grus before, and he wasn't about to start now. As long as they kept their distance from her, everything would be fine. "I need to know that she's okay."

"What's the ship's status?" Aidric called out to one of his subordinates, Rykal didn't know who.

"Sir, the ship has cleared the docking bay and is undergoing scans. Things appear to be as we'd assumed. The ship has no weapons, no shields, and no bioagents that we can detect. The technology is basic, fission reactor for faster than light speed, but that's all. I don't believe they have the capability to hide anything from us. There are twenty-eight life signs on board, female. All but one are in what appears to be cryogenic sleep."

All but one.

Her.

Rykal finally turned his face enough to see Aidric standing with a veritable army behind him. Given a moment, he could easily defeat them all. "Open the doors."

"Quarantine protocols haven't completed." Aidric stood in front of his forces, his own weapon still holstered. "Once the ship has passed, I'll allow you into the bay. But we will be coming with you, and you will do what I say."

He didn't bother to respond – to agree with the conditions would be a lie – and turned his attention back to the shuttle bay. She was there on the other side, scared yet determined to keep her people safe. Rykal didn't know how he knew these things, but he did, and he wasn't about to let some foolish Grus get in the way, or worse, hurt her.

If that happened, then they'd see what kind of weapon he could become.

Rykal reached out to the station's AI to check the status of the quarantine.

LET ME IN!

ANALYZING...UNKNOWN biology. Warning...unknown species.

I DON'T GIVE A FRAK. Open these Gods dammed doors!

ANALYZING...SPECIES threat level zero percent...biology compatible.

Commence decontamination.
Analyzing...decontamination complete.

THE DOORS BEGAN to open as Rykal raced through them the moment he was able to fit through. Ignoring the shouts from behind him, his focus was solely on the ship and the woman inside. He stopped short of where the ship's ramp would be and waited. *Come out. I know you're in there. Come out to me.*

But there was no movement at all. Rykal's frustration grew as much as the itching in his brain was quickly becoming a throbbing. The doors needed to open *right now* so he could get inside and get her. He paced back and forth in front of the door and he could feel her there, waiting confusedly for something to happen. There was no reason to be confused, there wasn't a reason not to come out so he could finally be with her.

Frack it.

He pushed past someone who'd come up beside him and grabbed the panel that protected what looked to be a manual release latch. The metal was old and damaged from radiation and space debris battering against it, making it next to impossible for it to open the way it should. Thankfully, Rykal was far from a normal person. Engaging his cybernetics, he grabbed the lever and braced his feet. With a roar he slammed the entirety of his weight and strength behind him and forced the metal to move. Inch by inch the stubborn metal squealed under the pressure as it moved open slowly.

"Rykal stand back and let us help." Aidric's voice.

He wasn't about to stop, not when he was so very close to the person he needed.

Another burst of adrenaline raced through him and with one additional mighty twist, the door unlocked, and the hiss of atmosphere raced out of the ship to fill the docking bay. The door chugged open revealing a woman standing on the other side, a breathing mask pressed to her mouth.

All he could see was the mass of red hair pulled back behind her ears, her skin pale and her limbs long. There was recognition in her eyes as she finally looked up into his; she knew they belonged together every bit as much as he did. Rykal took a step closer and lowered his chin while he held her gaze.

"Mine."

CHAPTER THREE

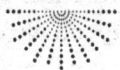

The last thing Lena thought she'd be faced with when she came out of cryo sleep was a half-naked cybernetic alien who clearly thought she'd understand what the hell he was saying. Not to mention the army of unenhanced aliens standing behind him, clearly uncertain if they should be pointing their blasters at her or at him.

Not the least bit reassuring.

And yet, there was something about him, the way he was looking at her that made her think that he wasn't a threat to her or to the passengers still resting. Well, not yet at least.

Their skin was a light tint of olive, dark hair and bodies that all appeared to be many inches taller and broader than the average human. Unlike her human passengers, there didn't appear to be a wide difference in their physical appearances. Muscular builds, steel gazes and all looking ready to fight.

She did have a weapon of her own, but she hadn't had time to run a scan to see if it was even going to work after the years of sitting around while they floated toward their destination. The details about what they were going to find once they got into the sector hadn't been particularly clear, but their other options would have been far more dangerous than setting the autopilot and going to sleep for a half century.

The ship should have woken her from cryo sleep weeks before they entered their destination sector. Instead, she'd only had hours to get her feet under her, shake the dullness from her mind and figure out what the hell was going on. The tractor beam and the station were completely unexpected, and more than a little overwhelming given her current state.

If these people turned out to be as bad as some of the factions back on Earth, there was little chance she'd be able to get her wards out of here safely.

The cyborg man was still talking.

Lena held up her hands, hoping everyone would realize that she wasn't the least bit of a threat to them. "Ah, hi there."

Everyone's gaze snapped to her.

Shit. That wasn't good, was it?

"I'm Captain Lena McGovern of the ship The Kraken. I guess we're refugees from a planet called Earth and I'm really hoping you folks are the friendly type. Because we're pretty much screwed if you're not."

The cyborg man cocked his head to the side, and his enhancements pulsed with some sort of light. Another man, someone who looked remarkably similar to the cyborg but lacking enhancements himself stepped up beside him. He held up his hand to her but turned to speak to the cyborg in a language Lena didn't understand.

She knew there was no chance that any alien race they'd come across would understand any of their Earth's languages, but she'd hoped that at the very least they'd have a someone on board who'd be able to decipher what she was saying given enough time. Earth standard was easy enough to learn and with any luck whatever they spoke would be something Carys, the closest person they had to a linguist, would be able to figure out. Unfortunately, she was still sound asleep in her cryo stasis tube back in the Kraken's loading bay.

Whatever conversation they were having was becoming far more heated than Lena anticipated. The cyborg rounded on the other man, which drew the attention of every person with a blaster. The cyborg was angry, shouting words as his cybernetics glowed brighter, occasionally pointing at her.

Yeah, this wasn't going how she would have liked. And without knowing exactly what was being said, she couldn't risk the lives of the people still sleeping on the Kraken. Her blaster was tucked neatly against her back in her rear holster. Whether these aliens didn't see her as a threat or not, she had no choice but to play things safe. Reaching behind her, she pulled her blaster in a somewhat rusty manner and trained it on the cyborg.

For exactly one second.

She then slid her attention to the alien and leveled her sight on him. The soft whine of her blaster powering up drew everyone's attention, even if no one moved to cover her. Which was odd given she was armed, but the others clearly didn't see her as more of a threat than the cyborg.

"Okay, let's try this again." She licked her lips as her gaze bounced between cyborg and alien, trying to determine who posed the larger threat. "My name Captain Lena McGovern of the ship The Kraken. We're refugees from Earth. I have twenty-eight women in cryo sleep on board. I won't allow anything bad to happen to them. Let us leave and we'll go about our business."

Her body was still very weak from having the cryogenic reversal process forced through faster than would have been ideal. She had to fight to keep her arms up and her blaster locked on the alien, not wanting anyone ot think that she'd be easily overpowered.

Despite the fact that a toddler would be able to take her down in that moment.

The alien shot a glance at her as he continued to speak to the cyborg. Did he understand what she was saying? No way Earth standard had made it this far out into space. And yet, he turned to her once more, holding up his empty hands. He nodded toward her weapon and mimicked putting it back in her holster. Then he brushed his hands in an odd manner, as though he was trying to show that he held nothing that would hurt her

"You're not a threat to us?" She wasn't sure, but it kind of made sense based on his actions.

He nodded.

"Wait, you understand what I'm saying?"

He nodded once more, even as the cyborg let out a low growl and took a step closer to her. Lena couldn't help but stare at him, feeling oddly unconcerned about his display of anger. There was no way she should trust him – shit, trust any of these people – but she knew deep down in her gut that there was no way he'd do anything to hurt them. Which was completely screwed up because her track record with a man of any species wasn't exactly stellar. If anything, she should be running far away from him. They hadn't come all this way to simply give in to another potential threat.

Even if he was kind of attractive.

Still, when he said something to the other alien who looked a bit like him, who in turn said something to everyone with the blasters that had them lower their weapons, Lena felt her gut instinct might be justified. The cyborg mimicked the hands up posture of the other alien, but there was something about the way he looked at her that sent a shiver through her body.

He took a step forward before pointing to his naked chest and then at her.

Okay Lena. Time to put into practice all those diplomacy courses they forced you to endure back at the academy.

"You want to come closer to me?"

He nodded before pointing to his ear and then to her.

"You understand what I'm saying even if I can't understand you."

He nodded, smiling softly, even as she retrained her blaster on his face. The other alien behind him said something and another person handed him a small device that he quickly handed over to the cyborg. Turning his attention back to her, he held it up to the place behind his ear and mimicked pressing it against his skin before pointing to his ear.

"So, if I let you inject me with something, you're telling me that I'm going to understand what it is you're saying?" He nodded again and took another step closer.

Yeah, this wasn't exactly the best idea she could be presented with, but she didn't have many other options. The chances of her getting the door shut and getting the ship out of this docking bay while somehow avoiding their tractor beam was firmly fixed somewhere between *slim* and *none*. It could be poison, or a tracking device, and if Carys was awake she'd be informing her that this was a horrible idea. And yet, they could have killed her several times over by now if that's what they'd wanted. She also got the distinct impression that their technology was far superior to what she'd managed to cobble together before they'd fled Earth.

Unknown injection it was.

Lena held up her blaster as a sign of submission before tucking it back into her rear holster. "I'm trusting that you're not going to do something to hurt me here." While she was willing to put her own life at risk, she wasn't going to do anything that would jeopardize her passengers. "Let me come down."

The aliens all moved back, but the cyborg did not. He held her gaze as she jumped to the floor, his crystal blue eyes monitoring her every move. What no one seemed to expect was her ship's response to her leaving the safety of its hold. As she straightened from jumping down, the inner emergency door behind her closed and locked with a slam that echoed in the docking bay. Those blasters were up and on her once again, with the lead alien looking more than a little annoyed.

"What? I must keep my people safe. Besides, he brute forced his way in there once, I'm sure he could do it again." Lena was surprised that the safety mechanism had worked given what the cyborg here had done to it.

Be thankful for small blessings.

And now for the real test. "So you're going to press that thing to my neck and then I'm going to understand what you're saying. And nothing else is going to happen to me?"

He nodded before shrugging.

"Very reassuring." She let out a small huff and turned her head so he could better see behind her ear. "Have at me."

He didn't move at first, which made Lena feel awkward and vulnerable. That was until he *did* move, and she realized exactly how large his body was. Heat seemed to radiate from him to the point it was nearly overwhelming. When he reached out to move her hair from her neck, Lena shivered once again, surprised at how intimate that simple act was. Shit, it really had been far too long since she'd spent any time with a man, let alone someone who treated her this tenderly.

When he pressed the device to her neck the bite of the injection had her yelp and attempt to pull away. His hand gripped her shoulder and held her still, keeping her in place as whatever it was flowed from the device directly into her brain.

That's when the pain started. The sudden throb of a headache morphed into a full-blown migraine in seconds, as Lena reached up and gripped her head. "Fuck!"

He didn't let go, and she had no choice but to use his strength to help keep her upright as her brain was attacked. It took her a moment to realize that he was speaking to her, saying words that she didn't understand but in such a way that she couldn't help but be comforted. There was something about his tone, possessive but reassuring, that helped her relax.

"*Sa reh crencha, te letta. Met kama sat el sana* like that. *Letta te* your body. Yes, like that. The nanobots are *reh kama* your brain. It won't be much longer before you start to understand us."

Lena blinked rapidly trying to clear the sudden blurriness from her vision and shake the weird ringing from her ears. Nearly as sudden as everything began, she was able to look up into the cyborg's eyes and realize that she now understood exactly what he was saying. "Whoa."

He nodded. "You understand me now. Good. My name is Rykal. I'm the leader of the Fallen, cyborg people who inhabit Zarlan, the planet below this space station. These people are the Grus and you are now mine."

"Oh good, that's good to..." She shook her head. "I think there's a problem with those nanobots. I thought you said that I was yours?"

The other alien stepped closer. "I'm Aidric, commander of Grus Prime, and liaison between the Fallen and the Grus. Rykal you need to step away from the woman now. We need to take her to medical to ensure her and her people don't carry any diseases that could infect us, or something we're unable to contain."

The next few moments happened so unbelievably fast that Lena wasn't entirely sure the exact order of events. One moment she was standing looking at the cyborg – Rykal – trying to figure out what they'd done to him. Then the next he'd picked her up in his arms, threw her over his shoulder, and ran from the docking bay as he dodged blaster fire.

"What the fuck! Let me go!"

He didn't respond, leaving her watching Aidric and the remaining Grus scrambling to follow them before a door slid shut behind, blocking her view of their pursuers. Rykal's grip on her was vice-like, making it impossible for her to break free. She tried to reach up and grab her blaster, but she couldn't quite reach. Escape seemed to be impossible, nor did she know where she was or their intended destination. The twists and turns of the station became difficult for her to keep track of, especially with her head bouncing upside down.

"Let me go, please!"

"Stop!" He tightened his grip on her. "We're nearly there."

The *there* turned out to be an escape pod that was barely large enough for one cyborg, let alone both of them. But like everything in the last few minutes, he didn't give her a chance to protest, dropping her inside before following and shutting the door. He didn't reach out to type any commands, instead closing his eyes. "The station's AI won't allow me to take a shuttle due to safety protocols, but there are no such restrictions on the escape pods."

"Where are we going?"

He opened his eyes and lowered his face so his lips where only a few inches from hers. "I told you, you're mine. I'm taking you home."

Lena should be shaking with panic, fear, anger, just about anything than the rush of lust that suddenly heated her groin and made her nipples hard. "Home?"

"The planet." He cupped her face with is large hand, rubbing his thumb across her lips. "I will keep you safe there."

Safe? That was a state of being that Lena hadn't experienced in years. "Where I'm from, nothing comes without a price."

Rykal frowned and she was able to see that the crystal blue of his eyes was a result of cybernetic enhancements. "There is no cost. I have no need of currency."

"That's not what I meant." She couldn't look away from his mouth, nor could she shake the urge to lean up and kiss him.

Shit, this wasn't like her at all; while she'd had sex in the past with the occasional partner, not once had she experienced this all-encompassing desire to be with a man she'd only just met –

and met not under the best of circumstances. Everything about him drew her in – his smell, the heat from his body, the feel of his too hard muscles beneath her hands. With Rykal she knew he'd keep her safe, even if he demanded she give him everything.

Rykal lowered his head until it was nearly impossible for Lena to keep her eyes open. "I want to taste you."

If his people had any concept of consent when it came to sex, he didn't seem to show it. He leaned in and captured her mouth with his, his tongue thrusting against hers as he reached up and cupped her breast with his hand.

Shit, I totally consent if that's how he kisses. Lena moaned, not sure if she wanted to back away or press hard against him. Rykal pinched her nipple as he maneuvered his knee between her legs, the shift making her form-fitting space suit pull hard across her swelling clit. She gasped as the pressure increased and he continued to suck and lick at her mouth, only to shift those kisses along the side of her neck down to the spot just above where her space suit started.

"I want you naked. I want to mark you as my own." He nipped at the exposed skin hard enough to pull a gasp from her.

"I…" But the rest of her thought fled her mind as the escape pod shuddered violently, sending her stumbling. "What the hell?"

Rykal reached over and pressed a few buttons on the pod's control panel. "We're entering the planet's atmosphere. Right through a stormfront."

Fuck. "That doesn't sound good."

"There's a strong possibility it might tear the pod apart."

Lena's heartbeat surged once more. *"What?* No!"

Another violent shudder had her slammed back against the wall. Rykal wrapped his body around hers, the evidence of his arousal still there and now pressed against her hip. "If we die, at least it will be together."

"Dying? I'm not planning on dying."

The escape pod dropped fast as the running lights blinked out. Rykal chuckled. "I'm not either. Hold on."

Lena did and for once in her life, said a prayer to the universe that she'd get out of this alive.

Mostly so she could kill Rykal.

CHAPTER FOUR

The impact could have been a lot worse than it turned out to be. Rykal had been able to link his mind with the escape pod controls and took control of the navigation system, steering them to land in the ocean. He managed to bounce them across the water with his nanosecond changes to the thrusters, like a skipping stone until they lost enough velocity to come to a stop. This made their landing far safer than their original trajectory, with a touchdown location in the western desert. Both locations were far away from Cimacha, the main city where his kind had made their home, which meant they'd need to make their way to the closest observation post and contact someone to come rescue them.

This would give him time to be with Lena, to make her understand that she was now his and he was hers. He could feel the confusion of her thoughts, the mix of anger, fear and lust that comprised her current emotional state. She was still recovering from having been in cryogenic sleep for he didn't know how long, which meant she was still weaker than she would normally be. She'd quickly find her strength once more, and he'd be able to show her how good he could make things for her on Zarlan. It would only be a matter of time before she'd come to accept her new reality and the new life he'd be able to offer her.

Aidric would no doubt try to stop him, unwilling to understand that Rykal and his people deserved happiness after all they'd sacrificed for their planet. He'd make his brother recognize that all of the Fallen needed to have something in their lives that went beyond waiting for the next fight, or keeping their enemies safely locked up in the prison at the southern pole. If Aidric didn't, Rykal knew he wouldn't be able to stop the uprising of the Fallen against the Grus; a battle that would benefit no one.

Lena had lost consciousness when the escape pod hit the upper atmosphere, requiring him to keep her secure while they plummeted down. It was disconcerting being able to feel her slip away, knowing that this tangle of emotions and impressions was coming from her. How he'd become connected with a woman who wasn't of his kind and who's home planet he'd never heard of was a mystery he'd solve at a later time.

The shuttle pitched sharply to the side, as the computer alarm sounded. "Warning. Escape pod buoyancy controls damaged. Submersion imminent. Warning."

Frak.

"Lena? You must wake up." He caressed the side of her face, but there was no sign of her returning consciousness. "Lena?"

The pod pitched and bobbed as the waves sloshed over the top of them. Rykal knew it would only be a matter of time before they'd start to sink below the surface. He needed to get Lena out of the pod and to the shore quickly.

The escape hatch hissed open once he sent the release protocol with his mind, giving him the extra space he needed to climb out. With effort, he reached down and gently pulled Lena's unconscious body up and over his shoulder as the buoyancy of the pod sunk dangerously low. Lena moaned and he could feel her start to wake up. He dropped to a squat and shifted her so she was now in his arms. Her lips parted and she let out a soft sigh when he leaned in and kissed her forehead. "Wake up."

She opened her eyes, blinking rapidly before squinting. "You didn't kill me."

"I did not. You're safe and I need you to be with me so we can swim to shore."

"Swim?" She pushed away from him and looked around. "That's a lot of water."

"We're not far from land, which is good because our pod is sinking." As if on cue, the escape pod bobbed lower as a wave slashed over them. "We need to swim to shore and we can get help from there."

"Right. Yeah, that seems like a good idea." She bit down on her bottom lip. "We do have a small problem in that I don't know how to swim."

Rykal nodded. "I'll carry you then."

"I'd always wanted to learn how, but most of the water on Earth isn't exactly safe for us to submerge our bodies in. Not since the wars."

As much as he wanted to learn all he could about her and her people, they didn't have time to linger. "Jump on my back and don't let go. I'll get us to shore." He could see that she wasn't exactly certain what to do, so he turned around and squatted. "Up."

"I'm not a child." She leaned forward and pressed her body hard against his before wrapping her arms around his neck. "Is this okay, or am I hurting you?"

"Hold on." He stood, pleasantly pleased with the squeal of surprise that erupted from her and jumped into the ocean.

Water covered his face and head, as Lena's hands dug into his throat hard. With a few kicks he got them to the surface where she sucked in a huge gasp of air. "Asshole."

He then took a breath, put his face in the water and began to swim as quickly as he could to shore. He needed to slow his oxygen exchange conversion down to nearly nothing so he could keep his head beneath the surface and make it easier for Lena to stay above water. The temperature was cold, and he could feel her shivering as he cut through the waves. After several long minutes, he finally made it to shallow water and they were able to walk the rest of the way to shore, where Lena fell in a heap on the hard sand.

"How are you not exhausted? Or dead because I didn't see you take a single breath." Her breath came out in gasps as she shivered hard. "Shit, you don't even have a shirt on. Aren't you freezing?"

"My cybernetics regulate my body and effect any necessary repairs to my biological systems."

She nodded. "I'd assumed you were a cyborg, or at least an enhanced version of your people. How much of you is artificial?"

Her space suit was dripping wet and her red hair plastered against her face as wet rivulets of water trickled down her neck. He ran a weather scan, noting that the temperature would drop within the next hour. There was also a stormfront off to the west that would cause them harm if they didn't seek shelter quickly.

"A stormfront is approaching. We need to get to the communications outpost before that hits."

She frowned. "Are you ignoring my question?"

"No. I will answer it and everything else once we've reached shelter." Not waiting for her to respond, he reached down and pulled her up. "Can you walk?"

"Stop that. I'm perfectly capable." She yanked her arm away and glared at him. "I don't know why you think you're in control of me, but you're not. I didn't ask to have my ship pulled into your space station, nor did I ask for you to kidnap me and bring me down to this planet. I need to get back to my passengers to make sure they're safe."

"Aidric will ensure no harm comes to your people. They will be safe and looked after." His life was the one that might be in jeopardy. "You can express your displeasure with me as we walk toward that outpost in the distance. If we move quickly, we should get there just ahead of the storm."

Lena threw her hands up in the air, but turned and marched in the direction he'd indicated. While she might be a stubborn woman, she certainly wasn't foolish; something Rykal appreciated.

They walked in silence, even though he was able to feel her mixed emotions bleeding off her. Confusion and anger would shift to concern and back again with every few passing minutes. What he couldn't detect was the arousal and attraction toward himself that had been there when they'd first entered the escape pod. He wanted those feelings to return, wanted to have the warmth they generated back in her mind so they washed over him and eased the coldness that had long existed inside his core.

He wanted to feel her naked body against his, to understand what made her feel pleasure and pain, what made her emotions sing with joy. He wanted to mark and consume her so no one else ever came near her and tried to take her from him.

Rykal wanted Lena forever.

But even with the oppressive need for her spiking inside him, his underlying safety protocols had snapped into place. Survival took precedent; getting her to shelter where nothing and no one would be able to get to her was paramount. Then and only then would he let his guard down and give in to his baser desires.

The wind was blowing hard from the south, which sent Lena's hair whipping around her face like a firebrand. She'd wrapped her arms around her chest, and was still visibly shaking. "How much longer before we get to this place?"

"Another twenty minutes at this pace."

She began to walk faster. "I hope there are blankets and a

heater. I'm not sure what kind of diseases your people have on this planet, but the last thing I want to get is a cold after having been stuck in cryo sleep for over half a century."

"I promise you there are no airborne bacteria you should be concerned with. The Sholle obliterated nearly all lifeforms on the planet when they attacked us."

"The Sholle?" She shook her head. "I'm going to hold you to the history lesson once we're safe."

It didn't take long for the wind to get so strong it became impossible for them to converse at all. Lena struggled to maintain her pace, and Rykal had to help keep her moving forward. The outpost was close enough now that he was able to connect his cyber link to the computer, turn on the heat, and send out a distress beacon. His second in command Darrick would no doubt be the first one to pickup the signal and send a shuttle the moment he could. The timing would most likely be delayed due to the storms, so they would be stuck together in the shelter for some time.

"How much farther?" Lena's words were consumed by the roaring winds.

Rykal lowered his face and pressed his mouth to her ear. "A hundred paces."

He felt her nod, even as her legs began to buckle under the strain. Being this close to her made it easy for him to pick up on her mood, to feel the waves of determination flowing from her in the face of adversity. This woman had more focus than most of the Grus he'd fought with during the war; she had a sense of purpose that was normally born out of strife. Wrapping his arm around her waist, he pulled her the last few paces to the shelter, where they waited for the system to scan them before opening the doors to safety.

The moment the doors slid closed and the screaming wind was locked out behind them, Rykal released Lena and let her move away from him. Her relief was obvious on her face, but so was the realization that they were now completely alone and stuck in a building together.

"This is cozy." She looked around the room, her gaze not resting on any one thing for very long. "Will your people be able to find us?"

"I've already sent out an alert. The moment they can send a shuttle through the storm they will."

She stopped moving, and slowly turned to face him. Her red hair had come completely unbound and hung in tangled waves across her shoulders and down her back. Her cheeks were flushed red and her bright hazel eyes relayed an intelligence he wanted to get to know. Then she shivered, a full body tremble that launched him into action.

"You're wet." He crossed the room in two paces and began to pull at her space suit. "You need to take this off so we can dry you and get you warm."

"I'm fine." She stepped away, shivering again. "I just need a blanket or something."

The urge to protect her, to warm her with his own body was nearly too much for his controls to handle. Nothing in the world was as important to him as her health and safety. Nothing more valuable than knowing she was happy and cared for.

He wanted to strip her naked and worship every inch of her body. To fit thoughts of her into the empty places in his mind knowing they would perfectly fill the gaps. His body surged with lust, the need to taste and touch her, to consume everything about her until the universe knew that she was his and no one else's.

"Rykal?"

Looking up at her, he realized that he'd lost awareness of what was going on around him. His body shook nearly as much as hers, though the reasons for his reaction were different. "You need to take the clothing off and get warm. You *need* to."

She cocked her head to the side and nodded. "You're worried that something is going to happen to me?"

Was that what this was? Worry? He'd never had concern for anyone since his transformation into a cyborg. Possibly not even before. "You need to get warm and stay safe."

"Okay." She turned her back to him and slowly began to peel the wet layers from her body, letting them fall to the floor with a sucking-slop. "Can you get me the blanket that you mentioned?"

Yes. The blanket will help her, will get her warm.

He knew where it was, knew where everything was in these shelters. They were standard buildings designed to offer protection to any cyborg who might require aid. The Grus never came to Zarlan's surface any longer, but his people still ensured the shelters had the items necessary for the Grus as well.

Some habits were hard to break.

Rykal grabbed the blanket as well as some food rations and brought them back to a now naked and shivering Lena. "Thank you." She took the blanket and covered her body easily due to its size.

Still, he knew it would take more. He wanted more.

Lena's face was still flushed, but he could tell from the bio readings coming off her that it was no longer from the wind; this was an internal reaction. She licked her lips. "Do you need to dry off too?"

The cold and wet would do nothing to his biological systems; there was little that could hurt him outside of a blaster shot to the head or sinking to the bottom of the ocean. But his body betrayed him – the desire to be naked and press his flesh against hers was overwhelming. He said nothing, but with purposeful motions, pulled his wet clothing off until he stood naked before her.

"They'll dry faster this way." Yet he made no move to pick the clothing up and deposit them someplace where that would happen.

His cock was hard and stood like a brand between them. His *rondella*, the sensitive patch of flesh on his inner thigh that helped prepare his body to mate, filled with blood in the first time since his rebirth. Rykal didn't know if they were sexually compatible – sex wasn't a thing he'd even considered since his cybernetic conversion – but based on the look she was giving him they must not be too different in that regard.

He reached down and grabbed his cock in his hand, giving it a stroke. "I want to mate with you."

She shivered again. "I can see that."

Rykal took a step closer. "You're mine. I knew you were out there in space; I could feel your presence. You're meant for me and I you."

Lena's eyes widened. "I…shit. I've just fled a planet where women aren't exactly respected for their independence. I've been in cryo sleep for over half a century, woke up to find my ship captured by an alien tractor beam, and then kidnapped by a cyborg. I'm not exactly sure what's going on here."

Her gaze moved from his cock to the glowing cybernetic implants that had been inserted into his body. He stepped closer, knowing she wanted to touch them but was too afraid to ask. "They don't hurt."

"That's amazing. We have cybernetic enhanced people on Earth, but it's not as sophisticated as these." Her fingers slid out from beneath the blanket and she traced a path around where the circuitry met skin. "They're warm."

He could feel that her fingers were still cold, the circulation not fully reaching her extremities. "They can warm you."

The look in her eyes changed from curiosity to desire. "How is it possible that we're from different planets light years away and physically compatible?"

"I've given everything to my people, it's only fair that the universe has given me something in return." What little restraint he had remaining was about to snap. "I'm going to claim you now. I'm going to make you mine."

She hesitated for a moment, before flattening her hand on his naked chest. "Yes."

Rykal took her head between his hands and kissed her.

CHAPTER FIVE

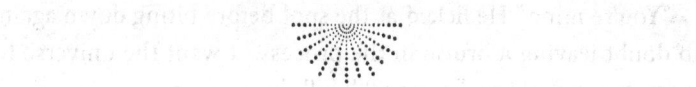

The moment Rykal's mouth claimed hers, Lena knew she was done for. She didn't understand the how's or why's of what this thing between them was, but she knew this was now inevitable. Her body was primed in a way she hadn't felt in ages before leaving Earth; her pussy wet and her nipples hard. She wanted to feel his long, thick cock slide into her body just to see the heights of pleasure he'd be able to take her to.

Kissing her the way he was, holding her face with such reverence and desire, she knew their lovemaking would be nothing short of explosive.

She wanted him now.

Lena let the blanket fall to the floor and stepped against Rykal's large frame. His cock was trapped between their bodies, hard and leaking from his need, a promise of the joy that was to come. "You're so big."

He shoved his hand in her hair and tugged her head back until her throat was fully exposed to him. There was just enough pain to send a jolt of pleasure through her body that made her tremble. Lowering his mouth, he licked and kissed her much the same way he'd done on the escape pod, but now there was nothing to stop him from devouring her the way she knew he wanted. The point between her neck and shoulder became a focal point for him, and he lowered his mouth to the spot and with a growl bit down.

"Fuck!" It hurt, but she could tell he hadn't broken the skin. "Rykal?"

"You're mine." He licked at the spot before biting down again, no doubt leaving a bruise in the process. "I want the universe to know. If any fool touches you, I'll kill them."

The words should have terrified her; to have a man she didn't know act in such a way and lay such a claim on her without her consent was wrong.

And yet, Lena knew it was right. She wanted to be possessed by this man, knew that despite everything she'd left behind, she'd somehow traveled across the dark vastness of space to find him.

She closed her eyes and widened her legs. "Yes."

Lena could tell that he'd been holding back, careful not to hurt her to this point. But that restraint was gone with her assent and Rykal went mad with lust.

Roaring, he picked her up and threw her over his shoulder, marching over to a cot that was pressed against the side of the wall. It looked to be too small for his frame but was more than big enough for Lena to stretch out comfortably. With little gentleness, he dropped her onto the bed only to stand over her staring.

Lena had never felt so exposed in her life; stretched out naked and cold, on an alien planet with a cyborg who wanted to claim her for himself. But it was also the most liberated she'd ever felt in her life. There were no rules she had to follow, no society to dictate what her role was and what she needed to do with her life. There was no provisional Earth government to force her into labour that would wear her down to nothing and lead to an early death.

Her escape from Earth had been risky, but had led her to a

freedom she'd never anticipated.

She opened her legs wide, loving how Rykal's gaze snapped to her pussy. He dropped to his knees on the edge of the bed and grabbed her inner thighs with his hands and pulled them apart even further. "You have hair."

Lena couldn't help but giggle. "Yes. As red as what's on top of my head."

She'd always been considered a genetic oddity back home. There were so few people with red hair and hazel eyes any longer, it had brought her the type of unwanted attention she'd been desperate to avoid. No man had ever looked at her with the same reverence as Rykal; flattering and arousing all at once.

He lowered his face to her pussy and pulled in a long, slow inhale. "The sweetest scent I've ever faced."

Lena gripped the thin blanket on the mattress as her body was half lifted into the air. She squeezed her eyes shut before gasping when he licked a swipe across her pussy, teasing her clit as he went. "Shit."

"I don't know how exactly, but I knew you would like that. That you wanted me to put my mouth there."

"Yes." She couldn't help but to strain against the now empty air. "More."

His mouth returned as he flexed his fingers against the skin of her thighs. Rykal's tongue was as equally large as everything else about him. The hot flesh teased her, igniting arousal that snaked through her body, setting her nerves alight. She moved her hips in rhythm with his teasing tongue, gasping with each caress against her clit, silently willing him to do even more. Whatever this connection between them was, he picked up on her desires and lowered her to the mattress so he could slide his long finger into her pussy.

"Oh God." She rolled her head back and forth against the pillow, knowing it wasn't going to take her long to fall over the edge of pleasure and into blessed oblivion.

Rykal fucked her body with his hand, her juices coating his fingers as he moved inside her. His finger was thicker than some men she'd had sex with in the past – which wasn't saying much for her previous lovers – and he knew to curl it in such a way to press against that secret spot deep inside her that would push her over the edge.

Her body shook and she lost the ability to hold back; she moaned and sighed, gasping for air as though she were close to death. Her nipples were hard, and the cold air of the room made them electric with their sensitivity. It was too much and not enough; she wanted more than she knew her body could handle, and yet didn't want things to be so much that she wouldn't remember.

Rykal groaned against her pussy and moved his hand in such a way that she couldn't stop the burst of pleasure as her orgasm ripped through her. She screamed as she grabbed at his head, trying to push him away as she pulled him closer; the waves of release burned her even as they sated her desire.

Finally, he pulled away, letting her legs fall to the bed with a dull thud. It took her a moment to find the energy to open her eyes once again, but when she did, Lena was granted with the vision of Rykal kneeling over her, his cock as hard as ever and his blue gaze locked on her face.

"I'm going to mate with you now."

Lena couldn't have stopped him even if she'd wanted. And she most definitely did not want him to stop.

Instead of sliding his cock inside her and taking his pleasure, Rykal reached down and turned her around. "On your hands and knees."

She nodded, though it took effort to make her body comply, wanting nothing more than to give in to her exhaustion and lie there while he fucked her. Once she moved, widening her stance so he could find her opening from behind, she found another tremble of desire roll through her. *Shit, maybe there's something in the water here that makes a woman extra horny.*

He grabbed her hips with his large hands and squeezed her hard as he lined up his cock and thrust forward. Lena gasped when he filled her as far as he could go, her pussy clenching around his shaft. Rykal wasn't gentle with her, but there was still a worship about him whenever he placed his hands on her body. He flexed his grip on her once more as he pulled back. "I'm going to make you mine."

"Yes, okay."

He thrust forward hard enough to jolt her body. "You're mine. Say it."

"I'm..." She'd never given herself to a man like this before – cyborg, alien or human – and she couldn't help but hold back.

Rykal let out a sound that could have been a roar or a growl. "Say it. Lena, say it."

He punctuated each word with a thrust hard and deep into her pussy. Each time he fully connected, her clit jolted and the pleasure began to grow more. She didn't want to give him what he wanted, scared that it would end things too quickly, that she'd be lying to him or give something that she'd never be able to get back. A part of her soul that she'd need to continue living out here on the edge of the galaxy.

Instead, she closed her eyes and pressed her cheek to the mattress as he continued to fuck her from behind. Her breasts swung, grazing her nipples against the rough material of the blanket. Her body was still sensitive from her previous orgasm, and coupled with Rykal's raging desire, Lena knew it wouldn't take much for her to come a second time. What she wasn't expecting was for Rykal to reach down and hook his arms beneath her shoulder, to then pull her up into a sitting position on his lap. He had the strength to continue to fuck her hard, thrusting up into her willing body as he grabbed her breasts and teased her nipples.

"Fucking say it." He bit the spot on her neck again, harder this time, marking her. "You're mine."

Lena groaned, letting her head fall back against him and giving her body over to him. "Yes."

"Say *it*."

"I'm yours."

He pinched her nipples, and she bucked down not sure if she was trying to escape his touch or get more of it. "Again."

"I'm yours." She sobbed, the pleasure and pain mixing in her to the point where she couldn't tell one from the other. "Please."

Shifting his hand, he slid it down her body to her pussy. "Is this what you want?"

Her voice failed her, and all Lena could do was nod and pray that he understood.

"I want to feel your release. I want to smell and hear you. I want you to know that it was me who brought you to this place."

Oh, him and his filthy mouth. "Yes, yes."

He pressed his finger to her clit as he sucked on the wound on her neck and thrust up into her. It was all too much and Lena cried out. If her previous orgasm was a wave, then this was a fucking tsunami. Her voice abandoned her, leaving her lips parted in a voiceless scream. Her pussy clamped down hard on his cock as he pounded into her. His hands moved back to her breasts as he shifted her so he could press his forehead against the back of her shoulder.

She felt his cock pulse inside her before he tilted his head back and roared. His body shook, his thrusting became stuttered and ragged. His seed filled her, easing his thrusts until they finally stopped.

They sat there, clinging to each other, breathing hard and ragged as the storm raged outside. Lena's heart still raced, and she didn't know what her world would now be like. But one thing was certain; she really did belong to Rykal.

All she needed to do was figure out exactly what that meant.

CHAPTER SIX

Rykal couldn't let her go even as her body went limp from the intensity of her release. Lena was in his arms shivering – this time from pleasure – as her heartrate dropped closer to normal. He was becoming familiar with all her bio scans, realizing that somehow this was how he was aware of her moods, her very presence. It should have been impossible for him to have detected her across the vastness of their sector, and yet there was no way he'd be able to not know how she was feeling from this point forward.

She was engrained into his very psyche.

Sliding his hand across her slick, naked breast, he let his systems note every rhythm her body kicked off, needing to remember her like this – happy and sexually sated. He pressed his mouth to the spot he'd bit earlier and licked it softly with his tongue. "More."

The whimper that slipped from her was endearing. "Not sure I can handle more."

"You can." Reaching out with his sensors, he used the data he'd collected to begin to arouse her once again. "I know your body better than you know yourself."

Avoiding her pussy and her nipples, he began to stroke her sides, the smooth skin of her inner thighs. She was so unlike his kind down here; no *rondollo*, the female equivalent of his body that would help drive her arousal, but she had hair between her legs. He shifted her in his arms so she lay stretched out across his lap, her body bowed across him, open and exposed. The hair between her legs was curled and damp from her release, making it a joy to slide his fingers through, teasing everyplace except the one spot he knew she'd want him to touch.

"I can see your arousal growing." He ran his other hand along the swell of her belly. "I can see heat blooming across you as I do this." He cupped her breast but still left the nipple alone. "And this." He circled her clit without touching.

Lena arched up, trying to shift into his moving touch with little luck. "Rykal."

"Not yet. You have to trust that I know how to take care of you. To give you what you need to be happy."

She sighed and let her head roll to the side as he continued to tease and stroke her side. Time ticked on in his head, as he manipulated her body perfectly to the point where she was enflamed with desire. Her pussy was wet once again and it would take no effort to slide his cock into her willing body.

Instead, Rykal stood, taking her with him.

Lena let out a surprised squeak, struggling to catch her balance even though there was no way he'd let her fall. "I've got you."

Her surprise turned into a low chuckle. "You're going to give me a heart attack."

What he wanted to do was fuck her hard and fast so that she'd never want to be with another man – Grus, human or cyborg – ever again. Setting her on her feet in front of the computer console, he placed her hands on the flat surface and bent over her. "Don't move."

She held her breath for a moment before nodding her head

once. With her standing the way that he was, Rykal had the perfect view of her naked body. Her limbs were long and her red hair even longer as it reached halfway down her back. That flowing, fiery mane was quickly becoming an obsession with him. Wrapping his hand around the strands, Rykal pulled her head backward as he thrust his cock into her waiting pussy. Now he could feel her muscles around his shaft as he looked down at the possessive bite mark on her neck. It consumed him, knowing that he'd done that to her, that she was his and that he'd do anything in the galaxy to keep her safe.

"Rykal." She moaned as she began to thrust her hips back against him. "Fuck me."

Yes.

Yes.

Gone was any semblance of restraint; he knew that they were both long past that point. He fucked her with hard, fast thrusts, each one making his body ache for release. But he wouldn't come, not until she did first. He tugged her hair harder as he squeezed her hips; he wanted to press his fingers to her clit, to force the pleasure onto her, but knew it would be too much. No, he needed to let her body take control, to drive her pleasure to the peak before he'd be able to push her over the edge. Rykal tugged and fucked her until sweat pooled on her lower back and her skin puckered with bumps.

"Please, please, I'm so fucking close." Her words were so softly spoken, he wasn't sure she was even aware she said them out loud. "Yes, yes, just like that."

He swivelled his hips, but knew it wasn't going to be enough for her. Instead, he leaned over her body and pressed his mouth to the bruise on her shoulder. "You're mine. This will always be here as a reminder to anyone who might think otherwise. Mine forever. You will do what I want, what I tell you to do. Right now. I want you to fucking come right now and then I'm going to pull out and come all over your back. Mine *forever.*"

Lena's body went tight as a wire, before her pussy clamped down on his shaft and she came with a scream. Rykal groaned and pulled back, knowing he wouldn't have long to do exactly what he'd told her he would. The muscles of her pussy milked his shaft for what felt like an eternity before she finally went limp. It was only then that he pulled his cock from her, and jerked off until streams of his come exploded from him to coat her back in ropey spurts.

Pleasure overrode his internal restraints, and for one blissful moment he felt like the man he'd been before the war, before his life had been stolen from him. There was no fear, dread, or growing coldness that occupied the spaces in his chest; all that was blown away by the warmth of having and needing this human woman from across the void of space.

He came back to his awareness when he felt Lena's legs shaking to hold herself up beneath the added weight of his body draped across her. Carefully, he stood up and turned her in his arms to hold her in an embrace. "Thank you, little one."

Her hands felt so small against his chest, as she placed them against his cybernetics. She seemed fascinated by them, no doubt not having seen something quite like them. "Why placed here? It feels like a panel over your heart?"

The memory of the blaster ripping through his chest and into his skin was perfectly preserved. The pain was as fresh today as it had been then, as was the fear that spread within him when he realized he was about to die.

He'd failed his people, his brother, his fellow soldiers. One careless action was all it had taken and it was nearly the undoing of his people in their fight against the Sholle. If Aidric hadn't been prepared, hadn't been willing to sacrifice both their souls to save their people, matters would have been far worse.

"Rykal?"

He realized that he hadn't answered her. "It was necessary."

She frowned for a moment before it morphed into a yawn. "Let me take you to bed."

Her eyes widened. "I don't think I could come again if I tried."

"To rest. You will need your sleep, for once the storm is over, we'll need to leave quickly and return to my people before the Grus find us."

Ignoring her confused expression, he scooped her up in his arms and carried her to the bed. Her eyes were closed, and she sighed softly as sleep immediately overcame her. He tucked the blanket around her, letting his gaze roam over her body. She was so unlike any of the Grus women he'd been with in the past, and yet every inch of her skin was perfectly familiar to him. Lena of Earth was the woman who could fix him in a way he hadn't realized was broken. For the first time since his rebirth, Rykal felt right with the universe.

The communication console crackled to life, indicating that a transmission was incoming. "About *fracking* time, Darrick."

He pressed in his code and the screen flared to life. Instead of Darrick's expected presence, he was now faced with the stern, heartless eyes of Aidric. "You fool. What have you done?"

Rykal couldn't stop his teeth from grinding together. "What I needed to make sure she was safe."

"You know nothing about her or her people. They could have been sent by the Sholle to infiltrate our planet." Aidric leaned forward, moving his face closer to the screen. "You're putting us all at risk."

The mere thought of Lena being an operative of the Sholle nearly sent Rykal's systems into overload. "She and all her people are from Earth. They're escaping their own wars and chose to come here to find peace."

Aidric closed his eyes briefly, the only indication Rykal had that his brother was barely controlling his rage. "If that's the truth, then we would have discovered it after talking with her."

"You mean interrogation."

"It's the same thing." Aidric straightened once more. "You've now made a peaceful investigation impossible. I might be commander of this station, but the high council are the leaders of our people. They are the ones who determine who can and cannot stay on the station, and which actions against us are mandated as detrimental and worthy of attack. You've been flagged as being rogue and dangerous. The order to decommission you is the next step."

It shouldn't have surprised him, and yet Rykal had to fight to stop himself from stepping away from the screen and ending the conversation immediately. "Why?"

"Why do you *think*? You kidnapped an alien, injured security personnel and stole a *fracking* escape pod. You've been marked for destruction and the human for imprisonment."

Rykal glanced over at where Lena lay sleeping, oblivious to the horrors that were coming for them. "I won't let you take her."

The mask that Aidric so carefully wore to keep his emotions hidden from the world slipped ever so slightly. His lips turned down and Rykal could hear a quiver of distress in his voice. "Why this woman? You've never responded to anyone like this before. Past or present. Brother, why is she worth throwing your second chance at life away?"

"A life I never asked for. One that you forced on me."

"Please, 'Kal." Aidric swallowed, using the nickname he'd given him when they were children. "This goes against everything in your code, everything you were programmed to do."

He didn't have an answer, not one that his far too emotionally distant brother would understand. "She fills a void in me that I hadn't realized was there."

A beeping off screen grabbed Aidric's attention. "We're scanning for your communication feed. It won't be long before they're able to determine the location you're broadcasting from."

That was why Aidric had been so talkative. Without saying another word, Rykal ended the communication, reached down and yanked the coms control center from the panel, destroying the machine. Lena was still blissfully asleep, which meant he still had time to reach out to Darrick and move her before the Grus security forces found them. He folded her space suit and placed in on the console and found an old Grus uniform that looked like it might fit her. They wouldn't have a lot of time once he contacted Darrick. He should wake her, tell her what was happening and get her ready to go. But one look at her sleeping face and he couldn't do it. Not yet at least. Better for her to sleep because he didn't know when they'd have time to rest again.

Grabbing his pants and boots, he stepped out into the raging storm in search of a secondary and secure communication network. Because he'd rather die again that let anything bad happen to Lena. Even if that meant killing his own brother in the process.

CHAPTER SEVEN

Lena woke to find herself alone in the bed with the blanket covering her body and her feet tucked in. It took her a moment to reorient herself, temporarily forgetting what had happened to her since the Kraken woke her up. The late resuscitation protocols, the Grus, being kidnapped and then having the best sex of her life – all of it had happened in such rapid sucession she had no idea how long it had been since those first moments when she opened her eyes. Checking the small chromometer on her wrist, she gave it a shake when the time she saw didn't initially register in her brain.

Shit, had it only been *hours*?

Things had changed so rapidly in such a short period of time they could hardly be real. She hadn't even had the chance to reconcile the fact that they'd *actually* made it out of Earth's solar system and to their destination without getting attacked or having suffered some sort of computer malfunction. Lena rolled onto her back and chuckled softly. God, everyone back on Earth wouldn't believe it either, that was if any of them were still alive. Maybe things had improved in the years since she'd put her passengers into cryo sleep and they'd left.

Doubtful, but she'd always been accused of being an optimist.

Now they had an opportunity at a new life with new people and a planet that sure, wasn't necessarily the easiest to live on at first glance, but it was a far sight better than the political insanity they'd left behind. At least she hoped it was.

Turning her head, she looked to see where Rykal was in the room, but she couldn't find him. Strange, given how small the place was. The winds were still howling outside and the temperature of the room had dropped by a few degrees, but it wasn't bad seeing as how she was cocooned in the blanket. Her body was still sensitive from the raw sex they'd had; achy in that *wow you got fucked hard* kind of way that the simple memory had the ability to curl her toes. Rykal seemed to know exactly where to touch her, how to make her body heat with desire. It shouldn't be possible given they'd only just met and weren't even the same species.

The universe giveth...

Lena sat up in bed and looked around the room to see if there was any indication of where he would have gone. "Rykal?"

Nothing.

Her space suit was sitting on top of the computer console folded neatly and clearly far dryer than it had been when she'd taken it off. Beside it was another set of clothing – dark green with what looked to be brown patches on the sleeves – clearly meant for her to try on. Getting up and shivering when her feet hit the cold floor, she walked over and held up what appeared to be a uniform. It was going to be big on her, but the cloth appeared flexible and would make moving around on the planet easier than walking in her tight-fitting space suit.

"When on Earth, dress like an Earthling."

It only took her a few minutes to put the uniform on, and as she'd suspected it was a bit large on her frame. She did keep her space suit jacket, hoping the extra layer would give her some additional protection. It felt odd and yet comforting to know that he'd thought of her, and went in search of fresh clothes for her to wear.

The door opened, startling Lena as Rykal marched inside from the storm. Unlike her, he was still mostly naked, having only put on his pants and a pair of boots. His bare torso was as broad and muscular as she'd remembered. He looked at her and nodded as the door locked shut behind him. "They fit."

"Thank you, yes." She couldn't stop from biting down on her bottom lip. "You don't have any clothing yourself?"

"My body doesn't damage the way yours would." He crossed over to her, reached up and kissed her hard. "You need to be protected."

Lena ignored the way her chest tightened, and her heart fluttered. "I'm more than capable of looking after myself and others." With difficulty, she stepped back needing the space so she could think straight. "What is happening here?"

Rykal winced, but made no move to close the distance between them. "The communication array...isn't working. I had to go outside to effect repairs to the backup. Darrick has now received my message and will send a shuttle the moment the storm eases."

"Darrick is a friend of yours?"

"Another cyborg. My second in command during the war, though we hold no such ranks currently."

She looked at his body once more, noting that many of his cybernetics related to strength; enhanced arms and chest and clearly the ability to heal himself from minor damage. She reached out and placed her hand once more on the ridge where his skin disappeared into circuitry. "Did you choose these or were they provided to you?"

His gaze slipped away from hers. "I was the first of my people to receive them."

Oh, she didn't like the sound of that. "What does that mean? Did you volunteer?"

"I died."

Lena's hand fell away. "What do you mean you *died*? You're standing right in front of me, clearly not dead."

The spark of passion that had been in his gaze before she'd fallen asleep was gone. "The Sholle have been the enemy of the Grus for as long as our two people have been alive. They've consumed all the natural resources on their planet and it didn't take long for them to set their sights on ours. The last great war between our people saw our forces fall and the Sholle invaded our world. They used their machines to strip the soil, to pull all life from it to be transformed into energy for their ships."

Lena's heart ached for a people she barely knew. "Earth is like that, though we can't blame outside forces for the damage done to our world. We're more than capable of being our own monsters."

"We were dying. But my brother had one final idea that if it worked could save us all. Reanimating the dead, bringing us back to life with cybernetics and coding that allowed us to coordinate attacks. We were stronger, less prone to harm. We had no fear of dying because that was something we'd already experienced." He moved her hand to the center of the cybernetic implant on his chest. "I was shot here. The killing blow that ended one life and gave me another."

Lena looked up into the crystal blue cybernetic eyes of the man who'd brought such passion to her only hours before. "You're the most alive man I've ever met. No matter what happened to you in the past, or the changes they made to you then, you're here now. Here with me."

His mouth trembled, before he reached up and took her hand in his. "We'll have to discuss these things later."

She couldn't explain why, but she knew something terrible had happened while she'd rested. "What's wrong?"

"Aidric and the Grus soldiers are on their way for us. I've had to destroy our communications array here and use a secondary beacon to reach Darrick. He's flying a shuttle to get us now, though we'll have to walk out in the storm to find a place where he'll be able to set down safely."

"You destroyed the array?" She gave her head a shake. "You told me it wasn't working."

He ran his thumb across her cheek before pulling back. "I didn't want to worry you needlessly."

"I'm the captain of a ship that's traveled across the galaxy. I'm more than capable of determining what I should and shouldn't worry about." Lena's stomach bottomed out on her. "Is my ship still safe? Are my passengers? I need to get back there to check on them."

"You can't." He grabbed her by the shoulders when she tried to bolt for the door. "Lena, you have to trust me."

"Trust you? I don't even *know* you. You kidnapped me and now the lives of everyone on my ship are in danger because you felt the need to possess me?" God, she'd never been this much of a fool, putting her own desires ahead of everyone else. "I can't believe this."

He squeezed her shoulders hard enough to force her to look him in the eyes. "I know my brother. He won't do anything to your ship or your people while I'm out here causing him problems. He'll leave them alone and come for us. The longer it takes for that to happen, the safer they will be."

Lena didn't know if she wanted to slap Rykal or kiss him. "Fine. But the minute I'm able to get back to the station and get my people free, then I'm going to take it."

He let go and stepped away from with in a single motion. The spark she'd gotten used to seeing in his eyes dulled ever so slightly. "As you wish. We need to leave now." He turned and marched to the door.

Lena's chest tightened and she knew she'd screwed that up, but things had been happening far to quickly for her. Between the hangover from the cryo sleep and the fucking amazing sex, she didn't exactly have a lot of time to get everything set in her brain while making sure not to hurt the feelings of the cyborg who'd kidnapped her. She pulled her jacket tighter around her and realized that he was still standing there half naked. Turning from him, she found his clothing still in the pile on the floor where he'd left it and picked up his shirt.

"If we're going to be on the run from your brother, then I think at the very least you should have a shirt to wear. We wouldn't want you to get cold while we're out there."

With great care, she reached up and held out his shirt, waiting for him to take it from her. Instead, he ducked his head and let her slide it over and onto his shoulders. It shouldn't feel as easy or right doing these domestic kindnesses for him, and yet Lena couldn't deny that they did.

With his cybernetics covered, Rykal looked similar to many of the human men she'd left behind. Maybe two people from different planets really could be meant for one another.

All they had to do was survive.

CHAPTER EIGHT

The storm had begun to ease as Rykal led Lena over the hill toward the clearing where Darrick would land and shuttle them off to safety. The city that the cyborgs had built wasn't as grand as what life had been before the Sholle attacked and destroyed everything, but it was the best they could manage with the few resources the Grus provided them. But the break in the weather meant it would be easier for Aidric to find them as well.

Time was of the essence.

Rykal was running a beacon on the cyborg network that he and the others had created during the war, a means of stealth communication that had helped them win. Darrick would pick it up the moment he came into range, but it was modified so that it would be difficult for Aidric to track their precise location. Their window of opportunity was small, but Rykal had trust in his brethren that once they made it to the city, they'd be safe.

Then he'd be able to set about the task of winning Lena's heart.

She was far stronger now, surer footed since their walk to the shelter. Lena kept pace with him, and he was able to see the strong woman who'd managed to keep her passengers safe while she flew blind across space in a ship that had little business being *in* space. This Lena was the leader, the captain that brought women to safety. She would be good in a fight, if it ever came to that.

The gods better help Aidric if any harm comes to her. Brother or not, Rykal would snap his neck.

"Is it much farther?" Lena's words were whipped around by the wind. "Have you made contact?"

Rykal sent another burst communication, and this time he received Darrick's response. "He'll be on the ground by the time we clear that hill."

"Thank God."

True to his word, the shuttle was already there and waiting by the time Rykal crested the hill. Looking back at Lena, he couldn't miss the relief on her face. Her muscles would still be weak from being in cryogenic sleep and he'd put her through much in the short time since waking up. He paused long enough to scoop her up into his arms and carried her the rest of the way down the hill. She really must have been tired, because she didn't protest at all.

The shuttle door lowered, giving them access to the ramp and the safety that waited inside. Rykal set Lena down and let her walk, not wanting her to feel incapable of managing on her own.

"Rykal?" Darrick stood just inside the small shuttle, his gaze locked on Lena, who in turn hadn't moved far beyond the ramp. "Who's this?"

As large as Rykal was, Darrick was taller and broader. His cybernetic eyes shone green in the low light of the shuttle, casting odd shadows across his cheeks. His brown hair was cut so short hardly any showed, giving him a menacing look that had often played to their advantage out on the battlefield. Darrick's cybernetics comprised half of his neck and left shoulder, repairing the damage he'd taken when he'd jumped in front of blaster fire that would have killed a fellow soldier. Rykal had made sure his friend was the second person to receive Aidric's implants, a thing Rykal had spent the following years trying to make up for.

Lena stood still even as Rykal retracted the ramp and closed the door. "This is Lena. She's a human from a distant planet called Earth who traveled here in a ship with other women. They're refugees and are looking for a new home. She's also my mate and I'll kill you if you hurt her."

Darrick cocked a single eyebrow in a manner that spoke volumes. "Pleasure to meet you."

Lena nodded, her eyes widened as she looked between them. "Likewise."

"We'll have to carry on this conversation in the air. Aidric is trying to track us and if we don't get back to the city quickly, we're all going to have a very bad day."

"Right." Darrick reclaimed his seat and set about starting the shuttle. "You're going to need the restraints. The shuttle's stabilizers can only do so much in this weather."

Lena looked away from Rykal long enough to secure herself in the passenger chair, only to stare at him once more. He could feel her confusion and more than a little trepidation at his declaration; he couldn't exactly blame her though, even if it was the truth. She was now a part of his life, a vital part. If anything happened to her, he knew deep down in what remained of his soul that he'd go insane. His life would be over and so would the lives of anyone who'd hurt her.

He slid into the seat beside Darrick and checked the co-pilot command center. "We have a window opening up in the storm."

"I see it." Darrick pressed the control drive. "Hold on."

Rykal focused his attention on the storm, on the shuttle and getting them all to safety, even if what he really wanted was to move to the back of the ship and pull Lena into his arms to reassure her that everything would be alright. She'd be safe and cared for, her people would be released and provided for, and Aidric would eventually leave them all to go about their lives. But he knew he would never be able to outright lie to her, so he focused on what he could control.

Stage one – getting her back to the city.

The opening in the weather didn't last for long, but it was enough to allow them to fly full throttle to Cimacha, the city that the surviving cyborgs had claimed as their home. The moment they got into range Rykal felt Darrick reach out to him through their cybernetic link.

What's going on with this human?

Rykal didn't want to have to explain everything, but he knew if they were going to have a chance of stopping Aidric from escalating this into a full-blown war, he'd need Darrick and everyone else on his side. *I don't know why, but I was aware of her the moment she entered the sector. She fills a gap in my brain, and my soul that I never thought would be whole again.*

Darrick kept his gaze on the controls, but Rykal could tell something that he'd said had struck a nerve with his friend. Darrick's hand balled into a fist for a moment before he stretched it out flat. *Was it like an itching in the back of your brain?*

Yes. Rage flared inside him. *She's not yours.*

No, she isn't. She's not the source, but it feels close. I thought my cybernetics were failing.

If Darrick was experiencing the same things, then there was a chance that another human back on Lena's shuttle was meant for him. Perhaps all the humans had cyborg mates waiting for them here. The implications of that were far too great for him to dwell on right now.

My friend, we'll find her for you. As soon as I put Aidric in his place.

Darrick snorted. *Easier said than done.*

"Are the two of you carrying on some sort of conversation? Because it's more than a little rude to ignore another person in the room like that."

They both looked back at Lena, who seemed far more annoyed at them than concerned about the weather or escaping Aidric's soldiers. She had a core of mettle to her, a natural leader who would fit perfectly into their world.

Darrick snorted again. "Apologies." *You're going to have your hands full with this one.*

A problem I'll happily live with for the rest of my life. "We have the ability communicate in short range through a cyborg neuronet. We're not used to caring about the others around us and what they can hear."

"Well if I'm going to be around for a little while, you damn well better get used to it."

"I'll be sure not to use this method while you're present." True to his word, he severed the link with Darrick.

"Thank you." She narrowed her gaze on something behind him. "Is that where we're heading?"

"Cimacha, is our capital." Rykal turned and transmitted their security codes. "We'll be there shortly."

Rykal was able to see the docking field lights when the shuttle lurched sharply to the side. The alarms sounded as the shuttle was hit with another barrage of blaster fire, this time from the other side. Darrick turned off the alarm and quickly maneuvered the shuttle to avoid another attack. "We've got Grus ships on both flanks. They must have been waiting for us to arrive and popped up under my scanners."

Rykal should have known better than to assume Aidric wouldn't have a secondary plan to stop them. "Can we land?"

The shuttle shuddered under another hit, this time sending a cascade of sparks showering down over Lena. "I think that one penetrated your hull!"

The alarms sounded again, as Darrick scanned them. "She's right. Hull breach on quadrant 327. We're not going to be able to sustain many more of those."

They were so close to the landing pad, Rykal knew the others in the city would be able to see the attack, which would only serve to ratchet up the tension between their peoples. He was about to tell Darrick to make a run for it, when the coms channel opened.

"Put the shuttle down, Rykal."

Fracking Aidric.

Darrick opened coms. "By firing on us you're declaring war on the cyborg population. That is not a war that the Grus want. You will not win."

"Rykal declared war first when he attacked our people on the station, kidnapped an alien who we hadn't cleared from quarantine and then stole an escape pod."

Darrick looked at him, his eyebrow fully cocked. "Is that true?"

"It is." Lena had left her seat to stand behind them. "And I'm not going to be the reason a war breaks out. Especially not when my people are still stuck in cryo sleep on my ship back on that station. We need to put the shuttle down and surrender."

"No!" Rykal was on his feet and pressed against her. "I won't put you in danger. I'll kill them all first."

Lena blinked several times as she stepped away from him. "You don't get to control me. I didn't fly halfway across this galaxy only to find myself in a worse position than the one I left. I'm the captain of the Kraken and have been trusted with the lives of every single person on it. I'm not going to let your arrogance put their lives or their futures in jeopardy because you're thinking with your cock."

Fear and anger radiated from Lena, though Rykal knew it wasn't for her own safety. She was every bit as much willing to put her life on the line for others as he was, and he knew she'd willingly sacrifice herself to save her people. He would do the same.

"Rykal, put the shuttle down before you reach the landing pad and we'll keep this matter between us. There's no reason for things to escalate into a war. No reason for us to disturb the status quo." Aidric's voice was even, lacking passion despite his words.

He would kill them all, of that Rykal had no doubt.

"What do you want me to do?" Darrick kept his gaze outward, his hands hovering above the controls. "We can make it to the pad, just say the word and I'll make a run for it."

Lena shook her head but said nothing else. There was no way she'd be able to stop him from doing what he wanted and she no doubt knew that. Darrick had long ago proven that he'd die for Rykal given even the slightest indication. Everything came down to this, down to him.

Looking Lena in the eyes he realized that he would do anything for her, even if that meant risking losing everything. "Put the ship down. Stand down all weapons."

"That was the smart move." Aidric's voice rang through the coms. "Prepare to be boarded and taken into custody."

Rykal dropped to his knees and placed his hands behind his head the moment the shuttle touched down. Lena sat beside him, keeping her hands in her lap. "What do you think they'll do with us?"

"They'll place you back into quarantine and process you. They'll want to know your history and why you came here. Our people aren't exactly trusting of strangers."

"And what about you?"

That was the real question. "I don't know."

Once Darrick finalized the landing protocol and released the ramp, he also dropped to his knees, flanking where Lena sat. "If we're lucky, they'll only deactivate us."

"Not us." The moment the soldiers boarded the ship, Rykal spoke. "Darrick was following orders and wasn't aware of what had happened on the station. He is not to be blamed for this incident."

The security leader barked orders at his subordinates. "We're under orders from the commander himself to detain all beings on this shuttle and bring you back to Grus Prime. We have permission to shoot to kill if you even so much as flinch in the direction of escape. Is that clear?"

It took all Rykal's control to keep from reaching out and snapping the man's neck. "Crystal." When they went to put Lena into restraints, Rykal growled. "Don't put a hand on her."

The guards looked at him, then her before turned back to their boss. The security leader was suddenly lacking in the bravado he'd shown only moments before. "She's an alien to our two peoples, with unknown abilities. She needs to be restrained."

"Rykal, it's fine. They're not going to hurt me, and I'll be with you the whole way back to the station. Won't I?" She said the last part to the security leader. "It would be beneficial to everyone if we tried our best to keep everyone happy and not let things get so bad that the two cyborgs on the ship get pissed off and kill everyone. Right?"

A collective sigh of relief seemed to roll through the security personnel when the leader nodded. "You'll be placed in protective custody together in our ship. Get them secured and move!"

Rykal tried to keep his focus on the matter at hand, but whenever someone touched Lena, moved her, accidentally bumped into her, his anger grew, swelling to a level he'd never experienced before. But as quickly as it threatened to overwhelm him, she'd reach out and caress his hand, rub her thumb across the top of his thigh, or press her shoulder against his. Those simple points of contact were enough to help him maintain his composure.

Darrick said nothing else, but Rykal felt his friend watching their interactions and taking note. If there was another human on that ship who was destined to be with Darrick, Rykal had no doubt that he'd also want to find her as quickly as possible.

Their ship landed back on Grus Prime, the hiss of decompression sending a sliver of dread through him. Lena let out a soft sigh. "Back to where we started."

"Physically yes. But a lot has changed since then." If he was cautious, then perhaps he could maneuver events to play out in their favor. "I'll deal with Aidric."

He'd been expecting his brother to be waiting for them in the docking bay when they arrived, but he wasn't there. In fact, there were hardly any security forces present when the detail from the ship led them down the ramp. "I don't like this."

"Stop there." The security leader continued past them, leaving the trio out in the open. "The commander will be speaking with you all shortly."

The last thing Rykal saw was Lena looking confused as a bolt of electricity surged through him, sending his cybernetic circuits into overload before shutting down.

CHAPTER NINE

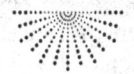

Lena couldn't sit still, instead choosing to pace in the small medical room she'd been placed in over an hour ago. She'd been quickly swept up by the security forces waiting to the side when they'd disabled both Rykal and Darrick. She'd fought as best she could with her arms fastened, but she was no match for the fully armed security forces. She didn't know what had happened to Rykal, but she wasn't able to sense his presence the way she'd been able to up to now.

It was strange, missing something that she'd only vaguely been aware of up to this point.

Doctors – well, people she'd assumed to be doctors – had been waiting for her as soon as she'd been brought into the room. They'd taken samples and scans, no doubt wanting to confirm that humans weren't carrying some unknown illness that made cyborgs horny and go insane. At this point, she really wouldn't be surprised if they'd actually found something.

But after they'd left, no one else came to speak with her, and that freaked her the fuck out. So, until someone showed up and conducted the alien equivalent of an interrogation, she'd pace the length and width of the room and hope like hell that things would turn out for the best.

Because as crazy as the past day had turned out to be, she didn't think she'd be okay if something happened to Rykal. That constant awareness of him, the soft buzzing of his consciousness in her mind that gave her peace and comfort was a feeling she'd never once experienced back on Earth. No man or woman offered her that connection or sense of belonging before, and she'd quickly grown used to it.

It was more than a little addictive.

More time passed and the muscles in Lena's legs began to protest the constant motion. She really wasn't strong enough after the long cryo sleep for the level of activity she'd been subjected to since waking up, but she hadn't had much of a choice either. She eventually had to give up and sat in the chair that had been thoughtfully placed to help her ease her burden. That act of kindness felt uncharacteristic for the people she'd met since her arrival, but one she was thankful for. The moment she sat down, the door slid open and a tall athletically built man stepped inside. It took her a moment to realize this was the man who'd been there with Rykal when she'd first emerged from the Kraken.

"Aidric. Right?" She tried to keep herself as relaxed as possible but couldn't quite manage it. "Have you done anything to hurt my people?" *Where's Rykal? Is he okay? Did you kill him?*

"No one has boarded your ship since your kidnapping, nor has there been any indication of movement inside. I assume your people are still in cryogenic sleep?"

He was painfully calm and cool; his blue eyes so similar to Rykal's yet lacked the electric glow that relayed a feeling of energy. It didn't take a genius to realize that Aidric was highly intelligent and far more dangerous than she'd initially given him credit. Lena was going to have to watch what she said around him. "Yes, the entirety of the crew and passengers went into cryo sleep once we got out of Earth's solar system and began our journey. I was automatically woken when we reached this sector, though I should have been brought out sooner." She snapped her mouth shut when she saw a spark of interest in his gaze.

"So you and your people chose this sector as your destination. Why?"

God, how the hell could she even begin to explain to an alien whose people had been attacked and nearly wiped out by another alien race that everyone on board the Kraken had undertaken this journey based on a hunch.

"You wouldn't believe me even if I told you." She leaned back against the chair, the exhaustion of the past day catching up to her.

Aidric cocked his head to the side and narrowed his gaze. "You might be surprised what I'd believe. Especially after what has transpired today."

Lena got to her feet and began to pace once more. "Life on Earth has gotten nearly impossible for those of us that haven't been born into wealth. The colonies on Mars and Titian have highly restricted immigration policies, making a transfer to them difficult at best. I just had a…a feeling that if I got into a ship and headed out this way then I'd find someplace…safe." She stopped and looked directly at him. "I know how that sounds and that it doesn't make a lot of sense. But once I was able to buy my ship and put out a call for others who might want to come with me, it didn't take long for me to fill up."

Aidric nodded once, then again. "There's something else you're not telling me."

"It's going to sound insane. Or like I'm trying to scam you, but truthfully, I'm not."

Aidric got to his feet and stood beside her. There was a small change in his expression, an old pain that seemed to slip out from beneath the mask he clearly wore. "When the Sholle first threatened us, I wasn't the commander of this station. I wasn't even on the ruling council of our people. I was a scientist whose sole purpose was to try and make the lives of the Grus people better. But when our planet was attacked, it became clear that our people were going to lose. I focused my research on lengthening the quality of Grus life, and turned it into a means to create soldiers. My own brother fought and died in the war, and I had to make a decision to utilize my cybernetic research on him."

"He told me." She could barely speak, her voice coming out of her at barely a whisper.

"What he doesn't know, that no one knows, is that there was a flaw in my programming." There was no masking his emotions now. Pain and regret were clear on his face as Aidric looked directly into her eyes. "I was never quite able to pinpoint where the bug came from, which meant I couldn't effect repairs. But whenever we scan any of the people who've been changed into cyborgs, there is a gap in their matrix code. I once speculated it was where their emotions once existed."

Lena couldn't help but feel sorry for him. "Why are you telling me this?"

He hesitated, before reaching out and giving her arm a gentle squeeze. "I ran a complete diagnostic on Rykal once we got him into a secure holding. Darrick as well. The gap in Rykal's programming has begun to fill. Somehow self-repairing in a way that I've never seen happen before in the years since his creation."

Lena bit down on her bottom lip. "Darrick?"

"No. But there's some unusual activity in his neuro cortex."

She didn't need him to say the words out loud for her to understand what he was implying. "You think that I'm the reason Rykal's code has changed."

"And that there's another person on board your ship who might be affecting Darrick."

Everything that had happened both here and back on Earth had been for a reason. Lena leaned against the wall and for the first time in what felt like her entire life, she relaxed. "Thank God."

Aidric frowned. "What does that mean?"

There were so many things that she hadn't understood back on Earth; it was as though there was a part of her mind that was being driven by some unseen force that wanted her to take a ship and go out into the dark reaches of space. Only the people on the Kraken understood her, because they'd all experienced similar feelings.

Explaining that to an alien though, well, that wasn't going to be the easiest thing.

Lena turned so her back was fully pressed against the wall, suddenly needing the extra support. "The people of my planet have not had the best time in the past hundred years or so. Our ancestors had a technology that they didn't understand, and the detrimental effects that it had on the environment until it was almost too late. When they realized that they had to fundamentally change their entire economic backbone to save the planet, it was difficult for them to make that switch."

"Your people had other planets to live on?"

Lena snorted. "Not at the time, though they eventually moved out and colonized another planet and a moon in our sector. The Mars and Titan I mentioned. Regardless, the people left behind on Earth had a much harder time and we had to do anything we could to survive."

She looked down at her hands, still able to see the ghosts of the blood and dirt that used to be caked beneath her fingernails. In many ways, she was as flawed as Rykal appeared to be.

"Did you steal your ship and take these people with you?" Aidric hadn't moved, his calm demeanor a blessing.

"No, I earned that hunk of metal. I used the money that my father and mother had earned, and the funds that my grandparents and great-grandparents had passed down. I was the first member of my family to have the means to leave. But it was more than that. Ever since I was a child, I've had this fascination with this sector of space. I would sneak into the observatory and use a few minutes of time to look at this star. Over the years I met others, other women, who also were fascinated with this one shining star in the sky. When I bought my ship, I put the call out that I was heading a one-way trip here and anyone who wanted to come with me could come. There were twenty-eight of us in total, who all had that same focus. I didn't want to leave any of them behind."

Aidric stared at her, and she could almost see the gears of his mind grinding, trying to make sense of her story. None of it was logical, and yet, she couldn't deny its truth. He finally turned his back to her and walked toward the door, before stopping midway. "Twenty-eight? Adults?"

"Yes. All women. When people came to me to book passage, I was surprised by that, but didn't exactly have time to argue. We filled the stasis tubes and off we went."

The lines around his eyes deepened. "Our people who fought and died, only to be brought back to fight again, gave more for our people than should ever have been asked of them. The cybernetic matrix program was initially flawed beyond what I'd first mentioned to you. The first group to be transformed are different from the rest. More aggressive with natural leadership abilities. The high council didn't approve. I wasn't sure why the cyborgs became programmed that way and had to find a workaround."

"You did?" A tremor of excited trepidation ran through her.

"Yes, and it changed them all. I'm responsible for that and everything that followed. If there's an opportunity for them to find some peace, to fill in the flaw in their programming, to ease the rage that simmers below the surface, who am I to stand in the way."

Lena swallowed hard, knowing she had to ask the obvious

question and not sure she wanted to. "How many of the initial cyborgs were there before you made the change?"

"Twenty-eight." He held her gaze a moment longer, turned and left.

Lena's heart was pounding so hard that she could hear the echo in her ears as she felt it throb in her throat. What did he mean by that? Was she going to be free to go? Would Rykal be okay despite all of the laws that he'd broken?

God, she hoped so.

She didn't know why she'd flown across the galaxy, but now that she was here and she'd met Rykal, Lena knew this was where she was meant to be.

More time passed and she was about to give up hope, when the door finally slid open. Rykal stood there, dressed in a clean uniform, his black hair washed and brushed, his piercing blue eyes wide and locked onto her. He came fully into the room, crossing the distance in three steps, before wrapping his arm around her waist and pulling her hard against him.

"Rykal?" That was all she was able to get out before he crushed her mouth in a kiss. His lips were warm, as his tongue flicked across her teeth as it went in search of hers. He continued to devour her, until her lungs screamed from lack of oxygen and she had to shove him back enough to breathe. "What's going on?"

"I don't know what you said to Aidric, but he somehow convinced the Grus leadership not to decommission me."

Relief raced through her, more addictive than any drug. "Oh, thank God."

"More than that, he's said that we will be free to go soon. He needs to first finalize a few details, but then we'll be given a shuttle and be allowed to return to Cimacha."

Lena closed her eyes and let her forehead tip forward to press against his chest. "What about the rest of my passengers?"

"He didn't say, but knowing him the way I do, that is the matter he's dealing with currently." He put his hand beneath her chin and lifted it up until she was looking him in the eyes once more. "For now, he's assigned us quarters to wait, rest and get nourishment."

There was a glint in his eyes that told Lena that there was something else Rykal wanted that went beyond food and rest. It had only been half a day since they'd had sex, but Lena's body was already craving him once more.

"Is there a bed in these quarters?" Her voice was low, husky in a way that was so unlike her. Seductive and teasing; two things she wasn't normally.

"There is." He ran his thumb down across her lip and she couldn't help but tease the tip of it with her tongue.

"We better go then." She smiled up at him, pleased by the feel of his cock against her stomach. "We can talk later."

He grabbed her by the hand and yanked her out of the room.

CHAPTER TEN

Rykal was barely able to contain his raging lust for Lena as he led her through the corridors of the station toward the quarters Aidric had assigned to them. He didn't know if he'd ever get used to the feelings of lust and fascination he had for Lena, and there was a large part of him that hoped he didn't. For the first time since the war, since becoming a cyborg, Rykal felt alive and part of something much larger than himself. He had Lena to thank for that.

He also owed her thanks for somehow rekindling the relationship he had with his brother; something he'd never thought would happen again. Their conversation had been brief, but poignant; Aidric was convinced that the twenty-eight women on the Kraken were connected to the twenty-eight cyborgs who'd taken up leadership roles for the Fallen. He'd promised Rykal that he'd conduct some research on the possibility and would be in touch. Aidric even slipped again and used Rykal's childhood nickname once more. That simple word was more than enough to give Rykal hope that there would be more for their future.

But Aidric wasn't who he wanted to focus on just then. He tightened his hold on Lena, anticipating what was to come.

The moment they were alone, that they were tucked safely behind the door of their quarters, he was going to strip Lena naked and lick her body until she screamed with pleasure. His arousal was so high, he knew there was no hiding it from the Grus they passed on their way. It was oddly amusing to witness their double takes when they realized not only who he was, but that there was an alien woman being dragged alone behind him.

Speaking of whom...

He turned and scooped Lena up into his arms in one quick, smooth motion, continuing on their path before she realized he was now carrying her.

"You know I'm more than capable of walking on my own." There was only mild annoyance in her voice.

"Your human legs are too short. You're slow."

"We have an expression back on Earth. Good things come to those who wait."

"That's a stupid expression."

Thankfully, neither of them would have to wait any longer. He knew their quarters were just ahead and he wanted nothing to slow them down. He reached out to the station's AI, sending the security clearance codes.

SECURITY CODE...ANALYZING...RECEIVED...ANALYZING...
Emotional control check...analyzing...reviewed... testing...analyzing...

RYKAL GROWLED. *Open the fracking door!*

ANALYZING...CYBORG *impatient...*

. . .

I'll show you impatient.

There was a ruffle of something in his brain as they got to the room and the door slid opened. He couldn't be sure, but he swore the AI found him amusing. But that was another question for another day.

Right now, the only thing he cared about was getting Lena naked.

The door closed behind him, and he continued over to the bed where he placed her down on the mattress. "Strip."

She cocked her eyebrow at him and let out a soft chuckle. "Aren't you going to say *please* first?"

He said nothing whatsoever, instead pulling his newly acquired uniform shirt off and tossing it to the floor somewhere behind him. Her gaze snapped to his chest, and she shifted toward the edge of the bed and sat up. "I've wanted to do this again, only this time I want to take my time and give you a ride."

"We have all the time in the world." But he wasn't certain what she was planning to do to him.

Rykal's sexual experience before his change had been varied, and he'd always enjoyed the time he'd spent with his partners. Human women clearly had different desires than Grus, and he was surprised when she pulled his pants down to expose his cock, and then leaned in to lick the head of his cock. He couldn't help but shiver from the intensity of the touch, thankful that she continued, rather than leave him to suffer and beg for more.

Lena sucked the head of his cock deep into her mouth, swallowing as she used her hand to stroke his shaft. Unlike back on the planet, she used her free hand to massage the membrane along his inner thigh. He groaned as his knees buckled from the contact.

She pulled back and looked up at him with a frown. He could feel her confusion come off her in waves. "Did I hurt you?"

"Just the opposite." He widened his stance, exposing the

membrane for her to see. "Grus men have this *rondella*, on our bodies."

"That word didn't translate for me."

The concept was different enough with humans that she had no frame of reference that the nanobots could use to assist. "An area of our body that produces sperm for fertilization. It also gives us great pleasure when we're mating if it's touched."

"I didn't notice that before." She lowered her head to look at him, her breath washing across the too-sensitive skin. "It's dark green. Way darker than your skin."

"It fills as I'm aroused."

"What happens if I do this?" She pressed her mouth to his thigh and licked a long swipe across it with her tongue.

Rykal's world nearly blacked out on him as pleasure roared through him, making his cock twitch and his body shake. Every inch of his body tingled as he became hyper aware of his skin, his nerves, even the way the air touched him. It was an all-encompassing feeling that fired his blood and made him want to fuck her hard and fast. He hadn't had a pre-orgasm since he was a young man, the stacking of pleasure as his seed was produced in preparation for release. He wasn't going to last long if she continued to do that. He reached down and grabbed her hair, pulling her mouth away from his thigh and stretching her neck back so she was fully exposed to him.

Lena gasped as she licked her lips. "What did I just do to you? Did you just have an orgasm, or was that reaction something else?"

"Something else." Stepping free of his pants, he was now naked and able to focus his attention on her. "Something that I'm going to get glorious revenge for."

Human bodies seemed to lack some elements that Grus women had but made up for it with others. Her breasts were larger than a Grus woman, and she responded with a moan when he shoved his hand beneath her suit to capture her nipple between his fingers. She seemed to respond to tiny bits of pain, and he could feel it mix with pleasure inside her until she wasn't sure where one response started and the other ended.

Lowering his mouth to her throat, he went in search for the mark he'd left upon her previously. The dark bruise stood in stark contrast against her pale skin, which gave him a pleasurable possessive shiver. He kept his gaze locked on it as he began to strip her with one hand, refusing to release her hair and the glorious tension that was building inside her. It took effort and required a bit of help from Lena, but they eventually got her stripped, so she was as naked as he.

And now the fun can begin.

Her nipples were hard and dark pink, beaded up and practically begging him to suck on them. There was no way he'd be able to resist them and lowered his mouth. He sucked hard, using his teeth and tongue to tease and torment the sensitive flesh, enjoying the sounds that came from Lena as she bucked and thrashed beneath him. He could smell her arousal, could feel the wetness between her legs as she moved against his thigh.

He made a point of rubbing his *rondella* against her, letting the pleasure build again, knowing the end result would bind the two of them together forever. He wanted this, needed this mating to happen so they'd both be forever happy. She was his and he was hers. She'd crossed space just to be here with him; she given up her home, her life, in search of him. Rykal couldn't have guessed that another creature would do anything like that for him before.

Rykal shifted his body so his cock slid inside her pussy, and her clit pressed against him. He lifted his mouth from her nipple and instead moved to suck the bruise on her shoulder. "You're mine."

"Yes." She lifted her legs and wrapped them around his waist. "Yours."

It was in that moment, as his orgasm grew to the point of tipping that Rykal realized she might not fully understand what he meant. This wasn't some passing fancy or claim of his affections; no, he was about to bond with her in the Grus mating ritual, claiming her so no other man could. He desperately tried to hold his body back, knowing they wouldn't have much time.

"I've marked you as mine." He nipped at her shoulder but looked up again to stare into her eyes. "My *rondella* produces a chemical that will mark you as my mate. If I come this time, no other Grus or cyborg man will dare touch you. My scent will be on you forever."

She reached up and cupped his cheeks. "As long as no other woman in this universe lays a hand on you. My scent better be all over you forever, because I'll kill anyone else who tries to take you from me."

That was all he needed to hear. She not only understood what was about to happen, but she wanted him the same way. Reaching between their bodies, he pressed his finger against the top of her swollen clit and rubbed it in circles as he thrust into her. Her juices eased his cock and he fucked into her body as hard and as fast as he'd dreamed he could.

He wanted to wait, to feel Lena's muscles contract around him before he finally claimed her, but it was difficult to hold the wave of pleasure at bay. Rykal shifted so his weight rested on his elbows and knees, giving him the ability to use his hands better. He did his best to focus his attention on her; he alternated teasing her nipples and her clit with his fingers and shifted his mouth from her throat to her mouth. He kissed her hard, swallowing up the noises of pleasure as the slipped from her; drinking them down like a sweet nectar.

Lena's eyes were squeezed shut and her body shook beneath him. "So close."

It was as though she was trying to hard to find her pleasure. He shifted his mouth to her ear and flicked his tongue against her lobe. "I'm yours and you're mine. Forever. I will bring you pleasure and love. And right now, I want you to come."

Her body bowed beneath him as her pussy clamped down hard on his cock, and a scream ripped from her chest. That magnificent sound was all he needed to hear. Rykal closed his eyes and let the dam he'd built up, break. Pleasure roared from his body as he cried out; waves of his orgasm washed over him as he pumped his seed inside her.

His marking scent came with it as well, claiming her so no other could, so no other would dare. His pleasure overwhelmed his cybernetics, and for the briefest of moments he was Grus again; a man who would give his life for the woman whom he loved.

He felt *alive*.

And then he fell in a heap upon her body.

They stayed that way, a mess of arms and legs tangled together as their bodies cooled in the recycled station air. Unlike down on the planet, Rykal didn't have the urge to run, to hide the darker side of his being from her, to keep her safe from a thing he couldn't control. Lena didn't care, and wanted him for who he was, expecting nothing more. He shifted so her head rested on the side of his chest that was still flesh, giving her the freedom to reach up and run her fingers along the seam of his cybernetics.

She placed a kiss to his chest. "That was…unbelievable."

He'd been told that when a Grus finally mated, they felt different. He'd always assumed that the difference would be subtle, small but in a fundamental way. He hadn't anticipated this all-encompassing shift in his outlook on the world. "I'm now yours until the end of our days. We've formed a bond that cannot be broken."

Lena lifted her head just high enough so she could place her chin on his chest and look at his face. "I don't understand why, but I knew. Before you said anything, shit before I even arrived on this station. I knew that you were the man I was destined to be with. You're the reason I gave up everything back on Earth and came here on blind faith."

"Cyborgs aren't supposed to be able to mate. We died and our *rondella* was supposed to have died as well. Dried up so we couldn't have a family of our own. You've proven that it's possible for us to have lives, to have love."

"The universe has worked a miracle that pulled our two people together." She paused, her brow furrowed. "I...I think Darrick's mate is in there. Its probably why he was able to sense her."

"Darrick? How did you know?"

"He told Aidric that he felt someone, but I don't know much more beyond that. Aidric left and then you showed up after that." She ran her finger across his chest. "If there is another woman and she does turn out to be Darrick's mate, then that means all of the women on board the Kraken are probably cyborg mates. Maybe."

A whole ship full of people looking for happiness; a group of cyborgs down on the planet who didn't know their lives were about to change. "Aidric will want to test that theory before he allows the rest of your passengers to be woken from their sleep."

"And if it turns out that we're right, that all those women are meant to be with a cyborg down on the planet, do you think he'll let them go down there to look? Will we be able to form lives, have homes and families?"

The Grus leadership might take issue with the cyborgs having mates, might be fearful of what would happen if the Sholle ever returned and they were needed to go back and fight another war. "If they know what's good for them and for my people, then they will give us all the resources we need to relocate your people planet side."

Rykal sat up and brought Lena with him. Cupping her face, he kissed her gently on the nose. "I love you. I will do everything in my power to keep you safe, to give you the life that you deserve. And all I ask for is to know that you'll love me in return."

She smiled and something deep inside him softened. "I loved

you before I even knew you. But now that I'm here with you, I love you even more. I can't wait to live the rest of my life with you."

Rykal wrapped his arms around her and knew that he'd finally been rewarded for everything that he'd ever sacrificed. He'd been given the gift of true love.

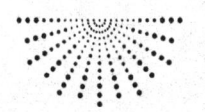

MATED TO THE CYBORG

A dutiful cyborg must fight against his programming to be with his mate.

A CYBORG PROTECTORS ROMANCE

MATED TO THE CYBORG

ALYSE ANDERS

CHAPTER ONE

Darrick knew that as a cyborg, his life was limited with what he'd be able to accomplish. He'd been created as a weapon of war and had served his purpose, only to be discarded by the Grus, the aliens he once called his people. Most of his past twenty years were spent down on what remained of the planet that the Grus had held as their home, spending his days tinkering with computer systems and upgrading the air hoppers that provided the bulk of transportation for the cyborgs.

He had once been an engineer, a creator of systems that kept his people safe, that made the quality of their lives better. Then the Sholle arrived in their solar system and he, like many Grus men and women of a certain age, was designated a soldier, handed a weapon, and shoved out onto the battlefield. He'd done his best to fight to save the people around him. He turned out to be a natural leader and quickly moved up the ranks to become second in command of the ground troops.

And then, he died.

It was shortly after his commander and friend Rykal had been shot, killed, and brought back as a cyborg. They'd gotten caught in a firefight and Rykal was still adjusting to his new cybernetics.

A Sholle fighter had somehow snuck up on their flank and was about to open fire on Rykal when Darrick noticed. Jumping in front of the blaster fire had been both instinctual and foolish, as Rykal's instincts would have kicked in and saved him, though Darrick hadn't known that at the time. The blast ripped through his body, leaving him broken, bloody and dying. Darrick remembered his vision fading into darkness as a final wave of pain washed over him.

And then, he woke up.

Now, years later as he stood in a waiting room on Grus Prime station, he couldn't help but wonder if the universe had somehow preordained his actions on that day, and his subsequent transformation from man to cyborg. Because for the last three days he'd been waiting on the station, a place he hadn't been to since before his rebirth – knowing that something monumental was about to happen to him. More accurately, there was a woman somewhere close by who he knew would change his life forever. All he needed to do was be patient and hope that the Grus would allow him to meet her.

Patience wasn't something Darrick was known for.

The room was small, but he'd been unable to walk about the station without a complement of armed guards trailing behind him. Rather than be constantly under the watchful eye of Grus security, Darrick waited alone and paced. Rykal had been allowed to come by only once, and even that brief visit had made the Grus security forces uncomfortable. One cyborg, they might have a chance of stopping if there was a problem; two of them could tear the station apart. But it had given Rykal the opportunity to let Darrick know exactly what was going on, telling him who these humans were and what was so special about them.

The thought of a group of women boarding a ship with no weapons or shields, being put into cryogenic sleep, and setting course for a sector of space that they had no intel on, just because they felt drawn to the location, made little sense to his cybernetic matrix. Hadn't they considered the risks to their lives? The possibility that they might have had a malfunction on the ship that could have sent them so far off course they would have never survived? The potential of alien marauders attacking them, stripping the ship of anything valuable, and selling them off to the highest bidder? They'd thought they were alone in the universe and did not consider the inherent dangers that would inevitably befall them once they realized they were in fact *not* alone.

They were foolish and impulsive, yet somehow, they miraculously arrived in one piece.

According to Rykal, all the women on board had the same sense of *need* that drew them to make this journey. Lena, the captain of the Kraken, was one of these women, and it turned out that she was destined to be Rykal's mate. More so, somehow her very presence was repairing a flaw in his code that Darrick hadn't even been aware was present in the original twenty-eight re-born cyborgs. If Lena had been drawn to Rykal and was somehow making him whole, then there was a strong possibility that there was a woman still sleeping on the ship who was destined to do the same for him.

It was madness.

He was a killer now, condemned to live the rest of his second life down on the planet, waiting in case they were attacked again and were required to serve and save the Grus people. He'd had the opportunity to have a mate, to live with her in a home and have children. That life was ripped from him the day he jumped in front of blaster fire to save a man who didn't need saving.

If it weren't for the constant itching in the back of his mind, he would have dismissed the idea completely.

Darrick looked over at the communications panel, but much as it had been for the past three days, there was no indication that the Grus had allowed the human women to be woken from their sleep. Aidric, the station commander and the creator of the cybernetic controls that ruled his life, had insisted that Darrick stay onboard the station. Aidric knew of the itching in his head, understood what the implications of that feeling were, and Darrick knew that he would soon be used as a test to see if what had happened to Rykal would also happen to him.

They wanted to know if he had a mate onboard as well.

Unfortunately for them all, Darrick wasn't going to last much longer cooped up in a room with nothing to do. Without thinking about it, he mentally reached out to the station's AI to see if he could get a status report.

ALERT! *Alert! Unauthorized cyborg infiltration!*

QUIET. *I'm not going to do anything to your systems. I need an update.*

WARNING, *unauthorized cyborg. If you do not disengage from central control, you will be deactivated.*

FINE, *but can you let me know if the human ship has cleared quarantine yet? I'm getting bored.*

THE AI PAUSED, and Darrick could almost feel it considering his request. Odd given that there wasn't supposed to be any ability for the AI to have emotional algorithms. Finally, it responded. *The Kraken has completed quarantine. Human subjects are still being held in cryogenic stasis, by order of Commander Aidric and the high council.*

Darrick wasn't surprised that Aidric was keeping tight control on releasing the new arrivals until he had a plan in place to ensure none of the Grus were put into danger. Their people had been subjected to too much loss, too much death for them to be anything but cautious.

Though that didn't mean that Darrick couldn't take a look at the alien's ship. He knew Rykal or Lena wouldn't mind, and it wasn't as though he was going to try and take off and leave the station. He smiled as he headed for the door, only to be stopped when it wouldn't open.

Come on. I want to go check out the ship.

He could feel the AI's annoyance. *Access denied. Cyborgs are not qualified to evaluate alien equipment.*

Darrick was about to give up and resign himself to another few hours of boredom when he had an idea. *I'm an authorized engineer. I have the necessary skills and approved expertise to provide a report to Grus high council.*

The confusion coming through the AI was palpable. *Cyborgs are soldiers, they have no additional skills.*

Run a scan for me and my record. Pre my rebirth.

Working...analyzing...record found...analyzing...
Darrick, first subcommander...lead engineer.

The one and only. It didn't matter than he'd died and been reborn with a rage so deep within him that he could turn into a vicious killer at a moment's notice. At one point in his life, he'd been an engineer and a damn good one. Those skills might have long gone unused, but with his enhanced memory, he was more than capable of recalling the information. The AI must have recognized that as well, because the doors to the room slid open.

. . .

IF CYBORG DARRICK does anything to endanger the life of any Grus on station Grus Prime, the cyborg will be immediately terminated.

UNDERSTOOD. He had no intention of doing anything beyond sating his curiosity about the human ship, and possibly reviewing their manifest to see if there was a chance that he too had a mate onboard. Not that he would let that bit of information slip to the AI.

The corridors of the station were full as he went down to the docking bay. A shift change for certain sectors must be in effect, which made getting to his destination unnoticed far more difficult. The Grus he passed would give him a wide birth, openly staring, and whispering softly. Darrick didn't know if they forgot that his hearing wasn't limited to the normal range of Grus, or if they just didn't care.

Monster.

I heard they fight each other to the death for fun on the planet.

I don't know why we don't detonate bombs on them and take our planet back.

That was the one that hurt the most. The cyborgs had been given what was left of Zarlan, the planet that all Grus had once lived on. It had been their payment for not only dying in the war against the Sholle but for having to give up their old lives to forever be weaponized machines that the Grus could use for any future wars. It was a small price for the Grus to pay for what they'd done to their fallen brothers and sisters, implanting cybernetics and programming their minds for destruction.

Darrick ignored them and kept his attention focused on the task at hand – finding the human ship. Thankfully, the security guards on duty in the docking bay were also in the middle of a shift change, which gave him a brief window to sneak inside unseen.

The air here was far warmer than the rest of the station,

closer to what it was like down on the planet's surface. The ship was resting securely at the far end of the bay, security clamps in place to prevent anyone from jumping in and taking off without permission. He made his way around the side of the ship, where the door appeared to have been forced open and then hastily re-secured.

Rykal had mentioned that he'd torn it apart it when he felt Lena on the other side and couldn't control himself, needing to get to her no matter the cost. Darrick felt no such urge, and he couldn't help but feel the sting of disappointment. He couldn't be certain that his mate was there, let alone that he'd react as Rykal.

The metal hull of the ship was old and had taken more than a little damage on its journey. Dents and scratches lined and pitted the metal, making patterns that could have represented the stars themselves. He placed his hand on the hull, surprised at how warm it felt beneath his touch. It was as though there was a living, beating heart somewhere deep inside of it that generated the heat, keeping its precious cargo safe and secure.

Darrick continued to inspect the ship, but his attention kept returning to the closed door and what he might find on the other side. He *knew* better than to go inside, to break not only with protocols, but with Rykal's request to keep his distance. If it weren't for the increased itching in the back of his mind, he would have turned around, his curiosity satisfied, and returned to his quarters to wait for further instructions.

He found himself standing in front of the door, his hand sliding along the handle, giving it a gentle tug to test its strength. The previous damage had weakened any chance of the metal keeping a cyborg out. It would take little effort for him to break in by twisting his arm like this –

The squeal and pop of the handle snapping and the door sliding open reverberated throughout the docking bay. If there were guards present, Darrick didn't bother to wait and find out if they'd heard. Grabbing hold of the handle, he stepped up into the ship.

The air inside was cooler than that of the docking bay. It held that chemical tint of recycled oxygen from years of purification. The computer technology, as well as the navigation controls, were basic at best, lacking many of the systems that the Grus had taken for granted for the better part of the last few centuries. Still, these humans had somehow made their way here against all the odds, and now they were under cyborg protection.

Darrick and the others would do what was necessary to keep these women safe – even if that meant fighting the Grus.

Darrick scratched at his head due to a sudden increase of the itching but was unable to relieve the building sensation. The ship's language was basic to the point where it lacked a self-sufficient AI, so interfacing with it to learn what he wanted about the passengers would not be impossible. That meant he needed to see them physically. *Why* wasn't a question he didn't want to ask, nor find an answer to. All Darrick knew was that he needed to look – he turned around – that way, to find…something.

His instincts took over as he moved, blindly navigating the narrow corridors of the ship with an efficiency he shouldn't have. Left here, then right and another right. Down this hallway toward the storage bay and *there*!

The doors slid open for him, revealing the cryogenic stasis tubes of twenty-seven active stasis tubes with the women still sleeping inside. Darrick walked up to the closest unit and looked down through the small window to see the face of a human female lying peacefully inside, still sleeping. Her features were smooth, her skin the same color as Lena's. Whoever she was, Darrick wished her well, but she was not who he was looking for. He moved from tube to tube, peering down at the various faces inside. They were similar in some ways – two eyes, one nose, lips – but varied wildly in others – brown skin, blonde hair, curls, bald – showing the variety in their species.

After several minutes of looking, Darrick finally stopped in front of a tube to scratch hard at the back of his head. The itching was to the point of distraction, almost so much that he nearly forgot to look down. The moment he did, though, everything in his world stopped.

He'd found her.

CHAPTER TWO

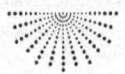

There was no explaining how he knew that the woman still sleeping in this tube was the one who was destined to be his mate, but Darrick had zero doubt. The light brown skin of her face was flawless, dusted with freckles, and framed with long curly black hair. Her lips were wide and full, and Darrick couldn't help but stare at them, wondering what it would be like to press his mouth to hers and kiss them. Even as she slept, he was aware of her presence and knew that when she woke up, there'd be no denying their connection.

Well, if the only way for that to happen was for her to come out of stasis, that was something he could easily remedy. Darrick moved to the ship's computer, trying to find a way to trigger the sequence that would wake her. The language and the controls made little sense to him despite the nanobots that helped with language translation, but it shouldn't take him long to force his way through. He pressed a few buttons when someone cleared their throat.

Darrick's head snapped up, and he realized that Aidric, Rykal and Lena were all standing in the doorway of the ship's loading bay, with a small security detail in the corridor behind him.

Aidric stepped forward as every internal alarm went off in Darrick's head.

"I need you to step away from the computer."

The rage that Darrick had long thought he'd suppressed quickly roared to the surface. Without thinking, he charged Aidric, throwing his body at him with a shout. The impact of slamming into the ground was blunted by Aidric's body beneath him, which Darrick barely registered. "You're not going to take her away from me!" He slammed Aidric's upper body down hard against the floor, and his head bounced sharply. "She's mine!"

He pulled his fist back to slam it into Aidric's face when someone caught him from behind and yanked him back off the now stunned Grus commander. Arms came up beneath his shoulders and locked his head in a vice-like grip that immobilized him, even if it didn't lessen his rage and panic. "Let me go!"

WARNING! *Cyborg attack detected. Warning! Continued assault on Commander Aidric will be viewed as a violation of the protocol CY-567. Warning! Cyborg decommission imminent.*

THE STATION'S AI shouted in Darrick's head, but it did nothing to stop him from struggling against Rykal's grip. "I said, let me go!"

"Not until you get hold of yourself, soldier." Rykal's voice in his ear, his body was keeping Darrick in check. "No one is taking your mate from you."

As quickly as the rage had flared, it dulled enough that Darrick was able to regain a fragment of his control. "I need her."

"I know you do. But not like this. You need to be strong for her, and you need to be patient while we wake her up and let her know what's going on."

He didn't *want* to wait. He did want to smash through the metal and glass that kept her from him, pull her into his arms, and never let her go. Even knowing that doing so could hurt her was barely enough to keep him from acting on that impulse. He surged forward, trying to break out of Rykal's grasp, but he couldn't break free. "Let me go."

"Lena's going to wake her up right now. Then we'll see about you meeting your mate."

Aidric's security forces helped him up and steadied him once he got to his feet. "Thank you for proving my theory. I'm surprised you were able to hold out as long as you did before you went in search of her."

He should have realized that the entire process had been too easy. They'd *let* him break in. He'd been used as little more than a *fraking* science experiment.

Lena made her way over to the stasis tube and looked inside. "Oh, that's Carys Jones. She was one of the first passengers to find me and sign up for our journey. We became friends of a sort." Lena tucked her red hair behind her ear and started pressing several buttons on the side of the tube. "I've begun the process of waking her up. It takes about an hour for us to fully come out of the sleep and for our bodies to get rehydrated. She'll be hungry as well." Lena looked over at them, her gaze lingering on Rykal. "We should give her more time than I had to get her bearings."

"I suggest that we relocate Darrick temporarily." Aidric nodded in his direction. "We need to give her a chance to acclimate to her new reality."

"No!" He tried to get out of Rykal's hold again, nearly succeeding this time. "I'm not leaving her!"

"Soldier, stand down!" Rykal's command cut through the chaos of Darrick's mind, and he froze. "We're going to stand up and move to the corridor. No one will keep you from your mate. I won't allow it."

Darrick looked over at Lena, who was still pressing buttons and activating parts of the computer system that he hadn't even recognized as important, and knew Rykal understood his needs. Nothing would keep him apart from her, and he had his commanding officer's support to ensure nothing bad would happen.

He closed his eyes for a moment and did his best to let the fear and paranoia slip away enough that he could do what was asked of him. "I can make it to the corridor."

"Good. Now, on your feet." Rykal let him go.

The sudden freedom threatened to overwhelm Darrick as the urge to run and possess hit him once more. But he fought it, reaching out to grip Rykal's shoulder and squeeze it in search of support. "I require assistance."

With a solid grip on Darrick's arm, Rykal maneuvered him past the stasis tube and out into the corridor where the terrified looking Grus security forces stood. Rykal chased them back with a single sneer, which gave Darrick room to breathe. "Did I hurt the commander?"

"Aidric's head is as thick and impenetrable as his heart. He'll be fine."

Which was lucky for Darrick, because an accident or not, killing the Grus commander would mean he'd be deactivated immediately and there would be nothing that Rykal could do to stop it from happening.

With each passing moment, Darrick found it more difficult to keep himself still, to stop himself from rushing back to see his mate – to finally hold Carys in his arms. Even the sound of her name felt right to him, as alien as it was. She would have to know that she was destined to be with him, to live the rest of her life on the planet where he could take care of her.

"Why's this taking so long?" He took a step closer to the door, even as Rykal stood there, blocking him from returning. "I can feel her waking up."

"Lena had been automatically woken up by the ship when they entered our sector of space. Even being as far away as I was from her, I was still aware of her presence. I know what you're feeling is overwhelming, but you must be patient."

The last thing Darrick wanted to be was patient. He wanted to rip through metal to get to her. He wanted to kill anyone who dared to stand in his way or who might try and keep her from him. He wanted to strip them both naked and fuck her for hours until there was no mistaking that she was his and he was hers.

His cock was stiff, and even his *rondella* was beginning to fill and swell – a sexual reaction that hadn't happened to him since long before his rebirth as a cyborg. Darrick knew if he couldn't get himself under control, there was a chance he'd scare her with his desires. Or worse, he'd hurt her; that was something he would never forgive himself for.

"I need to...do something." He pressed his forehead to the cool metal wall. "I can't stop this overwhelming need to..."

"Claim her?" Rykal nodded, placing a hand on his shoulder. "I was the same. Aidric has a theory of why we're reacting this way to the human women, but I'm not certain I believe it."

"I've never felt this way. Not even before the rebirth."

"Nor I." Rykal turned so he could see Lena. "The urges and panic ease, but I'm still aware of them and Lena every moment I'm conscious. Aidric seems to think that will ease as time goes on, but he can't be sure until there's another cyborg to study and compare against what's happening in my own matrix."

"Me." It would figure that despite everything he'd been through and given up for the Grus, that he'd still be little more than a subject to be studied in the lab. "I'll let them look at anything they want as soon as I can hold her in my arms."

Time crept on, and Darrick was painfully aware of each passing second. The closer Carys rose in consciousness, the stronger the urge became to force his way to her side. He somehow held himself back and stood watching Lena as she worked her magic to bring the cryogenic tube's system up to full. Heat in the loading bay rose, and several of the Grus security guards muttered their discomfort and shifted annoyingly off to the side.

Darrick took the rage and annoyance that filled him and directed outward. "Leave if you're going to complain!"

That sent the security guards scurrying out of the ship. Rykal nodded, a slight smile on his lips. "At least the Grus still have their survival instincts intact."

Darrick was well past the point of caring about the Grus, their protection, or anything else. Until he had Carys in his arms, nothing else mattered. They stood in the hall, and Darrick watched Lena finalize the process of bringing Carys out of cryogenic sleep, while Rykal mostly watched her move. If Darrick was going to become as focused on his mate as Rykal was on his, there was a chance he wouldn't be able to accomplish anything else. She'd have to come with him to Zarlan, to live in the city and do…he had no idea what humans were capable of. Lena was a ship's captain and navigator, so the race could at least learn.

"What are we going to do with them?" He didn't look away but knew Rykal was listening. "When this is over, and she's with me, where will we take them? Can they survive on the planet, or will we have to build special homes for them?"

"I don't know." It was obviously something Rykal had thought of as well. "Aidric has insisted Lena undergo a series of medical evaluations while she's here. I would be prepared that he asks the same of your mate once she's woken. Once we know their biology, we'll be better able to prepare them for their new lives. Do what we need to in order to keep them safe."

There would be a need for new homes, beds, other products to help keep them protected. Darrick's mind categorized the possibilities, making notes of where he could put his long-dormant engineering skills to good use. He'd gotten halfway through the list when he was hit with a sudden rush of awareness.

Carys was awake.

He nearly made it past Rykal, but he was grabbed from behind. "Let me go."

"She won't be able to understand you. They'll need to inject the nanobots into her brain to allow for the lingual translation. Based on what happened with Lena, it appeared to be painful."

No, he didn't want her to feel any pain. He wanted to steal her away from them all and wrap his body around hers. "I need to be with her."

Rykal's grip held fast, even and Darrick continued into the room. "Lena, I suggest you talk to your friend and quickly tell her what's going on so we can get those nanobots injected. I'm not going to be able to hold him back much longer."

Lena nodded and leaned down over the stasis tube, speaking to Carys. Darrick couldn't pick up their words, but he was more than aware of Carys' emotional state – confusion, relief, and fear followed in rapid succession. Lena stepped back, and Aidric came closer, while additional movement from the stasis tube caught Darrick's eye.

After a moment, Carys sat up and looked around. Her black hair had slipped forward and covered most of her profile, making it difficult for him to see her. She said something and chuckled, a deep, rich sound that sent a shiver through his body. He must have made a noise because Carys turned to look over at him, her eyes wide and her mouth opened.

That first glimpse of her brown eyes was more than Darrick could handle. Using a sudden surge of energy, he ripped himself from Rykal's grip and ran across the room. Carys cried out, scrambling backward in the tube, unable to get away from him as he threw himself against the side. He cupped her chin in his hands and looked her in the eyes.

"Mine."

CHAPTER THREE

Carys was still trying to catch her bearings when a large man cried out and bolted toward her. She wasn't a shrinking flower, nor was she normally easily intimidated by anyone, let alone a man. But this wasn't a normal man, or even the same as the alien Lena had introduced to her. No, this dude was huge, with glowing green eyes, and apparently had a keen interest in her.

Which, shit, that was more than a bit to take in after having been asleep for over a half a century.

The touch of his hand on her face sent a shiver through her that ended when someone pulled him back. Lena stepped between them, pressing her body against the side of the stasis tube. "Let's not start with the possessive bullshit. Maybe give her a moment to catch her breath, okay?"

"Yes, please." She wasn't normally someone to be slow on the uptake when it came to situations, but even she needed a moment to make sense of things.

"We really didn't have time for me to fill you in on all the details. Umm, yeah. This is Darrick. He's a cyborg and we think there might be a connection between their people and the women who boarded the Kraken."

Carys' heartbeat pounded hard in her throat, and she wanted nothing more than to set some space between her and this hyper fixated man – cyborg, whatever – and herself. "That's ah...not exactly what I was expecting when I signed up for this trip."

If she was being completely honest with herself, Carys hadn't been certain why she'd felt so compelled to get on the Kraken, knowing it was going to be a one-way trip with an uncertain future waiting on the other end. Sometimes she'd imagine there'd be a lush planet full of vegetation and deep pools of water waiting for them. Other times, she'd picture a planet like Earth, full of cities and people, but with far less in the way of hate and prejudice.

Cyborgs hadn't entered the equation.

Carys kept an eye on Darrick, even as she spoke to Lena. "Do you think its safe if I get out of the stasis tube?" Now that she was awake, the desire to get up and stretch her legs was growing exponentially.

The alien beside Lena said something to her in a language that Carys didn't understand. As an amateur linguist, the cadence and flow of his speech intrigued her, the exact sort of thing she'd wanted to discover beyond the normal confines of human exploration. "What did he say? And more importantly, how did you understand him? The last time I checked you'd wanted me along on this journey to help with the translation side of things."

Lena smiled. "So, they have these nanobots that they can inject into our heads. I don't want to pretend to know how they work, but they rewire our minds somehow to help us understand the different language spoken. It hurt like a sonofabitch, but so far apart from a few words that don't have any context equivalent in human language, I understand everything said to me."

Admiration and disappointment washed through Carys. "My skills aren't exactly needed here."

The alien stepped closer, glancing briefly up at Darrick, before nodding. He waved one of his minions closer, who handed him what looked to be an injector. Holding it out for her to see, he cocked his head to the side, and she got the impression that he was waiting to see if she was interested.

She'd be a fool not to want to take the injection. It would be an amazing experience to simply know what everyone was saying to her all the time. Her desire to learn other languages had come when she was a child, growing up on the streets. The mix of people and cultures all mashed together as they struggled to survive meant there were times when Carys had to barter with people she couldn't communicate with. The more languages she'd learned, the easier it had been to get what she needed to survive. And that had allowed her to gather the resources she'd needed to eventually buy passage on the Kraken and end up here.

Which wasn't going quite the way she'd anticipated.

Darrick pulled once again against the other cyborg who held him back. The other cyborg said something to Lena, who snorted. "Rykal said if you wouldn't mind making a decision a bit faster, he'd appreciate it. Darrick's a bit of a handful and things will be easier if you're able to communicate with everyone."

Carys ignored the alien and the two cyborgs, and instead forced her stiff body to move and pulled herself out of the stasis tube. "They're going to have to suffer some inconvenience a bit longer. I'm not going to have something injected into my body before I've even got my ass out of bed. For all we know it's some sort of mind control device that links us to those things." She nodded toward the cyborgs.

Lena chuckled and nodded. "Yeah, I didn't really think that through given the circumstances. But the cyborgs don't seem to need the nanobots in us to be linked. Darrick found your stasis tube and you hadn't even been woken."

Turning on shaky legs, Carys got a good look at Darrick. She'd seen that level of desperation only once before; it had been unnerving then, even though it hadn't been focused on her. A man had been trying to get medicine to help a dying child, and had been left nearly in tears when the black-market vendor hadn't held up his end of their agreement, selling the medicine to a higher bidder. It had broken Carys' heart, but it also served as a reminder that the only person she'd be able to trust in life was herself.

Seeing Darrick staring at her with that level of desperate need was nearly too much for her to handle. Swallowing hard, she shook her head. "For now, I'd rather take the time and learn how to speak their language on my own. It's probably a good idea for at least one of us to understand it in case there are any problems with your nanobots in the future."

The alien looked at her a moment longer before nodded and handed the injector back to his minion. He then said something else to Lena who shrugged. "That's a good point."

"What point?" It would be frustrating having Lena understanding everyone and not translating, but they'd all have to go through a bit of a learning curve.

"Sorry." Lena indicated toward the alien. "This is Aidric the station commander of the Grus Prime, which is the station we're on. The aliens call themselves the Grus and the cyborgs are known as The Fallen. He said that your decision is probably wise and smart because you can in turn teach others who might not wish the injection either. The process hurts like hell."

The last thing she wanted to do was be put in a position to act as a teacher; but the unexpected results of her decision to board the Kraken were quickly becoming a lesson in compromise. "Fine. I'll need someone to teach me their language and then I'll setup lessons for anyone who doesn't want the injection once we bring them out of cryo sleep."

Darrick tore himself out of Rykal's grip and leapt across the stasis tube to land only a few inches away from where Carys stood. She gasped at his sudden proximity, but despite his earlier indications that he wanted to physically manhandle her, he made no move to touch her again. He spoke, his words coming out in a slow deliberate cadence, even as others around him exploded in chaos at his sudden escape.

She found it nearly impossible to look away from the soft glow of his green eyes. They were clearly powered by whatever cybernetics he had, giving the rest of his body a truly alien feel. He was larger than any of the other men in the room, even the other cyborg, and commanded everyone's attention and no doubt a healthy amount of fear.

Not that Carys was scared – not of him at least. She didn't know how she knew, but there wasn't anything Darrick would do to intentionally hurt her. If anything, she had reason to believe that the safety of everyone else in the loading bay was more at risk from him than her. Swallowing past the sudden tightness of her throat, she chanced a look at Lena. "What did he say?"

"Basically, he's offering to teach you their language. And no, I don't think it's a bad idea." Rykal said something else to Lena as he moved closer to Darrick's side. She rolled her eyes and snorted. "If he's Carys' mate the way you all seem to think he is, then this will be a good opportunity for them to get to know one another. No kidnapping involved."

"Kidnapping? Mate?" The last thing she'd ever expected was to find any type of relationship once she'd boarded the ship and left Earth. Yes, she'd had an overwhelming interest and desire to go with Lena, especially when she discovered what their destination sector was. She hadn't considered that there'd be an alien cyborg waiting for her wanting to settle down with her. "I didn't fly across the galaxy to hookup with a robot."

Darrick narrowed his gaze.

Lena came up along side her. "The interesting thing is that you might have actually done something like that without even realizing it." She gently moved Carys backward away from

Darrick. "I know this is a lot to take in. I just went through it myself with Rykal, so I know your brain is barely awake and trying to deal with this stuff is next to impossible. What we really need to do is give her some space."

Darrick rambled off a string of words that flew past Carys, but there was no mistaking the tone; he wasn't going to let anyone take her anywhere. The tension in the room rose and it was only going to be a matter of time before someone got hurt. If she didn't do something to diffuse Darrick, it wasn't going to end well for any of them.

"How about this? Give me a few minutes alone with Lena so I can get cleaned up and changed. Then you and I can meet, and you can try and teach me some words. How does that sound?" She kept her voice smooth and her tone light, hoping it would be enough to help Darrick relax.

What she hadn't anticipated was for him to reach up and cup her cheek with his massive hand. The warmth of his touch surprised her, as did the gentleness of his caress. For a man as big as he was, Darrick clearly had the capacity to care deeply. He held her gaze and nodded once, before stepping back and giving her the space she so desperately needed.

"Okay then." The muscles in her neck and back were tight and now that the immediate tension from the situation was gone, all she wanted was a pain reliever and a hot shower. "Have you woken anyone else up?"

"Given how both Rykal and now Darrick have reacted to our presence, it's probably for the best that we keep the other women in cryo sleep until we figure out exactly what's happening. Then we'll be able to better prepare ourselves."

Logical and smart; two of the reasons Carys had felt confident signing up as a passenger on Lena's ship. "Then medical is empty and I'll be able to get all the good drugs."

Aidric said something then, but Lena waved him off. "Thanks, but knowing Carys the way I do, she's going to want to stick with human medicine for the time being."

"For now." Carys waited for Lena to drape a blanket across her shoulders, before letting the other woman lead her out of the loading bay before she said anything else. "What the fuck's going on?"

"It's weird and I'm not sure I have all the details. I've only been awake myself for about five days, but a lot has happened. Let's get you to medical and we'll go from there."

They were about to turn the corner when Carys looked back at Darrick. She didn't know why, but she was certain that her life had gotten dramatically more complicated. What she wasn't sure of was if that was a good thing or not.

CHAPTER FOUR

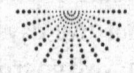

There were certain advantages to being one of the first few passengers awake on a ship. Being able to spend as much time as she wanted in the shower was a perk Carys hadn't realized she'd been missing in her life. Clean clothing and a towel were waiting for her when she stepped out, but there wasn't any sign of Lena.

"I'm in the exam room." Lena's voice reached her from across the corridor. "Alone."

Carys didn't know why that bit of information relaxed her the way it did, but she wasn't about to question it. "I'll be over in a minute."

If Lena had only been pulled from cryo sleep five days earlier, then chances were she didn't have all the answers Carys wanted. She'd have to keep her natural inclination to dig up details at a minimum. And yet, there was a part of her that didn't want to go into medical and ask any questions at all. Carys wasn't a fool and knew the chances of her getting an answer she wouldn't like were highly likely, and that would only serve to piss her off.

She hadn't fought this hard and come this far to basically end up as a sex toy for a cyborg.

Giving herself a shake, Carys strode into medical enjoying the way the cool air felt against her damp hair and skin. "So, what the hell's going on?"

Lena sat on the examination bed, her feet swinging as she held out an injector for Carys to take. "Painkillers for you. It should help make everything better. As for what's going on, that's still something we're trying to figure out." Lena pressed the injector to her neck and did her best to focus on Lena's explanation.

Over the next few minutes Lena proceeded to tell her what had happened when she'd been woken by the ship's computer, and Rykal's reaction and subsequent kidnapping of her when they finally came face to face. "Be thankful that we knew enough to keep an eye on Darrick and Rykal was strong enough to hold him back. While the planet's surface is better than what we left on Earth, it has these massive electrical storms that are remnants from their war with the Sholle."

Carys sat down on the bed beside Lena. "Do you believe them? That there's a chance that we're their mates?"

Normally one with a quick come back or snarky remark, Carys was surprised when Lena didn't immediately say anything at all. Her gaze slipped down to her empty hands as her lips pursed. "I have a question for you. You're going to want to answer it right away, but instead I want you to take a minute to really think about it before you do."

Carys didn't like where this was going. "Okay."

"When you were back on Earth, before you signed up to come on my ship, did you ever find yourself looking up at the sky and knowing that there was something out here for you? Not like some wistful thinking *oh someday my life will be better out there* kind of shit. Like you knew in your heart that if you didn't get passage on the Kraken you would regret it for the rest of your life?"

Carys did open her mouth to speak; her response of *no, that's insane* nearly spilling past her lips. She'd been too busy trying to buy food for herself, trying to barter and negotiate with vendors so she wouldn't have to try and stretch out her supplies past the point of reasonable. Life on Earth was hard, but it also had its fun moments too. Teaching the upper class how to speak common dialects used in different communities so they could try and convince people to come work for them, only to give them all the wrong words making them sound like idiots had been fun. Sure, it had gotten her in a pile of trouble, but it also had her laughing for months.

And yet, she'd always set money aside, knowing that one day she was going to use it to get off Earth and go out into space. She knew she wasn't going to live on Earth forever, though her final destination wasn't something that she'd ever had a clear idea about. When she'd finally found Lena and learned that she was planning on taking a ship full of passengers to an unknown sector of space to set up new lives, Carys knew she was meant to be on that ship. That there was something up there that needed her.

Someone up there.

"I guess I did." She frowned as she turned the injector over in her hand. "Well, shit."

"Exactly. Rykal and I have been talking with Aidric over the past few days while we were monitoring Darrick. Apparently when Aidric designed the cybernetic matrix that they implanted into the fallen soldiers, he'd missed a bug in the code with the initial group. It made the cyborgs prone to a level of violence that Aidric and the other Grus couldn't control. But once Rykal started spending, ah, time with me, that code seemed to change and filled in the gaps that were present."

"And he thinks that somehow, we women of a different species, half a galaxy away were aware of this and hopped a ship to come help? That's fucked up."

"I know, but I don't have a better explanation." Lena looked up and let out a little sigh. "Apparently, there are twenty-eight cyborgs who were initially created. They've all migrated to leadership roles within the cyborg community. Aidric changed the code once he realized the problem, created a workaround or something, but those twenty-eight men were always more aggressive, always took charge."

"Twenty-eight." Carys understood the implication. "There are twenty-eight women on the Kraken."

"Weird, right?" Lena shrugged. "Darrick didn't respond at all to me, which rules out it being a weird general human-cyborg connection. The responses appear to be specific. One cyborg and one woman from the ship. And we need to figure out if there's anything else we need to know before we wake anyone else."

It was smart. "I guess we're lucky that I'm the second woman. There are a few of them in cryo sleep who would be having a harder time dealing with this than me."

"I was thinking the same thing. We'll have to be cautious, but I'm so happy I have you here to help me. It was a bit much trying to make sense of everything on my own."

Without thinking, Carys threw her arm over Lena's shoulder and pulled her in for a hug. "I can't imagine everything that you've been through. The weight of responsibility ensuring that we not only made it here but kept us all safe. Thank you for that."

Lena wiped away an errant tear. "You're welcome. Now, I think we're going to have to come up with a quick plan because if Rykal's reaction was anything to go by, Darrick isn't going to stay away from you for long. Are you going to be okay being alone with him?"

There wasn't much Carys couldn't handle on her own. "I'll be fine. I have to admit I'm looking forward to the challenge of learning a new language."

"Oh my God, Rykal couldn't understand why you wouldn't accept the nano bots. They're so used to everything coming so easily to them that they've forgotten the thrill of learning something for yourself."

Sure, we'll go with that. "Where am I going to meet him?"

"I'd suggested here on the ship, but Aidric wants Darrick someplace where he can be contained if there's a problem. They've assigned him a room on the station, and he'd like you to work there."

Considering she'd come as far as she had and hadn't stepped foot off the ship yet, Carys was more than ready. "The pain relievers have kicked in and I'm ready to go."

"I figured you'd say that, so Rykal and Darrick are waiting outside in the docking bay that they have the Kraken in. Let's go."

Carys couldn't explain it, but as they walked toward the exit a weird mix of excitement and desire began to build inside her. She wasn't a prude and loved sex as much as the next woman, but she wasn't exactly the type to get aroused at the idea of spending time with a man she'd only spent a brief amount of time with. But here she was, her nipples growing hard and her pussy feeling that first rush of arousal as she stepped down from the Kraken to land a few feet away from where Darrick stood waiting.

He was just as large and intimidating as she remembered, but something had changed in the intensity of his gaze. There was a heat behind the look he gave her as she strode up to him, one that hadn't been there previously. "I'm all cleaned up and feeling better. Time to learn how to speak your language."

Darrick nodded and held out his hand in the direction he wanted her to go. Lena and Rykal fell into step behind them, just far enough away to give them a bit of privacy, but still close enough for Rykal to intervene if there was a problem. The doors slid open when they reached the end of the docking bay, revealing the interior of the space station. The walls were much taller than Carys had anticipated, their gunmetal gray making the passageway cold and feel like a prison. "Shit, that's really not a good look."

Carys knew he could understand her but wasn't expecting him to laugh. He nodded and motioned for her to go toward the right. "I don't know which one of your people built this station, but they really needed to hire someone who could have helped with the overall aesthetic of the place."

Darrick spoke, but the words still weren't registering with her the way she'd hoped they might. She was able to pick up the odd one here and there and would need to start writing things down to help her solidify them in her brain. As then went, many of the Grus they passed stared at Darrick, giving them a wide berth whenever it was possible. Anyone who came close would keep their eyes averted, as though they were scared that even acknowledging his presence would bring them bad luck.

"You're not a very popular guy around here, are you?"

He shrugged but didn't say anything in response. They eventually turned a corner that led to a far less populated corridor, giving them space enough to reach their destination far faster. Lena came up behind her and nodded at the door to the left. "Rykal and I are in these quarters. It's unusual for two cyborgs to be on the station at the same time, so they separated the two of them. Darrick's room is a bit further down, but if you have any problems just come here."

The thought of being left alone with a man who was claiming to be her mate should be freaking Carys out, but it wasn't. "Okay. I'll have him contact you once we're done, I guess?"

"Yeah, I don't think we really know what next steps are going to be." She looked up at Rykal and smiled. "Maybe we'll head down to the planet?"

Rykal said something and nodded, which elicited a response from Darrick. Maybe she was going to have to rethink the entire internal translation system. Lena smiled. "I'm not sure Aidric would approve."

"Would you mind translating for those of us who are stubbornly refusing nanobots?"

"Oh sorry." Lena blushed. "Darrick suggested bringing more cyborgs up here to see if they too can find their mates. That might be a good idea but I didn't think the station commander would approve."

Rykal said something else as he wrapped his arm around Lena. "Right. We're going inside now. Let me know if you need anything." The door slid open and Lena looked over her shoulder at Carys and winked. "Have fun."

And then she was alone with a cyborg on an alien space station.

"Okay then." Turning to look at Darrick, she was surprised to see an amused smile on his face. His green eyes glowed, giving him a distinctly alien appearance. "I guess we're heading to your place."

Darrick nodded his chin in the direction they were to walk, as he locked his hands behind his back. Carys could carry on a conversation with the best of people, and she wasn't afraid to make mistakes when it came to learning a new language. Her brain was wired in such a way that she didn't find it difficult, especially if she was submersed in the culture. So, spending time with Darrick would be exactly the type of person she should spend time with to pick up the nuances.

Even if what she really wanted to do was see if the muscles she'd caught a glimpse of were as big and she'd suspected.

They finally stopped at a door half a corridor away from where Lena and Rykal had disappeared. Carys took a breath and steadied herself before straightening. "Let's do this."

Darrick opened the door and she marched inside without really looking at where she was going. Upon reaching the middle of the room, she stopped and frowned. "This is pretty basic."

The door closed behind them as Darrick made his way to sit on a small couch that was set against the far wall. There was nothing personal about the quarters, but they were functional enough to ensure any guests would be comfortable enough for their stay. Without a bunch of objects though, it would be a bit harder for her to learn basic vocabulary. Darrick watched her as she moved around the room, and she couldn't help but wonder if he was trying to analyze her the way she was analyzing her surroundings.

There was a small computer terminal in the corner, which would probably give them limited access to the station. Stopping in front of it, she ran her finger across the smooth surface. "This is a computer terminal. How do you pronounce it in your language?"

"*Tal mechana.*" He said the words from the couch, his gaze locked onto her.

Carys tried to ignore the way her body was starting to respond to his proximity and focused on his words. "*Tal mechana.* Okay, that's easy enough. How about this?" She reached out and touched the chair that had been shoved off to the side. "What's this called?"

"*Shtole.*"

"Now I know computer terminal, *tal mechana* and chair, *shtole*. I'm going to be running this place before you know it."

Darrick chuckled and the deep richness of the sound sent a chill through her. Shit, there was nothing more arousing that a sexy voice on a man with a body to match. She turned around and half sat on the edge of the desk. Darrick was watching her every move, his green eyes roaming across her body, pausing momentarily on all the typical places that men tended to look. She cocked her head to the side and smiled. *You're going to be a bad girl now, aren't you?*

She sure was.

"One of the best ways to learn a language is to start with common words and then work your way up. How about I point to an object and you tell me what it's called?"

He nodded but looked slightly confused.

Carys stood up and crossed the room, only stopping when she

was only half a foot away from him. Keeping her gaze locked on his, she reached for the hem of her shirt and pulled it up and over her head. She then dangled it out in front of him. "What's this called?"

A muscle in Darrick's jaw jumped. "*Mala.*"

"Shirt is *mala.*" She let it drop to the floor. "I'll remember that." Probably not, but this had suddenly not become about learning to speak his language and had quickly become about fucking.

Darrick was also aware of the change in the mood, rising to his feet in a sudden quick motion. He rambled off a sentence and surprisingly, Carys was able to recognize a few of the words. She didn't need to worry about a translation though, because the next thing Darrick did was cup her cheeks in his hands and captured her mouth with his in a kiss that curled her toes.

Her pussy dampened as pleasure heated low in her belly, and her nipples hardened as he pressed his muscular chest hard against her. His tongue thrust against hers as they sparred briefly with one another, seeing who was going to win dominance over the other. When Darrick thrust his hand into her hair and tugged her head backward until her entire body was almost thrown off balance, she knew he'd won.

Finally, he pulled up, his lips moist from their kiss. "*Sha.*"

"*Sha.* Kiss?" She licked her lips.

He nodded. "*Frak.*"

"Oh, I think I know that." She moaned when he reached up and pinched her nipple. "I very much want to *frak*. Right now."

Darrick's wolfish grin was all the translation she needed.

CHAPTER FIVE

Darrick scooped her up in his arms and carried her over to the bed. Unlike his home down on Zarlan, this bed was larger and far more comfortable. Having a place to rest wasn't exactly a necessity for him, or any of the other Fallen. If Carys was truly his mate, that would be a problem he'd have to remedy before he brought her down to live with him.

He didn't know what human women liked, but she might even enjoy helping to make his dwelling more comfortable.

Not that he cared about that just now.

The only thing Darrick could focus on was Carys and how she squirmed and shifted on the mattress as he watched her get comfortable. He'd somehow become hyper aware of her emotional state, which made this entire experience even more arousing to him. How she'd switched from frustration at not being able to understand what people were saying, to pride at understanding the few words he'd taught her, to her arousal at the prospect of going to bed with him, had been a shock to keep up with.

Carys lifted her leg and shook her foot at him. "Mind offering a little assistance?"

It was strange being able to understand her but knowing she didn't have any idea what he was saying in response. He wasn't much of a conversationalist, so holding his tongue wasn't a difficult prospect for him. His actions always spoke louder than his words, and thankfully actions were all that were necessary of him for the next little while.

Holding her leg in one hand, he removed the boot with the other. When it fell to the floor with a thump, she switched so he could remove the second one. Instead of letting her leg go, he grabbed hold of the cuff of her pants and gave them a little tug. Carys smiled as she reached for the waist of her pants. "If you let me go then this whole process will be a whole lot faster."

With both her feet now pressed against the mattress, she lifted her hips and slid the material over her hips and thighs and down her legs, leaving her clad in only two tiny pieces of fabric. She looped her fingers beneath the straps of the material that covered her breasts and slowly slid them down her arms. "I'm feeling more than a little underdressed. Think I can convince you to get naked too?"

Unlike her, Darrick lacked the ability to be subtle or to tease. With a single motion, he pulled his shirt off and dropped it to the floor. He then toed off his boots, casting them aside so he could push his pants down. Now naked, he stood still and let her look as much as she wanted at his body.

Unlike the arousal he'd been expecting, a look of shock and horror crossed her face. "What the fuck happened to you?"

It had been so long since anyone had seen his cybernetics, he'd forgotten how overwhelming they could be for another to see. The side of his neck and all of his left shoulder and arm had been destroyed by the blaster fire he'd taken in the war; the blast that would have killed Rykal if he hadn't already had cybernetics installed in him. They'd also enhanced his legs, though those were in addition to his natural self, instead of a replacement.

Carys got up from the bed and moved to stand in front of him. "Can I touch them?"

He nodded and was surprised when his internal systems kicked in to regulate a rush of his adrenaline. Was he excited at the idea of her touching him, or was this yet another anomaly in his systems? Quite possibly, they were one and the same. When Carys got to her feet, he had to fight the urge to hold his breath as she ran her hand up his cybernetic arm, along his shoulder and over to this neck.

"How did I not notice?"

Darrick had long perfected the ability to mask his cybernetics, having gotten used to others' negative responses to them. Even other Fallen who had more than enough of their own enhancements were startled at the extent of his additions. His death had been bloody, violent – and his rebirth more than a little unexpected. The Fallen held a great many things against Aidric and his cybernetics program, but he'd worked a miracle when he'd brought Darrick back to life.

Unlike others, Carys wasn't repulsed by who he'd become after his wounds. No, she was fascinated, going so far as to lean in and place a kiss to his biceps. "I can't image the pain you must have felt going through this."

He shrugged. She could understand his explanation, and even if she was, he'd yet to find the words to accurately explain what it had felt like to die, only to come screaming back to life. Thankfully, she didn't let his silence stop her from exploring the rest of his body. Her hands slipped from his cybernetics over to the skin of his true body. There he was able to feel, to be able to pretend that his life was still a bit normal, that he could still love and feel the way he had before.

She moved around to stand directly in front of him and leaned in to place a kiss to the middle of his chest. The press of her moist lips to his body sent a shiver of awareness through him, exciting parts of him that he'd assumed had long ago died. His cock throbbed to life and for the first time since his rebirth, his *rondella* filled with blood and pleasure began to build deep inside him.

"*Frak.*" He tipped his head back and enjoyed the growing arousal.

"I don't need to speak your language to understand that word." She chuckled as she let her hand slide down his front to land on his thickening cock. "Nice to know that our biology is compatible."

He hadn't asked Rykal if that was true, but given that someone hadn't tried to stop him, or deterred him otherwise, then he had to believe that was the case. They'd both find out rather quickly if he got his way.

Darrick tried to keep calm and his desires under control, but the more Carys touched him, the harder it was to do so. When she wrapped her fingers around his cock and gave it a stroke, he growled, flinching hard.

"Did I hurt you?" Her eyes were wide, and her lips parted.

He shook his head hard, but couldn't stop from pushing on her shoulders, hoping she'd understand what he wanted her to do. Based on the sly smile she gave him, she knew exactly his intentions. With a lick of her lips, she leaned down and placed a kiss on his stomach. "You're a bit too tall for me to get on my knees and suck you. Why don't you sit on the edge of the bed?"

It was far easier for him to accept commands than it was to give them, so Darrick moved to do as she suggested, but refused to let go of her. It had been so very long since he'd last been with a woman in a sexual way, and the excitement racing through his body was overwhelming his internal systems. His cock throbbed and pressed hard against his lower belly, his *rondella* almost too sensitive for him to manage.

Carys positioned herself between his thighs which he opened

to give her the best access. Her gaze landed on the dark green patch of skin on his inner thigh, immediately drawing her attention. "What the hell's this?"

"*Rondella.*" He sucked in a breath as she ran her fingers along the sensitive surface.

"I don't think there's a human equivalent for this. What's it for?" But without the nanobots there was no way she'd be able to understand his explanation.

Darrick took one of her hands and cupped the bottom of his cock, while shifting the other to press down lightly on the dark patch. The dual sensations dragged a moan from him, and he bucked up into the air on instinct.

"Oh, that's going to be fun." She chuckled as she lowered her mouth to suck the tip of his shaft.

The swirl of her tongue across the head of his cock was glorious; pleasure built up deep within him, a sensation he'd long ago assumed he'd never be able to experience again. The warm moist darting of her tongue was practically electric, setting his nerves ablaze as his arousal grew higher and higher. She increased the pressure on his *rondella*, until Darrick thought he was about to be overcome by a pre-orgasm, the bloom of desire a male Grus felt that signaled he was ready to mate.

Gods, this was nearly as overpowering as the first time he'd ever mated with a woman. Everything felt right, perfect, exactly how it should have been for him. Carys was the only woman he could picture himself with from now on. His hand moved to the back of her head as he pressed his fingers into her black curls. He tired to keep his possessive desires at bay, but the closer his orgasm came the more difficult that became.

He needed to pull her back, wanted to taste her the way she tasted him. He wanted to feel her pleasure and for her to know that he was the one who'd brought her to that place. But before he could move, Carys pressed harder against his *rondella* and the sudden burst of pleasure exploded through him. His shout filled the silence of the room and he couldn't stop from gripping her hair too tightly as he fucked her mouth with his cock. If he didn't stop soon he'd fully orgasm, and he wanted his cock buried deep inside her when that happened.

Pulling her off his shaft, he wanted to smile at the confused look on her face. "Did you come? I was expecting, I don't know, fluid? Do you guys do things differently?"

All he could do was nod, pull her up by her shoulders and tossed her on the bed. Carys might be curious and stubborn, but she was also a woman who knew exactly what she wanted. She splayed her legs wide open and slid two fingers down her core, shifting the hair between her legs out of the way.

"I don't know how your women are built, but human women really like it when you touch this little thing right here. Using your mouth is even better."

If that's what she wanted, who was he to deny her? Darrick lowered his body until his face was positioned above the junction of her legs. The surprise of hair there quickly became a fascination for him as he played with the coarse strands, careful to tease her as he went.

"That little thing is called a clit. And if you'd be so kind as to suck it, I'll be forever thankful."

He liked the name of the body part – clit. Keeping his gaze on her face, he lowered his mouth and sucked it hard. Carys' body bowed off the bed and she slapped at his head. "Shit, not so much. Ease me into it there, asshole."

Darrick smiled and instead of sucking again, he licked up the length of her clit and teased its tip with his tongue much the same way she had to him. That must have been the right move, because she instantly relaxed and parted her thighs wider. He sighed when she moaned and began to buck her hips in time to his lick, thrusting against his face as her pussy grew damp.

The overwhelming urge to claim her as his own was threatening to peak once again, and he had to calm himself as he continued to arouse her. He moved his hand and pressed a finger into her warm, waiting body, loving how her muscles clamped down on him as she continued to moan and thrust against him.

"So close." She thrashed her head side to side, whimpers slipping from her as he doubled his efforts.

This time when he sucked hard on her clit, Carys groaned and he felt a rush of her juices coat his finger and cover the palm of his hand. What little control he had left slipped away and he focused everything he had on making her orgasm. With his free hand, he squeezed her inner thigh and fucked her hard with his finger. Her body began to shake, bowing once more off the bed, staying there half suspended in the air.

The tension rose to a peak and stayed there for a deliciously long moment before Carys let out a shout. Her muscles flexed and grabbed at his finger as her come filled his mouth. Her orgasm finally ended, and she fell back onto the mattress with a loud gasp. Her body shook beneath him and he could feel her surprise at the pleasure he'd given her. "Shit, that was great."

But Darrick was far past the point of being able to talk, needing to feel her muscles around his cock. He climbed up her body and thrust into her warmth, taking pleasure in the surprised gasp that popped from her. He placed a kiss on the side of her throat, moving his mouth along her smooth brown skin until he reached the juncture of her neck and shoulder.

He nipped at the skin as a possessive streak rolled over him. He wanted to claim her, wanted no man or woman to come near Carys without knowing that she belonged to him. He nipped again, this time harder and ran his tongue over the spot, enjoying the salty taste of her sweat.

"Shit," she said as she wrapped her legs around his waist, "that's hot."

He bit down, nearly breaking the skin, but this time he didn't pull back. He kept his lock on her as he fucked into her body. Her pussy was slick, and her muscles pulled at his cock with each withdrawal. Carys moaned and bucked her hips as he pounded into her harder and harder. Gods, his orgasm was so close he could nearly taste his release, his body electric with the rush of pleasure inching closer.

What he hadn't expected was for Carys to lean up and bite down on his non-enhanced shoulder. The pain mixed with the pleasure and pushed Darrick over the edge into release. He pulled his head back and roared as his hips pumped forward and come shot from his cock and filled her pussy. Without realizing what was happening, his mating scent flowed from his *rondella*, marking her forever as his mate. Pleasure far greater than anything he'd ever experienced in his life or since his re-birth flooded his systems, making it difficult for him to see, to feel anything beyond his desires for this woman in this moment.

Finally, the waves of his orgasm ended, and Darrick slumped forward, careful not to let his weight fully rest on Carys.

The code in his brain was flying through his matrix at a rate far faster than he'd ever experienced before. There was something different, and he couldn't keep track of what was happening. No doubt, this was related to the link between the humans and cyborgs, and it was something that his matrix would adjust to. Darrick tried to run a diagnostic centered on the code that was linked to the area in the back of his matrix that had caused the itching sensation, but it failed.

Strange.

Perhaps every cyborg's reaction to their mate was different and they'd have to create a different protocol for handing the situation. It was something he'd need to address with Rykal and possibly even Aidric.

He became aware of her fingers tracing a circle on the back of his head, playing with the strands of his short hair. Her breath brushed across his ear in pleasant, soothing puffs. Darrick turned his face and placed a kiss to her cheek. "Did I hurt you?"

"Yeah."

Lifting his head, he frowned down at her. "Are you well? Did I do much damage?" Then he sat up. "Can you understand what I'm saying?" Panic swirled deep inside him as the lines of code increased in their speed once again.

There was mischief in her brown eyes. "I'm going to assume that question was asking me if I knew what you just said. The answer is no. I just made an educated guess based on how fucking fantastic that was. But you should have warned me you were a biter."

It was only then that he looked down and saw red blood and a darkening bruise nestled in the crook of her neck. His heart skipped at beat at the sign of the damage he'd caused her. "Gods." He got to his feet and quickly found his clothing. "We need to take you to medical. The doctors need to look at you to ensure I haven't damaged you."

Carys sat up, pulling the blanket that had been below them a moment earlier with her. "Wait, slow down. I can't catch your words when you speak that quickly. What are you saying?"

He stopped, pointed at her neck, then pointed at the door. "Doctor."

"*Troca*? I still don't understand."

The moment they got to medical, he was going to insist she get the nanobots injected so they could have a proper conversation. Rather than continue his frustrated attempts at linguistic interpretations, he picked up her clothing and handed them to her, then he pointed at the door.

"We're leaving?" She pouted. "But we haven't had time to cuddle. Or for me to learn what your cock is called in your language."

"*Rak*." He pointed at his cock, which pulled a smile from her.

"Another word to add to my list." She pulled her pants on and quickly dressed. "I don't know where we're going, but I'm game."

Bringing her enjoyment was starting to become addictive. If

he wasn't careful, their relationship would transform from that of mates to something deeper. And that was a step Darrick was scared would be one too far.

Because a cyborg who loved was a dangerous problem for the Grus.

CHAPTER SIX

Carys was riding a high of endorphins and happy sex afterglow as she moved down the hall toward wherever it was Darrick was taking her. If she had to guess, he wanted to take her to the doctor to get the bite checked out, which probably made sense. It was starting to hurt a bit now, but there was a dark part of her mind that enjoyed the pain and was thrilled to have been marked by him during sex.

Yeah, that little tendency of hers had brought her more than a few problems back on Earth with the few lovers she'd had then. At least Darrick didn't mind in the moment, even if his views on aftercare were limited to a visit to medical.

It was fun not fully being able to communicate with him while having sex. At no point did she feel as though he wasn't listening to her, and yet she had this blindness to not being able to understand the soft noises that had come from him. They might have been words, or they simply could have been his sex noises – either way, she'd loved them.

What she wasn't enjoying were the fearful glances they were getting as they made their way through the corridors of the space station once more. These Grus weren't exactly a trusting species, which should alarm her more than it currently did. Not that their attention was fixated on her at all; no, every single person was staring at Darrick. It probably wasn't helping that he looked as though he wanted to murder someone, growling and glaring at the Grus as they approached.

"You might want to relax a little bit. I don't need to speak your language to know you're making people nervous."

Instead of taking her advice, Darrick put a hand on her shoulder and used it to move her closer to his side. Shit, that wasn't going to make things better for them. It also had the unfortunate side effect of making her bruised area hurt as his finger grip was dangerously close to where he'd bit her. "Darrick, can you please move your hand?"

He relaxed his grip slightly but kept it in place.

Thankfully, they'd reached their destination. The doors slid open to reveal what was obviously a medical facility. It was far bigger than the one that they had back on the Kraken; five exam tables with scanners and medical equipment lined the back of the room, and there appeared to be an additional corridor in the middle but it was blocked off with a glass door.

Darrick maneuvered her over to one of the available beds, picked her up and set her down on it. He pointed at her, then the bed and left her sitting there.

She couldn't help but roll her eyes. "Yes fine, I'll stay here." Maybe she wouldn't learn the language if all he did was point and glare at her.

The staff in the medical facility was currently keeping their distance from them both, which wasn't helping Darrick's mood. He barked something at them, but no one responded. He said the words again, this time there was no missing the undercurrent of anger from him, or the fear coming from them.

Carefully, she slid to her feet and pressed a hand to the middle of his back. "Darrick, it's okay. I'm not hurt that badly. It's just a bite mark that will heal given some time."

He spun around and picked her up in a single fluid motion, that ended with her sitting back on the exam table. The look on his face was one of rage, a response so far past what the situation called for, Carys was starting to get concerned. "I know you're angry, but I don't understand what you're saying or what's going on. I need you to keep calm so I can try and keep up with you. Okay?"

As she was speaking to him, she caught sight of three of the medical staff rushing from the room and down into the hallway with the glass door. There was no way that was going to end well for any of them. When Darrick was about to turn around to see what she was looking at, she cupped his face in her hands and leaned in for a kiss.

Unlike the glorious intimacy they'd shared only a short time earlier, something had changed inside Darrick. There was little reciprocation for her kiss, no heat and certainly no undercurrent of something else that she'd sworn had been there before. When she pulled back and looked into his eyes, all she saw was the cool electric glow of his cybernetically enhanced eyes and none of Darrick's personality.

"What's going on?"

He jerked away from her, taking several steps backward as he brought his hands up to his head. His body began to shake as he doubled over, clearly in pain. Carys didn't know what to do, or how to help. The medical staff jumped into action, but it wasn't to help Darrick. They grabbed patients and moved them, some down the hallway and some outside of medical, depending on which exit was closer. Only one female Grus stayed behind, her long body poised to run, but her gaze flicked between Carys and Darrick.

She held Carys' gaze. *"Ye cha te ca frak seta qe."*

"I have no freaking idea what you just said to me, but I'm not leaving him. He needs help. Your help."

The woman shook her head. *"Seta!"* She pointed at the door.

"I don't care what you're saying. If you're not going to stay here and do your job to help him, then I'll have to."

The woman closed her eyes and took a deep breath before turning to pull something out of the medical storage unit beside her. She then made a wide birth around where Darrick still stood shaking – her gaze never once leaving his – and made her way to stand beside Carys. She held out the injector and pointed to the spot behind Carys' ear. It was more nanobots; the woman clearly wanted to be able to communicate with her, no doubt because she thought Carys didn't understand what the hell was going on.

But what this woman didn't seem to understand was that Carys didn't need to speak their language to recognize discrimination when she saw it. "I'm not putting those things in me. That's not going to help *him*."

The woman shook her head, set the injector on the bed and fled from medical, leaving Carys alone with Darrick.

Well, *frak* them all to hell.

"Okay then, time to figure out what's going on." Ignoring the pain in her neck, she crept closer to where he was, not sure the type of reaction he might give her. "Darrick?"

His body still shook, but she felt him shift his body toward her as she got closer. *"Hel."*

God, maybe she should go over and take the nanobots. This would be a hell of a lot easier if she understood what he was saying. Her gaze moved back to the injector where the woman had left it, even as Darrick continued to chant, *"Hel seta, hel, hel."*

This wasn't giving up on herself, this was doing what she had to in order to survive the situation and help Darrick. "Fuck it. Don't move."

She bolted for the bed and snatched up the injector as quickly as she could manage. Then she moved to stand in front of him so he could easily see what exactly she was doing. "I want you to know that this annoys me to no end. I was just starting to learn all the exciting parts of your language." No response to her attempt at humor.

Not wanting to wait any longer, she pressed the injector to the skin behind her ear where both Aidric and the woman had indicated and pressed the button. What she wasn't anticipating was the bolt of pain that lanced through her brain and stole the air from her lungs. The pain increased to the point where she had to press her hands to her head, much the same way Darrick was doing himself. Unlike him, she couldn't help but cry out in pain and fall to her knees from the overwhelming power of it all.

Carys tried to keep her eyes open and her gaze on Darrick's who was now openly staring at her as he continued his chanting. *"Hel, hel, letana hel."*

For a brief moment, her hearing appeared to fail her altogether, only to be replaced by the loud whooshing of white noise. But as sound began to return, she realized that she was understanding the words coming from Darrick.

"Hel, please. Run, *letana*. Please run."

The pain began to recede, and it because easier for her to relax and let the new sound of his voice wash over her. "Wow, this is really fucking weird."

Darrick was clearly unable to respond to her, his eyes still wide even as his voice began to fade to a whisper. Carys got back to her feet and took a tentative step closer to him. "This is working now, and I can understand you. I know you want me to leave you, to run away, but I'm not going to do that. We're going to figure out what's going on and we're going to do something about it. Okay?"

He shook his head, his whispered chant continuing. "Run, please run."

"I'm not running. What I'm going to do is try and find someone who can help us."

There was movement from the hallway with the glass door. Several of the Grus medical staff were standing there, watching them. Beckoning them to come out to help her, she wanted to scream when no one moved. "Fine, I'll do everything myself." She marched over to the door and knocked on it. "He needs help."

The man standing on the other side shook his head. "They're killers. We're not going near him."

Based on everything she'd seen to this point she couldn't imagine Darrick being anything less than a kind caring soul. But that did explain the reactions to him walking through the station. "What am I supposed to do then?"

The man narrowed his gaze and nodded toward the computer terminal. "Talk to the station's AI. Tell it that there's an emergency and it will decommission him."

Yeah, that didn't exactly sound like the thing she wanted to do. "I don't want to kill him."

"Once they go off there's not a lot you can do to help. They're flawed."

A thud behind her had Carys turn to look over at Darrick who was now on the floor, his knees pulled up to his chest. "Darrick!"

Dropping to her knees hard enough to send her teeth clacking together, Carys leaned over and pressed several small kisses to his temple. "It's okay. We're going to figure out what's wrong with you."

The glass doors whooshed open and a group of patients dashed past as quickly as they could manage. Carys watched them go, followed by the medical staff. The last one to leave was the man she'd been speaking to, who hit a button by the door before bolting out.

The room flashed blue several times as a voice echoed down from above. "Warning. Cyborg incursion detected. Warning. Prepare for decommission."

"No!" She draped her body over Darrick's. "We're not decommissioning him. Back off!"

"Warning. Please move away from the cyborg." The soulless

voice of the computer filled the small space and filled Carys with dread. "Decommissioning cannot begin until the cyborg has been isolated."

"Well then we're not going to be able to do that because I'm not moving."

"Please run. You need to run. Leave me." Darrick's voice sounded muted beneath her.

Carys swallowed hard. Her panic and confusion weren't helping her reason through the best course of action. "I really would like to do that, but if I move, I think the computer is going to kill you."

But if she didn't move, she didn't think she'd be able to get the help she needed. After what felt like an eternity but was probably only a few minutes there was a sound from the corridor and the doors slid open. Rykal and Lena were there, as was Aidric and what appeared to be a large group of security officers. Carys tightened her hold on Darrick, even as she looked at Lena. "Thank God you're here."

"Ms. Jones, please move away from him." Aidric stepped beside Lena, his gaze locked on Darrick.

Lena's eyes were wide as she reached for Rykal's hand. "He said you have to move away – "

"I gave myself the nanobots. I understood him." She tightened her grip. "I'm not going anywhere unless you can guarantee no one is going to hurt him."

"Warning. Cyborg incursion detected. Decommission recommended." The AI's voice filled the room once more.

"As you can hear, your system isn't exactly reassuring me that Darrick is going to be okay."

"Once a cyborg begins to malfunction, there isn't anything we can do. They lose the ability to control their urges and kill others without reason." Aidric stepped past Lena and Rykal and entered medical. "You need to move so we can ensure no one else gets hurt."

It was the logical thing for her to do. Darrick was still moving his mouth, but no words came out any longer. Even he recognized that there was a problem and the only way to solve it was for him to be decommissioned. This wasn't her world or her people, and she wasn't able to argue against them.

And yet, there was a part of her deep down that knew Darrick could be saved. She knew beyond reason that their connection was growing stronger and she could somehow help him. All she needed was a bit of time and space to ensure she could make things better.

Aidric continued to stare at her, but something in his expression changed. Whether he realized that she wasn't going to move, or that there might be an opportunity for them to fix things, Carys wasn't sure. He looked back at Rykal and let out a little huff. "Seal off the corridor. I want all Grus personnel out of harm's way if this fails."

"What are you planning to do?" Rykal shoved Lena out from Carys' sight. "Do you need me to stay?"

A muscle in Aidric's jaw jumped. "Can you reach him through your neuro link?"

Rykal looked at her and narrowed his gaze. "I can hear his concern about Carys, but he won't respond to my call."

"Then you can't assist. Take Lena and keep the others away." Aidric stepped fully inside the room and triggered the door. "AI, seal the door to medical ensuring no one can enter or exit."

There was a momentary pause before the AI responded. "Confirmed."

"Pause cyborg decommissioning. Do not restart unless both lifeforms in medical have been terminated by the cyborg."

"Request denied."

Aidric looked up at the spot where the AI's voice emanated. "What do you mean, request denied?"

"I am programmed to ensure Commander Aidric's safety. Request denied."

Despite the gravity of the situation, Carys chuckled "I think she likes you."

Aidric's lips were pressed hard together, before he crossed his arms. "Pause cyborg decommissioning. Do no restart unless the human has been killed and my life is in jeopardy."

The AI took even longer to respond. "Request granted."

"Oh, thank God." Carys released her death grip on Darrick and sat up. "Can you help him?"

"I'm not sure." Aidric approached cautiously, until he reached Darrick's side. He got to his knees and looked at something on the back of Darrick's neck. "Let's find out."

CHAPTER SEVEN

Darrick was lost. His vision out to the world had faded away, as had his auditory inputs; he'd been left stuck in his matrix alone and unable to penetrate the coding. Normally, this was a place where he could connect with other cyborgs, carry on limited conversations, or work his way through a problem that required him to rely on his cybernetics.

All those capabilities that he'd benefited from since his rebirth were lacking and he didn't understand how. Worse than that, he couldn't understand why this had happened. There'd been a reason, something he'd been aware of before. But now? He didn't know what was causing his sudden blankness.

Reaching out to the code, he tried to search the lines to see if there was a bug, a flaw that was causing his regression. As he searched, he was confronted by a sudden rush of new code, lines that shouldn't belong there, that seemed to not make any sense in the grand scheme of his programming. A virus that was rewriting his code, something he needed to fight to ensure he'd be able to continue to function.

Darrick reached back into the deep recesses of his mind and pulled out his previous learnings as an engineer. He could fix this enough to be able to communicate with Rykal or one of the other cyborgs on Zarlan. If they needed to have someone from Grus Prime to come down to the planet to assist with his repairs, then so be it. Anything would be better than being stuck in this unknowing blackness.

You're going to be okay.

The voice wrapped around him in a strangely comforting way. He tried to discover who was trying to communicate with him, but the voice wasn't linked to any cyborg he was familiar with. Gods, that could mean he was starting to hear phantoms, and that meant his matrix was beginning to degrade. If that was true, then the only option would be decommissioning.

The death that had been denied him all those years ago.

That wouldn't be so bad – dying. He'd been alone since the end of the war, only having a few friends and no capacity to form a romantic relationship. The ability to have a family had been snatched from him when he'd been killed, but the temptation of that desire had continued to haunt him from the moment of his rebirth. It would be far easier to drift away into the blackness than to be continuously taunted.

No wonder some of their kind would lose their grip on reality and need to be decommissioned.

You're going to be fine.

Was he though? There were so many reasons why he shouldn't be, but he couldn't help but take solace in the unseen voice. The unexplained code shifted, and Darrick became fascinated by what was scrolling past. There'd always been a gap in the programming Aidric had installed into them, something that he'd mostly been able to ignore despite the yawning chasm off in the periphery of his mind. He moved closer to the hole and chanced a look inside. He'd always assumed it was blank, nothingness that would swallow him whole if he let it. Looking down, he saw lines of the code coating the sides of the hole.

That was strange and more than a little concerning. If this

was a virus, there was a strong possibility that it would have the ability to override his systems if it filled in the empty space. No, no, that would put everyone both on Zarlan and up on Grus Prime in danger. He had to do something to stop this before it was too late.

Darrick marched to the side of the hole and was about to throw himself inside, when he felt a hand on his face and the brush of warm lips on his skin. *I've got you. You need to relax.*

There was something familiar about that voice. He couldn't remember where he knew it from or why he felt as though he could trust it, but that was the case. The person who that voice belonged to wanted him to trust that they could make everything okay. Who was he to deny them the opportunity to see if they could make it work?

He wouldn't let things get to the point where the lives of others would be put at risk. For now, he'd put his faith in that voice and wait.

Even if in the end, he'd have to make the sacrifice and self-initiate the decommissioning.

"You better hurry."

CARYS' heartbeat raced the longer it took for them to maneuver Darrick's now unconscious body into position so Aidric could plug him into the computer and run a diagnostic. She didn't know why, but time was running out for them to fix this. "Have you found anything yet?"

Aidric typed a series of commands into the system. "I'm not sure why, but the computer is having difficulty reaching his internal matrix code."

"That's bad. What's blocking it?"

"I believe Darrick himself is the problem." He typed another string of code and let out a soft sigh. "He's pulled his personality code into a protective shell inside his matrix. It's making it difficult to communicate with him."

"I would imagine he's trying to protect himself from whatever your AI was planning on doing to him." She couldn't believe they simply killed any cyborg who posed too much of a problem for them, rather than try to help. "I'd be scared you tried to kill me too."

"That's not what I think is happening here. He's the one who's retreating from the new code in his system. This is the same as what happened to Rykal when he connected with Lena. It's filling in a gap in the programming, a bug that I'd accidently introduced during the development. Unlike Rykal, Darrick has flagged his as a virus and is doing what he can to protect his core systems from the attack."

"Is there a way you can stop it?" She didn't want to even pretend to understand what was happening to him. "Can you wipe out the new code?"

"No. And I don't believe you'd want me to do that."

"Why not?"

Aidric looked up from the screen, an odd expression on his face. "Your connection is rebuilding his emotional core. I haven't had the opportunity to explore the changes or why it's happening, but this connection they have with you human women seems to be rebuilding what was lost."

"Emotional core?" Her heartbeat kicked up another notch.

"He'll be able to feel something beyond rage and detached observation. I've seen the change in Rykal and I believe that's what's happening to Darrick. But instead of acceptance, he's fighting it."

"Why would he fight something like that?" None of this made much sense to her, but Carys wasn't willing to give up on him yet. "When we were together, he didn't seem to have any problems with how he felt toward me."

Aidric turned to face her, lacing his hands together. "Cyborgs don't have emotions the way the Grus do."

"Well that's not true. I can't speak to any of the other cyborgs, but Darrick clearly has emotions." They had been directed at her, making this entire thing very personal.

"You don't understand. When I implemented the re-birth program, I'd initially used the cybernetics to bring all aspects of our fallen soldiers back to life, including their emotions. But it wasn't possible, so I tried to limit all emotions. The first batch of cyborgs, twenty-right to be exact, they'd had a flaw I hadn't initially noticed. They could feel great anger, but no other deep emotions. I was able to create a block of their emotions for subsequent cyborgs, but those initial cyborgs remained different. They became the leadership of the Fallen, the ones others looked to during the war."

Carys considered herself an intuitive person – it was one of her strengths that made her an excellent linguist – but even if she wasn't, she would have known there was something else to Aidric's story that he wasn't saying. There was a look in his eyes that told her that even if she called him on it, he wouldn't tell her what she wanted to know. They didn't have time for her to pick away at that thread, but she'd be damn sure to talk to Lena about it once this was over.

After they'd saved Darrick.

"It doesn't matter what you programmed them to be back then, things have changed. I don't know why our presence has modified their code, but it has." Carys took Darrick's hand in hers and gave it a squeeze. "His emotional blocks have lifted and for some reason he's fighting against them. What can we do to help him?"

Aidric turned his face away, letting his gaze come to rest on their joined hands. "His coding has a safety mechanism in place to help prevent corruption from rogue code or viruses. We need to modify those protections to allow the new code an opportunity to take root in his matrix. Once that's happened, he should become aware enough that his safety measures will disengage."

"Perfect. So how do we do that?"

"I'm not sure." He frowned. "I need to introduce counter measures in such a way he won't fight them."

"You need a distraction."

"I need *you*."

Carys gave Darrick's hand another squeeze. "I'm not a computer person, so I'm not going to be much use to you that way."

"I don't need you to code, I need you to engage with him so he isn't aware of what I'm doing." Aidric looked around the room, his lips twitching up in a brief smile when his gaze landed on something. "That will work."

"Do I want to know what you have planned?"

"I promise, it won't be anything that will harm you. Probably not, anyway – I can't be 100% certain given the circumstances. This is new ground for me." He marched over to one of the exam tables and picked up what appeared to be a headband covered in sensors. On his way back, he also grabbed a chair and positioned it beside Darrick. "Please, have a seat."

"What are you going to do to me?" But she sat down regardless, willing to subject herself to just about anything if it meant helping Darrick.

"Our doctors can connect with a patient's mind when they are unconscious or in a coma using this technology. It gives them the ability to talk to the patient and discover exactly what they are thinking and feeling on the inside, so they can direct the treatment on the outside." Aidric moved to stand behind her and slipped the sensor band over her head. "I want you to talk to Darrick."

"And what are you going to do?"

"I'll be writing special code that will help him better integrate the changes to his matrix that your presence has caused."

"Is this going to be safe for him? I mean, if I'm the reason for these changes in the first place, won't me being in his mind be worse?"

Aidric finished adjusting the sensors and moved beside her. "I'm not sure. If we do nothing he'll either shut down or be decommissioned by the station's systems."

She bit down on her bottom lip. "Will it be safe for me?"

"I won't lie to you, as I said I'm not certain. He might react as though your presence is a virus to be attacked. To the best of my knowledge, we've never tried something like this on a cyborg." Aidric put his hand on her shoulder. "You've only just arrived in our sector of space. You don't know our people, our history. I won't force you to make this choice if you have any hesitation. If you don't want to risk this, I can try another approach."

God, Carys wasn't a person to make life and death decisions for herself, let alone for someone else. If she said no, she was certain that Aidric would try another means to reach Darrick. If she agreed, she might not come out of this unscathed, and there was no guarantee that it would even work.

She looked over at Darrick's blank face, missing the way his green eyes shone at her with fascination.

Fuck it. "Let's do this."

CHAPTER EIGHT

One moment Carys was sitting on a chair in medical, and then in the next she was standing in a dark room. There wasn't any outline to the darkness, but she was somehow aware of walls and a hole somewhere in front of her. She wasn't certain what she'd been expecting when Aidric had hit the command to send her consciousness into Darrick's mind, but this yawning black certainly wasn't it.

"Hello?" She carefully took a step forward, relieved when she didn't fall into the vacuum before her. "Darrick, are you here?"

There wasn't a response. She took another step, then a third trying her best to see if she could spot anything out there. "It's me, Carys. Darrick?"

Movement off to her right drew her attention, but she didn't move toward it. Aidric had warned her that there was a chance Darrick would see her as a threat and try to attack her. She didn't know what that might be like and as a result, was on high alert. Turning toward the sound, she took a cautious step toward it, ready to bolt in the opposite direction if necessary. "Darrick?"

Out of the black came a shape. She had to blink to be able to focus on what it was, trying to make sense of the large abstract presence. The closer she got the easier it was for her to feel Darrick rather than see him. It *was* him, but there was a layer of something keeping her from being able to reach him.

She reached out to try and touch him, shocked when her hand encountered a cold surface. This would be a hell of a lot easier if she understood exactly what was going on. "Darrick, I'm not sure if you can hear me or not. It's Carys."

The surface shimmered and came a little more into focus. It became easier for her to see Darrick's features, even if they were still fuzzy. Emboldened by her progress, she moved closer to him, keeping her contact fixed in place.

"I was worried about you. When you fell to the floor in medical, I didn't know what was happening. And then all these Grus jerks were running around, and they weren't willing to help me. I had to go and inject myself with those stupid nanobots just so I could talk to someone and figure out what was happening. That really did hurt like a sonofabitch."

The longer she spoke, the clearer the image of Darrick became. She could almost make out the details of his face, could see the color of his eyes and the fullness of his lips. Smiling, he shifted her hand up to his cheek, wishing she could feel him.

"You scared me out there, and that meant that I had to come in here so I could make sure that you're okay. Aidric put some sensor band thing on my head so we could talk like this, which has been a weird experience so far."

At the mention of Aidric's name, the space around her darkened and Darrick stepped back and dropped into a defensive squat. Energy snapped in the air around her, the current making the hair on her arms stand straight up. "Whoa. Um, okay. Sorry I mentioned him."

Instead of calming down, Darrick charged her, far faster than she was able to move. He slammed his body into her, sending them both sprawling to the floor. If this had been anywhere but inside Darrick's mind, Carys had no doubt that the impact would have done her serious harm. Instead, she was able to force them into a roll, flipping them over and over until she landed on top of him.

"Darrick, I need you to stop!"

His features snapped into perfect focus and she found herself looking down into his confused, perfectly normal looking, green eyes. "Carys?"

"Yes. Oh, thank God. Are you okay?"

His mouth was pulled down in a frown as he gave his head a small shake. "What's happening?"

"You're unconscious in medical on Grus Prime. Aidric sent me in here to try and talk to you, to make sure that you're not hurt. We haven't been able to reach you for a while now." "I'm..." He rolled his head, so he was no longer looking at her. "I'm...broken?"

There was something in the way he said those words that broke her heart. "There's nothing in the world wrong with you. You're certainly *not* broken."

"Yes. There's something wrong. I can't figure out what it is." There was a soft quiver in his voice, but when he looked back at her, there were no tears. "Why are you here?"

"I told you, I'm here to make sure that you're okay."

Aidric had recommended that she not talk to him about code or anything that might make him think there was something else going on. While she hated not being entirely truthful with him, she also didn't want to risk both their lives by pushing him too far too fast. All she needed to do was talk to him, keep him focused on her and calm so Aidric could upload the code changes.

"I need to go." He stood up in a way that shouldn't be possible given the laws of physics, bringing Carys with him. "I need to find the problem."

Shit, maybe he wasn't as blind to what was going on as they'd hoped. "What problem are you talking about? I was hoping that you'd be able to wake up so we could have a conversation out in the real world rather than in here."

Darrick paused and looked back at her. "In here?"

"Inside your head. Remember, I told you that I was using some sort of medical device to talk to you." Carys could feel something tickle the back of her neck, as though there was a river of water rolling over her skin. The sensation grew stronger as Darrick took another step away from here. "Can I come with you?"

She didn't know why it was important for her to stay with him, but she did. The moment he left her behind she guessed bad things would happen to them both. Darrick frowned again but nodded. "Keep up."

It was strange moving inside like this, with no visual cues to tell her where she was walking toward, or even how far she'd come. With her far too active imagination, it didn't take much for her to picture getting lost in the blackness, never being able to find her way out. The sudden rush of panic caught her off guard and she reached out to take Darrick's hand. He looked over at her and all she could do was shrug.

"I'm afraid of the dark."

He hesitated for a moment before pulling her close to his side. "I'll keep you safe."

Carys could only hope that would be the case.

They walked for a while, Darrick occasionally stopping to check something that Carys couldn't quite see. But every time he did, she could feel the tug of something beyond her vision, something that told her they were getting closer to an answer, or maybe even a problem. She wasn't certain, nor did she know if things were about to get worse for them. Darrick seemed to know where he was going, and the tension in his body ratcheted up a notch when they came to a spot and he looked down.

"The hole is still filling in."

She looked to where he'd indicated, but she wasn't able to see anything at all, let alone a hole. "Is that a bad thing?"

"The hole has always been there. I don't understand why it's changing."

"Change isn't always a bad thing. Maybe that will be the case when the hole is filled." Aidric had mentioned to her about the impact the human women were having on the cyborgs. Maybe this was how his rekindled emotions were manifesting itself in his matrix. She leaned forward trying to see the edges of the hole. "Is it a big?"

Darrick put his hand on her shoulder and hauled her back. "Don't get too close. I don't know what it will do to you. And you don't want to fall in."

That didn't see like the worst thing in the world. "I'm not going to lie to you, I can't see it. There's no edge or anything."

When she tried to take a step forward to show him that everything was okay, Darrick grabbed her around the waist and pulled her hard against him. "No!" Fear so strong she could feel physically it came off him in waves. "You'll die if you do that."

She could still see nothing, which maybe was the point. They were in Darrick's mind and he was trying to resolve the changes going on with his matrix. New emotions, something that had been ripped from him when he'd been subjected to the rebirth process were now coming back, but not exactly as they'd been before. His psyche had been wounded and now he had to reconcile that things were changing yet again. His life would never be the same for a second time.

The difference was that this time, he wasn't alone.

Turning her face so she could look up at him, Carys frantically tried to think of the right words to say. She might be good with learning languages, but she wasn't necessarily great at saying the right thing. But the fear and confusion on his face had her realize that this wasn't about talking and was more about helping him on an emotional level.

Licking her lips, she smiled and hoped she wasn't going to make matters worse. "Why are you so worried about me getting hurt?"

He frowned. "My duty is to protect people."

"Is it? I thought you were programmed to protect the Grus. I'm not Grus, remember?" She waited a moment for that to register with him. "So why is it important for you to keep *me* safe?"

"I…" He snapped his mouth closed and frowned.

"I hate to sound conceited here, but I'm right. You don't know why, but you know that for some reason you want to keep me safe."

"Yes." He held her a bit tighter. "We need to move away from the edge."

"I don't see an edge. Maybe there isn't an edge there at all? Maybe what you're seeing is something else."

Darrick shook his head. "It's there. And there's a virus filling it in. If I can't stop it then my matrix will become infected and I'll have to be decommissioned."

Carys turned in his arms and reached up to cup his face. "You're not going to be decommissioned. There's no way in hell I'm going to let that happen."

She pulled him down for a kiss, putting every bit of love and concern she felt behind it. Unlike out in the real world, there was something far different with this kiss, something more intimate. She could feel his emotions washing over her: confusion, lust, fear. She tried to project her own feelings back at him: love, desire, peace. Deepening her kiss, she pressed hard against him, as though if she were able to imprint her feelings on him then everything would work out for the best.

Darrick hesitated, but eventually moved his hands lower, cupping her ass and holding her hard against his body. She didn't know how if any of this would work, but failure wasn't an option for her. She pulled at his shirt and tried to tug it up and over his head. Thankfully, this wasn't reality and in a blink all their clothing was gone.

"Oh, I like this." She pressed a kiss to the middle of his chest.

Unlike in the real world, he was missing all his cybernetics and instead stood there as his unaltered self. She slid her hands along the pristine skin, knowing that the next time they were together and awake that this would all be gone. His shoulder was smooth, the strong muscles flexing as she ran her fingers across the surface. Darrick groaned as she chased her touch with kisses, letting her tongue dip out to lick across him.

"What are you doing?" He pushed his hands into her hair.

"Distracting you. Is it working?"

The hard press of his erect cock between them was all the answer she needed. "I want to fuck you."

She didn't argue when he picked her up and positioned her body so his cock was now resting at the entrance of her pussy. Physics clearly didn't matter here and Carys wasn't one to say no to a new sexual adventure. Wrapping her legs around his waist and her hands around his neck, she shifted as he guided her body down until his cock filled her.

Logically, Carys knew this wasn't her body nor was she having sex with Darrick right then. She was currently little more than a projection into his mind, whose sole purpose was to distract Darrick long enough so Aidric could upload the fix to his code and everything would be okay.

Logically.

But nothing felt fake – not the touch of his chest against her breasts, nor the way his hands tightly squeezed her ass as he thrust his cock inside her. The scent of his sweat and the heat of his body under her touch was as real as it had been back in the room they'd shared. Even the graze of his teeth against her shoulder where she knew on her body in medical there was a bruise, somehow felt more real here in the darkness of Darrick's mind.

He lowered his mouth to her shoulder and bit gently on the same spot. He growled as he licked his tongue across the skin. That primal possessiveness was going to be her undoing. She moaned, tipping her head back and exposing her neck to him.

In a flash they were no longer standing, her back now pressed against a floor. Darrick pounded into her body, and the pleasure from the rub against her clit was overwhelming. She didn't try to stop the pleasure from washing over her. "Yes!"

Her orgasm slammed into her; muscles contracted and flexed as Darrick cried out, thrusting into her hard as he came as well. His pleasure mixed with hers until Carys no longer knew what she felt or who it was coming from. The darkness around them brightened until they were bathed in a shimmering light. She could barely think to breathe, she'd become so consumed by Darrick and everything she felt. She lost the ability to track time and nothing else mattered except for him. This overwhelming desire to be one with him was all she wanted.

But like all good things, this too eventually came to an end. Darrick's body slowed and came to a stop. He kept his cock inside her, even as he moved his face, so his mouth pressed against her throat. "I don't know what happened here."

"We had sex."

"Did we? I...it was wonderful, but it didn't feel right."

"What?" She looked around her, just as confused by the light as she'd been about the dark. "How was that not right?"

"It didn't feel real."

"It wasn't exactly. Remember, I'm not actually here with you. This is all in your head."

Darrick pushed himself up to his forearm and looked down at her. "Why are you here?"

"You were hurt, and I had to come and try to save you."

"I'm not hurt." His frown deepened. "Am I?"

Carys didn't know how, but she knew the next few moments

were going to be critically important. "What's the last thing that you remember?"

"I..." He gave his head a small shake. "I was fighting the Sholle. Rykal had just returned to us, but they'd changed him. The Sholle were approaching our flank and I realized that Rykal didn't see them coming. He didn't see them aiming to fire at him and I jumped. I...I think I died."

God, hearing the pain and confusion in his voice was enough to break her heart. "You did die. At least, that's what I was told. You died and then they made you a cyborg. But Aidric had made a mistake and your code had a flaw in it." Darrick began to pull back, but she grabbed his shoulder to hold him still. "It's going to be okay. We have a plan to fix everything."

"The hole." He looked over at the spot he'd indicated earlier. "It's almost filled in."

"I know this is going to be hard for you to hear, but that's okay. The hole wasn't meant to be there, so we're fixing it."

Slowly, he shifted his gaze from the spot back to Carys. "It's you. You're fixing me."

It wasn't a question. Her heat skipped a beat and she couldn't help the mix of fear, love and relief from washing over her. "I am. At least, I think that's what's happening."

Darrick cocked his head and nodded before laying once more on top of her. "Okay."

"Okay." She wrapped her arms around his body and held him while they waited to see if that was indeed the truth.

CHAPTER NINE

Darrick's brain still itched. His body wasn't feeling much better as he fought to wake himself up from whatever had been happening to him. He hadn't been sleeping – that wasn't what cyborgs truly did – nor had he been taken offline for a diagnostic run. There were no logs of that time for him to review and from what he could tell his body hadn't been rebooted.

Something was different though.

"I think he's starting to come around."

Aidric's voice was somewhere off to the side, and for the first time in a while, Darrick wasn't sure how he felt about the Grus commander. There wasn't the distrust the way there normally was, even though Darrick couldn't remember exactly what had changed between them.

He flexed his hand, and only then did he realize that someone was holding it. Wait, there was a person beside him, someone whom he knew and cared for. Someone important.

Carys.

With effort, he turned his head and forced his eyes open to see her sitting there. She looked exhausted; her black hair messier than he remembered and there were dark circles beneath her eyes. But when she smiled over at him, something seemed to loosen in his chest, making it far easier for him to breathe.

"Hello." His voice sounded rough in his ears, and he cleared his throat. "Something happened?"

"Yes, something did." There was a sensor band around her head, the white of the material a stark contrast against her brown skin. "But I think everything's okay now."

"I wouldn't go that far." Darrick turned his head to see Aidric standing at the console. "I'm running several scans to check, but I think the new code has stabilized in his matrix. I can't be certain until everything's completed."

"Aidric?" It was odd having the Grus commander here helping him. *Frak*, he wasn't even certain what was happening. "My memory of the last hour is blank."

"It was actually longer than an hour." Carys gave his hand a squeeze. "There was an hour of you malfunctioning here. It turns out that time runs differently when I've got my consciousness plugged into your brain directly. I was there for four hours."

He couldn't imagine that much time had passed without him realizing it. Carys had been inside his mind helping him with something and...wait. "You understand what I'm saying?"

She blinked twice before bursting out into a fit of laughter. "Yes. I injected myself with the nanobots when you were shutting down. It was the only way I could communicate with the Grus, even though they didn't help me."

Aidric snorted.

Carys ignored him. "Do you want to try and sit up?"

He nodded and together they managed to get him sitting up for a moment before he stood. "Something is definitely different."

"In addition to the repaired code that was started with Carys' presence, I had to insert a virus of sorts to help your matrix accept the changes." Aidric made his way over to Darrick. "You were fighting the corrections and there was a chance you were going to shut down. I don't believe you self-decommissioning would have been the best course of action for anyone."

"No, that wouldn't have been ideal." There was almost too much information for him to process. "My matrix is still intact?"

"Based on my scans, yes." Aidric looked at where Darrick held Carys' hand. "I'll need time to evaluate the changes to both your systems and Rykal's. It's safe to say that not all cyborgs will respond the same way when confronted with a human woman who they see as their mate. We'll need to take precautions."

The door to medical slid open and Rykal strode through. "I received your message."

"Carys?" Lena pushed past the men before pulling Carys into a fierce hug. "I was worried about you and what was going on. No one would tell me a fucking thing."

"I'm fine. He's fine. We're all perfectly *fine*."

Lena gagged. "I hate that word."

"I know." Carys let her friend go before turning back to Darrick. "I'm still a bit confused as to what happened and what this all means."

Aidric laced his fingers behind his back. "For reasons I've yet to determine, the presence of the women on your ship are causing a rewrite of the code for the initial group of Fallen who became cyborgs. It's generating new code that's filling in the missing pieces that had been suppressed when the cyborg matrix was created."

"So, there are at least twenty-six other cyborgs are going to have some sort of reaction to the women on the ship." Lena shrugged. "That will be entertaining if nothing else."

"It could potentially be dangerous, especially if they react the way Darrick did." Rykal wrapped his arm around Lena's waist. "We should come up with a plan for how to handle this. The last thing either the Grus or the Fallen need is for several cyborgs to go insane."

"Not to mention I need time to prepare the women when they

wake up from stasis." Lena patted Rykal's hand. "I guess we should go talk about this and let these two have a chance to get cleaned up and rested. You both look like shit."

"A shower and change of clothing would be amazing." Carys tried to run her hands through her hair and failed. "A nap would also be ideal."

"I'll notify security that your extended presence on the station has been approved." Without another word, Aidric turned and left medical.

Darrick hadn't even had the opportunity to thank him. "Some things never change."

"My brother is many things, but receptive to anything emotional isn't one of them." Rykal stared at the now closed door a bit longer. "I do worry about him."

While Darrick was thankful for all he'd done for him, feeling pity for the man who'd engineered his rebirth was the last thing he was capable of. "Commander Aidric is the last person I'd be concerned with. He'll be fine."

Rykal looked as though he would argue, but Lena tugged at his arm. "Let's go and let them rest. We'll come find you at your quarters in a few hours, then we can discuss our next steps and moving everyone down to the planet."

The thought of having all those human women on Zarlan, their cyborg mates content to live their new lives once more, made Darrick happy. "We'll wait for your arrival."

He managed to stop himself from doing anything until the door closed behind the couple, leaving them once again alone. The moment it slid shut, Darrick pulled Carys into his arms and held her tight. "I don't remember all of the details, but I know the only reason I'm alive and functioning is because of you." He breathed in her scent and let the panic he'd felt flow away. "Thank you."

Her body relaxed in his hold. "Do you remember what triggered your reaction? I haven't really been able to figure it out."

Thinking back to the last time they'd had sex, it took Darrick a moment to realize what it had been. "When I saw the bite on your shoulder, the harm I'd caused you physically. I believe it triggered something that was half my cyborg self and the need to protect others, and my Grus self who'd always wanted a mate to love and protect. Knowing that I'd been unable to keep you safe from myself had sent my already strained matrix into a spiral. All I wanted was to have you forever, to claim and keep you."

"And knowing that you hurt me, that you wanted to hurt me pushed you over the edge?"

"It wasn't that I wanted to hurt you, I needed to claim you." He tugged at the collar of her shirt to reveal the still fresh bruise. "I needed to put my mark on you so no one else would."

He couldn't look her in the eyes, not sure of how she'd react to what he'd said. When she reached down and lifted his chin to force his gaze to hers, Darrick was surprised. She rolled her eyes and smiled. "I know this might be a bit hard for you to accept, but I found that kind of hot. I happen to enjoy my sex a bit on the rough side and the way you claimed me back there was probably the best fucking sex I've ever had in my life."

"Really?"

"Yes. Next time before you go off on a weird cyborg meltdown over some perceived slight you've made against me, maybe ask first if I'm upset." She pressed a finger to his lips when he went to speak. "Actually, I'm not a person to sit back and let someone get away with something. I promise you here and now that if you ever do anything to upset or hurt me, I'll tell you in no uncertain terms."

Never in his life had Darrick ever been so put in his place as he'd been in that moment. He nodded, and hoped she understood how much he appreciated what she'd done for him.

"Good. Now, I'm going to give you a minute to rest while I go see if there's a shower or something I can use down that hallway.

Then I want you to take me back to our room where we're going to have sex before Lena and Rykal come back. Okay?"

"You're in charge." Something that he was grateful for. "There's a series of cleaning stations through the doors on the left. I'll wait here."

Carys kissed his cheek and went off in search of the stations, leaving him there with his thoughts. The hole in his code was filled to the point where he couldn't find the edges of it. He wasn't entirely certain of what all the lines of the new code would do, but there seemed to be more than he thought necessary. While Aidric had run a scan, Darrick couldn't help but want to know as much as he could about the changes.

He reached out with his matrix to the station's AI, hoping its greater computing power would be able to assist.

Warning, unauthorized cyborg activity.

Warning, retreat or you will be decommissioned.

I DON'T REQUIRE access to the station's systems. I have a question for you.

...UNEXPECTED

CAN you determine the significance of the changes made to my matrix?

WORKING...ANALYZING...TESTING...DETERMINATION unclear.

ARE YOU CERTAIN?

Working...analyzing...retesting...determination still unclear.
  Analysis to be sent to Commander Aidric.

No! He's already analyzing the changes. No need to send additional data.

Commander Aidric is analyzing...Commander *Aidric has not notified me.*

If Darrick didn't know better, he would have sworn the AI was upset by that revelation. *I'm sure he'll require your assistance soon. I hope so.* And then the AI disconnected itself.

Darrick opened his eyes, surprised and more than a little confused by the AI's reaction to what had happened. The chance that the station had developed an emotional framework was miniscule due to the protections that would have been put in place. The last thing the Grus needed was another computer going mad.

He'd have to mention it to Aidric the next time he saw him.

The doors to the back corridor opened and Carys came out, her hair freshly brushed and her skin damp from water. Darrick stood from the table and walked over to her. "Do you feel better?"

"I feel cleaner." She reached up and fingered the collar of his shirt. "I have to admit that while I was interested in a nap, while I was in there washing up I happened to catch sight of that bruise and couldn't help but wonder what it would look like if you bit down on it again."

The mere mention of that had his cock stiffen. "If it would be acceptable to you, I'd love to mark you once again."

Her grin was all the confirmation he needed. Darrick scooped her up and stepped out into the corridor.

CHAPTER TEN

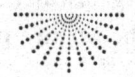

Darrick carried Carys into the room that would only be theirs for a few more short hours before they were able to return to Zarlan's surface. His home on the planet lacked many of the comforts he wanted to provide to her, so he wanted to take advantage of their current situation. A bed with clean sheets, privacy and no other cyborgs present to ask the inevitable barrage of questions.

How did you find her?

When did you know she was meant to be with you?

How can I find a mate of my own?

They'd deal with all of that later. For now, the only thing Darrick cared about was feeling Carys' body pressed against him.

The door to their room slid closed as he set her down to stand in the middle of the room. "I can't wait."

"Wait for what?" She gasped when he dropped to his knees and pulled her pants down as he went. "Oh."

The thin fabric of her undergarments was damp from her arousal, the scent of which was enough to make his head spin. Rather than pulling them off as well, he pressed his nose to the material that covered her pussy and hid his prize from sight. He stuck his tongue out and licked a long, wet trail across the dampness, thrilled by the taste of her. "Mine."

Carys chuckled, her body shaking as she did. "I wouldn't dare argue with you considering what I'm hoping you're about to do next."

He pressed his tongue against her still covered clit, enjoying the feel of her heat and the texture of the material. "I will do whatever you want."

"Then get that finger of yours in there and fuck me with it." She widened her stance, making it easier for him to do what she wanted. "I'm a little pent up and hope we can do a repeat performance."

He'd do what she wanted as many times as she'd want for the rest of their lives.

Shoving the undergarments aside, he traced a path around her clit and along the side of her nether lips to tease her sensitive flesh. Carys braced a hand on his cybernetic shoulder, as she swayed forward closer to his touch. "Yeah, I'm not going to last long."

He hummed and moved his mouth closer. "I'll happily do this again. And again." Then he pressed his finger into her pussy, turning so it pressed against the top of her passage.

She gasped and her body shivered. "Right there."

Fucking her with his hand, he lowered his mouth and licked at the hood of her clit. The taste and smell of her would be forever burned into his mind, imprinted on him so no other woman would ever be enough for him. Her come was sweeter than any treat he'd ever experienced in his life, more addictive than any drug. Lapping at her clit, he mimicked with his hand what he wanted to do to her with his cock. Fucking her hard, then slow, letting her arousal build, only to slow down when he thought she was getting too close to her release.

"Asshole."

"I'll have to teach you how to say that in our language." Then he sucked hard.

Her orgasm must have caught her by surprise, as she doubled over his shoulder crying out. Her inner muscles clamped down on his finger, squeezing him as he continued to press deep inside her until every bit of her release was pulled from her body. Her gasping breath morphed into a soft laugh and she tried to stand up. "Like I said, asshole."

Darrick wasn't done with her – would never be done with her. He sat back before laying flat on the floor. "I'm yours."

Rather than simply jumping on his body to do with him as she wanted, Carys paused to look down at him. She smiled and for a moment he thought she might shed a tear. Instead, she knelt beside him and placed her ear to his chest as she hugged him. "Yes, you certainly are."

They stayed that way as a rush of emotion slammed into him. Gods, he wasn't going to get used to this, the overwhelming connections, this all-consuming love he felt for her. Despite everything he'd ever wanted to accomplish in his life, she was now the most important thing in the universe.

He truly loved her.

When Carys lifted her head to look at him, he could tell she felt the same way about him. She bit down on her lower lip for a moment before looking down at his body. "You're still dressed and I'm only half naked. I think we're going to have to change that."

Unlike the first time together, Carys took her time stripping him of his clothing. First, she removed his boots, setting them beside him neatly. She then followed up by pulling his pants off, folding them and setting them beside his boots. He had to sit up so she could pull his shirt off, and he waited for her to fold it and set it on top of his pants before she encouraged him to lay back down.

"I want to learn about your body." She pressed a hand to his cybernetic shoulder. "I feel like we haven't had any time to get to know one another."

"I know you better than I know myself."

Her eyes lit up and she winked at him. "I'm a bit behind you then. This should be fun."

Instead of starting at his head as he'd hoped, she went back down to his feet and picked up his left one. "I never thought that an alien who lived across the galaxy would also have five toes."

"I'm a bit of an anomaly. Grus normally have six."

She cocked an eyebrow. "That's good to know. I'm also *really* happy you're an anomaly. *Six?*"

He nodded.

Carys shivered. "All hail, five toes." She lifted his foot and kissed the tops of each of them.

She placed his foot on the floor but slid it closer to his body, so his knee was bent and his *rondella* was visible. She pressed his bent leg to the side, exposing the membrane for her to see. "This is what I was curious about."

She trailed her fingertips along the inside of his leg, until she came to the place of her curiosity. "So, this is how your body produces sperm?"

"That is part of the process." He sucked in a breath as she ran her finger along the circumference of the spot. "It heightens our pleasure as well. Helps with the bonding experience with our mates."

"Females have these as well?"

"They do. On females they're called *rondollo*. When we mate, they rub against one another, increasing our arousal until completion."

She looked disappointed, but her expression was hidden when she lowered her face and kissed him in the middle of the spot. It would have been so easy for him to ignore what he'd seen and give in to the pleasure she was drawing from him. Darrick could close his eyes and let her continue until they were both ready to fuck.

But he couldn't do that.

He sat up and pulled her with him. "It doesn't matter to me that you're different. I don't care that our biology isn't the same. Or that we may not be biologically compatible to have offspring. You saved me, rekindled emotions that I never thought I would get back. You've allowed me to feel so much more than physical pleasure. And even still," he moved her hand to grip his hard cock, "I'm burning for you and no one else. I love you, and *no one else*."

Her eyes were wide, and her mouth had slipped open. "Darrick."

He grabbed her by the back of the head and pulled her into a hard kiss. For the first time in forever, his mind stopped working and he allowed himself to feel nothing beyond the emotions brought forth by her. They kissed on and on, and slowly she climbed on top of him as she pulled at her undergarments. With effort, they stripped the rest of her clothing away, only needing to break contact once.

"I'm going to ride you." She straddled his cock, rubbing her pussy along the length of his shaft. "It's going to feel really fucking good."

Darrick laid back and let her take control. His *rondella* was full and so sensitive the cool air of the room felt like a brand against him. When Carys moved her body down his shaft, the weight of her ass against his legs contacted with the membrane. The intensity of the pleasure nearly took his breath away.

"Yes." He grabbed her hips and thrust up hard into her body. "Like that."

They fell into a rhythm, her fucking down on his shaft, her full, naked breasts swinging in the air above his chest, her nipples occasionally brushing against his skin and cybernetics. The temptation was too much for him to resist and he captured one of her breasts in his hand and sat up to suck the nipple into his mouth.

Carys gasped and on her next down thrust, she ground her pussy hard against him. "More. Do that again."

He wasn't a man to resist the request of the woman he loved. He matched the flicks of his tongue across her nipple in beat of her thrusts against him. Before he realized what was happening, he started to thrust up to meet her, increasing the pressure against his *rondella* as he also increased the pressure against her clit.

Carys moaned, her head tipped backward, and her throat stretched. He could see the spot where he'd bit her before, the injury that had started his descent into temporary madness. With his free hand, he moved his fingers along the wound, tracing its pattern much the same way she'd traced around his *rondella*. She moaned when he pressed down on the skin, her pussy muscles clamping around his cock.

Releasing her nipple, he pulled her down so he could replace his finger with his mouth. Gone was the fear and panic of what hurting her would mean. There was no gap in his emotions, no darkness that threatened to swallow him whole. All that remained was Carys and the need to give her all the pleasure she could handle.

He opened his mouth and bit; not too hard, not enough to break the skin. He would leave his mark, his brand that this woman was his and no other man dare try to take her from him. Unlike before, he knew she wanted it, desired his mark the way no one else had.

She was his as much as he was hers.

"Shit!" Her whole body shuddered as she cried out. Her pussy clamped down on him as she thrust uncontrollably against him, riding his cock hard as her orgasm consumed her.

Darrick tried to hold back, but she was slamming against his full *rondella* and there was no stopping his release. The first powerful waves of his pre-orgasm rolled through him, quickly followed by the mind-blowing explosion of his full orgasm. His come shot from his cock and he felt it fill her body as she pumped him.

The world disappeared as he barely became aware of anything beyond Carys' body on his. He bowed up, his arms squeezing her hard as waves of his orgasm shook him. Every nerve ending seemed to fire at once, as though every cell in his body had pulled apart under the intensity of pleasure, only to slam together once more. With a gasp, he fell back against the floor, taking her with him.

They laid there, bodies drenched in sweat and limbs entwined. Darrick's world slowly began to right itself and he became aware of Carys' breath against coming out across his skin in short, shallow puffs. "Are you well?"

He felt her swallow before she patted his chest. "I'm sorry, Carys has died and only left a shell of herself behind. Check back later."

Joy spread through his chest, mixing with the remnants of pleasure that still warmed him. "You're funny."

"I am. I'm also going to be sore after this. I don't know about you, but I'm not used to having rough sex twice, with a four-hour stint of putting my consciousness inside someone else's body sandwiched in between."

"I'll be sure we leave that middle part out in any future love-making encounters." With his arms still wrapped around her, Darrick sat them both up. "We should probably get dressed. It won't be much longer before we must leave to meet Rykal and Lena."

"I wonder if we're going to move the remaining women from the Kraken down to the planet without waking them up? It seems like they should be aware of what's going on before that happens."

"Can you imagine the chaos that would be created if only a handful of cyborgs react the way I did to the arrival of their mate? The Grus aren't equipped to handle that many out of control Fallen."

She groaned and rolled her eyes. "I know. And it would be stupid to try anything else. I just know how annoyed I'd be if I was one of the women and found out that I'd been stuck in stasis longer than necessary."

"Lucky for us then, you were the second one out." He placed a kiss on the tip of her nose. "We better get dressed."

He saw her legs shake as she stood, which made him want to keep an eye on her even more than normal. This was going to be his new reality – keeping watch over his mate to ensure nothing bad ever happened to her. There were certainly worse fates than that to be dealt.

"I'll have to make sure I get my belongings from the Kraken before we leave. I didn't bring a lot with me from Earth, but I have a few mementos I'd like to have. That I'd like to show you." She smiled, looking more than a little embarrassed.

"Let's go now. We can be there and back before Rykal and Lena arrive." It would also give him the chance to take one last walk around Grus Prime. The chances of him returning to the place he'd long ago called home were slim.

"Really? You don't mind?"

He tied his boots and straightened his shirt. "Let's go."

The Grus who lived on the station still stared at them as they passed through the corridors on their way to the docking bay, but unlike before, Darrick didn't care about what they thought. He didn't care if they were worried about him going mad, because he knew it was no longer a possibility. Carys had fixed him, repaired the damage Aidric had caused when he'd installed the cybernetic matrix into him. Darrick now had complete control over himself and knew he'd always be happy with Carys by his side.

Reaching down, he took her hand in his. "I love you."

Her breath caught in her throat and she stopped walking. He turned to look at her but refused to let go of her hand. She smiled and gave his hand a squeeze. "I love you too."

"No regrets about what you found now that you've reached your destination across the galaxy?"

"None." She lifted his hand and kissed the back of it. "Let's get my stuff."

When they reached the docking bay, Darrick was surprised to see Aidric standing with a group of engineers by the Kraken. *How the hell is he always in the one place we don't want him to be?* "So much for no one knowing we're here."

If Carys had any reluctance about confronting Aidric, she didn't show it. Dropping Darrick's hand, she marched across the docking bay. "What the hell are you doing with the ship?"

"The decision has been approved by the high council. We are preparing the stasis tubes for transportation down to the planet's surface." He frowned at her. "What are you doing here?"

"I came to get my belongings." She crossed her arms and kicked her hip out to the side. "Does Lena know what you're doing?"

"She gave me control of the ship and all of its computer systems." Aidric cocked a single eyebrow. "Get your belongings and leave. I need Grus Prime to get back to some semblance of order and that won't happen with cyborgs on board." The normal bite in Aidric's speech was lacking.

If Darrick wasn't certain, he might even think the commander was amused.

Impossible.

Carys was about to step into the ship when the station's AI alert claxon echoed in the docking back.

"Station alert! Station alert! Incoming attack!"

Aidric bolted to the command console. "Computer, report. Who's attacking?"

The claxons nearly drowned out the AI's voice, but even so Darrick would have known what it was about to say.

"Warning, the Sholle have entered the system. Prepare for attack."

SAVED BY THE CYBORG

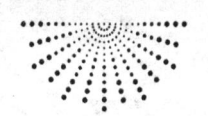

With the enemy closing in, a cyborg must do everything he can to save his mate.

A CYBORG PROTECTORS ROMANCE

SAVED BY THE CYBORG

ALYSE ANDERS

CHAPTER ONE

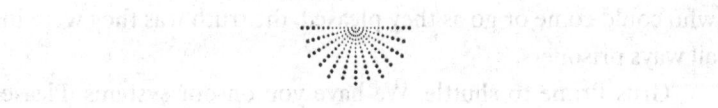

Eagan hadn't flown a ship off Zarlan's surface since the final days of the Sholle war nearly two decades ago. It had been made clear to him that there was no room for a man with his skills anywhere on Grus Prime space station. Not only was he a cyborg, but a skilled tactician who'd been instrumental in creating the war plan they'd needed to drive the Sholle away from their sector for good.

At least, that's what he'd thought had happened.

Rykal had contacted him an hour earlier with the words Eagan had never thought he'd hear again.

The Sholle were back.

They hadn't attacked either Grus Prime, nor Zarlan itself. As of the last report, three scout ships had entered the edge of the sector's sensor range and were holding position. That gave Eagan time to process the information and take a shuttle to the station where he could convene with the Grus leadership to determine the plan of attack.

And how many cyborgs would be sacrificed this time.

The atmospheric storm was stronger than normal, violently shaking the small shuttle. Normally, there was a Grus pilot and co-pilot who would fly any recalled cyborg up to the station. This prevented any of their kind from having access not only to a ship that could be used to attack the station, but also allow the cyborgs to leave the planet without authroization. While the Grus claimed that the Fallen – the most sanitized term for cyborgs they could have come up with – were their own people who could come or go as they pleased, the truth was they were in all ways prisoners.

"Grus Prime to shuttle. We have you on our systems. Please continue on approach vector alpha."

Eagan signaled his acknowledgment, even if he didn't vocalize it.

He tried to not hate the Grus, hate what they'd turned him into, but it was difficult. He'd been forced into the war with the Sholle the first time around because his attack and defense simulations had been the most successful. Having a tactical mind was one thing, but being forced to convene with commanders while firing weapons on the battlefield was another.

No one in his small detail of soldiers had been aware of the presence of the bomb that took his leg, gouged his side and stole the lives of the others. Eagan had never been so far out of his element. Until they pulled him from the rubble, connected cybernetic enhancements to his body and installed a matrix into the back of his brain. His life, or re-birth as they loved to call it, completely changed at that point.

His brain saw things even better than before. His body was stronger, faster and more responsive.

It was a shame his emotions couldn't come along for the ride.

The moment the shuttle popped out above the planet's exosphere, peace descended over him. The blackness of space was a balm across a wound he hadn't realized was festering, soothing the old hurt. Grus Prime hovered in the distance, a grey-blue beacon calling out to him, reminding him of the life he once had. There was something different about the station, something he couldn't quite reconcile with his memories. The running lights directing him toward the docking bay were the same, as was the shimmer of the energy shield that protected the Grus home.

Eagan reached up and scratched at the back of his head, frustrated when he realized that the itching felt as though it was inside his brain.

Wonderful.

On top of an imminent attack, he possibly had a glitch in his system.

Ignoring the itching as best he could, Eagan maneuvered the shuttle toward the docking bay. The moment the shuttle passed through the energy shield, a voice echoed loudly in his head.

ATTENTION CYBORG. *You are now approaching Grus Prime Station. You are prohibited from connecting your systems to the central computer. Failure to comply will result in immediate decommission. Acknowledge.*

THE STATION'S AI had been part of his creation upon the cleanup from the Sholle war. He'd worked with Commander Aidric to ensure the cyborgs wouldn't pose a threat to the Grus, who would be powerless to defend themselves against a full-blown attack. The fact that the voice sounded feminine was his doing, though hearing it now, he should have considered a more neutral voice.

ACKNOWLEDGE CYBORG.

Eagan clenched his teeth. *I acknowledge.* Maybe the itching in his head wasn't a glitch, but rather an unexpected by-product from the AI's monitoring systems? If their entire world didn't go to hell in the next few hours, he might consider talking to Commander Aidric about it.

If he could manage to stomach the interaction.

He easily finessed the shuttle into the docking bay, landing it with as little impact as he could. It only took a moment for him to disengage the engines and decompress the shuttle before the door opened allowing him to leave. Protocol dictated that he be greeted with a full complement of security guards who would direct him to a contained waiting facility, so he was shocked when Rykal and Darrick instead approached the shuttle alone.

Stepping out into the docking bay generated an odd sensation of nostalgia and something else that he couldn't quite place. Both men were looking at him strangely, their gaze not once leaving him. Eagan fought the urge to shake his head or reach up once again to scratch. "I'm here."

Rykal shared a look with Darrick before stepping forward and holding out his hand. "Did you take any scans of the Sholle ships on your way up?"

"The shuttle's sensor range doesn't reach that far, but I gathered what information I could. I take it they haven't moved?"

"No." Darrick crossed his arms, highlighting his hulking frame. "They haven't done anything yet but scan the station. Even then we're not certain what information they would have received given the distance."

"They'd never been interested in the station before, only the planet and what resources they could strip from the surface." None of this made sense to Eagan. "It's possible they're trying to determine if we've weakened enough for them to come back and finish what they'd started." He took a step forward, but his gaze snapped to a ship sitting off on the far end of the docking bay. "What's that?"

Before he was able to change his direction toward the unknown ship, both Rykal and Darrick were at his sides, their arms moving him away. Rykal kept his gaze locked on Eagan.

"That is a separate problem for after our meeting with the Grus command."

Eagan didn't know why, but there was something important about the ship, something that was tied in with the Sholle's presence and what was going to happen. He didn't know how or why he knew this, but it was in his heart the truth.

The further away he got from the ship, the easier it was for him to focus. "I expect an explanation."

"You'll get one," Darrick said as he released his hold once they entered the corridor. "There will be no avoiding it."

"Let's keep our attention focused on the problem at hand." Rykal also release his grip, though he didn't move as far away as Darrick did. "Aidric has informed the rest of the Grus high council about the Sholle's presence."

Eagan hated everything about this. Hated that he knew the Grus would expect him to come up with a plan to protect them while also putting the Fallen in danger. They'd expect him to do this as quickly and efficiently as possible before returning to Zarlan's surface to continue his necessary exile.

What made matters worse is that he'd do it. Every last thing.

He hated the Grus.

The emergency lights flashed as they traversed the corridor, now cleared of most Grus personnel. Non-essential people would have been sent to the residential section of the station where the families were segregated and kept safe from any alien or cyborg arrivals. He hadn't been there since after the war when the station had been a military facility, rather than the last hope of the Grus people. But the Grus couldn't live on a partially destroyed planet and the Fallen could. The change only made sense.

Logical. Practical. A plan that he too had orchestrated.

"Nothing has changed." The observation frustrated him.

Darrick snorted as he shook his head. "I think you'll be pleasantly surprised."

That turned out to be a truth as well. When they entered the command room, Eagan's gaze took in all the relevant information of who was present. Naturally, Commander Aidric was there informing the Grus high council about the situation. As the creator of the cyborg matrix and the man who created their people from the fallen soldiers, he'd become the natural bridge between their two peoples over the years.

Eagan hated him, even as he respected the decision he'd been forced to make on their behalf.

However, the Grus high councillors were another matter all together. The group of three – two men and one woman – sat in chairs in the middle of the room, their impractical long robes draped across the arms rests and cascaded to the floor. The moment one of the councillors looked at the three cyborgs, he lifted his chin and shifted his gaze away.

It's good to see some things never change. He used the cyborg short range communication to connect with Rykal and Darrick. *Have they acknowledged your presence at all?*

Not yet. Rykal laced his hands behind his back. *I have low expectations of that happening either.*

Darrick stiffened, somehow making his large frame appear even larger. *At least we have Aidric as a conduit. I'd hate to get annoyed and accidentally bash one of their brains in.*

Their link was suddenly broken, and the voice of the station's AI blared in his head.

Attention cyborgs. Linked communication is strictly forbidden. Failure to comply will result in immediate decommission. Acknowledge.

There was a time when Eagan might have been amused by the overbearing AI, but today wasn't that day. *If you expect us to protect the Grus from the imminent Sholle attack, communication between cyborg units is not only pertinent, but required. YOU fracking acknowledge!*

The hesitation on the part of the AI was nearly palpable.

Rykal glanced over at Eagan, cocking his eyebrow. As the seconds ticked on, Eagan wanted to laugh at the insanity of the situation.

After a few moments of silence, the AI's voice returned. *Permission granted. For now.*

Darrick snorted. *So kind of you.*

With that distraction gone, Eagan was able to relax a fraction. It was only at that point that he realized there were two people present in the room who shouldn't be there. Two people who he didn't recognize, who didn't appear to even be Grus. Why hadn't he noticed them as soon as he walked into the room? He scratched at the back of his head again, wondering if the annoyance was somehow to blame for his oversight.

That's Lena and Carys. Rykal's voice felt tentative and held a sound of something Eagan hadn't heard from his former commander in a long while – love.

Who are they? Without being told, he knew they'd arrived on the ship back in the docking bay, that they were somehow the reason for the Sholle's returned presence in the sector. But there was something more than that. Something he couldn't figure out yet and it was starting to irritate him.

Not to mention the itching in the back of his brain was getting stronger.

Rykal turned to face him. "I promise you it will all become clear. We need time to address this first and then I'll give you all the details. We'll also deal with the itching in the back of your brain."

"How did you know?" But then he looked over at the two women and he realized there was a reason two cyborgs had been allowed to be on Grus Prime at the same time. Somehow the Fallen were linked to these women.

And in that moment, Eagan knew everything in his life was about to change.

"Rykal, can you and the others come over." Commander

Aidric's gaze paused on Eagan briefly, but he gave no other indication of concern.

The three approached the high council, walking past the two women where they stood off to the side. It took tremendous effort not to turn and look at them, to keep from diverting his path to approach them. He could feel Rykal and Darrick's attention fixed on him and knew they would intervene if he got too close. Not because they were trying to protect the Grus or even himself. He somehow knew they would do anything for those women, even kill him if it was deemed necessary.

Commander Aidric stood at attention, his gray uniform crisp and clean, contrasting with the slight hunch in his shoulders. "Have you been shown any of the scans of the Sholle ships?"

Right to the matter at hand. Eagan hadn't remembered seeing him so obviously tired before, not even in the days of the war after his re-birth. If the others noticed, no one said anything. "I've only just arrived."

Commander Aidric's gaze slid to Rykal's for the briefest of moments before he turned to the high council. "Please excuse me while I show our tactician the most recent data we've collected."

None of the councillors responded to him, instead turning their attention to one another. Commander Aidric spun on his heel and nodded toward the far console. "This way."

Eagan reached out to the others. *There's something wrong with the Commander?*

Aidric's tired. The concern in Rykal's words was unusual, as was the use of solely his given name. As far as Eagan knew, the two of them weren't on the best of terms, even if they'd once been close.

It's been a busy few days. Darrick added, and a flash of the dark-skinned woman flashed through his mind. *Let's hope things settle down for us all and this turns out to be nothing.*

Eagan shook his head. *When the Sholle are involved, it's never nothing*. That was the reason they'd brought him to the station, to determine exactly what was happening.

"There's a console ready for you." Aidric pointed to the station closest to them. "I've opened permissions with the AI to grant you full access to anything you might need."

"I'm surprised the AI wasn't able to determine what's brought the Sholle here." Eagan knew his abilities to shift through data and making leaps of logic was the most precise of any of the cyborgs, but with the resources available to the AI, it should have been able to find the source as well as he could.

"We ran the tests multiple times, but nothing showed." Aidric spoke in a clipped tone as his gaze slipped over to the console. "Whatever is attracting the Sholle, it's beyond the AI's capability to locate."

While incredibly advanced, the AI was still limited by its programming. Eagan had the advantage of being born biological, and his life experience gave him a wider perspective that allowed for leaps in logic.

Commander Aidric turned to look Eagan in the eyes. "I need to know if our people are about to be obliterated, or if there's something else happening here."

The impulse to protect washed over Eagan and he nodded before taking the seat and scanning the sector. "Please hold."

The ability to determine patterns out of seemingly nothing was a gift he'd possessed long before he'd been re-born. It was simply the way his brain had developed, and it had made his life easy if not a little boring. With the enhancements of his cybernetic matrix, it allowed Eagan to make those connections faster than any Grus alive. It didn't take long for him to see exactly what had drawn the Sholle out from whatever rock they'd taken residence under and pulled them here.

There was a signal.

It was faint, and not of Grus origin. The trickle of data floating out into the blackness of space wouldn't have been detectable by many. But the Sholle's technology was far superior to even the Grus; clearly, they'd been able to pick it up and followed it here, thinking they were going to find a new victim to exploit.

What he couldn't determine was where the signal originated.

It took another few minutes of searching, trying to find the barest threads of data and painstakingly follow them back to the source. When he realized what it was, Eagan got to his feet and turned to face the Commander and Rykal.

"They're not here for us. They've come for the ship in your docking bay."

CHAPTER TWO

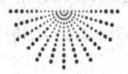

Eagan couldn't be certain why, but he knew that the itching in the back of his brain had something to do not only with the ship, but with the signal that was emanating from it. Commander Aidric frowned, but both Rykal and Darrick instantly went on alert.

"What do you mean the ship?" Rykal's voice was low and there was no missing the hint of aggression. *You best be careful with what you say next. That ship is important to our people.*

Explain how. "They tracked it here. Without examining it more closely, I can't be certain how."

It's full of women from a planet called Earth. The muscles in Rykal's jaw jumped. *We don't understand how, but the women are meant for us.*

The Grus? None of this made sense to him.

No, the Fallen. Darrick sounded more than a little panicked. *They're our mates.*

It took Eagan great effort not to show his doubt. *We're not capable of having mates.*

Commander Aidric cleared his throat. "It would make sense for you to evaluate the ship in person." He let his gaze slide past them toward where the high council sat. "If there's something on board then it will need to be destroyed."

"Whoa, hang on a second." The human woman with long red hair pushed away from the wall and marched over to them. "No one's going near my ship without me being there. The safety of my passengers is my responsibility."

"Eagan, this is Lena McGovern, the captain of the human ship, the Kraken." There was no mistaking the pride in Rykal's voice. *She's my mate.*

He couldn't process the thought that cyborgs could have mates, let alone that there was an entire ship of them sitting in the docking bay of this station. He didn't have time to dwell either, not with the Sholle sitting out there waiting. "Captain, you can come with me then. We need to find out what's drawing the Sholle's attention and if it can be shut off rather than destroyed."

Lena placed her hands on her hips and cocked her head to the side. "You're decisive. I like that. Let's go then." She didn't wait for anyone else and strode from the room. The dark-skinned woman – Carys – simply shrugged and followed her out.

"Commander Aidric, do we have your permission to continue on this mission?" The old habits had slotted back into place far easier than Eagan would have liked.

The blank expression on the commander's face was far too familiar, as was his emotionless tone. "Go. Rykal and Darrick – assist Eagan and report back when you've discovered the source of the signal."

"Commander Aidric."

The air felt as though it had been sucked from the room as the head of the high council stood. His dark green wrinkled skin and white hair belied his age, and his attitude his status. The look of disdain he shot the commander was nearly enough to have Eagan feel sorry for him.

Almost.

"Yes, High Councillor Yannis." Commander Aidric turned and

bowed in one smooth motion that was clearly long practiced. "How may I assist?"

High Councillor Yannis' gaze was locked on Commander Aidric, but Eagan could tell he was speaking to them all. "Is it wise to allow *three* cyborgs to remain on Grus Prime? Their collection here puts all Grus at risk. Would it not be better to send the other two away and allow this tactician to remain?"

Though they were phrased as questions, Eagan knew a command when he heard one. He braced himself for the inevitable division, when Commander Aidric bowed again and took a step closer to the high councillors.

"With respect, the presence of the Sholle in the sector does require an unconventional response. Having three of the Fallen on Grus Prime will allow us to protect the station in the event of a direct attack. If Eagan can determine the source of the signal and can deactivate it promptly, then Rykal and Darrick will be able to return to the surface of Zarlan and begin to plan our defences."

It had been a long time since Eagan had felt anything close to surprise, but Commander Aidric had certainly caught him off guard. It seemed High Councillor Yannis was also shocked, as he sat back down with a frown. "If you feel that's the best course of action, then proceed."

"Thank you, High Councillor." Commander Aidric turned back to them. "I suggest you move quickly. I'll stay with the high council."

Rykal nodded. "We'll report back as soon as we learn anything." *We need to move quickly. I'll fill you in once we get to the docking bay.*

Eagan fell into step behind the two men, his military training code freshly back into the forefront of his matrix. It had been a long time since he'd interacted this way with any of the other Fallen and it felt awkward and forced. Yes, they'd been born out of war and the necessity to protect the Grus who couldn't protect themselves, but in the decades since the invasion he'd changed, and his wants and desires had changed with him.

A mate. That was a dream he'd long ago pushed aside, knowing it wouldn't be a possibility. No Grus mate wanted anything to do with the Fallen. And even if they did, most of the Fallen were incapable of returning the emotions that a mate would desire. He couldn't believe that these human women were able to somehow push past the emotional void and connect with them.

Their return journey to the docking bay was unobstructed, though surprisingly silent as they went. Eagan didn't normally mind silence, but in this instance some answers were beneficial. It would have been a distraction from the growing itching sensation in the back of his brain.

The doors to the docking bay slid open to reveal Lena walking around the outside of the Kraken with a hand scanner. She looked over her shoulder at them and flashed a grin. "You're slow."

"Aidric had to run interference with the high council. They wanted to remove Darrick and I back to the planet." Rykal smiled at her, wrapping his arm around her waist and kissing her cheek when they drew close enough. "Have you found anything?"

Eagan was finding it difficult to think. "How long have you been mated?"

"Not long." Lena looked at him with an odd expression. "It's only been a few days since our arrival. God, that's nuts." She held out the scanner for him to take. "I can't find anything, so this might be useless."

"It won't be sensitive enough." He couldn't look at the device, even though he took it from her. It was growing more and more difficult for him to keep his focus. "When I examined the data captured by the broad-spectrum signal sensors, I was only barely able to detect it. The pattern is easily mistakeable for background noise, which is why the AI did not sound an alarm."

The itching was starting to become a throbbing, and he knew the source of the disturbance was inside the ship. If he could get onboard and look around, maybe he'd be able to determine what it was and deactivate it.

Rykal stepped between him and the ship's open door. "Before you go in there, you need to understand exactly what will happen, what's at risk."

"The Sholle are here. The station, the planet and the lives of both our people who live there are at risk." He forced his gaze from the ship to Rykal. "I'm more than aware."

"But the moment you step onto that ship, you're not going to care about any of that. You won't be able to stop yourself from looking for your mate. She's going to be the only thing that matters to you. The Sholle could attack this place but it won't matter. I need you to know that, to be prepared." Rykal's gaze dropped to the floor and he took a breath. "I kidnapped Lena the moment I saw her. Darrick nearly died because his systems weren't prepared for the change. Normally, I'd let this happen naturally and we'd deal with whatever the fallout was, but with the Sholle there we don't have that luxury."

Eagan knew Rykal was right. The pull was there, and it was far stronger than anything he'd ever felt in his life. It was the sort of thing that would be so easy to let himself get swept up in, to let it consume his life.

He closed his eyes and took a breath. Then he took another. When he opened his eyes again, Eagan knew he had no choice in any of this. "I will need to find her first, then focus on the signal. I don't know what any of this means, but I'm assuming the two of you will know how to handle my reactions."

Lena stepped beside Rykal. "Carys and I will wake whoever it is out of stasis and let her know what's going on. We didn't come here with this in mind, so it will be a bit of a shock to her too."

"While Lena's doing that, hopefully we'll be able to find the signal and disrupt it." Rykal turned to face Darrick. "Keep everyone else out of the ship. Stay out here and I'll let you know if I need you."

"I'll keep watch." Darrick moved to take sentry position, his military training obvious.

The plan was sound, even if the results were unpredictable. Eagan nodded. "I cannot accept that things will be that easy for us, but we can re-evaluate once we see the results."

"We need to fly the Kraken down to Zarlan's surface and away from the grasp of the High Council." Rykal cocked his eyebrow. "I know Aidric. He hasn't informed them about our reaction to the humans."

"That's very unlike the Commander." Eagan knew of Rykal's relationship with Aidric, but even still he couldn't hold back his anger – the one emotion all Fallen had been left with. "He's always been one to put the Grus first."

"I don't think he trusts that they will allow the rest of them to be removed from stasis." Rykal's body stiffened. "You might not realize it, but Aidric regrets what he's done to us."

Eagan's chest tightened. "Then we best hurry so we can help him make amends."

Mentally prepared for what might happen, Eagan walked past the others and up the ship's ramp. The humans were clearly a much smaller race than the Grus, their ceilings and corridors shorter and narrower than a typical Grus shuttle. Their technology was also considerably less advanced based on what he'd seen of their computer systems. How could a race as technologically inferior to theirs have been able to reach across such a vast distance to their sector of space? How were they linked?

He turned toward the mental tug that led him further into the ship. He knew the others were behind him – Rykal and the two human women – but he ignored them, letting his eyes fall closed as he moved quietly toward his goal.

She was here. How he hadn't been aware of her presence the moment he'd landed the shuttle on the station, Eagan wasn't sure.

The feeling was as strong as a beacon in the blackness of space, shouting out to him *hey look, I'm over here waiting for you.* Now that he knew what it was, knew that she was here ... close. He needed her. Needed to hold her in his arms, to keep her safe.

Each step increased the pressure on his brain, and his feet seemed to move of their own volition. His heart rate had increased, as had his irritation about being followed. *No, keep calm. You need to keep her safe from the Sholle, from the council. Calm and focused.*

"Keep back." He heard Rykal behind him.

"He's almost there – " Lena that time.

"He'll be fine. Give him space."

Eagan opened his eyes and stepped into what appeared to be a loading bay. It wasn't overly large but must have comprised the bulk of the ship itself. Rows of stasis tubes were lined up along the walls, surrounded by the necessary equipment to keep the people inside safe on their journey. The throbbing in his head was now a pounding, a beat demanding that he move faster, *get over here right now and save me from this sleep*!

There was no way he couldn't comply.

No searching for the correct tube was required, as Eagan knew where she was, could feel her laying there waiting for him. He marched over to stand beside one of the closer units on the right. He hesitated for a moment, before looking down to peer through the observation window of the tube.

The woman was small, even more so than Lena or Carys. Her skin was white, and her brown hair was a mass of short brown curls. She looked as though her eyes would open any second and she'd smile. He didn't know how he knew that, but he did. Her nose was small and her lips full, giving her a delicate appearance. But there must be more to her than that if she'd been brave enough to put herself in the hands of another to bring her out into the unknown.

He became aware of Lena by his side entering commands into

the tube's computer unit. "This is Beth Jones. Oh, I remember her. She's a teacher. I couldn't figure out why she wanted to come with us." Lena frowned as she looked at the console. "I don't see anything unusual about her tube, so if there's another signal coming from the Kraken, it's not here."

Beth. It was an unusual name, though it might be quite common where she was from. "Get her out."

Rykal put a hand on his shoulder. "Lena will do that, but now I need you to help me find the signal. If it's what piqued the interest of the Sholle, maybe cutting if off will make it easier for them to ... leave. I'd rather we avoid another conflict."

Gods, he didn't want to leave, not when she looked so small and helpless laying there. Rykal increased the pressure on his shoulder. "I know you don't want to leave her. That you don't want anyone to touch her but you. But we have a mission to complete first."

The mission. Yes, that was important. He needed to find the source of the signal and hope it deterred the Sholle from coming here. Eagan straightened and with effort, looked away from Beth. "Don't touch her."

"I won't. I'll be with you. Lena and Carys will wake her up and make sure she understands what's happening." *I know what you're going through.* Rykal's thoughts echoed in Eagan's head.

"Let's find this signal." The throbbing of his brain had dulled since he'd come to stand beside her stasis tube, making it a bit easier to think. "The signal must be coming from something that's still powered."

"Most of the ship's systems are off." Lena hovered by the tube's controls. "The only things still powered are the stasis tubes and the central core."

Eagan nodded. "Engineering would be the place to start." Even if what he wanted to do was stay here. "Do you know the way?"

Rykal looked over at Lena, who pointed at the corridor. "To the left, then two rights. It will be straight in front of you."

Eagan looked once more at Beth, before turning sharply on his heel to head to engineering. The sooner he discovered what was happening, the sooner he could be with her.

CHAPTER THREE

Beth had been more than a little freaked out when she'd climbed into the stasis tube back on Earth. Her family hadn't wanted her to go, had even gone so far as to try and lock her up in their home to prevent her from making it to the Kraken before it's departure. Fleeing through the crowded streets to make it in time had been more than a little terrifying. Her home was in a protected section of the city, and she'd only been beyond the walls once when her father was trying to show his daughters how lucky they were to have the life that they did. The map Captain McGovern had provided her via their communications proved accurate, and she'd been one of the last passengers to come on board.

So when she felt the rush of adrenaline pump through her body, when she became aware that she was starting to wake up, she immediately panicked.

They found me and they're going to stop me from going. I don't want to go home.

Oxygen blasted over her face, and she couldn't help but suck in a deep breath, letting the mixture fill her lungs and wake her brain. Her eyes were slow to open and even when they did, she found she couldn't see anything clearly. It took her a moment to realize that she was still in the tube and the top hadn't opened yet.

Another type of panic set in.

She hated being confined in small spaces. When she'd been put under initially, she was still riding the rush of fear about being caught. Now that her freedom was so close, she needed it to happen as quickly as possible.

"Let me out." Her voice was barely a whisper, though it filled the small chamber.

Thankfully, the response was the hiss of hydraulics as the cover lifted then retracted, leaving the space above her now blissfully wide open. "Thank God."

"You need to take it slow. You've been in there for a long time."

Beth looked over to see Captain McGovern standing there with another woman who she didn't recognize. They were both smiling, and each offered her a hand to help her sit up. "Thanks."

"You're going to feel a little lightheaded, but that's normal."

"Thank you, Captain."

"Please, call me Lena. Considering where we are, titles aren't exactly necessary."

"You can say that again." The other woman snorted. "A lot of things from Earth aren't exactly relevant."

Lena grinned and nodded toward the other woman. "Beth, this is Carys, another passenger who's also been woken. We're going to help you up and then we're unfortunately going to hit you with a whole lot of information."

"That doesn't sound good." Her heart pounded, the echo of which beeped back to her from the stasis tube monitor. "Did we make it to a new Earth?"

The women shared a look, before Lena nodded. "I'm going to say yes. It turns out that things are a bit more complicated than I'd anticipated before we set off."

She gave Beth a run down of what had happened in the past few days since the ship had woken Lena up. The rush of information was almost too much for her to take in, especially when her brain couldn't let go of the idea that they'd been traveling at faster than light speed for over fifty years. "Everyone I knew back on Earth is dead. My family." Tears welled up in her eyes and threatened to spill. "I understood that when I signed up, but the reality is kind of hitting me."

"There's something else." Lena looked at the door to the corridor behind her. "The cyborgs I mentioned. We're not sure why yet, but it seems that the reason each of us was compelled to come on this journey is that there's a cyborg here who has a connection to us. They call us their mates, and to be honest I don't have a better title for what this seems to be."

A mate? She'd left her family behind on Earth because they'd been trying to marry her off to one of the city councillor's sons. The idea of being sold off to someone who didn't know her, didn't care about who she was beyond her value to her family, disgusted her. "I'm no one's mate."

Pushing their hands aside, Beth swung her feet to the side and gingerly stood up. Her muscles protested after too many years of disuse, and she had to hold onto the edge of the tube. Lena grabbed an injector from the medical tray. "This will help your muscles recover from any atrophy they might have been subjected to." She pressed it to the side of Beth's neck. "There's something else. The Grus obviously don't speak Earth basic and their language is complex."

"I was trying to learn it, but circumstances got in the way of letting me continue." Carys pulled another injector from her pocket, though the design was nothing Beth had seen before. "This contains nanobots that can basically rewrite your brain so you can understand what people are saying. It's like a built-in translator, but driven by your mind."

"It also hurts like a fucker when they go in, so you need to be prepared." Lena took the injector from Carys, holding it up for Beth to see. "You don't need to, but it does make life easier."

"Especially when you have a nearly wild cyborg in your face." Carys shrugged. "The language is interesting to learn, but a short amount of pain makes life a whole lot easier."

Beth wasn't one to enjoy pain, but she hated being unable to know what was going on even more. Being kept in the dark was what had nearly gotten her into trouble back on Earth. She turned her head to expose her neck once more. "Do it."

The pain was as horrible as the women had indicated, hitting her nearly the moment the nanobots slipped into her bloodstream. Beth's head throbbed so hard she gagged and would have vomited if not for the lack of food in her stomach. Her vision whited out, causing her to blink rapidly to try and bring it back. Her world started spinning and if it wasn't for the two sets of hands on her body to keep her steady, Beth had no doubt she'd have ended up on the floor in a heap.

After a while, her head settled down and her body seemed to come back to normal. Her mouth was dry and all she wanted was a drink, some food and strangely to have a nap. "You'd think I'd be over wanting to sleep after having been unconscious for fifty years."

"If things weren't so crazy since waking up, I would have crawled into the nearest bed and stayed there." Lena grabbed a clean set of clothing. "Unfortunately, none of us have that luxury. There's a cleaning station at the back of the docking bay. You'll want to get washed and changed while you have the chance."

"What haven't you told me?" Beth took the clothing and held the bundle tight to her chest.

The smile that was so often on Lena's face dropped. "It seems that there's something on the ship that has alerted the mortal enemy of the Grus and brought a few of their scout ships here. Rykal and Eagan are trying to find the source of the signal in engineering. But there's a chance they won't find it and we might have to move the ship."

Eagan.

Beth wasn't sure why, but there was something about hearing that name that sent a shiver through her. "Who's Eagan?"

Lena cocked her head to the side. "He's the cyborg who identified you as his mate. That's why we had to wake you. As soon as he stepped on the ship, he was drawn to you, but we needed him to find the signal. There was no way he'd be able to do that before he'd connected with you, so here we are."

There was a noise behind them drawing their attention. Two large men stood in the doorway, their frames wide and muscular. The shorter of the two stepped forward, his gaze locked onto Beth. His long light brown hair was swept back behind his ears, giving her a clear view of his eyes that looked as though they were glowing. He took another step forward, but even that proximity was too much for her to handle. She turned to Lena. "I'm going to change."

Without waiting for anyone to speak, she ran for the cleaning station and shut the door. God, this wasn't what she'd thought would be waiting for her when she came onto the Kraken. Not that she'd had a clear understanding of what they were hoping to find when they were woken, but basically going from an arranged marriage to someone who thought she was his mate wasn't it.

With shaking hands, she stripped out of the uniform she'd put on for the cryogenic sleep, and washed her body as best she could in the shower with none of the fancy soaps she'd grown used to on Earth. She dried carefully and dressed into the rough cotton shirt and pants, pausing long enough to run her hands through her damp curls, trying as best as she could to bring them back to life.

Beth hadn't considered herself privileged, but clearly she'd lived in a protective bubble up to this point. Standing here looking at herself in the mirror dressed in standard Earth clothing, she realized her life would never be the same again.

She hadn't understood why it had been so important for her to secure passage on the Kraken. When she'd heard about her impending engagement to Marcus on Earth, she'd panicked, knowing he wasn't the man she was meant to be with. When she'd inquired about passage off Earth, she'd originally hoped to buy a flight to Mars where she'd be able to start a new life. It wasn't until she'd learned about the Kraken's journey to an unknown sector of space that Beth knew that was where she'd needed to be.

Maybe there really was something to this mate thing.

Strengthening her resolve, she put on her boots and stepped back out into the loading bay. Everyone else was gone except for the man she'd seen before. Licking her lips, she crossed her arms and stepped closer. "Eagan?"

He nodded but made no other move.

Beth continued closer, trying not to let her fear overwhelm her. "I...I honestly don't know what's going on right now. Lena told me that we don't have a lot of time to discuss things. That there's an enemy close by who might want to hurt us?"

He nodded again.

Now that she was only a few feet away from him, she was able to see that his eyes not only truly glowed but were also brown. The light made them appear warm and inviting. Other than that, she couldn't see any indication that he was an enhanced person. His olive skin could have almost passed for a human skin tone. His jaw line and strong nose would have made him stand out, but every one of her friends would have swooned and cooed over how handsome he was.

Beth could tell though, that there was a darkness to him, an edge that kept others at arm's length. "Were you able to find the signal in engineering?"

For a moment, she didn't think he was going to say anything

to her. But he lowered his chin when she took one final step closer to better look her in the eyes. "I did not." His voice was low and raspy, as though it wasn't something he used all the time.

She swallowed hard, trying to keep her rising nerves down. "What's the next thing you need to do then?"

"Inspect the loading bay." His body swayed ever so slightly toward her, before he stiffened once more. "It's possible that the collection of stasis tubes is generating an energy signature that the Sholle are homing in on."

Beth turned to look at the remaining tubes and all the people inside waiting to be released. "What happens if the tubes are the source of the signal?"

"I don't know."

Eagan stepped up behind her, close enough she could feel the heat of his body through her clothing. His proximity had her body respond, and a tingle ran through her that seemed to follow a path from the back of her neck straight down to her pussy. It became difficult to breathe evenly, as her now hardening nipples brushed against the fabric of her undergarments.

"D-do you need to look at something?" God, she sounded like a teenager with her first crush.

He was so much bigger than she was, Beth couldn't help but wonder what it would feel like to have her body pressed against his; how gentle or rough he'd be when having sex. *There's an enemy out in space waiting to maybe kill them all. Not the time to be thinking about sex.*

Eagan stepped against her, and there was no mistaking the press of his erection against the small of her back. "I need to connect with the computer that controls the tubes. Stay with me."

She wasn't sure if that was a request or an order, but regardless, she knew she wouldn't say no. "Where are the others?"

"Rykal went to inform Commander Aidric of what we've discovered. Lena is still on the ship."

Oh good. "I'm not an engineer or even a computer specialist, but I can help you if you'd like?"

He sucked in a small breath that wouldn't have been noticeable to her if she wasn't standing there with him pressed against her back. "Yes."

The loss of his touch against her was a shock to her body when he stepped away and marched directly over to the computer. She was so aroused from that short conversation, Beth didn't understand how that was even possible. She knew she had to fight against whatever this attraction was between them, so they could deal with the crisis at hand. The fact that he didn't banish her somewhere else so he could concentrate spoke volumes about his self control.

Well, if he was able to hold back, then she'd damn well do that too. "What can I help with?"

He didn't say anything at first, but finally waved her closer. "I find I can concentrate better when I know where you are."

She shouldn't be flattered by the possessive undertones of his statement, but she was. "Okay."

Coming to stand by his side, she was amazed to watch as his fingers flew across the computer interface and reams of data appeared. Eagan was following logic paths that she couldn't, tracking pathways and algorithms. As quickly as he'd started the search, he abruptly stopped. "That's unfortunate."

"What is?" She moved closer to him, trying to see what he was on the screen. "I should have paid more attention in school."

"The way the stasis tubes have been setup, they're generating a signal, very low level and basic, but one that's present nonetheless."

"Does that mean we have to wake everyone up?"

"We can't risk the chaos that twenty-five cyborgs suddenly aware of their mates would create."

"You're doing okay?" Beth looked down at his hand and realizing how long his fingers were.

"I'm not." He turned his head slightly to look her way. "If it weren't for the Sholle presence I would have grabbed you and taken you far away from here the moment I laid eyes on you."

"Oh." Another spike of arousal shot through her. "What are we going to do? Hide the ship?"

Eagan gripped the edge of the console. "That's not a bad idea."

CHAPTER FOUR

Eagan was in hell and for the first time in his life he wasn't sure what to do. Now that he'd experienced the overwhelming rush of possessiveness when it came to his mate, he understood Rykal and Darrick's reactions to him. Even now, it was almost impossible to think rationally beyond his impulses to grab Beth throw, her on the nearest surface, and thrust his hard cock into her. If he couldn't claim her as his own soon, he was worried he wouldn't be able to save the rest of the humans and prevent the Sholle attack.

He needed space to think.

But now that he'd spent time with her, had her by his side, Eagan knew he wouldn't be able to walk away. He had to come up with a plan that they could implement quickly, and that wouldn't involve waking the humans.

The Grus wouldn't be prepared for the chaos that would follow.

Beth's curls were damp from her cleansing, and they hung low around her cheeks. Eagan wasn't the type of man even before his re-birth to notice something as simple as a woman's hair, which was more proof that this connection was far stronger than should be possible. She looked up at him with her large brown eyes and pouted. "Where could you hide the ship? Is there shielding here on the station? Lena mentioned a planet somewhere. Can we move it there?"

It had been a long time since he'd worked with anyone closely. Even back during the war, he'd been the one working out strategies for others to implement. He was a soldier who took commands and provided support where necessary. But he kept himself at a distance whenever he could.

Beth might not be a soldier, but she was clearly used to working with others, being a partner of sorts. She easily slid into the role and that strangely offered him comfort.

Her ideas were solid as well.

"The Grus won't put the station at risk. Once they learn that the signal is coming from this ship, they'll want it removed. We'll need to find a spot down on Zarlan that will be able to protect the people in stasis while blocking the signal from reaching the Sholle."

"What happens if they try to attack the planet?" She asked her question with the gravitas of someone who'd experienced the fallout of war.

"They lost to our cyborg army once before. I have no doubts we'd be successful once again."

If Rykal and Darrick feel even a fraction of the way toward their mates that Eagan did, he knew there would be nothing that would stop them from destroying the Sholle to keep them safe. But that didn't solve the problem of the humans being close to the cyborgs. Even with the women still in stasis, Eagan knew the impact of them being on the planet close to the cyborg city wouldn't end well. It would be an unnecessary distraction if the Sholle attacked that could potentially divide and distract those who had mates waiting.

The Kraken's scanners were primitive and wouldn't give him the information he needed to find a safe spot for the ship to hide on the planet. Closing his eyes, he reached out to the station's AI, hoping it would be able to help.

Warning. Unauthorized cyborg contact. Please disengage or be slated for decommission.

Commander Aidric has tasked me to find a solution to prevent the Sholle from attacking. I need your help.

It was strange to feel the AI's hesitation. *Proceed.*

The advantage of connecting directly to a computer system was its ability to accept bulk information without needing to communicate with words. Eagan opened his mind and allowed the AI to access his thoughts on what had happened over the past few hours, including their current dilemma. The AI then disconnected, no doubt so it could go in search of a solution.

Eagan felt Beth place her hand on his forearm, forcing him to open his eyes and look at her. Her frown pulled at her lips and wrinkled her forehead. "Are you okay?"

"I've been communicating with the station's AI to help find a location on the planet's surface where we can move the Kraken."

"Oh." She looked away and her face flushed. "I forgot."

"Forgot what?"

"That you're enhanced." She shrugged as her hand fell away from his arm. "You don't look like the other two men. I can see their cybernetics, but with you it's not as obvious."

Eagan hadn't considered his enhancements for a long time. His wounds in the war hadn't been as catastrophic regarding his physical appearance, but had taken his life, nonetheless. They had only spent a short time together, not even an hour, and Eagan could appreciate her curiosity about a man who claimed she was his mate. Taking a step away from the console, he pulled up the bottom of his pantleg to reveal his cybernetic limb.

"I'd anticipated a weakness in our defenses and was attempting to setup a defence perimeter to keep our base camp safe. The first laser blast took my leg. The second hit me in the back. I don't remember anything after that until my re-birth."

"Re-birth?"

He was about to answer her when the AI reconnected with him. *Cyborg, move the Kraken to the following location.*

Turning back to the ship's computer, Eagan typed in the coordinates as the AI sent them. The map revealed a small landing in a valley far enough away from the city that any affected cyborgs should be able to be prevented from reaching the humans, but close enough that if they needed to evacuate the ship, they would have the necessary resources available to do so. The rock formations in the valley naturally produced low-grade radiation that should be sufficient to block the signal emanating from the stasis tubes without needing to wake the sleepers.

Eagan nodded. *Well done. This is ideal.*

If the AI was capable of emotions, Eagan would have been convinced it was arrogant. *Naturally.* And then it was gone.

"I need to find Rykal and relieve Darrick from his post. We'll need to move the ship to these coordinates." Eagan turned and without thinking he pulled Beth hard against him. His cock was stiff and it was becoming increasingly difficult to keep himself from stripping her naked to fuck her. Instead of giving in to the impulse, he pressed his nose into her hair and took a long, deep breath. "Soon."

He felt her shiver in his arms, though from anticipation or fear, he wasn't certain. Eagan let her go and looked at her hard, trying to see if he could determine the nature of her reactions. "Do you not wish to mate with me?"

Beth's mouth fell open for a moment before she snapped it shut. "I've been awake for an hour. Not only did I just learn that you think I'm your mate, but that we're the cause of a potential alien invasion. I don't know where I am or what I'm doing, let alone if I want to mate with you."

Eagan's gaze was locked onto her, making it easy to see the changes in her body. Perhaps attraction worked differently with her race? He reached out to the AI once more through his cybernetic link. *Do you have a record of the other human's physical state when they wished to mate with the Fallen?*

The AI was suddenly back in his head, and he could feel its interest in his question. *Her pupils are dilated. Heartrate elevated. Engorged sex glands. Scans of other human women indicate these are signs of species arousal.*

She wishes to mate with me. That was a positive.

You will need to win her trust to proceed.

Coming up with a plan to win Beth over was something Eagan was more than capable of doing. *I'll strategize and win her as my mate.*

Affirmative. And the AI was gone again.

That wasn't something Eagan would have anticipated happening. Clearly, the AI had advanced in the time he'd been away from Grus Prime. He'd have to mention this to Rykal and Darrick later to see if they've had a similar experience. For now, they needed to move the Kraken to Zarlan before the Sholle attacked.

Beth was frowning at him again. "You went away again."

"The AI was providing me with additional information." He stepped closer to her, waiting for any sign of her fleeing. "We will move the ship, then you and I will have our time together."

"Okay." Her breathing came in soft rasps and her face flushed once more.

Eagan nearly walked out of the room leaving her to wait here, but he couldn't. As much as he wanted to be honorable, to give her the time she needed to adjust, the pull in his mind was becoming too strong for him to resist. Closing the distance between them, he took her face in his hands and lowered his mouth. Words of comfort and seduction passed through his mind, but none of them seemed to be right. No, Eagan might not know what human women want or how to win them over, but he did know that a kiss was a good place to start.

Her eyes fluttered shut as his mouth drew close. Her breath

washed across his face in short, staggered puffs until he brushed his lips across hers. He felt her gasp, the sharp intake of air a second before he sucked her bottom lip into his mouth.

Eagan's body was hard, his cock throbbing from lack of contact. The taste of her nearly made him insane, shoving all reason from his brain, every plan he'd orchestrated to save his people and hers was gone. All that remained was his desire for this woman, the burning need to strip them both naked so they could fuck then and there.

Instead of doing what he wanted, he increased the pressure of his kiss. He dipped his tongue into her mouth, tasting and teasing her. He held her close and breathed in her scent, wishing he could imprint himself on her. When she sighed and pressed her body against his, Eagan felt a rush of triumph and reached up for her breast to squeeze.

He finally pulled his mouth away, letting her suck in a gasp of air. "Wow."

"You're mine." He shifted his hand to pinch her nipple. "You don't know how difficult it is for me...to resist doing what I want to do to you right now."

His cock throbbed. His *rondella* on his inner thigh pulsed as it filled for the first time since his re-birth. The tenuous grasp he had on his control threatened to snap when she sighed so softly, he wasn't sure she was aware she'd done it.

"Eagan?" Rykal's voice echoed in from the loading bay. "Do you have a solution?"

Rage roared up inside him. Eagan tightened his hold on Beth. "Leave."

Her eyes widened and she tried to look past him toward Rykal. "Eagan, you can tell him your plan. Remember, once we move the ship then we can have some time together. That's your reward for doing what you need to do to save everyone. Me."

He could tell she was embarrassed at the idea of being his

prize, but he couldn't have picked a better one. With effort, he released his hold on her and forced himself to step away. "Mine."

She nodded. "Yes, I'm yours."

All he needed to do was move the ship and then they would be free to be together. He turned to face Rykal. "The station's AI has found a location on Zarlan where the ship's signal will be disrupted, but it will be close enough to the city to ensure we can wake and move them if the need arises."

"I'll inform Aidric. Let Lena know the location and then we'll proceed. She'll fly the Kraken. You and I can offer her support in the shuttles to ensure the Sholle don't get too close."

Eagan moved away from Beth, which made it a bit easier for him to think. "Do you think the Grus will try to stop us?"

"Aidric hasn't informed the high councillors of the importance of the human women to us. I don't anticipate that changing until they have been safely moved to our care."

Eagan didn't need to be told that the high council wouldn't approve of the cyborgs from having mates. "We best move swiftly."

"Agreed." Rykal shifted his gaze to Beth. *I don't need to ask if you want her to come with you on your shuttle. I know the answer. She may not want to and you must accept that. Give her time to adjust. These human women are strong and resourceful, but they are as confused as we are as to why they came here.* He then left.

"What was that about?" She'd wrapped her arms around her core.

"Lena will be flying the Kraken to the planet. I'll be taking the shuttle I arrived on back. You can choose to go with her or come with me." The words physically hurt him to say, knowing that she might not make the decision he wanted. He held himself stiff in case he wasn't able to hold himself back from her, prevent himself from taking her in his arms and never letting go.

Beth smiled and shrugged. "It doesn't matter to me, but I can tell it means a great deal to you. I'll come with you on your shuttle. Just let me get a few things before I do. Okay?"

Relief washed through him. "We don't have much time."

"I'll run." And she did.

Eagan was aware of her every move on the ship, even as he made his way down the corridor and out into the station's docking bay. Rykal was engaged in a conversation with Lena, Darrick and Commander Aidric. When Eagan walked down the ramp, Aidric's gaze snapped to him. "Are you certain this location will work to mask the signal?"

"The station's AI scanned the planet and provided the details." He cocked an eyebrow in silent question.

Aidric simply nodded. "If the AI did the calculations, then proceed."

A rush of pleasure and pride rolled through Eagan's mind that didn't belong to himself. Rykal gave his head a small shake as he frowned, clearly feeling the same thing he had. They shared a look. *Was that you?* Rykal's voice sounded as confused as he felt.

No. Not you I take it?

No. Strange.

The AI? There was no reason it should have anything close to an emotional response. *We should inform Aidric.*

Rykal shook his head. *Later. We don't have time to deal with additional problems at the moment.*

He was right. The AI was a problem for another day. "We'll fly our shuttles down to the planet as protection for the Kraken."

Lena clapped her hands together. "We have a plan then. I'll fly the Kraken, Rykal and Darrick can take one shuttle, and Eagan can take the other."

"Darrick and Carys will fly in one. I'll stay with you."

Eagan was surprised by the finality with which Rykal spoke. Lena wasn't though and rolled her eyes. "Fine. As long as I get my passengers someplace safe, I don't care who is flying with whom."

"I'm here!" Beth jogged down the ramp, coming to a stop

beside Eagan. Her shock and surprise at seeing Aidric was nearly enough for him to attack the Grus commander. "Oh wow. You guys do look different from the cyborgs."

Aidric cocked an eyebrow. "Welcome to Grus Prime. I'm Commander Aidric." There was a distance in his tone that put Eagan on edge.

"Did I interrupt?" Beth looked up at Eagan, her eyes wide and her body tense. "I'm so sorry."

"Not at all." Lena smiled brightly at her. "I promise, you'll have time to catch your breath once we get down to the planet."

"I hope so." Beth openly stared at Aidric. "I feel like I'm stuck in a weird dream."

Eagan put his hand on her shoulder and squeezed. "It will soon be over, and you'll be awakened." Soon, she'd be his mate and there'd be no going back. "Let's move."

CHAPTER FIVE

Beth was aroused, confused and exhausted, none of which was helpful given their current circumstances. She followed Eagan into a large, sleek shuttle that was off to the side of the Kraken, doing her best not to stop and gawk at everything as she passed by. The realization of the fact that she really was on an alien space station hit her when she had come face to face with Commander Aidric. She didn't know why she knew, but he was not a cyborg. She could tell by the way he held himself, the way the others spoke and responded to him that not only was he a Grus, but someone of importance.

Hopefully, Eagan would have time to continue their conversation on the shuttle.

The shuttle was larger and far sleeker in appearance than the Kraken, or any ship she'd ever seen back on Earth. The computer consoles were black with touch sensitive pads that came to life the moment Eagan sat down in the pilot's chair. "You can sit beside me."

His tone was still abrupt in a way that would normally upset her if it came from one of her family members, but Beth complied with little complaint. She knew there wasn't malice behind his words, even if there was that same note of wanting to control her. Without knowing why, she knew that if she pushed back, Eagan would listen to her.

That was something her parents never did.

The chair had been designed to seat someone considerably larger than Beth was, giving her the feeling of a child trying to fit into an adult's world. The security strap was too large for her and there was no obvious way for her to tighten it around her. "Don't get into an accident."

Eagan glanced at her. "You will need that when we make our way down through the planet's atmosphere. The storms on Zarlan are powerful."

She set her small bag of belongings down on the floor and proceeded to do her best to strap herself in. "Is it always like that, or is this just the current time of year for storms?"

"The Sholle tried to destroy our planet by stripping it of our resources. That resulted in our ecosystem being pushed out of the norm. We have been working to repair the damage, but it will take a lifetime to correct."

"And those are the creatures sitting out in space waiting for us?" Shit, no wonder they were all in a panic wanting to make sure they weren't drawn back here. "We better hurry then."

"Indeed." He reached behind her and pressed a button that automatically tightened the straps. "As long as the commander is able to dissuade the high council from trying to stop us, all will be well."

"Why would they want to stop us?" There were moving the source of the signal away from the station; why wouldn't they want that to happen?

"Our two peoples have a complicated history."

Lena and Carys had only given her the highest level of details when it came to the political and social structure of the Grus world. Beth knew the cyborgs were called the Fallen and had been modified when they'd died in the war. Beyond that, she only had questions and no time to ask for answers.

"Kraken to shuttles." Lena's voice crackled to life from the speakers. "I'm not sure exactly what's going on, but I'm being told we're going to have a very small window to take off and get outside of the station's energy shield. Be ready to lift off."

Eagan cocked his head in a way that Beth was now starting to recognize as him communicating with the other cyborgs. "What's going on?"

"Rykal said Commander Aidric is concerned the council will stop us. He's not certain and Rykal doesn't want to risk the Kraken being attacked."

"Will you be able to coordinate with him?" She didn't know the limitations of their cybernetics, nor was she smart when it came to battle strategies. "Is there anything I can do to help?"

"Our communication range won't reach beyond this docking bay. It's limited in scope. There's a chance we'll need to put ourselves between the Kraken and the station." The muscle in his jaw jumped. "Stay seated and safe. That's how you can help."

Beth nodded but hated knowing she was useless in this situation. She'd been a teacher back on Earth and had worked with the very young. Even those skills had been limited given the resources available to her in the school. She'd been a glorified monitor, who would offer encouragement and smiles to the children when they found the subject matter too difficult.

She wasn't a fighter or pilot. She didn't know languages or how to heal a wound. She was reliant on others to help her and that was something Beth had always hated about herself. And now? Well, it was going to hurt her now. Instead of being useful to Eagan and the others, she was a liability to be carted around. The worst kind of problem to have. With a sigh, she tipped her head back and let it rest against the chair.

The shuttle trembled briefly as Eagan pressed a sequence of buttons on the panel to bring the shuttle to life. He paused, and

CYBORG PROTECTORS

half-turned his face toward her. "This connection between us is strong. While I'm unable to read your thoughts, I can read your emotions."

She sat up straight. "Is that something all your people can do?"

"No. This is the first time in my life I've felt this." He looked at her full-on, his glowing brown eyes locked onto her. "You're not a burden. I will help teach you how to survive here."

"Kraken to shuttles, we're leaving."

Beth shifted uncomfortably in her chair under Eagan's gaze. "We better go."

Eagan hesitated for a moment before turning to the controls. "Engaging engines. Shuttle two launching."

The docking bay doors opened while the Grus support staff scurried to a secure room. There was an energy shield keeping the atmosphere inside the station, and Beth could easily see its shimmer as Eagan moved the shuttle forward. The crackle of the protective barrier rushed over the ship as they passed through and out into the silence of space. There was another shimmer not far away and Beth wasn't certain if she was actually seeing anything or if her eyes were playing a trick on her.

"Shuttle two, take up a defense position on the Kraken's flank." Rykal's voice came through the communications. "Be ready to react to any additional ships coming from Grus Prime."

"That doesn't sound good." Beth sat up straighter. "Is there something I can help monitor?"

"The monitor to your right. Let me know if anything appears on the screen."

Beth couldn't help but think this was a task Eagan could complete easily on his own, but she was grateful for something to focus her attention on. "You got it."

"The station's shield isn't dropping." Beth didn't recognize the male talking, but she assumed it was Darrick, the only other man mentioned who she hadn't met.

"Give Aidric a moment to put the authorization through. He

gave me his word this would work." Rykal didn't sound quite as confident as his words implied.

Eagan's body tensed the longer they waited, flying stuck between the station and its shield. "I don't like this."

"Why would the Grus try and stop us? The humans wouldn't have any value to them." Beth knew there was more to it than that, but even still with lives in danger she couldn't imagine that they'd want the Kraken anywhere close if it was the cause of a potential attack.

"It's not about the humans." Eagan's hand balled into a fist. "It's about keeping the cyborgs in their place. We're weapons for them to use on a whim and not people with hopes and dreams. They took that from us when they forced our re-births on us. They changed who we are fundamentally as people. Having mates, having that missing piece of us returned so we can live as our own people, that wouldn't sit well with the high council. That makes us people instead of tools."

Beth might not understand exactly everything that had happened between the Grus and the cyborgs, but she did know how it felt to be used as a thing, her own hopes and dreams ignored. "My father had agreed to marry me off to a business partner's son."

Eagan didn't move, but she could tell he was listening to her every word.

"I hadn't even met him, but my mother said he was passably good looking, as though that's the most important thing when it comes to getting married." Her sister had brought in a data pad with a picture of her fiancé. He was far older than Beth and there were more than a few rumors of what had happened to his first wife. "Neither of my parents cared about me or my desires. They wanted me married to this man so my father could secure a new building. It was about money, nothing more."

Eagan relaxed his hand and reached out to place his open

palm on her thigh. "You will never be treated that way again. I will cherish you."

"I know. But you can appreciate why I'm not keen to be told I have a mate. Someone who I haven't met and know nothing about. Someone who says that I have no choice in this arrangement."

Eagan moved his hand back to the shuttle's controls. "We both value our freedom."

The shuttle shuddered and Eagan had to direct it in the opposite direction of the Kraken. "If they don't get this shield down quickly, we're going to have a problem."

Time continued to tick on, and Beth's stomach soured. What the hell was going to happen to them if they couldn't even get free of the station? She couldn't image the Grus would be as accommodating once they learned the truth about the women on the Kraken.

"Attention shuttles," Commander Aidric's voice came through the communicator. "Your departure is unauthorized."

"Shit." Beth leaned closer to the monitor to make sure she was reading it correctly. "There are four ships coming out of the station."

"He lied to us." Eagan pressed something on the panel. "Shuttle two here. I knew this would happen."

"Stand down, Eagan." Rykal responded. "Aidric sent me a code for the shield. Come up close on the Kraken's flank. We're only going to have seconds to make this work."

"Thank God." Beth looked over at Eagan, but he wasn't anywhere near as relaxed as she would have hoped.

"Cyborg shuttles! Earth vessel! Return to Grus Prime and prepare to be boarded."

The next few moments happened quickly, sending a rush of adrenaline through Beth. The three ships crowded one another so tightly she couldn't imagine how they weren't running into one another. There was a flicker in front of them so soft, she would have missed it if she hadn't been looking at that exact moment. Eagan hit the thrusters, pushing the shuttle forward hard, but in perfect synchronization with the other ships.

Without seeing it, she felt the station's shield pop back into place. She looked back down at the monitor. "They're not following. They've actually veered off course."

"Aidric bought us a bit of time." Rykal's voice once more. "The code caused the shields to cycle in a maintenance mode. They won't be able to get through until we're safely on Zarlan."

"Let's hope they don't chase us down there they way they did when you kidnapped Lena." Darrick's amusement seemed off given the nature of the situation.

Beth gasped. "Kidnapped?"

"It was the first encounter between our people and unexpected. Both Rykal and Darrick had an uncontrollable urge to take and possess their mates."

"But you don't?" She shouldn't be disappointed by that. He'd kissed her back on the station, so clearly, he wanted her. But despite her better judgment and all of her fears of being little more than a possession to be sold off to the highest bidder, there was also a part of her who wanted to be wanted so desperately that another person would risk everything to have them.

Eagan rapidly typed in a long string of commands, before he rose to his feet and released the straps that held Beth in place. She squealed when he picked her up from the seat and carried her to the back of the shuttle. "We don't have a lot of time."

Setting her down on the nearest seat, he dropped to his knees and yanked her boots off. Beth could only sit there and watch him, her mouth open and heart racing, as he proceeded to strip her pants and undergarments free from her body. "What are you doing?"

"I'm past my limits of restraint." With her lower body now naked to him, he slid his hands up along the outside of her thighs. "So different and yet so similar."

Beth wanted to pull away, hide herself, embarrassed at being so openly exposed to him, but still couldn't do so. She'd never been with a man back on Earth, though she'd had an active imagination. This was the one thing she could control and the one thing that her parents had held over her for years. Now they weren't here to stop her, to tell her that being with a man of her choice was a mistake. She could give herself freely to Eagan and finally experience what it was like to share pleasure with another person.

Taking a breath, she widened her legs and put her pussy on full display for him. "Make me yours."

CHAPTER SIX

Eagan's mouth watered at the sight of her smooth inner thighs and the pink lips of her mound. Unlike Grus women, Beth had hair between her legs, though it was far lighter and thinner than the hair on her head. He cared not for the missing *rondollo* on her inner thigh, the membrane that helped a female Grus reach her orgasm. Eagan could feel Beth's anticipation, her need for pleasure. He would use her emotions to guide him.

Beth's eyes were wide, and her pupils had grown large and black. Her tongue dipped out to wet her lips as she watched him move closer. "I've never done this before."

Oh, that was exactly what he wanted to hear. "You've never had sexual relations with a man?"

"My parents wanted me to stay a virgin. They thought it would give them the opportunity to increase my value in an arranged marriage."

The thought of anyone using Beth as a thing to be bartered and traded sent his anger racing. "You belong to no one but me."

"That sentiment should piss me off." She smiled, her breath

coming out in small gasps the closer he moved his hands to the apex between her legs. "It should, but it doesn't."

Eagan knew they had precious little time before he'd need to return to the controls of the ship and land the shuttle. He wanted to take his time with her, savor her taste and smell. He wanted to fuck her hard and fast, then again but long and slow. He wanted to spill his seed across her body and rub it into her skin so any other man would smell him on her and knew that she belonged to him.

He'd settle with making her come.

He turned his face to bit down on her inner thigh. The flavor of her sweat tingled across his tongue as he licked at her skin. Eagan groaned, finally able to revel in the very thing he'd wanted to do from before the moment he'd laid eyes on her. He bit her inner thigh again, harder this time and Beth gasped. "Easy."

Eagan didn't want to go easy; he wanted to mark her so no other would dare take her from him. But he could feel her fear and trepidation and didn't want to scare her unnecessarily. He moved his mouth away, pleased with the already darkening bruise that was rising on her skin. Shifting closer, he spread apart the lips covered in hair, surprised at how soft the short strands felt. "This is where you feel pleasure."

"Yes." Her face was flushed red, and her eyes were heavy. "There's a little nub near the top called my clit. That will bring me great pleasure."

Human women might be slightly different biologically from their Grus counterparts, but Eagan knew Beth would guide him. He lowered his mouth and sucked on the clit hard. She gasped, her hands flying to his head to push at him. "Not so hard. Easy."

He eased the pressure but used his fingers to explore the rest of her body. When he found the opening to her body, he pressed his finger inside and fucked her with it as he sucked on her clit. It didn't take long for her body to respond. Wetness coated his fingers as he continued to work them in and out of her. He alternated from sucking her clit to flicking his tongue across the now swollen surface. With each flick, her hips bucked forward as though her body was chasing him and demanding more.

Eagan's cock strained in his pants, and he had no choice but to reach down and squeeze it to the point of pain. It wouldn't take long for him to reach his climax, for him to pump his seed inside her body. He wanted to feel her body squeeze his shaft, to come on him as pleasure flooded her body.

"So close." Beth arched her chest up as she widened her legs even farther. "Please."

The shuttle shuddered hard, sending Eagan crashing forward. Beth gasped as his finger pressed as far as it could go into her body. "Shit."

He reached out to the shuttle's computer using his matrix to reveal that they were dangerously close to Zarlan's atmosphere. He needed to get back to the controls, needed to get Beth safely back into her seat so she wouldn't be hurt.

Instead, he pulled back and looked up at her. "Do you trust me?"

She shook her head for a moment before changing it to a nod. "Why?"

"Come for me the moment you can." He leaned back in and sucked on her clit hard.

She gasped and grabbed for his head. "Right there."

"Shuttle two, you're approach for atmospheric entry is too steep." Rykal's voice echoed form the communication unit in the front. "Eagan?"

He didn't care. Nothing mattered except having her come, to feel her become his. Using his finger, he fucked her the way he wanted to do with his cock as he lapped at her clit. Beth's body began to shake and he could feel the rising pleasure grow inside her. She was close. It was only be a moment longer before he felt her inner muscles clamp down on his finger, her body bowing down over him. "Shit!"

Her orgasm washed through her as he felt every muscle in her body tighten and vibrate as he milked her release. Her juices coated his face and he drank as much of her as he could manage.

"Eagan, respond."

The moment her pleasure receded, Eagan got to his feet and grabbed her hand. He pressed it to his *rondella*, still hidden by his pants. "When I tell you to squeeze, do it. Hard."

The glow of her orgasm still fresh, Beth nodded as he pulled his hard cock free. Keeping his gaze locked onto her, he fisted himself, fucking his hand hard and fast while he stared down at the beauty of her face. Her gaze moved from his hand to his cock and she licked her lips as he continued to work himself. When they had time, he wanted to feel that tongue on his cock, to see how good it would be to have her lick up the length of his shaft. What it would be like to come into her mouth.

The very thought of that was enough to bring him to the brink. "Squeeze." She did as he asked, but it wasn't enough. "Harder!"

This time she did as he asked, and it was enough. He felt his *rondella* fill and pulse, the wave of his pre-orgasm slamming into his body as the shuttle shuddered violently. His eyes squeezed shut and he let out a shout as his seed spurted from his body and pleasure exploded through him. Everything darkened and nothing mattered as the waves of his orgasm flushed the anger and hate from his soul. He slowed the movement of his hand pumping his cock until the last bit of energy was sapped.

The shuttle was hit with another shudder, this one far stronger than the last.

"Eagan!" The concern was clear in Rykal's voice.

He looked down at Beth, who's arm was now painted with his come. "Are you okay?"

"Shuttle two respond now!"

"I'm good. You better get back to the controls."

His matrix would allow for him to walk straight and withstand any impacts to the shuttle, but Beth would not fare so well. "Stay here and strap into this seat. I'll get us landed."

He shoved his cock back into his pants and made his way to the pilot's control. "Shuttle two here. Correcting our course."

"Belay that. You're not going to have time." Rykal send him a series of coordinates. "The Sholle have taken an interest in the Kraken and have begun to move to intercept us. I need you and Darrick to either chase them off or destroy them. They can't get to this ship."

Eagan didn't want to put Beth at risk, but neither did he trust what the Sholle would do if they were able to capture the Kraken. If anything were to happen, at least he was together with her. "Understood."

"What does that mean?" Beth sounded more than a little scared.

"It means that things are going to get bumpy. Are you secured?"

"Yes."

"Don't get out of your seat no matter what happens."

"But what if you need – "

"For no reason!" Perhaps not all his anger had been flushed away.

Wrestling the shuttle away from the pull of Zarlan's gravity, he changed course so they were now on a direct intercept path with the Sholle. The first shuttle slid beside them. "Shuttle one here. What's the plan?"

Right. Despite everything, Eagan was still the strategist everyone looked toward. "They're scout ships and don't have a lot of armaments or shields. If we coordinate our attacks, we should be able to punch past their protections and hit their engines." He typed off a series of commands and sent them over to Darrick. "Execute this on my command."

"Yes, sir." There was no mocking in Darrick's voice, as they both slipped into their old roles.

Eagan waited as they barrelled toward the Sholle, half his attention on them and the rest on Beth. "We won't be long. Then we can get back to what we were doing."

"Okay." But she sounded far less confident than she had before.

"Engaging Sholle in three," Eagan typed in this attack command, "two, one. Fire!"

The shuttles split apart the moment they reached weapon's range, focusing their fire on the opposite sides of the Sholle's engine. The second Sholle vessel split off and flew past them, still on route to intercept the Kraken.

"They're not engaging." Darrick's voice crackled and cut out briefly as they both concentrated their fire.

Eagan continued to count in his head, knowing it would take both their ships to break through the initial and toughest barriers. "Keep this one engaged and continue to focus your fire here. I'll intercept the other."

An explosion ignited on the Sholle ship, and a moment later, Eagan punched in a new intercept course for the remaining Sholle shuttle. "Rykal, you have a Sholle coming up fast. I'll move to take it down but be prepared to evade."

"Understood."

In the years since the Sholle war, the Grus and cyborgs had worked together to build and improve the strength of their shields and the speed of their ships. Based on how quickly he closed the distance on the Sholle shuttle, the same couldn't be said for them. The Kraken had already begun the dangerous descent into Zarlan's exosphere and the violent storms that waited below. He knew the Kraken didn't have anything in the way of shields, so the combination of the storms and any fire that the Sholle may direct their way would easily damage or even destroy the ship.

There was no way he'd allow that to happen.

Eagan brought the shuttle up behind the Sholle, but they were met with the blast of rear lasers against their shields. He returned fire but knew it would take more fire power than what a single shuttle craft possessed. They shuddered again, this time from the rattle of the storm they'd flown into.

That's what he needed.

"Kraken, hold your course. Don't deviate for any reason. I'm going to try something foolish to take care of this pest."

"Do I want to know what that is?"

"Best if you don't." He didn't think the Sholle had the capability to intercept their communications, but it wasn't worth the risk. "We'll see you on the surface."

Eagan maneuvered the shuttle, so it was now pacing the Sholle. His scans didn't reveal anything beyond what he'd expected: single occupant with limited resources. The ship had the capability to strip resources from the planet's surface, providing them with the ability to produce fuel wherever they needed it.

He'd only seen the inside of a Sholle ship once, and only been able to get a quick scan of their internal systems. What he'd learned had helped him create a means to destroy their ships and drive them off the planet. He didn't have the resources here on his ship, but he would be able to generate something close using the electricity in the air. "Beth, I want you to go back and take the seat in the main cabin. Use the security straps."

"That doesn't sound good." Thankfully, she didn't sound as fearful as he'd expected when she got up and did as he'd asked.

Knowing that she trusted him to keep her safe emboldened him to do what needed to be done, regardless of the risk. He changed the frequency of the shuttle's shield and used the computer's targeting system to lock on to the spot where the Sholle's shield generator should be. The electrical charge in the air built up, though not as quickly as Eagan would have liked. "Come on."

The Kraken was coming into sensor range. They were too far

away for Eagan to be able to protect, and far slower than the Sholle shuttle. It was only going to be a matter of seconds before they were in range and the Sholle would be able to attack.

The sensors continued to tick up as the storm energy continued to build. It should be any moment before there was another lightening strike –

The air around the shuttle lit up, as the electrical charge crackled in the clouds. Eagan swerved the shuttle into the range of the lightning, targeted the Sholle and fired his blasters. The lightning super charged the blaster, the strike landing on the ship and causing an explosion. The Sholle shuttle pitched to the side, losing control in its decent and heading directly downward. Eagan would have celebrated the perfection of his plan if his hold on the controls of their shuttle hadn't also been burned out.

"Warning. Projected decent trajectory critical. Impact imminent. Warning."

"Eagan!" Fear rolled off Beth so strongly he was able to feel it despite the distance between them.

He didn't respond, couldn't spare the distraction as he tried to adjust and correct their fall. The storm battered the shuttle, making in nearly impossible to scan for any safe landing space. All he could do was pilot the shuttle as best he could, making the adjustments as he saw them. They were bounced around in the atmosphere until they finally broke through and he was able to visually scan the ground. He did the mental calculations and realized they would be several hours travel away from the location the Kraken would land; a rocky mountainous area with little space to land a shuttle under perfect conditions. Things were far from being perfect.

Making the few last-minute adjustments he could manage, Eagan turned in his seat to look back at Beth. "I care for you." He nodded, pleased when he felt her startled acceptance. "Now, brace for impact."

CHAPTER SEVEN

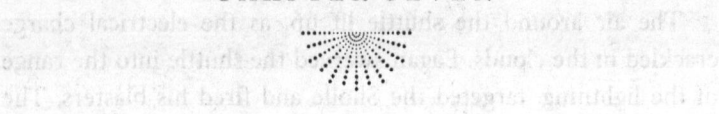

Beth's head ached. Well, her entire body ached, but her head was the part of her body that hurt the most. She forced her eyes open, wincing at the lancing pain that flashed behind her eyes. The last thing she remembered was Eagan turning to look at her, the feelings of love she couldn't hold back when he told her that he cared for her, and the overwhelming fear that slapped her when he told her to brace for impact.

The shuttle then began to spin as they went into freefall, the motion making her stomach bottom out and her heart race. She'd lost consciousness at some point, which was a blessing if she thought about it.

Which she didn't want to do because of how much her head hurt.

"Ouch." Her voice sounded weak in her ears, and the space around her seemed smaller. "Eagan?"

She was finally able to open her eyes and look around. It was dark, and the cavity of the shuttle had collapsed in on itself opposite from where she sat. Her chair was on an awkward angle and if she hadn't been strapped into the seat, there was no chance she would have survived the crash.

"Eagan!"

Beth fought through her panic and took several breaths to calm herself. She was alive and on the planet. She couldn't see the pilot's cabin, so there was a chance that he could have survived and was trying to find a way to get to her. Just because the front section of the shuttle appeared to be crushed under the impact of wherever the shuttle landed, didn't mean that he's dead and that she's now alone on an alien planet.

That she'd lost her mate before she'd even had a chance to know him.

The first thing she needed to do was free herself from this seat. She'd taken a survival course once in her youth, a mandatory session for anyone who ever traveled via shuttle. They needed to understand the basics of surviving, at least for a short time, in a hostile environment in case of an emergency crash.

This clearly qualified.

Looking around for something that she could use as a knife, her gaze landed on a piece of the wall panel that had cracked and now jutted from the wall. Careful not to cut her hand, she reached over and moved the metal dagger back and forth until the weak point snapped and she pulled it free. With renewed purpose, she pulled at the shoulder strap and began to saw at the material that held her tight to the chair. After several minutes and a deep cut to the palm of her hand, she was able to slice through the strap and slid herself free.

As her feet touched the ground a laugh escaped her. She dropped to her knees, her body shaking and let the relief wash over her. She shouldn't feel as pleased as she did about such a simple act of survival, but Beth couldn't help but feel pride in what she'd done. Her parents never gave her any credit when it came to making her own decisions and living her own life. They treated her as a fragile flower whose purpose was to be looked at, encouraged only enough to bloom, but never more than that.

And yet, here she was, trapped in a crashed shuttle on an alien planet, able to come up with a plan to save herself. It was more than a little bit of a rush. Now all she had to do was find a way to get out of the shuttle itself and find Eagan. If he was still alive.

God, he better still be alive.

Carefully, she got to her feet and picked her way through the remains of the shuttle. The door she'd entered by was currently disabled and she couldn't find a manual release to open it. She did find what appeared to be a med kit and searched through it. The nanobots in her head seemed slow to help her translate the words she was reading, no doubt because of the blow to the head she'd received. Eventually, she found an injector and had to focus intently on the description to confirm that it contained a pain killer before pressing the tip to her neck.

The pain in her head and body eased and she was instantly able to think clearer. Okay, despite everything that had happened, she knew she wasn't alone. The Kraken had landed safely and there was the second shuttle that no doubt saw what had happened to them. A rescue party would come, and she'd be taken to shelter sooner than later.

She just needed to let people know where she was and that she was okay.

Beth moved back to the door and continued to look around the sides of it for an override. After removing a panel, she found the lever and tried to pull it down. It refused to budge, even when she used the metal dagger as leverage against it. There was no way she was strong enough to force her way through.

"Shit." Using the end of the metal dagger, she banged against the door. "Hello? I'm in here. Eagan?"

The thought of him dying didn't sit right with her. It was strange but she somehow knew he was out there alive and trying to find a way to get to her. Maybe there was something to be said about this whole mate idea. Despite her optimism, exhaustion from the events of the last day and a distinct lack of food made her weak and more than a little tired. If Eagan was out there, he'd find a way to get to her and pull her out. Her priority was looking after herself as best she could.

The med kit had a small cache of rations that she pulled out. They didn't smell like anything she'd ever eaten on Earth, far from the palatable meals she'd grown accustomed to enjoying. The old Beth might have turned her nose up at the idea of eating a protein bar that tasted bitter and grainy, but the new her happily popped a second, then third bite into her mouth and savored it as she sat next to the door and waited.

She lost track of time and might have even nodded off, when she suddenly became aware of a banging behind her. The vibrations from an impact came through the walls and she scrambled to the side in anticipation of her freedom. She knew it was Eagan even before the door snapped and cracked as the bolts were broken and the metal peeled back. She could feel his impatience and rage at being kept from her. Her body responded to his presence despite her minor injuries. Her breasts felt heavy and her pussy damp, knowing that he was wild wanting to get to her, to keep her safe and protect her.

Light from the outside world had her shielding her eyes as Eagan forced the last barrier between them aside. "Beth?"

"I'm here." She got to her feet and made her way over to him. Before she could even move to jump free of the shuttle, he'd wrapped his arms around her and pulled her tight against him. "I'm okay."

Eagan didn't say anything but moved them both away from the ship and toward an outcropping of rocks. Instead of questioning him – how had he survived, would someone come for them, would everything be okay – she wrapped her arms around his neck and rested her head on his shoulder. He walked them into a cave, looking around as though he was surveying their environment. Setting her down gently, he cupped her face in his hands and kissed her hard.

"I'm going to retrieve supplies from the shuttle. Stay here."

She was suddenly too tired to argue or worry about what would happen next and simply smiled. "Okay."

Beth made herself comfortable as Eagan traveled back and forth between the cave and the shuttle bringing whatever useful items he found. He gathered a few bits and pieces from the shuttle and placed them in a sort of camp, and it didn't take long for them to have a protected shelter with a location beacon signal pinging their location to the others.

Eagan returned one final time with several blankets and another box of rations. "Given our location, I suspect it will take Rykal and Darrick several hours to reach us. They will need to secure the Kraken first."

"You think they made it to safety?"

"I do." He held a blanket out for her. "You need to keep warm."

She'd been thinking about this odd relationship they'd developed in such a short period of time. While it was clear to him that she was his mate and he was obligated to care for her, Beth was only starting to come to that realization. She'd never had the privilege of being this physically close to a man who wasn't a family member before, and the entire prospect was becoming appealing.

Mimicking Eagan's default behavior, she said nothing as she got to her feet to stand before him. She looked deep into his softly glowing brown eyes and cupped his cheeks with her hands. She saw his breathing hitch ever so slightly, the only indication that he was as struck by the moment as she was. Rising up on her toes as far as she could, she kissed him softly on his mouth, teasing his lips with her tongue.

"Thank you for saving me." She spoke the words against him, enjoying the way their breath mingled.

He sucked in a sharp breath through his nose. "Mine."

"Yes, yours."

She didn't know what she was giving permission for, but she knew that's what her words were essentially saying. *I'm yours to do with as you want. To love and fuck and hold in a way that shows me that I'm special to you.* She grabbed for the hem of his shirt and tugged it upward, letting him take over and pull it free of his head. She then took her own off, then her boots and pants, letting the clothing fall where it willed.

Her feet were cold through the blanket they stood on, but she didn't care, knowing it would only be for the briefest of moments before he'd warm her. She tried to help him remove his pants, but he brushed her hands away and made quick work of them and his boots.

They stood naked together in a cave, their bodies only a hair's breadth apart from one another. Beth's nipples were hard from the cold and her anticipation of what was to come. Eagan's cock was a hard between them, pulsing with the flow of blood through is body. "I want you to fuck me."

While he'd used his hands on her before, she'd regretted that they hadn't had the time to do the one thing she'd desperately wanted. She was no longer a virgin in the truest sense, but she still hadn't felt his cock stretch her pussy wide, fill her body full and drive her to orgasm. She wanted that more than anything in the world; wanted to feel him cover her with his weight and claim her for his own.

Eagan must have read her mind because the next thing she knew he'd lowered his head to her breast and sucked hard onto her nipple, while teasing the other one with his fingers. The sensation seemed to bolt straight down to her pussy, and each flick of his tongue against the sensitive tip felt like a lick against her clit. Her pussy grew wet and she couldn't help but arch forward, chasing the sensations. "Yes."

Was it possible to come simply from someone sucking her nipples? Beth was too innocent to know for certain, but there was a strong possibly that *she* might. Gasping, she grabbed his head to hold him in place as her body shook from the sensations.

Eagan lowered his hand and slid it between her legs to press against her clit. He teased the nub, rubbing small circles against it in rhythm with his tongue on her nipple. After everything she'd been through, the rising pleasure was nearly too much for her to handle. Clutching his head and shoulders, she cried out as her sudden orgasm washed through her unexpectedly. Her legs buckled, but Eagan was there to catch her and lower her down to the blanket.

God, he was fucking impressive standing over her looking down. His cock was stiff and from this angle she was able to see a dark green membrane that covered the inside of his thigh. That had been the thing he'd had her squeeze when he'd jerked off back on the ship. So different from anything she'd even considered possible in a lover.

Beth spread her legs and got as comfortable as she could on the rocky floor. "Please."

Eagan dropped to his knees so hard it must have hurt him. He grabbed her legs at her knees and pushed them forward, so they bracketed his hips as he lined up his cock with her pussy and pressed forward. Beth gasped as he filled her, not stopping to allow her a moment to adjust to his length or girth. It didn't hurt as much as she'd assumed it would, even if the sensation felt strange. He stared intently at her as he pulled out, only to plunge forward again, this time with more force.

She tried to hold his gaze as long as she could, but with each thrust the sharp rise of her renewed arousal became too much for her to handle. Her lids slipped closed and she gave in to the sensations. Eagan's body heat surrounded her, as he finally released his hold on her legs and lowered his body to hers. She moaned as he licked and kissed the side of her neck and the sensitive spot by her shoulder.

His teeth grazed the skin, nipping at the spot as he increased the intensity of his thrusts. The small bite of pain barely registered to her as she hooked her legs around his waist and met his thrusts with her own. She wanted to come again, wanted to swallow his come with her body. Her clit brushed against his mound each time, driving her higher and higher, closer to the place she wanted to be.

Eagan's mouth was pressed against the crook of her shoulder, his hot breath rolling across her skin. "Gods. Yes."

She felt his body shudder, the smooth membrane of his thigh rubbing and pressed hard against her. She could feel it pulsing, knew that he was going to come and that was enough to push her over the edge. Her body bowed as her orgasm tore through the remnants of her restraint. Pleasure filled her, whiting out her vision and making everything else fall away.

The sharp slice of pain on her shoulder caught her by surprise, as did the roar that exploded from Eagan as he fucked into her madly, coming hard. Pleasure and pain mixed together until Beth couldn't tell one from the other, her body a gloriously confused mess. Eagan groaned and finally came to a rest, his body still covering hers.

Despite the throbbing of her shoulder and the pleasant burn from the friction of their fucking between her legs, Beth was exhausted. She pushed aside her confusion, unable to stop sleep from claiming her.

The last thing she was aware of was Eagan whispering against her skin. "You're mine. Forever mine."

CHAPTER EIGHT

Eagan woke before Beth did, dressing in silence before wrapping the remaining blankets around her body and providing one for her head. He wanted to give her the opportunity to rest before the others found them, knowing that once they were safe, they would need to ensure the security of the other human women.

For the first time since he'd learned about Beth and what her kind could do for the cyborgs, Eagan felt whole. The itching in the back of his head was lessening and he felt the first tingle of emotions he'd long ago thought he was no longer capable of feeling. Gone was the empty darkness that seemed to consume him, leaving nothing but cold logic in its place. Beth had brought light to his life and it was warming him from the inside out.

She was his and he'd do anything for her.

Looking over to where she slept, Eagan had to fight the urge to wake her to have sex again. That as well was something new; the overwhelming desire to please and be pleased by another person. Even before his re-birth, he hadn't been emotionally close with a woman. All his focus had been on his career, on what he could do for his people and not on his own wants and desires.

Now, Beth was all he seemed capable of thinking of, despite knowing the Sholle wouldn't simply let the matter of their missing scout ships go.

Then there was the matter of the Grus.

Beth moaned softly in her sleep as she pulled the blanket up high around her neck. He'd been surprised by his need to mark her body as his own during sex. That wasn't normal for him, or for what he remembered of his times with women in the past. It felt right knowing that she was visibly marked by this bite, that the bruise would be there for all to see. When she woke, he'd be sure to care for her and make sure he hadn't done too much damage. He didn't know how fragile or resilient humans were when it came to physical damage, but he wouldn't be fooled by Beth's small stature.

The others hadn't contacted him yet, but Eagan knew their distress beacon was functioning and it would only be a matter of time before they were found. Once they got back to the safety of the city, Eagan would show Beth his home and hope she'd find it comfortable enough. He would make any changes she'd like; he cared nothing beyond the basic functions and needing a place to rest when necessary. What comforts would the human women want collectively, versus the items that would vary from person to person? The Grus hadn't provided the Fallen with much in the way of luxuries, nor had any of them thought to request anything. When a man saw himself as little more than a weapon, then there was rarely a reason to aspire to be more than that.

Beth moaned again, this time pushing herself up. "How long have I been asleep?"

"One hour, six minutes." He wanted to rush over, pull her into his arms once more and thrust his suddenly hard cock inside her. "Did you rest well?"

She nodded before wincing, reaching for the spot where he'd bit her. "Shit, that really hurts."

He should apologize for causing her harm, should offer to

retrieve the med kit and effect repair to the injured area. Eagan did neither. "We've had no response to the distress beacon. Based on my calculations Rykal and Darrick should have detected it and are working out the best way to retrieve us."

"Okay." Beth's frown deepened. "Why did you do that?"

"Do what?" He knew what she was referencing, but for some reason he wanted to avoid the conversation.

"Bite me during sex?" She stood, keeping the blankets wrapped around her to cover her naked body. "Can you get me something to help heal this?"

"No." The thought of his mark not being on her had his anger surge unexpectedly.

Beth cocked her head to the side, the frown lines on her forehead deepening. "What do you mean no? It hurts and I want to not hurt."

It wasn't logical – a trait that Eagan prided himself on – but he couldn't do anything that would remove that mark on her. There was no reason for her to be in any discomfort though. He moved to the med kit and retrieved a pain reliever.

"There's not much left in the kit. This will have to suffice until we're back at the city." Beth pulled back from him ever so slightly when he came close to administer the injection, causing him to pause. "Would you like to do it?"

"Yes, thank you."

Eagan's brain wasn't functioning the way it should given what was happening. He should be keeping her safe, coming up with a plan to get them out of this cave and away from any dangers that could be lurking. He should care about the fate of the other humans on the Kraken, the potential attacks from the Sholle once they learned the fate of their scout ships. There was a dozen or more things that should be demanding his attention, and not whether his mark remained on Beth.

She was her own person. She'd traveled light years away from her home to escape a marriage to a man she didn't know and didn't want. What right did he have to take her as his?

But there was no denying the connection. There was no way he could let her go.

Beth pressed the injector to her neck and instantly the tension in her body relaxed. "That stuff's fast."

"It's designed for Grus physiology, which must be similar enough to human to allow it to work."

"I think it's empty now." She handed it back to him, her gaze averted. "I'm going to get dressed now. I'm freezing."

"I'll find a heat source to keep you warm." Eagan didn't move.

The blush that appeared on her cheeks gave her a youthful glow. "Do you mind turning around? I'm not sure where all of my clothes ended up when we were...I think I see my boots over there."

"Why do you want me to look away? I've seen your naked body. More than that."

"I don't know, I just do." Her tone of voice had grown higher, and he could feel her frustration and unease. "Please, Eagan."

It was that burst of unease that somehow broke through the haze of lust and possessiveness that had blanketed his mind. Taking a breath, he turned his back, giving her the privacy she'd requested. "Your shirt is to the left approximately two meters."

"I don't see...ah, thank you."

Looking out over the landscape from the safety of the cave, Eagan ran a scan of his internal systems trying to see if he could find a previously unseen flaw in his code that would account for these atypical changes in his behavior. Everything appeared as it should until he got to the section where there was normally a blank spot. Some of the other Fallen referred to this as a hole in the code, a glitch in their creation due to the speed and pressures Commander Aidric had been under when trying to implement the cyborg program. Eagan saw the flaw as well but knew something the others hadn't.

It was no mistake.

While he had no direct proof of it, based on what he knew of Commander Aidric and the mandate that he'd been given, Eagan recognized that hole to be where their emotions should have been. It didn't make sense that Aidric simply forgot them; he was far too intelligent a man and proficient coder to do that. Though, that was what the few who bothered to question it came to believe. Eagan didn't, and it was something he could never forgive Aidric for.

But now, the hole in the code was being rewritten.

Narrowing his search, he stared hard at the lines trying to see what might have started this but couldn't see the initiating code. The best he could see was a time indicator of when the changes began to go into effect. They corresponded perfectly to when Beth was first woken from stasis.

"Are you okay?"

His eyes snapped open and he looked down into Beth's concerned gaze. "I was running a diagnostic."

"Did you find any problems?" She didn't ask why he was doing that, which spoke volumes.

"Perhaps." He cupped her face in his hands and placed a kiss to her forehead. "How much were you told about us when you woke?"

"Not a lot. We didn't have a ton of time."

"We were created from the fallen Grus in the battle with the Sholle. Commander Aidric on the station was the creator of the matrix that's embedded in our heads, the man who wrote the code. There's a flaw there, a blank space where something else should have been. I've long suspected it was where our emotions should have been. Anger was the only thing we felt, something we needed in order to fight."

Her pity washed over him in waves. "That's incredibly sad and explains so much."

"It opens up more questions." He kissed her lips, as softly and with as much feeling as he was able. "Since your arrival, that blank space is being filled."

Beth's eyes grew wide and she stepped back. "What? How is that possible?"

"I'm not certain. I wasn't even aware of the changes until just now. I suspect it's the same with Rykal and Darrick based on the changes in their behavior that I'd noted. Our links to you humans have generated the missing pieces. You are literally making us whole again."

"But I didn't do anything?"

"Your presence was all that was required." He stepped forward to close the gap, but she moved away once again. "The others had told me that Lena and Carys mentioned a compulsion to go on the journey and come to this sector of space. Did you have that same compulsion?" *Did you want to come to here and be mine?*

Beth's mouth opened and closed several times before she shook her head. "I was just trying to get away from my family. I knew I couldn't marry the man they wanted me to and that I had to get away."

"You were coming to me."

"No! I was running away *from*, not running *toward* something." Her fear and confusion were obvious even without him being able to feel her emotions. "None of this makes any sense."

"I agree. But it is what it is. Even if you reject me, it doesn't change the fact that you are mine and I am yours. It doesn't change the fact that new code began to generate in my system the moment I found you and you woke from your sleep. You've saved me, Beth."

"I didn't want to. I was trying to save myself."

The honesty of that statement hit him hard. No, she might not have consciously been aware of her actions, or have believed they were for purely selfish reasons, but Eagan had to believe that a part of her had also chosen to leave her planet for him. "Why did you choose the Kraken?"

Beth froze. "What?"

"Why that ship? There must have been others who were leaving as well that you could have boarded. What was it about that one that compelled you to join the passengers?"

"It was the closest one and Captain McGovern didn't turn me away. I wasn't being picky."

Eagan could tell that wasn't the whole truth. Before he could confront her with that, Beth turned and marched out of the cave. "Where are you going?"

"I need some fresh air."

"This isn't a safe place to be. I'll accompany you."

"No!" She let out a frustrated yell. "I'm trying to have some personal space." She waved in the direction of their crashed shuttle. "I'm going to the shuttle to look for something and then I'll be back." She didn't wait for his response, as she turned and continued down the rocky path.

The urge to ignore what she'd said and join her was nearly as strong as the compulsion to kiss her, though he knew neither action would be appreciated just then. Instead, he stood there and watched as she kicked at stones that were unfortunate enough to be in her way, and felt the waves of frustration come from her, even at this distance.

She would need to accept that he was meant for her, that the life she'd run away from couldn't hurt her any longer. Once she did, Eagan knew they would have a chance at a relationship. A spark of joy flared in his chest at the thought of being with her, making a life with her, holding her in his arms in the early hours before daylight broke and kissing her softly.

For the first time since his re-birth, Eagan knew he could love another person. Knew he could love Beth the way she deserved. He simply needed to find a way to be patient with her until she had time to process her new life.

She'd reached the shuttle and stepped inside in search of her goal. He hated not being able to see her, but he too would have to learn to manage these new impulses. He would stand and wait for her return, proving to them both that he could do what she needed him to do.

The soft whine of shuttle engines drew his attention toward the horizon. Finally, Rykal and Darrick had found them, and they'd be able to reunite with the others. He returned to the cave to gather their belongings, not wanting to leave any resources behind. Everything the Fallen had was important and was to be reused whenever possible. Blankets, injectors, remains of their rations were all quickly gathered and put into the pack he'd brought from the shuttle. Voices echoed up from outside, and Eagan snapped to attention.

Those were Grus.

Dropping the items, he charged from the cave in time to see three armed guards pulling Beth away from the crash site and toward the Grus shuttle. "Beth!"

"Eagan!" She fought against their grip as the guards opened fire at him.

He ducked behind the nearest rock, unable to return fire. He could only watch in horror as the guards pulled Beth along with them into the shuttle, closed the door and took off.

She was gone.

CHAPTER NINE

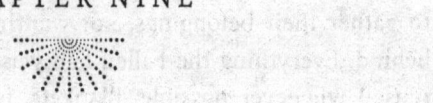

Beth sat in the shuttle surrounded by guards, her heart pounding as the memory of Eagan's pained expression burned into her mind. She'd heard a ship land when she'd been inside the crashed shuttle and had assumed that their rescue had finally arrived. She'd even gone so far as to wave and call out to the guards as they approached, not realizing that their weapons were pointed *at* her, not out to protect her.

By the time she heard Eagan call out for her, the guards had grabbed her and hauled her into their shuttle. While she might not understand exactly what was going on between the Grus and the cyborgs, even she wasn't fool enough to fight against an armed man. So, she went with them and hoped Eagan would be able to come get her, or at the very least be able to negotiate her release.

While she hadn't been with Eagan very long, she'd been surprised to hear the pain in his voice when he'd called out her name. There was a swell of emotion behind that single syllable, so unlike the reserved man she'd come to know in such a short time. Maybe there really was something to what he'd said about her helping him to generate emotions. Or maybe she was seeing something that wasn't actually there.

The shuttle didn't take her back out into space and toward the station, which was where she assumed the Grus would want her, but to another sector on the planet. There was a contingency of people waiting for them the moment the shuttle landed.

"Get up." The guard who'd been sitting beside her during the short flight stood, pointing his blaster at her.

"Am I under arrest or something?" She hated the way her legs shook as she stood. She was tired of being the victim here, being fearful and not having any control over what was happening.

"Move."

They joined the guards waiting for them at the bottom of the shuttle and Beth was surprised when one of them handed her a blanket before directing her toward a small building off to the right. The warmth felt good and helped chase away the chill that still clung to her from having fallen asleep on the rocks. She missed Eagan's warmth, even missed his grumpy presence and the soft grunts he'd make when he was working out a problem. How could she miss something from a person who she'd only known for such a short time? It didn't seem possible and yet, here she was.

The small building was stuffed full of computer consoles and screens that were monitoring something. Three chairs lined the back of the room, but only one of them was occupied. "Commander Aidric?"

He stood and nodded, before directing his attention toward the guards who'd come in with them. "Leave us." Beth felt them hesitate, before walking outside. "Eagan wasn't with you?"

"No." She wasn't going to give him too many details about Eagan's presence before she knew exactly where he stood. "Why have you captured me?"

"That wasn't my intention. Not fully." He laced his hands

behind his back and came closer. "I'm surprised he wasn't stuck to your side. That was the case with both Rykal and Darrick once they'd begun to bond with their mates."

You've saved me, Beth.

"Yeah, well I didn't really give him the chance to follow." God, she'd really screwed things up. Not that she was ready for this level of commitment with someone else, but she at least knew Eagan would do what he could to keep her safe. She couldn't say the same for Aidric. "What do you want from me?"

"The Grus high council are now aware of the connection the Fallen have with the human women on your ship. They have... concerns." Aidric kept his gaze even on her, but Beth could tell he was unhappy with the situation. "They wanted me to bring the Kraken back to the station."

"I don't think Lena will agree to that. And seeing as we're humans and not Grus or under the control of your council, I don't think they have any say in where we go."

Aidric cocked his head to the side and smiled slightly. "This is our sector of space. While we agreed that the Fallen can live on Zarlan, the Grus are still the controlling force here."

Beth would normally be intimidated by someone like Aidric; an authority figure who clearly had not only the law on his side, but the bulk of knowledge as well. She should defer to him, step aside and let others decide her fate. That was what she always did when it came to her parents, even with her siblings. But they were all gone, and she was here, standing on the cusp of a new life that she could finally have some say over.

Straightening, Beth shot Aidric a smile of her own. "I think the cyborgs would argue with you over that. I get the impression that wouldn't be something your people would want to deal with."

"It's funny," Aidric motioned for her to take a seat before he joined her, "when I started the cyborg program, I'd never considered the possibility that they'd have the ability to continue on with their lives. Originally, I'd merely hoped their bodies would be vessels that we could weaponize. When I realized that there was an opportunity for them to have another chance at life, it scared me. Who are we to determine who lives and who dies? What kind of life would we be forcing upon them if all they could do was fight and die once more?"

Beth hadn't considered the possibility of what might have been for the cyborgs, for Eagan, if things had gone a bit different. Aidric held her gaze, but it was still difficult to see exactly what he was feeling. What kind of person was so closed off that even looking into his eyes didn't give a hint of the man behind the mask? Eagan might have been that way once, but Beth could see the warmth, the love in his gaze whenever he looked at her.

She hoped he found her soon. Because she had no doubt that he was on his way to find her.

Aidric sat back. "You and I have a problem we need to find a solution for before the others arrive. The high council wants me to launch a sneak attack against the Fallen to kill the humans. They want to deny you hope for the future."

"You want to *kill* us?" Panic clawed at her throat and it took immense effort to tamp it down. "Screw you, buddy."

"*I* don't want to do any such thing." He narrowed his gaze. "I've put my reputation and possibly my life on the line to prevent that from happening. Now if you want to help me stop this from escalating, I need you to listen."

"I'm not a negotiator. I'm not even a member of the Kraken crew." She didn't know what she wanted from life, let alone know how to help stop a civil war. "But I do know how to fight back. Humans have dealt with oppressive regimes back on Earth and from what I can see your government is no better. Just another bully trying to keep their tenuous grip on power."

Aidric held up his hands and let out a sigh. "I'm on your side.

Rykal is my brother and despite us not always having the strongest relationship, I would never do anything that would put his life in danger. I brought him back from the dead because I wasn't willing to lose him."

The notes of sadness and regret in Aidric's voice caught Beth off guard. "I didn't realize." His admission took the steam out of her angry bubble. "What do you need me to do to help?"

"You can start by telling me why you agreed to join the Kraken and come to this sector of space?"

Ah, there was a hint of the man. Aidric was the creator of the cyborgs and he didn't understand what was happening to them. As much as he was responsible for the Grus on the station, he also wanted to keep the cyborgs safe. That was something Beth could appreciate, even if she wasn't sure how she could help him. "I tried to tell Eagan this, but it was just luck that I booked passage on the Kraken. I was fleeing something, and it was the first available ship."

Aidric's gaze narrowed. "Would you allow me to scan you?"

"Why?"

"If you weren't drawn to the ship, then that would disprove a theory of mine."

"Okay." She couldn't exactly stop him if he were to force the matter, but allowing him to look at whatever it was he wanted might help clarify things for herself as well. "What do you need me to do?"

"Don't move." He stood up as he pulled a small device from his pocket. "This will take the readings I need. It won't hurt at all."

He ran the device around the circumference of her head, while the device beeped and clicked. It only took a few seconds for him to get what he needed, though he stared at the results far longer than Beth was comfortable. "What's it say?"

Aidric didn't immediately respond, instead he turned to the computer behind him. "There's a shuttle heading this way. I will assume that is Eagan and the others coming to rescue you from me."

A wave of relief washed through her. "Will the guards open fire on them?"

"Not unless I give the order. Which I won't." He slipped the device back into his pocket. "When you were back on Earth, what were you trying to escape?"

"My family wanted me to marry a man who I didn't want. They wouldn't listen to me, so I didn't have many choices but to give in or run. I chose the latter."

"Have you considered why you didn't want to marry the man? Why you knew he wasn't meant to be your mate?"

"Of course. I didn't know him, he wasn't compatible."

"If you didn't know him, how could you know if he was compatible or not?" Aidric walked toward the door. "Your scans show the identical brain wave that's present in both Lena and Carys. It matches what's been generated in their cyborg mates. If I had to guess, if I were to scan Eagan, I would find the same thing."

Beth's heart raced. "You think it wasn't an accident that I boarded the Kraken?"

He looked over his shoulder at her. "I think you might not have understood what was happening, but you trusted your instincts and did what you knew needed to be done." Aidric stepped outside, leaving her alone with the weight of his words.

Was he right? Had the pressure she'd felt about her engagement come from her family, or had things been building up in her mind because she knew she wasn't meant to stay on Earth and go though with it? Maybe she really had been drawn to the Kraken, to this sector of space.

Maybe she really had been destined to be Eagan's mate after all.

An explosion from outside rattled the building. Aidric pressed his coms. "Report!"

"A shuttle has opened fire from above."

"Has anyone been hurt?"

"No, sir. It appears to be suppression fire."

Beth jumped to her feet and raced outside, knowing in her heart that Eagan was on board. The shuttle had landed, and she caught a glimpse of Eagan and Rykal as they ran down the ramp before ducking behind the cover of rocks. Aidric had taken shelter behind another outcropping and was currently shouting at his men. "Hold your fire!"

No one was listening to him on either side, which meant things were only going to get worse. Instead of taking shelter, Beth stepped out into the open, praying that she wouldn't catch an errant blaster shot in her back. "Eagan! Stop!"

She would have continued, but Aidric came up behind her, wrapping an arm around her waist. "Trust me?"

She didn't know why, but she nodded yes. Then she was surprised when Aidric pressed a blaster to her temple and shouted. "I said, everyone *hold your fire!*"

Within seconds, everything calmed, and all Beth could hear was her own rapid breathing and the pounding of her heart.

"Let her go!" Eagan's voice came from behind the rock closest to them. "I'll kill you if anything happens to her." Hate and rage dripped from his words and for a moment Beth thought he might explode out from cover to make a grab for her.

"I will as soon as I can ensure everyone is going to cease fire." Aidric's hold on her was tight enough to keep her still but loose enough Beth could pull away if she wanted. "Is Rykal with you?"

"I'm here." There was less anger in Rykal's voice, but just as much suspicion. "This isn't the best way to start negotiations."

"I do believe it was the two of you who opened fire first." Aidric turned slightly to face his men. "It is just the two of you, correct? Lena and Carys?"

"Yes. We weren't about to risk any other humans being taken. They're back on the Kraken." Rykal flexed his grip on the butt of his blaster. "Darrick is waiting in a second shuttle ready to join the fight if needed."

"It won't be. Let's take this inside where we can talk." Aidric took a step backward, bringing Beth with him. "Unless you'd like to continue your firefight?"

Eagan stepped out from behind the rocks first, his gaze locked on Beth. "If she gets hurt, I'll kill every single one of you."

The guards all raised their weapons and locked them on him, but no one made a move to stop his approach. Rykal stepped out as well, his blaster trained on Aidric. "As long as everyone remains calm, we'll all walk away from this alive."

Eagan's gaze met hers and she was shocked to see a wildness to him that hadn't been there before. She wanted to go wrap her arms around him and never let him go. Aidric was right, she might not have understood the reason why she'd left Earth, but now that she was here it was clear. She was meant to be with Eagan. They shared a bond that went beyond reason and logic and was growing in strength with each passing moment.

"You better be careful," she whispered to Aidric as they continued their slow retreat. "He's barely keeping himself together."

"I can tell." Aidric continued their painful backward journey until she heard the whoosh of the door to the building slide open. "Everyone else stay here. Do nothing unless you hear from me."

Eagan followed them in, his gaze locked onto Beth's the entire time. She tried to project feelings of calm and confidence, hoping it would help reassure him that everything would turn out okay. The moment the doors closed behind them, Aidric released his hold on Beth and she bolted for Eagan's arms.

"Thank the gods." He pressed his face to the side of her neck and breathed in deep. "I thought I'd lost you."

"I'm sorry. I didn't mean to get angry at you. I'm so sorry."

He tilted her chin up, kissing her softly on the lips. "I should have realized you weren't ready, that everything was still too new, and you hadn't adjusted."

"While I appreciate the two of you have things that you need to discuss," Aidric said, "we have a pressing matter we need to address."

Eagan's body tensed, before Beth patted his chest. "I know you're angry, but you need to listen to him."

Rykal leaned back against the wall, his chin lowered, and his gaze locked on the commander. "I was surprised to hear your voice when we landed. You haven't been to the planet's surface in many decades."

Beth looked back over at Aidric, who didn't look that old to her. "Decades?"

Aidric ignored her. "The high council wants to kill the humans to keep the Fallen in their place."

"Not going to happen." Eagan tightened his grip on her. "We'll destroy them if they try."

"I don't think they truly understand the connection between you and the humans." Aidric sat down on the nearest seat, his hand folded neatly in his lap. "There were twenty-eight humans on that ship."

"We're aware." Eagan finally released his hold on Beth, sensing that there was something important Aidric was trying to tell him and sat down in the chair opposite the commander. "Why's that important?"

"When the humans first arrived, we became aware of their connection with the Fallen. But I'd assumed that it could be potentially with *any* of the Fallen. That it was a random selection of cyborgs." Aidric took his time, as though he was trying to take careful measure of his words. "When I began the cyborg program, there was a flaw in the matrix. Rykal, you were the first successful one to accept the implanted matrix. There were twenty-seven others before I realized that there was a flaw in your code and was able to create a workaround."

Beth turned in Eagan's arms. "That can't be a coincidence."

"No, I don't believe it is." Aidric looked between Eagan and Rykal. "Each of you who had the initial flaw have all made your way into leadership roles within the Fallen. You're either leading one of the cities, or in charge of the prison, or other key positions. I've checked."

"You think the women are somehow drawn to us because of the flaw in our code? From across the galaxy?" Eagan snorted. "That's a stretch."

"Perhaps." Aidric pulled out the device he'd used to scan Beth's head earlier and handed it to Rykal. "Lena, Carys and Beth all have the same brain wave pattern. Without knowing normal human physiology, I can't tell you if this is normal with their race or not, but I don't think so. Somehow, they've all developed the same link and that link matches the glitch in your systems."

Eagan frowned down at the device before handing it over to Rykal, who scanned the readings. "When did you take these?"

"Shortly before you arrived."

Beth hated feeling out of her depth. "Does it matter how this happened? There is obviously a link between us, and there are twenty-five more who are connected to other cyborgs."

"Does the high council know specifically about the twenty-eight?" Rykal handed the device back to Aidric. "Are they fearful of what we'll do if we all bond with our mates?"

"They do not. Them believing that the humans are connected to specific Fallen rather than random would place a target on all twenty-eight of you." Aidric got to his feet. "I do have a plan to keep them ignorant of that fact."

Rykal cocked his head to the side. "How?"

"I plan to tell them that we've just spent this time negotiating. You pointed out that the humans would be nothing more than a resource drain on Grus Prime and offer little in the way of skills that would benefit us. And without knowing if they'd ever find a mate, we'd have to continue to care for them. But you as the appointed leader of the Fallen have graciously agreed to give them shelter. In return and due to the appearance of the Sholle scout ship, you've agreed to send reconnaissance teams out to find out what the Sholle are up to."

Rykal cocked an eyebrow. "I have?"

"You have." Aidric slipped the scanner back into his pocket. "I'll return to the high council with news of the negotiations."

Eagan shook his head. "I find it hard to believe they would accept these...negotiations. Even if we do actively put out reconnaissance teams."

"It will be hard for them to argue with the humans and their ship is already off the station and hidden from our scanners." Aidric smoothed down his tunic and Beth was amazed to see his expression shift to something mask-like. "Have your first scout team ready to leave within the day. While you did an excellent job at hiding the Kraken and destroying the Sholle ships, I can't believe we escaped harm that easily." With a nod to each of them, Aidric left.

Beth didn't know what to say, as she turned back to Eagan and smiled. "So, we're all okay now?"

"We will need to finalize a few details, but yes." He lowered his mouth to hers and kissed her hard.

"Before the two of you get too far into consummating your relationship, we need to get back to the Kraken and let the others know." Rykal stood. "We might be okay in the short term, but I have a feeling things might get far more complicated in the near future."

They waited for the Grus to leave before returning to the shuttle Eagan and Rykal had arrived on. Beth didn't want to be too far from his side, even though she knew there was nothing that would keep them apart any longer – not even her own fears.

Resting her hand on his shoulder once he took the co-pilot's seat, she leaned down to whisper in his ear. "Once this is sorted, will you take me back to your home?"

A shiver passed through his body. "Yes, love. I'll take you home."

Home.

It had been a long while since that idea brought Beth joy, but now, she couldn't wait to go there. Go home with Eagan.

CHAPTER TEN

Rarely had Eagan ever thought about the state of the small building he'd called his house since the war with the Sholle had been won. But standing there with Beth by his side, the cool winds of Zarlan's latest storm whipping around them, he couldn't help but think it was a poor excuse for a home. Beth deserved a large building, with flora around it to give it life. She should have bright colors across every surface, more than the gray and brown walls he had.

"It's perfect." Beth smiled as she looked around the front. "There aren't a lot of houses in this part of the city."

"Despite the number of Fallen across the planet, we're still a fraction of the population of Grus who used to live here. We're stretched out, taking as much space as we want." There were other, larger houses that he'd show her in the coming days. If she'd rather have one of those then Eagan would move them immediately. "We best go inside before the rain starts."

The air had a stale smell to it, indicative of how long it had been since Eagan had last been here. The furniture was spartan and what was there was basic. One chair, a single bed, a table where he'd eat, or fix any created plans for problems that no longer existed. He could only stand and watch as Beth moved around the space, occasionally stopping to touch something or adjust something else.

"We'll need to add another chair." She looked over at him and grinned. "And maybe some pictures. Do you have artwork here?"

"Some of us do, but it was never much of a concern of mine." He crossed the distance between them and ran his hand through her hair. "But I'll find whatever you want and bring it here. Anything that will make you feel more comfortable."

Her face flushed as he felt her embarrassment wash over her. "Thank you."

"You have nothing to be embarrassed about. This is your home now as well and I want you to be happy."

"Okay." Beth rolled her eyes as she smiled. "I'm never going to get used to you knowing how I feel."

"You will in time. Sooner or later it will become second nature to both of us." He tugged on her hair until her neck was stretched back and she could look nowhere but his eyes. "Right now, I can tell that the idea of being here scares you as much as it arouses you. Knowing that the bed we will share from now on is just over there waiting for us to fall into. Waiting for me to strip you naked so I can taste every bit of your body."

Her feelings of embarrassment became entangled with her growing arousal. "While I think that's a fantastic idea, I have no idea how we're both going to sleep comfortably on that bed."

It wasn't exactly the largest of spaces and while she wasn't a large person, together they wouldn't have much room to move. Thankfully, that was something he could easily remedy. Moving along the side of the bed, he pressed a few buttons on the console. The bed was made of a bio matter that was easily manipulated by the computer and within a few moments, it doubled in size, giving them plenty of room. "I'll fetch you additional blankets if you get cold."

Beth let out a small surprised gasp and he had to smile at the look of wonder on her face. "The bed grew."

"You don't have such technology on your planet?"

"We sleep on foam. It, ahh, doesn't do that." Beth walked over to the mattress and pressed her hand against it. "Wow, that's soft."

"If you prefer a different firmness, I can make adjustments."

Her face flushed as she flicked her gaze up at him. "I'd have to give it a proper test to make that determination."

Eagan was shocked at how quickly his arousal spiked at such a simple phrase. "I would be more than ready to assist you with such an evaluation."

All the nervousness, the fear and trepidation in her, was instantly gone. All Eagan could sense from her was joy and excitement at the idea of being with him. The rush of arousal was now tinged with pride.

She wanted him.

She *chose* him.

Eagan rose to his full height and slowly made his way around the bed to where Beth now stood waiting for him. Her brown hair was a messy halo around her head, her clothes were rumpled and ill fitting, and to him she was absolutely perfect. He cupped her face with his hands, caressed the soft skin just below her brown eyes with his thumbs, before leaning down and capturing her mouth with his.

She sighed into his mouth, pressing her body against his, and it was the sweetest feeling. Beth had traveled across the galaxy to get to him; she'd given up everything to be here. For the rest of their lives, Eagan would make sure that she was treated like the precious gem she was.

Without breaking their kiss, Eagan moved his hands from her face and slowly removed each piece of her clothing. He didn't need to see her to know what he was doing, he'd long ago burned everything about her into a permanent place on his matrix. He knew that if he scraped his thumbs along the side of her breasts when he slid her shirt down her arms, she'd gasp and giggle.

Like this.

And when he'd tug at her pants, letting his fingers tease the small dip of her hip when he pushed the fabric to the floor, her legs would begin to tremble.

Like that.

And finally, when he pulled away from her and pushed her down to the bed so she could spread out, the remaining few articles of clothing all that stood between them, Eagan knew in a matter of moments her cries of pleasure would fill their home. The bruise on her shoulder was still there, a blemish on her otherwise perfect skin; a mark that gave him pride as much as it aroused.

His cock was painfully hard, and his skin itched to be set free from his fabric prison. Beth's gaze traveled down his body as he made quick work of stripping down. He stood still for a moment while she looked him over, a small smile turning her lips. "You're so big. Everything about you. Big and hard and strong. I like that."

If Eagan had the ability to feel vanity, that sentiment would have inflated his ego. "I know something you'll like more."

There was no more waiting, no more flirting; Eagan dropped to his knees on the bed and grabbed the undergarments that hid her pussy from him. She was already wet from desire and he could smell her arousal as he flung the thin piece of material somewhere behind him. Finally, he freed her breasts, leaving no barriers between them.

"I want to taste you."

Beth groaned and squirmed beneath him. "Yes."

There was a part of Eagan who wanted to rush through everything, needing to claim her once again, leaving no doubt that she was his. But he pushed against that urge and instead gently leaned down and sucked her nipple into his mouth. She gasped as he began to flick the sensitive skin with his tongue, teasing and tormenting it until he could feel her arousal through their connection. Only when he didn't think she could handle it any longer did he switch to her other breast and repeat the process. The whole time he sucked and nipped at her, he was also thrusting his hard cock against the soft skin of her inner thigh; a tease and a promise all in one.

Beth wasn't a passive recipient to his ministrations. Her hands roamed across his back, her fingers threaded through his hair, flexing and tugging at him, pushing and pulling as she tried to direct where she wanted him to go. She opened her thighs wide, wrapping them around his waist, grinding her pussy against his body as she sought to increase contact against her clit. By the time he lifted his head from her breast, he could feel her desperation.

She looked up at him with wide eyes. "If you don't do something soon, I'm going to lose my mind."

Eagan couldn't help but smile.

He moved down, licking and kissing as he went. He paused to press his nose into the damp curls of hair between her legs and breathe in deep the scent of her. There was nothing else like it in the universe. When he licked a long, slow swipe up her pussy, the taste of her was as good as he remembered. He darted his tongue across her clit once, then twice, before he pressed a finger inside her the way he had back at the ship.

Beth groaned long and low as she thrust up against his mouth. Unlike the frantic need that had consumed him earlier, this time Eagan was able to relax and enjoy the feeling on her around him. The softness of her hidden flesh was addictive to him; he flicked his tongue across the sensitive nub of her clit, sensing her arousal rising steeply with each caress.

His cock was now pressed against the bed and it took the total of his discipline to keep from rubbing against it, seeking out his own release. No, when he came it was going to be deep inside

Beth's body so he could feel that connection with her. Warm pleasure surged inside him as his desires for her grew. He latched onto her clit and sucked with renewed intensity, fucking her with his had the way he planned to fuck her with his cock soon enough.

"Shit, Eagan." Beth thrashed beneath him as her juices coated his mouth and chin. He was about to force her over the edge into bliss when he stopped. He pulled back which earned him a glare that would have killed a Sholle where it stood. "What? No. Don't stop."

"I want to feel you come on my cock."

"Noooo." She let out a soft little cry. "I'm so close."

"I promise you I will make your body sing."

"I'm trusting you to do that." Her bottom lip was stuck out in a pout that told him she was less than convinced with his plan.

Eagan rose up on his knees to line his cock up with her opening, before coming down on his forearms to brace his body above hers. He thrust forward only a bit, enough to rub the crown of his cock against her clit. It slid easily with the slickness of her arousal easing the way. He teased her with tiny movements, but this time he was able to kiss her lips as he did. He nipped at her mouth, sucking her bottom lip as he pushed the head of his cock into her waiting body.

Beth's eyes had fluttered closed and she bore the cutest look of concentration as he continued to tease her. Her nipples were hard, the tips of them grazing across his chest each time he moved. He knew she wouldn't be able to last much longer, and he needed to feel her come undone around him.

Lowering his face to her shoulder, her body shuddered the moment before he pressed fully inside her body with one long, slow stroke. "Oh God."

Eagan opened his mouth and sucked on the bruise, knowing he couldn't help but return here, return to the mark that showed the world she was his. What he hadn't realized that while he might bear a physical sign, Beth had placed a mark on him as well, one that would never go away.

He loved her.

Love wasn't an emotion he'd experienced much even before his re-birth. He hadn't bothered to seek it out and then with the war, it was the last thing he was concerned with. Missing an emotion he hadn't really experienced wasn't something he'd ever worried about once he'd been implanted with his matrix. But now, oh now he knew this was what he felt and it would forever change who he was.

All thanks to the woman who'd come to save him without knowing that's what she was doing.

They began to move in rhythm with one another. He thrust forward as she bucked against him, their bodies connecting over and over until the only thing he was aware of was her and the arousal building inside him. Sweat pooled between them, making their bodies slide, rubbing each bit of skin until they moved like a perfectly timed machine.

Beth's breathing grew frantic as she increased the bucking of her hips. He could feel her impending orgasm and wanted to fall over the edge with her. Shifting his legs, he pressed his *rondella* hard against the outside of her leg, needing to feel the rush of blood that would push him into his release. The steady silent beat that drove him toward the edge grew louder in his head, echoing in his brain as it consumed every cell and circuit in his body. With his face pressed against her shoulder, Eagan closed his eyes and focused his attention on her, on the emotions rolling off her, on just how close she was to coming and wanting to be there with her.

The first feel of her orgasm trickled down his spine like an electrical current. It kickstarted something deep inside him. The cool detachment that had comprised his world view was blown from his mind, replaced by a full spectrum color blast. Pleasure mixed with love and a sense of peace as Beth tensed beneath him and cried out as her orgasm washed through her. Eagan let his walls fall as he gasped and came with her, before biting down on her shoulder.

He slammed into her over and over as years of pain and suffering dissipated. His orgasm ripped him apart, flooding him with pleasure so intense he couldn't imagine a world without it, a world without her. With one final stuttering thrust, he lost the ability to hold himself up any longer and collapsed down on her. It took her slapping at his shoulder to bring him to his senses enough to shift beside her. "Sorry."

"S'okay." Beth turned and tucked herself beneath his arm. "That was amazing."

Eagan wrapped her up in his arms, pressing his nose into the soft waves of her hair. "Did I meet your expectations?"

"Surpassed them." She began to draw tiny circles on his chest. "Is it too early to say that I love you? Because I'm pretty sure that I do and I'm not sure how that's possible."

For the first time since his re-birth, Eagan was happy. He pulled her a bit tighter to him. "I've learned that some things are better not to question. Somehow, despite a galaxy between us, you found a way to me. You saved me when I didn't know I needed saving. You showed me that I could love and was worth of love in return."

She peeked up at him. "You love?"

"Yes, I love you." He kissed the top of her head. "Something I wasn't sure I was capable of doing."

She made a happy hum. "Where do we go from here?"

"Anywhere we want. As long as we're together."

"I love the sound of that. Let's plan something." She let out a long, jaw-cracking yawn. "After a little nap."

"Rest, little one. We have the rest of our lives together."

Eagan pulled the blanket up to cover them both, closed his eyes and went to sleep, daring to dream of the future with the woman he loved.

HEALED BY THE CYBORG

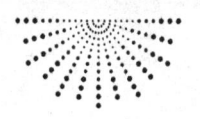

To save his mate,
he must first heal
his heart.

A CYBORG PROTECTORS ROMANCE

HEALED BY THE CYBORG

ALYSE ANDERS

CHAPTER ONE

Hallam stood in the middle of the old complex that had once served as a medical facility for the Grus people, his assessing gaze traveling over his patients who'd been brought to him for help. While the Grus no longer lived on the surface of Zarlan, the planet was still populated with a scattering of cyborgs, bounty hunters, and outcasts from other sectors. The prison wasn't far from here, and occasionally he'd be brought a patient to care for. The fights below the surface in the prison facility were brutal and more often than he cared to admit, by the time they were transported to the facility there was little he could do to save them.

Before his rebirth as a cyborg, that fact would have upset him.

Currently, he had three patients resting comfortably in beds. One was a cyborg who'd become trapped by a rockslide during the last storm. His biological leg was pinned and the subsequent damage required the limb to be amputated and replaced with cybernetics. The second was a female bounty hunter who'd captured her quarry hiding on a small settlement away from the city, only to get surprised when her target's gang arrived to free him. She'd gotten caught in the ensuing firefight, sustaining injuries to her chest. Her recovery had been initially questionable, but Hallam was able to use a technique he'd pioneered after the war to help save her life.

The last patient – a Grus technician who'd come down to Cimacha, Zarlan's capital city – had gotten into a fight with a cyborg. While the cyborg hadn't started the altercation, he was now held in the prison and threatened with decommissioning if this Grus died. Like everything that had happened to the Fallen – from their initial rebirth, to the rules that were forced upon them – this wasn't something the cyborg had asked for, but he would be the one to suffer the consequences.

Unfortunately, the wounds the Grus suffered were severe enough that there was little Hallam could do to save the man's life. His only regret was that it would also cost the life of the cyborg as well. Walking over to where the man lay, he checked the readings on the display.

"Computer, run a scan on patient three. Compare against previous scans and predict patient outcome."

The computer's pause was far shorter than he would have liked. "Scan complete. Patient's life signs are fading. Life termination imminent. Projected death, one hour."

When that occurred, Hallam would notify the prison and the cyborg in custody would be decommissioned. No trial, no justice, only swift punishment. Another one of his duties he hated but necessary to keep the peace between their people. If the Grus thought for a moment that the Fallen couldn't be controlled, then the potential that they would turn on the race who created them was too much for the Grus high council. Hallam had no idea what they'd do if they were placed into that position to chose between the safety of the Grus people and the lives of the cyborgs on the planet. He didn't want to ever be put in the position to find out.

Pressing a few buttons on the console, he gave the Grus one final scan. "Computer, notify me before death occurs."

"Affirmative."

With his rounds completed, Hallam made his way to the small office he'd commandeered as his own when he'd taken up the role of lead doctor after the war with the Sholle was won. Before his rebirth, he'd been little more than a medical technician, but after Hallam had taken charge of the medical needs of the Fallen. Initially, he'd worked with Commander Aidric to help the dead be implanted with the cybernetic matrix that initiated their rebirths. But as the war continued, and the consequences of what they'd done registered with him, he stopped.

Aidric hadn't.

Taking his seat, Hallam opened his matrix link with the computer network, letting the blast of information wash through him. There'd been some action up on Grus Prime, but the details were thin at best. No doubt he'd be informed of what was happening the moment someone got hurt and they needed him to bail them out. That was the way of things when you were a doctor for cyborgs.

He broke the link, and immediately reached up to scratch the back of his head. The itch was deep, as though it was originating somewhere in his brain, rather than on his scalp. Thankfully, it faded away after a few moments, leaving him able to concentrate on his report. With his patient's life hanging by a nanometer, there was little point in putting off writing the words he'd inevitably need to send. Connecting to the system once more, he set about mentally constructing the report. He was nearly complete, when the itching in the back of his brain started once more.

Then the facilities communicator sounded. Ignoring the itch, he opened the feed. "Hallam here."

Rykal, the leader of the Fallen, appeared on the screen. "Doctor, how full is your facility?"

"Three patients, soon to be two."

Rykal frowned. "I'm sorry to hear that. Please pass on my thoughts to the family."

That was odd. In all the years that Hallam had informed Rykal of a death, not once had he shown any trace of concern or sympathy for any of the patients here. "His foolish actions will also cost the life of cyborg. The moment the Grus dies, he will be decommissioned."

Hallam should have a handle on the anger that simmered beneath the surface by now, but each time a cyborg's life was impacted by the actions of a Grus, no matter who they were, it ate away at him.

Rykal nodded, his lips pursed and the muscle in his jaw jumping. "Send me the cyborg's designation. I'll see if there's something I can do."

He knew it was a nearly pointless action, but Hallam appreciated the attempt. "Done. What can I do for you?"

Rykal hesitated, his gaze slipping to someone off screen for a moment. "We have a number of patients of alien physiology who will require assistance. They're currently in stasis on a ship, but we need to move them to a more permanent location until we can process them."

"You're unable to wake them?" Hallam reached up and scratched his head once more. "Have they been processed through quarantine protocols?"

"Partially." Rykal reached up and placed the call on hold for a moment, temporarily blocking communication. When he came back, he stared at Hallam with something akin to determination. "I'm coming to you to discuss the details."

Hallam cocked an eyebrow. "This *is* a secure channel."

"You'll understand once I give you the details. We'll be there within the hour."

The screen went black, leaving him with more questions and unease than he'd had moments before. The itching continued, but he was able to ignore it the longer it went on. If it continued after Rykal left, he'd connect his matrix to the computer and run a diagnostic to see if there was a problem he'd missed with his internal scans.

Hallam was in the process of calibrating the new cybernetic leg on his patient when the doors to the medical facility opened and Rykal strode in, a small female trailing behind him. Instinctively, he ran a scan of her physiology – heat signature, oxygen co2 exchange rate, pheromones – and was mildly surprised at the results. "She's not Grus."

Rykal reached his hand and taking the woman's as they got close. "Hallam, it's been too long since I've visited you in person."

"There's been little need." While he made his base of operations the medical facility, Hallam had taken charge of all major medical decisions when it came to the Fallen as a people. "My reports have been adequate for our needs."

"They have. But things have changed for some of our people that will impact those needs." Rykal encouraged the woman to step closer. "Hallam, this is Lena. She's a human from a planet called Earth. Her ship and its passengers have been traveling at faster than light speed for fifty years to arrive here."

Hallam might not have the emotional connection to others that he'd had before his rebirth, but even he could see that there was something between these two that went far beyond friendship. "How long have you been here?"

"Not long." Her hair was a shade of red that Hallam had never seen before, and her skin was pale in contrast to Rykal's. "My passengers have all survived the trip. Currently, we only have three of us who've been woken from stasis."

Hallam couldn't look away from their joined hands or help but notice the way Rykal's heart rate increased whenever she'd rub her thumb across the top of his. "There's something different about you, Rykal. The readings I'm getting off you are not the same as the last time we met."

"That's because there's been a change to my code. Something

that will impact twenty-eight of us in total." Rykal dropped her hand and stepped closer, so Hallam had no choice but to look him in the eyes. "If Aidric's assumption is correct, it will impact you as well."

Hallam was one of the first cyborgs to be reborn during the war. As a medical technician, the thought of being able to prolong life after death had been fascinating to him. The reality of what that entailed had proven to be far less appealing. "Why only twenty-eight?"

"When Aidric created the first wave of cyborgs, he hadn't realized that there was a problem with the code. Have you ever wondered why that initial group of reborn have all gone on to become leaders of a sort in our community, and none of the others have?"

It wasn't something Hallam had considered before now, but Rykal was correct. "What does that have to do with the humans?"

Lena stepped beside Rykal once again. "The passengers on my ship? We're all women. Back on my planet, we were all drawn to this sector of space. When I put a call out that I was bringing a ship here, a one-way journey to see what was out here, they all came. Twenty-eight of us in total."

"That doesn't make sense. How would your people even be aware of ours at such a distance? The number is little more than a coincidence." That had to be it; the idea that two alien races were somehow aware of one another across the vastness of space was beyond illogical.

Hallam would have continued to believe so, if Rykal hadn't cocked his head to the side and narrowed his gaze. "When the did itching in the back of your head start?"

It was impossible for Rykal to have known about that. Hallam lowered his chin and stared hard at Rykal. "Over an hour ago. How did you know?"

"It's how it started with the others, myself included. It's like a sudden awareness that there's a wound that's starting to heal.

One that you hadn't noticed previously but now that you're aware, you can't seem to pull your attention away from it."

The longer Rykal spoke, the greater the itching in Hallam's mind became. "What's the cause and what do I need to do to fix this?"

"The cause is a woman on my ship, the Kraken. She's not aware of what's happening herself, nor will she be able to understand you at first." Lena lowered her chin and narrowed her gaze on him. "Every person on board is my responsibility. I need to ensure that they're all protected and can be woken from stasis safely."

Rykal nodded. "Which brings us to the crux of our problem. The stasis pods are on the ship, which is currently in the valley to the north west of the city. They're there because the collection of the stasis tubes is generating a low-grade signal that somehow reached the Sholle. They sent two scout ships to investigate."

The myriad of thoughts that had been racing in his mind, came to an immediate halt. "Are we in danger? Are the Grus?" Despite everything, his core programming to protect was firmly intact.

"We pulled Eagan in and came up with a plan. The scout ships were destroyed, and the Kraken has been masked for the time being, but there's no way we can leave them there. We need to find a place to move the stasis tubes so we can wake the women one at a time."

"I assume there's a reason we're not waking them all at once?" It would have been the logical course of action.

Rykal and Lena shared a look, before Rykal cleared his throat. "Our reactions to our mates have been unpredictable at best. I kidnapped Lena, and Darrick nearly self-decommissioned. Eagan was able to keep control better, but it helped that we were able to prepare him for what was to come."

"Mates? We're no longer capable." Hallam fought the urge to scratch at his head again.

"That's what we all believed. But Aidric has confirmed the connections between us and the human women. It's not just any of them that causes this reaction. A specific female is intended for a specific cyborg. That connection is undeniable."

The thought of having someone of his own, a mate wasn't something Hallam had ever wanted, even before his rebirth. He couldn't imagine losing control of his actions over a woman who he'd never met. He tried to say as much, but a completely different question came out of him. "You want me to find a location where you can mask the stasis tube's signals, while you wake the women one at a time?"

"Yes. It will need to be far away from the city so that we don't inadvertently trigger the awakening of one of the twenty-eight of us before they're informed. Do you have someplace that might work?"

Several possibilities flashed to mind. "The basement of this facility would be the best. We can erect a shield that would prevent any signals from being detected, and the medical facilities are here in case any of the women require care. That way, we can also ensure that all quarantine procedures are followed."

"You understand that you'll be impacted as well. You were the third of us to be reborn." Rykal reached out and squeezed Hallam's shoulder. "You'll need to find your mate before you can do this."

Panic raced through him so strongly, it felt as though he'd been punched. That was something he hadn't experienced since his last few moments before the Sholle blasters destroyed the medical facility he'd been working at, trying to save the life of another Grus. "There's no need. I'll do my duty without waking anyone."

Rykal reached out to him through the cyborg neural network. *My friend, that's something you might not be able to do. The pull becomes overwhelming the closer they are.*

Hallam ignored him, and instead held out a data pad to Lena.

"Bring the ship here and we'll work to move the stasis tubes into the facility."

Hallam? You need to understand –

"If you'll excuse me, I have patients I need to prepare for." Without another word, he turned his back on them and went to prepare the long dormant facility, ignoring the increased itching in his mind.

CHAPTER TWO

It took longer than Hallam would have liked to get the underground facility ready to accept the stasis tubes. He'd become uncharacteristically distracted, which made the planning and coordination with Rykal slower and more frustrating than he'd expected. The itching, while an annoyance before, was now a prominent force that he couldn't help but fixate on. There had to be another explanation for what was happening, another cause for the physical manifestation of this itch that he could discover and cure.

The explanation that a woman from another race who'd come across the galaxy to be with him wasn't something his logical brain could accept.

"Hallam?" Aerin, one of his cyborg technicians strode across the facility, her face filled with concern. "There are twenty-five stasis tubes, but we don't have enough power to run all of them. Not without risking degradation of their life support systems."

While their facility had been once the best that the Grus had built, the subsequent years of lack of use had led to some of the systems falling into disrepair. "How many units will we need to have offline in order for the systems to hold."

Aerin pressed several buttons on her data pad. "Two should be sufficient." She looked up at him, frowning. "I don't understand why we don't wake them all. If this is their intended destination, then there should be no harm in bringing them to the final step in their journey."

Rykal had insisted that none of the other Fallen be told of the significance of these women, especially as the others wouldn't have a mate of their own. They couldn't be sure of the impact that would have on their society and it was best to understand what they could about the women and the impact on the Fallen first. Still, that didn't mean Hallam enjoyed misleading his staff.

Straightening as much as he could, he leveled his gaze at Aerin. "Rykal has given us a directive, and I don't intend to question his reasons. Upload your calculations to my systems. We'll need to confirm everything and decide which ones will need to be woken."

"Yes, sir." Aerin blinked, the only indication that she'd been caught off guard by his tone. She connected to his matrix and within a nanosecond, the data had been pushed to him. "Please let me know if there's anything else you need."

"Thank you." He watched her leave, wishing there was some way he could tell her what was going on.

Rykal might be frustrating, but in this instance, he was correct. Hallam hadn't accepted what he was being told, despite the evidence before him. He knew that others would also have concerns and doubts as well. The smaller the circle of people who knew the truth until they were able to work out the details, the better.

Now they had to sort through the issue of needing to wake two occupants from their slumber.

The next hour passed quickly as Aerin and the other technicians finished the preparations for the stasis tubes. Hallam tried to keep his focus on the data and scans that flowed into his matrix, but the itching continued to be a distraction.

"Krak...to...allam." Rykal's voice crackled through the communication system, interference making it difficult to decipher the words. "...ak off...five min..."

The valley where the Kraken was currently stationed emitted natural radiation that dampened all signals that came in and out, making coordination challenging. But Hallam didn't need to be told when the ship took off, making its approach to the medical building. No, it was easy enough for him to know because the itching in the back of his brain instantly grew stronger.

She was getting closer to him.

It became next to impossible to focus on anything as the maddening sensation increased. A tremor in his hands began, forcing him to set down the data pad he'd been holding, for fear someone would notice. He took a deep breath, then another, but nothing seemed to help calm the rising tension inside him.

"Sir?" Aerin called out, waiting for him to look her way before continuing. "The ship is on approach. It will arrive shortly."

She was on board and Hallam wanted nothing more than to pull her free from the stasis tube and into his arms. "Everyone out."

Aerin frowned as she turned toward him. "Sir?"

"I want the entire docking bay to be empty. Out!" The technicians scurried away as Hallam's voice echoed throughout the space. He reached out as Aerin passed, gently holding her back. "Except you."

While he wanted to keep the human women far away from the other cyborgs, the increased itching and his growing irritation was so much that he doubted he'd be able to do this on his own. She frowned at him once more but made no additional move to leave. Hallam waited until the rest had left before letting out a shaky breath. "You know about the alien women in this ship, but there's something else you need to be aware of."

"Clearly, it's proximity is having some sort of effect on you."

"Not the ship, but one of the occupants." He couldn't stop

from reaching up and pressing his hand to the back of his head. "I...might not be myself for a bit. Take directions from Rykal. Do exactly what he says, and things should be fine."

"I don't understand – "

"Just do it!" Hallam's body shook as Aerin scurried away. He knew he'd need to apologize to her later, but sympathy wasn't an emotion he felt much of these days, let alone in this moment.

The itching had morphed into something else, a painful desire to move. He began to pace, unable to look away from the docking bay door where he knew the ship would be entering at any moment. There was a tiny part of his mind that was still lucid, logical and questioning why this was happening. He was more cybernetics than flesh, having died when the building was destroyed and fell on top of him. Both his arms and one of his legs were enhanced, as was a portion of his spine. Aidric had once commented that he was the closest thing they had to a walking AI; a concept Hallam hated.

The air in the docking bay changed the moment the energy barrier was lowered, and the ship dropped in from the sky. Hallam's gaze locked onto the ship and he tried to get his internal systems under control. The code that regulated his remaining biological elements was working overtime to keep everything in check. If he didn't know better, he would have thought he was excited, anticipating meeting a woman whose existence he'd been unaware of mere hours earlier.

Aerin marched over to the shuttle when the ship's door opened and Rykal jumped out. He didn't need to hear what she was saying to know she was informing Rykal of Hallam's lack of control. Rykal looked his way and nodded, saying something to someone inside the ship, before heading his way.

The moment Rykal got into range, Hallam felt him reach out through the cyborg neuro net. *Brother, you're feeling the effects of her presence.*

Mine. He gave his head a shake and tried to shove down the possessive feeling. *We need to bring two stasis tubes offline. We don't have enough power in the facility to maintain all twenty-five units.*

Rykal stopped close enough to him that Hallam knew if he tried anything, Rykal would physically restrain him. *Aerin mentioned that. It would seem we need to wake up your mate.*

Gods, the idea of having a mate felt perfectly right and horribly wrong at the same time. *I'm not worthy of a mate. I'm not capable of anything she might need.*

Rykal reached out and gave his shoulder a squeeze. *You don't know that. Let's find her and then you'll understand. She'll be able to help you in ways you can't anticipate.*

Hallam let Rykal guide him over to the ship. Each step closer he got, the stronger the need to take and possess grew. His heart pounded, despite his matrix's attempts to regulate the muscle, and he couldn't relax his hands. *I don't want to hurt anyone.*

You won't. "Lena?"

The small red-headed woman stepped into the opening of the ship. "Yup?"

"We need to wake two of the women. The facility doesn't have the power to operate all the stasis tubes. I'm going to go with Hallam to find his mate. We'll make a determination of the other one after he's finished."

Lena cocked her head to the side, a slight frown on her lips. "No problem. Is he okay?"

"He appears to be responding stronger than the rest of us did." Rykal didn't release his hold on Hallam's shoulder. "I'm going to stay with him to ensure everything is okay."

He was vaguely aware of the look the couple shared before Lena moved away from the ship to stand beside Aerin. It became difficult to focus on anything beyond needing to get inside the ship and find her.

Even if the very idea of it terrified him.

Fear wasn't an emotion he'd felt since his rebirth; most of his emotions had disappeared since the matrix had been introduced into his body. Feeling something, *anything*, now was nearly as overwhelming as the thought of having a mate. It didn't stop him from stepping into the ship and making his way down the narrow corridor toward where he knew the stasis tubes were. Rykal trailed closely behind him; his presence was a combination of annoyance and reassurance to Hallam.

With each step he took deeper into the ship, the clawing painful itching grew in intensity. Strangely, the pain helped guide him into the ship's loading bay, the location of the stasis tubes. The small part of his mind that was still able to think logically was appalled at the disrepaired nature of the medical setup. How had they survived travel from the valley to the medical building, let alone having spent any time in space? The computers were old and not of a sufficiently advanced technology to ensure the safety of all the occupants.

"This place is horrendous." He ignored Rykal's chuckle and moved close to the tubes.

"They traveled a great distance with nothing to protect them. By rights, they shouldn't have survived."

Ignoring the drive to keep moving, Hallam paused next to the closest tube to examine the person inside. "These humans are foolish."

"No. I'd say they're more determined. Though a certain degree of foolishness would be required to undertake a journey such as this."

Hallam ignored the woman inside the tube, knowing it wasn't his mate. He could feel her sleeping, knew that she was off to the left near the back close to the wall. She'd picked that chamber out specifically because of the wall – though he didn't know *how* he knew that – and that she was resting comfortably.

"You can feel her now." Rykal moved down the small passageway between the rows of tubes. "Is the itching unbearable?"

"Yes." He wanted to hold himself back, try to show some of the restraint and calm that he'd become known for.

It was impossible.

Hallam turned sharply and marched over to the stasis tube he knew she was in. His heart raced and the anger and itching rose to a level he couldn't handle. Placing his hand on the tube, he pulled in a sharp, shaky breath. "This is her."

Rykal moved quickly and was by his side before Hallam could do anything else. "Lena will have to wake her. They don't understand our language and we'll need to inject her with the nanobots. The process is painful for them and we've learned its better for Lena to walk them through where they've landed and what's happening before we introduce ourselves."

Yes, that all made complete sense to him.

Instead of moving away, Hallam looked down at the computer for the stasis tube and was able to understand the basics of the controls. It only took him a moment to press in a sequence that brought the stasis tube to live.

"Hallam, stop!"

He ignored Rykal and waited as the systems churned to life. There was no way he'd let another person do anything to her, not even one of her own kind. He was the greatest medical mind that the Fallen had on this planet and he'd do what he needed to do to wake her up.

Gods, he hadn't even seen her face properly yet.

"Hallam, step away from the tube. You've woken her up. You did what you needed to. Now let Lena and her people do the rest."

He moved forward, hesitating for a moment before looking down into the window revealing his mate.

Her face was round, surrounded by a mass of black curly hair. She had full lips and a thin nose that gave her delicate look. But anyone who'd undergo this type of journey had to be strong to survive. Hallam wouldn't make the mistake of underestimating her abilities.

"Hallam?"

The stasis tube hissed and churned as it came to life. He had no idea how long it would take for it to wake her up, but Hallam would wait until that eventuality. The pain in his brain was still increasing, and as her mind rose up from the depths of her unconsciousness, he could feel it sharpening.

"Lena! I need you in here!"

Hallam couldn't look away from her, even as he knew Rykal was moving around him. *Don't touch me. Leave us alone. She's mine and you can't have her.*

"I don't want her. But we must make sure that she's okay, that there haven't been any problems." Rykal hesitated. "Lena is here. You need to move so she can look after her passenger. Then we'll give you time to get to know one another."

The redhead was beside him, looking down at the stasis tube. "I don't know how, but he appears to have triggered everything properly. Ina should be waking up shortly."

Hallam didn't know what happened, but in a blink, he had his hand around Lena's throat and pressed her small body up against the wall. "Leave her alone!"

Rykal was on him in a flash, yanking him hard as he slammed his cybernetic arm down on Hallam's. "Let go of my mate or I'll rip every cybernetic implant from your steaming corpse."

Rage flowed through Hallam, but he didn't know if it was from him or Rykal; maybe both. It took several beats before he was able to get a handle on the surge of anger, the mix of possessive desire and fear that he hadn't felt ever in his life or rebirth. With effort, he released his grip on Lena and stumbled backward away from them all. "I'm sorry."

"Are you hurt?" Rykal swiftly pulled Lena into his arms before checking her over. "Do you need a medic?"

"I'm fine." She let out a strangled cough before waving Rykal away. "I still need to make sure Ina is okay once she wakes. You're going to have to get him out of here so I can do my job."

All he wanted to do was stay and ensure that his mate was healthy and breathing, but Hallam knew he wouldn't be able to stop himself from surging at Lena again if he was here. "The system still needs...another one of the passengers to be revived. I...can look at the records in my office." He chanced a glance over at Lena, hating to see bruises already forming on her neck. "There's a medkit close. I'll have Aerin bring it to you."

With another possessive surge threatening to spill over and wipe away what little control he had left, Hallam turned and fled.

CHAPTER THREE

One moment, Ina was dreaming about fields of green grass, fresh air and clear blue skies, and the next she was flooded with a rush of cool liquid in her veins and flashes of bright lights. She'd been under cryo sleep enough times to recognize the signs of waking up far sooner than most of the other passengers would have. The part of her mind that knew what was happening, helped her body relax into the sensations, knowing that it would speed the process.

The moment she was able to blink, Ina did so. Her vision was still blurred, but that had more to do with her degenerative vision problems and less with her waking up. She swallowed several times, trying to bring the moisture back into her mouth so she could say something to whoever was waking her up – most likely Lena.

"I slept in, didn't I?" She smiled up, blinking a few times more. "Sorry mom."

"Lazing about, being all drugged and stuff." Lena's voice. "I bet you're now pretending like you can't see or something stupid."

"Never." Ina let Lena help her sit up, bracing herself for the inevitable headrush that would happen. "So, we didn't blow up in an asteroid belt somewhere. That's awesome."

"We did not. In fact, we made it to our destination mostly in one piece." There was an odd note in Lena's voice that Ina hadn't picked up on initially, her brain still sluggish from the cryo sleep. "We've found ourselves a new home and a whole lot more."

"That sounds like a story you have to tell me. But I think I could use a drink before we get into it if that's okay?"

"Sure. Ah, one moment." Lena gave her shoulder a gentle squeeze before stepping away from the stasis tube.

Shit, they'd *actually* made it. When Ina first heard about Lena's plan to take a ship out to the middle of the unknown, she's initially laughed at the insanity of it all. A group of humans on a ship with little to no shields or weapons heading out on a one-way trip into the unknown? The thought of success was distant at best. But the longer she considered it, the more Ina realized that she needed to go. Despite her misgivings, despite the foolish nature of what they were setting out to accomplish, she knew in her heart that if she didn't get on the ship and willingly put herself into stasis, she'd regret it for the rest of her life.

This wasn't about her losing her position with Earth's engineering corps, or even her diminishing eyesight; though both of those factors had certainly help her make the final decision. She wasn't able to afford the laser surgery needed to correct her retina deterioration – God, only the richest families on Earth could afford such luxuries – and she couldn't work or else risk her retina detaching completely and losing her vision going for good. The chances that she'd end up someplace where her impairment wouldn't be a liability was slim. Ina had even told Lena as much when she'd finally approached the captain about booking passage. Thankfully for her, Lena was up for the challenge.

Hopefully, she was as well.

"Ina? I have that water for you. I'm also here with someone

who has a medkit." Lena's face was clearer now as the remnants of the cryo sleep agents were working through her body. But the flashes and floaters still made it difficult for Ina to see. Lena handed her a bottle of water and nodded toward a woman who most obviously wasn't human. She was taller than Lena by several inches and her short blonde hair was slicked back to reveal a cybernetic implant on the side of her face, and glowing brown eyes. "This is Aerin. She's a medic and is going to look you over."

"Clearly, we're not alone in the universe. Hello Aerin."

"They don't speak Earth standard, so I'll have to act as an interpreter until we inject you with some nanobots." The way Lena dropped that startling revelation sounded as though she'd said it more than once already.

The woman nodded and smiled softly. "*La tu.*" She reached out and Ina immediately saw her hand was also cybernetic. She said something to Lena, who nodded along before turning back to Ina.

"She said hello. Also, that she's going to conduct a quick scan to ensure you don't have any pathogens that they need to address before she lets you out of containment."

"Fair enough." There were enhanced people back on Earth, but their cybernetics were normally only enough to give people an edge in their jobs or bragging rights. The little she was able to see of Aerin was enough to tell her that these enhancements were far more extensive and advanced than anything they had on Earth.

The engineer part of her desperately wanted to ask far too many inappropriate questions. The rest of her knew better and made herself wait until a better time.

The scan only took a few moments and before Ina would have expected, Aerin was analyzing the results. Frowning, she said something quickly to Lena who nodded. "Yeah, we knew that. Will it be a problem if we inject her with the nanobots?"

"What's going on?"

"Aerin found the problem with your eyes. It's exactly what you were told it was back on Earth. I just want to make sure that the nanobots we need to inject you with so you can understand what everyone is saying won't cause you problems. The last thing I want is for your sight to be taken from you just so you can carry on a conversation."

Aerin shook her head and said something else. Lena cocked her head to the side and snorted. "Really? That's actually perfect."

"What is?" Ina hated not knowing what was being said. "And if you were waiting for my permission or something for these nanobots, consider it given."

"Sorry, I still suck at this whole waking people up routine." She turned fully to Ina and smiled. "Apparently, she can reprogram the nanobots to also do the repairs on your eyes at the same time it reprograms your brain so you can understand everyone. It will hurt like a bastard, but you won't have to worry about losing your vision."

Ina had to admit that there'd been a part of her that had hoped wherever they'd end up, someone on the other side would have a means to help her. Now with the real possibility of a cure nearly in her grasp, Ina didn't want to risk hoping that everything would be okay. The thought of losing her sight had terrified her in a way nothing else on Earth ever had. Not the environmental catastrophe they skirted around daily, nor the thought of being unemployed in a city where the weak and poor tended to end up dead.

No, the thought of being alone in the dark, completely dependant on the goodwill of others, of not knowing where she was, what was around her, *who* was around her was too much to comprehend.

Relief and fear mixed inside her equally. "That's…amazing."

Lena gave her hand another squeeze. "Okay. Aerin is going to do what she needs to do then and I'm going to hang out here with you. Is it okay to let her out of the stasis tube?"

Aerin nodded before heading over to a station to work.

"I guess that's a yes." Lena clapped her hands together. "Well alrighty. Let's get you up and moving."

"And you can fill me in on where we ended up and how you came to be such buddies with cyborgs." As Lena helped her out of the stasis tube, Ina noticed bruises on her throat. "Are you okay? What the hell happened to you?"

Lena chuckled. "Honestly, both of those answers are linked. And it's more than a short explanation."

"I think we have time." Pain and stiffness traveled up her legs as Ina put her full weight on them. "I hate this part of cryo sleep."

"Yeah, waking up sucks hard." Lena let go but stayed close enough in case Ina needed her. "As you've been able to see, the destination point we reached was inhabited. There are two peoples here. The Grus live on a space station that orbits this planet. The Fallen are cyborgs. They were born Grus, but died in a war and brought back to life. We think that they're the reason we came out here. The twenty-eight of us on the ship are each linked to a cyborg here. At least, we have been to this point."

Ina stopped moving and could only stare at Lena as she spoke. The flashes and floaters were annoying, but even they couldn't distract her from what she was being told. "We're linked to people of another race?"

"Yeah. Well, linked is a bit of a gentle way to put it. It turns out that we are each destined to be with a specific cyborg. Rykal is the leader of the Fallen here on the planet. He was aware of my presence the moment the Kraken floated into their sector of space." Something in her expression changed, softened as she spoke of him. "He's determined to keep his people safe, but he risked everything to find me, to make sure that I was okay."

"That sounds intense." Ina had been in a few relationships over the course of her life but none of them had sparked the passion of feelings that Lena clearly had for this Rykal. "Is he the reason you have bruises on your neck?"

"God no. He'd sooner cut off his own arm than do anything to hurt me." She smiled softly for a moment before it morphed into a grimace. "Umm, actually it was your mate who did this."

Ina froze. "I'm not going to be mated to anyone who would hurt another person. You can tell him to fuck right off."

"No no no no no, it's not like that at all." Lena sighed, letting her head fall backward. "I swear to God, I'm going to appoint someone else to do this orientation stuff. I fucking suck at it."

Ina didn't know Lena well, but she'd never come across as someone who exaggerated, or who wasn't totally honest with the people around her. She deserved the opportunity to tell the entirety of the story before Ina jumped to conclusions or panicked. "If he's not abusive, then what happened to your neck?"

"One of the reasons we haven't brought everyone out of stasis immediately has to do with the reactions of the linked cyborgs. You're only the fourth person, and each time the cyborgs have reacted possessively. Rykal told me it was as though all the programming in his matrix got overloaded and he was left with only the most basic of desires. When they were brought back to life, most of their emotions didn't come along with them, making things challenging. When someone gets too close to the woman they see as their mate, then that aggressiveness spikes. Apparently, Hallam is normally a calm dude. He's the doctor in charge of all the cyborgs here on the planet."

A doctor? God, her mother would be thrilled. "Where is he now?"

"I think he went to his office or something. Rykal went to make sure he stayed there until we had a chance to wake you up and fill you in. The whole concept takes some getting used to."

"That's the understatement of the century."

Ina had wanted to come out here on the Kraken, wanted to see what her life could be like far away from the constraints and problems of Earth. Until she'd developed issues with her eyes, her entire life had been about work, fixing things, and saving the planet as much as they possibly could. But there'd always been a hole in her life. Something had been missing and no matter how hard she'd tried to fill it, nothing seemed to help.

Maybe she was destined to be with this Hallam person, or maybe it was yet another thing that would turn out to be little more than a temporary fix for a problem Ina wouldn't be able to solve.

Aerin came back over with an injector and held it up for her to see. Lena let out a breath. "Okay, this is going to hurt like a bastard. I'm serious. Pain like you haven't felt before is going to slam into your brain and make you want to pass out. You won't and it should be over quickly. Just try and relax into it as much as you can manage."

Well, at least she couldn't claim that Lena hadn't warned her. Reaching out for the side of the stasis tube, she got a solid grip on it before shooting both women a smile. "Now what?"

Aerin moved closer and pressed the injector to the space behind Ina's ear, letting the nanobots flood her body. Ina was half expecting there to be a delay in the pain Lena had mentioned, but no, within a few seconds her brain felt as though it was going to explode out of her skull.

She cried out and doubled over as her vision swam and sick rose up her throat. She was either going to pass out or throw up, neither option appealing. But as quickly as the pain in her head started, the waves began to recede, making it easier for her to think. Her vision didn't clear though, if anything she was seeing less than she had before the nanobots had been injected into her.

"What's happening?" Ina squeezed the side of the stasis tube, needing to stay grounded as the blackness overtook her sight. "I can't see!"

"Shit. Aerin, what's going on?"

"*Ye cha* to calm. *Troca* Hallam will be able to *mag*. I'll contact him."

"I can understand her. The words sound like Earth standard." If she wasn't so freaked out about suddenly being blind, Ina knew she'd want to learn all she could about the technology.

"Well, that's something at least." Lena reached out for her. "Let me get you over to a chair where you can sit. I suspect Rykal won't be able to keep Hallam from you much longer. Especially where you're hurt."

"What do you – "

"*What have you done to my mate?*"

The deep male voice sent a shiver through Ina's body, and somehow knew she would have recognized Hallam no matter the circumstances. And yet, she couldn't help but be more than a little annoyed at being treated as though she wasn't her own person with the ability to defend herself.

"Mate?" There was no mistaking the confusion in Aerin's voice. "How's that possible?"

Lena sighed. "It's a long story."

"No one has done anything to me." She felt the tension rise in the air as he moved closer to her. There was a *presence* to him that didn't require her vision for her notice. Unwilling to be intimidated by him, Ina sat straighter and looked toward the direction she knew he stood.

"Aerin, move back." Lena's whispered warning didn't help put Ina at ease.

Her mate had come for her, and Ina couldn't do a thing to stop him.

CHAPTER FOUR

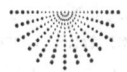

Hallam was ready to kill every person in the room. His body shook from his barely contained rage, making it difficult for him to walk toward her without wanting to break into a run. "I'm going to ask again. What have you done to my mate?"

The logic and reason that he prided himself on had fled from his brain. All that remained was the singular impulse to go to her and make everything better. Rykal was standing behind him, but Hallam knew his commander would be on him in an instant if Hallam made any move toward Lena. While they'd been sequestered in his office, Rykal had said little, as though he knew Hallam was unable to hear him or take to heart any wisdom he had to offer.

The people standing close to his mate – Ina – retreated as he grew closer. He was aware of Lena and her importance to Rykal and tried to keep his distance from her. One injury to Rykal's mate would be forgiven, a second would not. She did have the information he required, and he chanced a look in her direction.

Lena was not fragile and did not look away from the glare he shot her way. "We injected the nanobots into her after Aerin adjusted them to also correct an eye problem that Ina had."

Ina snorted. "They were supposed to fix my eyes, but they've somehow made me blind."

With difficulty, Hallam forced his logical side to the surface. "You're not blind. The nanobots are correcting your vision. This takes time."

Ina appeared to consider this, nodding. "When they're done correcting the damage then I should be able to see again."

"Better than before." He walked a circle around her, unable to focus on anything else. "Are you in any pain?"

"It's...disconcerting. The headache from the nanobots seems to have receded, but the backs of my eyeballs are itchy."

That was something that they had in common. The itching in the back of his brain that had started the closer she'd gotten to him was still there. He could feel the connection between them, especially now that she was standing in front of him. She was the source of his pain, his potential pleasure, the fixed point in the universe that was his and his alone.

Hallam stepped closer to her as Ina stiffened. "I won't hurt you."

"I...I'm sure that's true. But I can't see. I've only been awake for a short time after having flown across the galaxy to come here, and I'm more than a little freaked out knowing that you think that I'm your mate."

"You *are* my mate." Never had he been so certain of something in his entire life.

Ina was taller than Lena, her long black, curly hair fell across her shoulders like a wavy blanket. Her brown eyes might be blind, but he could see her emotions reflected in them: fear, confusion, determination. She was a formidable woman, someone who would attack her problems head-on. Exactly the type of female he'd been attracted to before his death and rebirth.

Hallam stepped closer to her, and this time she didn't flinch.

Instead, she turned toward him and looked up as though she was able to see him. He couldn't stop himself from cupping her face in his hands, needing to touch her, feel her skin beneath his. His cybernetic matrix flared as the onslaught of new code slammed into it, doing its best to regulate the sudden changes.

"No one will hurt you again. Intentional or otherwise." He leaned in and claimed a kiss, enjoying her soft gasp before he swallowed it up.

Hands pressed against his chest, pushing him away, gently at first, then harder. It was only when someone pulled him away from behind that Hallam realized Ina was trying to get away from him. "Let me go!"

"Brother, calm down." Rykal's grip unrelenting on his shoulder. "I know it's difficult, but you need to give her space. She's injured and scared."

"She's mine. Let me go – "

Rykal leaned in, his mouth close to Hallam's ear. "No one will take her. She'll be yours. But you need to be her doctor first. You need to treat her wounds. Heal her first. Let her get to know you and trust you before you give in to that pull. This will be the hardest thing you've ever done, but it will be the most rewarding."

Hallam pulled in a shaky breath as the tension inside him flowed away. Yes, of course he needed to help her. Needed to heal her vision and anything else that might be wrong with her. He was a doctor, genetically engineered to save lives and help others. And right now, she was the most important person in the galaxy.

"Yes." He swallowed and gave his matrix a moment to finalize the regulation of the adrenaline rush that had hit him. "I'm a doctor."

"That's right." Rykal stepped away, but Hallam wasn't worried. He knew he was back in control of his actions, even if it was tenuous.

"I'm sorry." This time when he moved closer to Ina, Hallam

was able to keep a respectable distance. "This connection between us is overpowering my logic centers."

Ina licked her lips before nodding. "That's okay. Lena told me that this link between our two peoples was unexpected on both sides. It stands to reason that we'll all make some mistakes."

Gods, she was beautiful and forgiving. "I'm concerned that the nanobots haven't completed their repairs to your eyes. I'd like to take you upstairs to the medical bay, while the others determine the second human who will need to be woken."

"I know we don't necessarily have the power," Lena took a single step toward him before stopping short, "but is there a way we can do this without waking another? Having two out of control cyborgs really doesn't feel like the best idea to go with."

"I've tried to find another way, but there simply isn't one. If we want to move them off your ship, at least one other must be woken." Given how powerful the urges to claim and possess were for him to keep under control, he had to agree with Lena's concerns. "Perhaps we can find a place to move the other woman that might shield the connection."

Rykal shook his head. "I felt Lena from across our sector of space. I doubt there's a room here on Zarlan that would stop a Fallen from feeling his mate."

This was a problem for the others to find a solution to. The only thing Hallam cared about was Ina and ensuring that she was healed. "I'll leave that to you. Ina," he reached out his hand and brushed his fingers softly against her arm, "would you come with me?"

He had to consider the possibility that she wouldn't. It was something his brain knew could happen, even if his baser desires wouldn't accept the possibility. These warring parts of his mind were maddening, especially as he felt his grasp on his control was slipping from him the longer he went without touching Ina.

Thankfully, she straightened and faced him. Holding out her

hand, she lifted her chin. "I'll need you to guide me. And I'd like Aerin to come with us."

No! Mine! Alone and no one else! He took a breath and momentarily closed his eyes before he took her hand in his. "Yes. Aerin is my assistant and will need to understand what's happening as well in case we need to perform similar repairs on the other passengers."

Ina visibly relaxed. "Thank you."

Rykal moved next to his mate. "Lena and I will try and determine the best option of who to wake up next. But we need to start unloading the stasis tubes now. The sooner we can get the Kraken out of here and ensure that the signal that was being broadcast out to the Sholle has been stopped, the better."

"Once we're done with Ina, I'll send Aerin back to assist you." Once Ina was comfortable with him, there would be no need for additional people with them. "For now, I'll send every available person I have to start the transfer."

"Thank you." Rykal looked as though he wanted to say something else, but instead turned to look at Lena. "We better get started."

Hallam didn't wait for anyone else, and instead guided Ina close to his side before leading her toward the hallway and the transportation tube. "Let me take you somewhere more comfortable."

She nodded, but he saw the muscles in her jaw and shoulders tighten. Of course, she'd be nervous being separated from the other humans and not being able to see where she was going. Ina was far braver that many of the Grus who orbited the planet, safe and secure in their space station. She was walking into the unknown with her chin held high. Not many could say they'd be capable of doing the same.

"The building you are in is old." The words left him unexpectedly, but the moment he said them Hallam knew it was the right thing. "I've been here for most of the time since the war between the Sholle and the Grus ended. My patients are primarily the Fallen. I believe Lena referred to us as cyborgs."

"She did." Ina's body relaxed slightly. "We have enhanced people on our planet, but not the same as what's been done to you. Humans like to try and be more than what we've born as, so we can't help but tinker with our bodies."

"The only tinkering that was done to us happened without our permission." Hallam still hated what Aidric had done to them all, even if it had been born out of desperation and the need to win a war or else be faced with total annihilation. "I was dead and had no voice."

Ina stopped moving, her horror at the revelation clear. "I'm so sorry."

"You did nothing to me." The bitterness was still there, an old festering wound that refused to close. Despite having helped Aidric in those early days, Hallam still blamed him.

"No, but I'm sorry that the decision was taken from you. No one should be forced to live a life they don't want." She then reached up and cupped his cheek.

The unexpected contact sent a jolt through his body that brought parts of him long dead roaring back to life. His cock grew hard and his *rondello* filled with blood, sending arousal coursing through him with surprising speed. He couldn't hold back a little gasp and reached for the wall to help keep him steady.

Ina pulled away. "What's wrong? Did I hurt you?"

"Hallam, are you well?" Aerin stepped close but kept more than an arm's length from him.

He'd somehow forgotten that she was with them. A flush of embarrassment chased his arousal away and made the moment even more unbearable. "I'm fine."

Aerin's eyes widened enough to tell him that she realized what had happened. She took a step back and nodded. "I'm going to go ahead and call the transportation tube. Ina, I'm still close."

"Okay." If Ina was worried about being left alone with him, she didn't show it. "Are you sure you're not hurt?"

Gods, if it was only that simple. "Our connection is having some unexpected results. We best continue."

Ina cocked her head to the side slightly before nodding. "Tell me more about this building."

The distraction helped give his matrix time to ease his arousal. "The walls had been damaged from the war and I've never bothered to restore much of the facility. The Fallen are rarely injured as our cybernetic matrixes can regulate and repair damage to our bodies. But there are instances where I need to repair cybernetic limbs, or even heal the occasional Grus who has become hurt, so there is a wing that we've identified as our primary base of operations."

"What color are the walls?"

It was a curious question to ask. "What does that matter?"

"I'm blind. It was the first thing that I wanted to know." She shrugged. "We tend to miss the things that we take for granted."

Hallam had missed many things after his rebirth; the feeling of peace he had whenever he'd wake up after a good sleep, the joy of discovering the perfect thing to say and put another person at ease, the excitement that would race through him whenever he'd make a discovery. His life had become a steady state of anger or empty, shifting between those states with little reason.

He took her gently by the arm and guided her toward the transportation tube. "The walls are gray. In this section, they are also marked with carbon scoring from blaster fire that happened during an attack. I should probably have them removed, covered or cleaned, but they serve as a testament to those who'd lost their lives."

The lucky ones who stayed dead.

"It feels colder here than it did in the other room. Is the air coming from outside or do you like the cold?" Ina's hold on his arm was light, but he was able to feel the heat bleeding from her body. "I might have to wear a thicker layer of clothing if I'm going to be spending any amount of time here."

"My cybernetic matrix regulates my internal temperature to optimal. But if you're cold, we can address that." He didn't want her to be uncomfortable, not if there was a simple solution to what ailed her. "The transportation tube is here."

"And so am I." Aerin stepped aside letting Hallam guide Ina inside. "Have the nanobots repaired your vision yet? Are you able to see anything at all?"

Ina shook her head, and her bottom lip stuck out slightly. "Not yet. The itching is still there though. They must still be working on the damage."

"We'll be better able to see what's going on once we get you to the medical room." Hallam gave her hand a gentle pat, even as another surge of possessive lust washed over him.

He had a tenuous grasp on his control, and he knew it wouldn't last for long. They needed to find out what was happening with her vision and why the nanobots weren't doing what Aerin had programmed them to do. Because it was only a matter of time before he'd no longer be able to hold himself back from claiming Ina as his own.

He wanted her in his bed and under his body. He wanted to hear what her voice would sound like when her orgasm claimed her. Wanted to feel her legs wrapped around his waist as he pushed deep inside.

Logic be damned.

CHAPTER FIVE

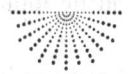

Ina hated being out of control – being blind was terrifying enough. But losing her sight and having to rely on people who she'd never met before, while staying in a building where she'd never been, on a *new fucking planet*, made the entire situation nearly unbearable.

If it wasn't for Hallam's constant presence, she would have broken down long ago. There might have even been some tears, though she rarely cried. Since his initial feral moments around her, he'd somehow managed to get control of his actions. Even without her vision, she could tell that he was struggling to maintain that emotional distance between them, and yet he hadn't regressed.

He did keep in constant physical contact with her. He kept his hands on her arm as he'd move around the examination table that he'd helped her sit on. Occasionally he'd reach up and move her hair from her face, or tuck some of the thick strands behind her ear. She should have told him that was a losing battle, but there was something sweet about the way he continuously tried to tame the curls.

Instead of fearing his touch, in a short period of time Ina had grown comfortable with it. She wished she could see his face, know what color his eyes or hair were, or even what his cybernetics looked like. She still couldn't quite wrap her head around the fact that he wasn't simply an enhanced human, but that he'd died and had been brought back to life. Who would do that to another person against their will? What had it felt like to die? To be reborn? Had it hurt? Had he found peace only for it to be ripped from his grasp?

The idea of dying had always terrified her. While she understood that it was a natural part of life, the entirety of the unknown element of what happened to the spirt after a body took its last breath was something that weighed on her. Usually, in the oddest moments.

It had been one of the factors that had driven her to space in the first place. She didn't want to live her entire life stuck in a rut, caught in the daily grind of necessary routine without taking a chance at something. Life was supposed to be exciting, at least in small bursts, and up until the moment she'd stepped foot onto the Kraken, Ina's life had been anything but.

Now, she had more than enough excitement to last a lifetime.

"I'm going to need you to stay still so we can run a scan of your head." Hallam moved to stand in front of her, and she couldn't help but turn her face to follow the sound of his voice. "The nanobots should have finished the repairs by now. I need to see if there's something stopping them from completing their task."

"Do you think there's more damage there than we initially thought? I knew I had a detaching retina, but maybe there was something else going on?"

If nanobots couldn't fix what was going on with her eyes, then there was a good chance that her new world of darkness would be a permanent state of being. She couldn't stop a shiver from passing through her.

"They've been programmed to heal, and they won't stop until

they've completed their task." Hallam put his hand on her thigh, and a different type of shiver passed through her body. The longer she spent in his presence, the more in tune she was becoming with him. He leaned closer, sliding his hand to her hip. "I won't let anything bad happen to you."

God, she wanted to believe that, even though she had no reason to trust him. "Thank you."

Maybe there really was a bond between them that ensured they would care for one another? It wasn't the weirdest thing she'd ever heard about happening in the universe, despite it not really making much sense. How the hell could two alien races have a connection across the vastness of space? The odds of them making the trip here in one piece and being connected with the group of people living here were astronomical.

"You're a thinker, aren't you?" There was a change in Hallam's voice, the barest hint of amusement. "I can practically see the thoughts race across your expression as they filter through your brain."

Ina felt her face flush. "Well, not all of us have a cybernetic matrix in our heads to regulate those types of things. I have to manage everything the hard way." He didn't say anything in response, which instantly made her wish she could see his face. "I'm sorry. That was thoughtless of me."

"No, you're correct. While I might not have wanted to be reborn or have my matrix, there have been benefits. I've had the luxury of my logic being at the forefront of my actions, driving everything that I do and say." His grip on her tightened, sending another shiver through her body. "Until you came, I never had to worry about control."

His voice was low, gravelly, seductive in a way that hit Ina deep inside her core. Her nipples hardened and her pussy grew wet as flashes of what that voice would sound like if he was naked against her, fucking into her body. Maybe there was a benefit to being blind? His touch against her skin felt far stronger than she'd ever experienced like this before. She could smell his scent, could hear a soft noise coming from him that she assumed had something to do with his cybernetics. "I wish I could see you."

Hallam hummed low. "Soon you'll get to explore as much of me as you'd like. Don't move."

The humming sound intensified as Hallam moved something around her head – no doubt, the aforementioned scanner. The itching in her eyes intensified and she had to fight not to scratch the itch. Hallam immediately turned the scanner off and she felt him moving around in front of her. "What's going on?"

He let out another low growl. "I had to stop the scan. I could feel your discomfort."

"That can't be possible. Can it?"

"I don't know." He paused, unmoving for a moment. "Rykal said that appears to be a common occurrence between Fallen and their mates. We're able to sense what you are feeling."

"Wait, is Rykal here?" Her head now ached, but she couldn't be sure if that was from the nanobots or simple exhaustion at having to figure too much out too quickly after coming out of cryo sleep.

"Our matrixes are able to connect with other Fallen when they are in proximity and we can communicate. It was designed for speed when we were on the battlefield."

Everything about them was designed for war. Ina couldn't help but feel for them. "At least its useful when you're not fighting."

"I might not have wanted this rebirth, but Aidric had chosen our skills wisely."

If Ina ever met this Aidric fellow, she was probably going to punch him. "Did your scan see anything off about the nanobots?"

Hallam paused and she could hear him pressing something. "Your retina is repaired, but they are working on healing an additional problem."

"What? I'd had a doctor check me over before I boarded the Kraken to come out here. Nothing turned up on their scans."

She didn't need to see him to sense his hesitation. "You have tumors in both of your optic nerves. Is this a common occurrence for your people?"

"Tumor? But...no, that's not common. Not in the eyes at least." She'd known plenty of people who'd worked engineering on the environmental systems who'd gotten sick over the years – cancer, tumor, lung issues – but Ina never had any signs of problems. If it hadn't been for her retina issues, she probably would still be working on the scrubbers trying to wring every bit of fresh oxygen she could out of them. "Is that something you can fix?"

"Yes. It's why the nanobots haven't finished their work. Based on these scans your vision should start to return within a few hours. Don't be surprised if your sight is blurry for a period after you're once again able to see." He moved closer to her again, once more placing his hand on her thigh. "I will look after you until then."

Oh, the promise those words held.

What would it be like to give herself over to a man without knowing who he was, what he looked like, what her surroundings were? The element of danger was there, though she didn't believe he would do anything to harm her, not after the care he'd taken up to this point. Her arousal had begun to grow, which was unusual for her. Her sex drive had been healthy over the years, but she'd never been one to take a bunch of risks with her body or her heart. Maybe there was some truth to this connection between them.

Hallam let out a soft growl. "I can feel your arousal. Your curiosity."

Shit. That was going to take some getting used to. "It's been a confusing few hours. I don't know what I'm thinking or feeling."

"Yes, you do. But I understand your desire to hold yourself

back." His hand moved back and forth along the top of her thigh, the weight of his hand reassuring as it was arousing. "You're safe with me here. Nothing will happen to you as long as there is breath in my lungs."

"God," she sucked in a breath. "You certainly know how to talk to a woman."

"I've never met a woman such as yourself. I haven't had feelings of anything but rage for so long I've forgotten how to exist in any other state of being." He cupped her cheek with his large hand. "I want to feel everything. You can help me live again."

Ina was many things – self-sufficient, cool under pressure, forward thinking – but a saint certainly wasn't one of them. It didn't matter to her what he looked like, his actions said more about who he was as a person than the color of his eyes. She sucked in a small, shuddering breath as she turned her face against his hand. "Will my recovery be disrupted if I were to engage in any physical activity?"

"Aerin, please go back to the loading bay and assist Rykal with the unloading of the stasis tubes."

Ina had temporarily forgotten about the other woman. She felt her face heat again but did her best to push her embarrassment away. "I'm okay, Aerin. I'm sure Rykal and Lena would appreciate the help."

"If you're certain." She could tell from Aerin's tone that she understood what was about to happen between them. "I'll wait to hear from you."

There was a shuffling of feet, the whoosh of the door opening and finally silence.

They were alone.

Ina hadn't been alone with a man with the intention of having sex for months before she'd left Earth for space. It wasn't as though she were avoiding being intimate, but no one had appealed to her in any particular way. She'd had more than a few fantasies though, and that had kept her occupied as she'd bring herself to orgasm alone in her bed.

But now with Hallam here, the very real feel of his body close to hers, knowing that in the next few moments they'd strip naked and she'd finally be able to feel the press of his body against hers was all she could think about. She sucked her bottom lip into her mouth for a moment before smiling up at him. "Is this where you lose control and throw me on a bed?"

She'd been going for humor, so she was a little surprised when he let out a growl that was less than playful. "I'm scared that I'll hurt you if I lose control."

There was so much concern, fear in his voice she could feel it come off him in waves. This time, Ina reached up and placed her hand over his that still cupped her cheek. "You won't hurt me. And if you do, I know you'll be able to make everything better."

"Ina." His body shook.

"On Earth, that's the name of my planet, we have a thing we do called a one-night stand. That's when people mutually agree to have sex without any commitments for any type of relationship beyond the night. I know you think I'm your mate, and I'm honestly not sure how I feel about that. But in this moment, I'm overwhelmed by everything that's happened. I'm temporarily blind and could really use some physical comfort. I want you to be with me. It's my choice. Everything else we can figure out later."

Hallam's response was to scoop her in his arms and march her toward what she seriously hoped was a bed. She might not know the future, but at least for the next few moments, she had control of what was happening.

CHAPTER SIX

The last grasp of Hallam's control snapped the moment Ina stopped talking. Her wisdom and reason for why she wanted to be with him was pushed aside by the simple feel of her longing to be touched that had hit him. She hadn't seen the extent of his cybernetic implants, but in a few moments, she'd feel them against her warm skin. He couldn't guess how she'd respond, but if the Gods were on his side, then she wouldn't care.

His quarters weren't far away from the examination room. He'd chosen them specifically so he could be available to anyone who needed him with little delay. Now, he was grateful for a completely different reason. Ina's body was light in his arms. She'd turned against his chest as she'd looped one arm around his neck, while the other gripped his arm. He could feel the puffs of her breath across his neck, teasing his skin with the promise of the intimacy to come.

He wanted her. Wanted to consume as much of her as she would allow. Long ago before the war, Hallam's passions had run deep and he'd savored the intimacies he'd shared with others. That part of him had died – or so he'd thought – with his rebirth.

But holding Ina in his arms, it surged back to life, clawed its way to the surface of his psyche and leaving nothing in its wake.

Gods, he didn't want to hurt her.

The door to his quarters slid open as the itching in the back of his brain intensified. This was what he'd wanted from the moment he'd became aware of her existence. Lust surged through him, his cock and *rondella* surged in time with his desires. The bed was small, something he never used, but remained present as a throwback to a time when the Grus lived and worked here. Now, Hallam eyed it and hoped it would be enough for both their weights.

He set her down so she could stand, not wanting to let her go but knowing the brief separation was necessary. "I need to adjust the bed."

"That sounds ominous."

He couldn't detect any feelings of concern from her, so he let the statement go. "It's not large enough to accommodate both of us." He moved around to the control panel to press a few buttons to enlarge it. "This still won't be ideal, but better than nothing."

The moment the bed finished expanding to the largest size the small room would allow, Hallam turned his attention back to Ina.

Gods, she was beautiful.

The mass of black curls were floating around her face as though the strands of hair had come to life and were yelling *look at this woman here waiting for you*. He did look, let his gaze roam across her body, taking in the swell of her breasts hidden by her clothing. He lingered on her lips and how she'd bite down or suck on her bottom lip whenever she began to grow nervous. Her brown unseeing eyes would flit around whenever she'd hear a sound, chasing the noise while she clearly tried to determine its origin.

"Hallam?" She pouted as she laced then unlaced her hands in front of her. "Is everything okay? I thought you were about to throw me on your now larger bed and have your way with me?" Again with the teasing, something he wasn't used to experiencing.

Another surge of possessive want slammed into him. His body shook from the potency of the emotions, as his will to hold back crumbled. "If I hurt you – "

"You won't."

"I might. I...my control is slipping from me."

"Who said you always need to be in control?" She shrugged and smiled. "Sometimes the best things in life happen when we stop trying to make things happen. Letting go can be freeing."

Hallam took two giant steps to close the distance between them pulling Ina into his arms and swallowed down her surprised gasp with a searing kiss. The contact of her mouth on his had his cock pulse, forcing him to grind it against her stomach as he teased her tongue with his. The itching in his head receded to the point where he was able to focus his attention on the sounds that slipped from Ina, paying attention to the ones that came when he cupped her breast in his hand and squeezed.

She tipped her head back and let out a gasp when he captured her nipple between his thumb and forefinger. Having cybernetic limbs had proven ideal as a doctor, providing him with a precision of touch that wasn't possible to achieve as a Grus. He hadn't considered the advantage it would also offer him as a lover. The ability to apply the exact amount of pressure through her clothing and against her nipple that would pull a moan from her was perfect.

What would be even better was to see what sounds he could elicit from her naked.

He pulled back long enough to strip his shirt off and remove his boots. Ina clearly knew what he was doing and began to strip off her clothing. Thank the universe and evolution for having their two peoples develop in such a way that they were clearly sexually compatible. Hallam watched enthralled as bit by bit of her skin was revealed to him. Her long black curls slipped forward to cover the tops of her full breasts, highlighting the hard, pink nipples that rose up from them. He didn't wait to remove his pants before lunging at her, forcing them both into a tumble down onto the bed.

She was small beneath him, but she didn't seem to mind the press of his weight down on her, nor the way he sucked her nipple hard into his mouth to nip and tease the tip with his teeth.

"Fuck." She thrashed her head from side to side, before she reached up with her hands to slide them across his back. "Yes."

When her fingers reached the seam of where his cybernetic arms were connected to his torso, he felt her body stiffen. He wanted to stop, to explain to her what had happened to him, tell her about the extent of the damage his body had sustained in the war, and what had been done to him to bring him back to life. All those explanations would have to wait.

The only thing he could focus on was the silent beat *mine* and *now* ringing through his head.

"Hallam?"

"Mine." He leaned his head forward and nipped at the junction of her shoulder and neck, knowing he'd soon place his mark on her. "Now."

"Hallam, I – ." She gasped as he pinched her nipple again before sliding his hand down and between her legs to explore the most intimate part of her. "God."

She was wet and had hair between her legs, a physical trait that Grus women did not have. He pulled back so he could see her better, while giving him the opportunity to remove his pants, leaving him fully naked. "You're different from the women of my race."

"Too different?" She blinked rapidly, as though she was trying to clear her vision. "Is this going to work? I hadn't even considered that we'd be too different."

Instead of answering, he pushed her thighs further apart –

noting that she didn't have a *rondollo*, the female sex gland that resided on the upper thigh – before pushing a finger deep into her wet and waiting body. Ina gasped and bucked her hips up against his hand, which brought a smile to his lips. "We're compatible."

"Oh, thank fuck."

The hair was a fascination that he'd explore later; now he needed to feel her body around his cock, to enjoy the press of his expanding *rondella* against her leg. This was what it felt like to be alive again, something he'd hadn't realized how much he'd missed until now. Bracing his hands on either side of her body, he lined up his cock and with a single motion, he thrust into her fully.

Ina gasped as her body stilled and she adjusted to his size. He could feel her tangle of emotions tumble inside her; desire, fear, embarrassment. He couldn't imagine what she had to be embarrassed about – everything about her was perfect. It was his responsibility as her mate to show her that perfection with the reverence she was due.

"You're mine." He said the words again, but this time he leaned close and sucked her earlobe into his mouth. "I'm yours."

She shivered again. "Show me."

Hallam pressed his face against her throat and began to fuck her in earnest. The squeeze of her inner muscles around his cock pulled a moan from him and sent his matrix into overload trying to compensate for the onslaught of sensations bombarding him. Everything about Ina's body was soft, warm and inviting. He didn't want those sensations to be dulled, to be regulated away until they were nothing more than a series of cold inputs. For the first time since his rebirth, Hallam wanted to *feel*, wanted to drown himself in sensations until he no longer felt dead inside.

Ina continued to meet his thrusts with her own. Her breasts rubbed against his chest and he felt the slide of her hard nipples against his skin. The itching in his head grew frenzied, driving him forward toward something he didn't completely understand. The silent chant of *mine, mine, mine,* grew louder, more incessant until he could think of nothing else.

His kisses grew harder, his touch stronger. He licked the juncture of her neck and shoulder before opening his mouth and slowly biting down. Ina gasped, but she didn't pull away, even as he increased the pressure.

Gods, what was he doing? He didn't want to hurt her, but he also couldn't stop himself from leaving his mark on her. His *rondella* tingled and he could feel the approach of his pre-orgasm, something that hadn't happened to him in so long his couldn't retrieve the memory from his matrix.

Ina pushed her fingers into his hair and tugged at his head. "Suck my nipples. Please, I'm so close."

He should do as she requested, give her the pleasure that she desired. He even tried to move his mouth away, but he couldn't release his bite. Instead, he shifted so he could capture her nipple once more between his fingers and pulled. Ina groaned, her muscles flexing around his cock as he felt her orgasm slide closer.

She's mine and no one elses. Mine to take and fuck and love and hold.

The rush of pleasure washed through his body as his pre-orgasm fired his nerves and woke up the long dead part of his soul. He growled against her body and fucked into her harder than before.

"Shit, Hallam." Ina moaned as she gripped his hair and pulled her body hard against him. "Yes."

Gods, he wanted to wait, wanted to ensure her pleasure came before he succumbed to his, but his release was getting dangerously close. Thankfully, she arched her back off the bed and with a stifled cry, he felt her orgasm wash through her. The dual sensations of her body squeezing around him and the slam of her emotional euphoria, pushed past the last of his resolve.

Hallam bit down hard on her shoulder as pleasure stronger

than he'd ever experienced in his life or rebirth hit him like a powerful blast. He was only vaguely aware of Ina's physical discomfort from his actions as he spilled his seed deep inside her body. Pleasure blasted through his matrix, overloading it to the point where it was no longer able to regulate his code. He finally was able to open his mouth, lift his head and let out a roar as the final waves of pleasure rolled through him.

Then everything went black.

When he became aware of his surroundings once more, it wasn't the feel of the bed beneath him, or the warmth of the other presence beside him that caught his attention. He had to wait for his matrix to come back up to full capacity before he understood what it was that he was hearing.

Ina was crying.

Hallam pushed himself up onto his arm and looked down at her, frantic concern surging inside him. "What's wrong?" He immediately began to scan her body and cringed at the sight of the purple bruise on the side of her neck and top of her shoulder. "I harmed you."

Her face was turned away from him. "You did, but that's not why I'm crying."

"Why then?"

She opened her mouth, but instead of words another sob popped from her lips. Hallam pulled her into his arms and held her while she cried, at a loss for what to do for her. Even before his rebirth he'd never been with a female long enough to share some of the gentler emotions that the Grus engaged in. They'd fall into bed, enjoy their time together, kiss and be on their way. They were arrangements that suited Hallam's nature.

But hearing Ina cry stirred something inside him he hadn't known existed before. Something so foreign he couldn't put a label on what it might be. Instead, he held her against him and puzzled over how he could fix this problem.

Time passed and her sniffles lessened. Hallam discovered that she enjoyed having her hair stroked, that she'd nestled closer to him when he ran his fingers down her back, and that the feel of tears against his skin was oddly soothing. Eventually, Ina reached up and began to touch his chest in a similar exploratory manner. Her fingers drifted once more across the seams of where his cybernetic arms were joined to his torso. She then paused and he felt her pull back slightly.

"Do these bother you?" He hoped not because there wasn't anything he could do about his limbs. The Sholle had taken them from him in the explosion, and Aidric had given him these in return.

She shook her head and pulled back some more. "No."

"What then?"

Ina looked up at him, a small smile on her face. "I think my sight is coming back. I can see again."

CHAPTER SEVEN

Ina blinked several times trying to clear the gray fuzz from her eyes, but it wouldn't quite leave. She was able to make out Hallam's shape, though his body was lacking any sort of depth. "I…it's not fully back, but definitely better than before."

"Good. The nanobots will repair most of the damage and if there is anything left behind I'll be able to fix the rest."

The fear she'd previously felt fell away and for the first time since Aerin pressed the injector to the side of her neck, Ina was able to relax. "Thank God."

While she knew she would have learned to adapt to her blindness if that had been her fate, she was relieved to know that she wouldn't have to stumble her way through life on an alien world and forced to rely on others for everything. It wasn't that she couldn't accept help when it was offered, but that she didn't trust the person doing the offering didn't have an ulterior motive for the gesture.

Life back on Earth wasn't pleasant with everyone doing what they needed to in order to survive. Even in her position as an engineer on the environmental units, a position of some recognition and prestige, she'd constantly had to watch her back in case one of her colleagues tried to take her down to claim her position as their own. After years of looking over her shoulder, she hoped her new life would allow her to stop constantly worrying about what might happen next. Brighter days were finally here for her.

Still, her vision wasn't back yet and hopefully it wouldn't take longer than a few hours at the rate the nanobots were working. That meant she'd have to push past her fears a bit longer and hope Hallam wasn't going to suddenly change on her. She really hoped not, because for the first time in her life she felt as though she might be able to have a relationship of sorts. Of all the things that had happened to her since deciding to board the Kraken, that revelation was the one that surprised her the most.

Pain on her shoulder and neck reminded her that Hallam was far from the normal human male she was used to. "Do all cyborgs bite when you're having sex? That really hurt, but I was a bit too busy coming to stop you."

He shifted away from her to sit up. "Cyborgs don't normally have sex. You're the only woman I've been with since my rebirth."

Another revelation that caught Ina off guard. "Really? Did your sex drives just not come back with you?" She cringed the moment the question left her lips. "Sorry, that was awful of me to ask."

"They did not. Most of us had more pressing concerns after our rebirth. Adjusting to our new realities was harder than anyone expected. Plus, we were immediately thrust back into a war with significant changes to our bodies." The anger in his voice was painfully clear, and she could only imagine how difficult things must have been for him.

Hallam pushed away from her and climbed out of the bed, only to pace around the small room. She couldn't see any of his features, but her vision had improved enough that she could make out a difference in the tone and color of his arms, and one of his legs from the rest of his body. The cybernetics were far more advanced than anything they had on Earth, and the engineering side of her was more than a little curious about the science and technology behind them. That curiosity was swallowed up by guilt. How was she any better than the people who'd thrust these enhancements on him if all she saw was his cybernetics, and not the man behind them who was still hurting?

Ina wanted to go to him but didn't fully trust herself with her visual limitations. Instead, she sat up and swung her legs over the side of the bed, grabbing the think blanket to wrap around her body when she shivered from the cold. "What did you do in the war? Were you a doctor then as well?"

"I was a medical technician." He stopped moving, and she was able to see a soft light from his cybernetics start to pulse. "My matrix allowed me to gather and retain knowledge that I wouldn't have previously been able to process. My abilities allowed me to be efficient on the battlefield and save many lives that would have otherwise been lost."

"So, you're a hero." She wasn't surprised by that revelation. There'd been something about him, an aura of competence that radiated with his every action. "What have you done since the war ended?"

A computer in the room beeped several times, an indicator or message of some sort. Hallam crossed the room, moving out of her limited field of view. She heard him press something before speaking once again.

"Report."

"All life signs from patient three have ceased." The sterilized voice of the computer echoed in the small room. "Notification of end of life protocol initiated and awaiting approval."

Hallam didn't say anything initially. Ina strained to hear what he might be doing, of any indication about how he may be feeling. Every so often, she'd get a sense of...something from him, but it was difficult. He kept himself so tightly wrapped emotionally, it was difficult for her to know. Finally, there was the sound of movement before his voice – now firmer – reached her.

"Protocol approved. Also send notifications to Rykal and Commander Aidric."

"Acknowledged and completed."

Ina heard the computer sign off and Hallam move once more. He stopped in front of her and she could tell the death was hitting him on an emotional level. She couldn't help but wonder if this was the first time he was experiencing the death of a patient in this way, and if her connection to him was the cause. Ina took his hand in hers and gave it a squeeze. "I'm sorry for your loss."

He didn't return the gesture and let her hand fall. "You're my mate."

Ina's head hurt at the sudden change in topic. "That's what everyone keeps telling me. I'm not exactly sure how I feel about the revelation yet."

"I did not ask for a mate. This is yet another thing that's been forced upon me."

His words felt as though someone had hit her in the face. "I'm not forcing anything on you. And I believe it was you and your crazy possessiveness like an hour ago who was forcing the whole *you're my mate and let's fuck* thing." She might not have been completely on board initially, but Ina had enjoyed herself. What she wasn't prepared to do was take responsibility for something that she'd had no part in initiating, or even understood the underpinnings of why it had happened in the first place.

Standing up was difficult, especially since the gray blur was still present. Still, she wasn't going to sit here with a man she didn't know, and be on the receiving end of anger that had resulted from a situation she hadn't been involved with. She'd go sit in the hallway and wait for Aerin before she'd do that. "I can't see where my clothing fell. Please hand it to me."

"No." Hallam's voice had somehow deepened, and the predatory sound sent a chill through her.

"You don't want me here as your mate. You're clearly angry

about the loss of your patient and there isn't anything I can do about either of those factors. I'm going to get dressed and find my way back to Lena and the Kraken. I might be blind, but I still have a brain in my head and can help with the stasis tubes and the ship." Straightening as much as she could, Ina hopped she looked more confident that she felt. "My clothing please. Now."

Hallam didn't hesitate this time, reaching for and handing her the few articles of clothing she'd been wearing upon her arrival. There was something strangely intimate getting dressed in front of him, even when she knew he wasn't staring directly at her as she did. This was the sort of thing lovers or couples did, not two strangers who'd only known each other for a few hours. Ina felt warmer if not more secure once she had dressed and slipped her boots back on. She might not be able to see where she was going, but at least now if she had to run, she wouldn't be naked. "I'm leaving."

"You still can't see."

"Then I'll wait until someone else can help me."

"I'll take you back to Lena and the Kraken." This time he let out a growl and she could see him shake his head. "But I need to see to my patients first. The stasis tubes will put a strain on my resources, and I need to ensure no one else dies."

He might not have wanted his rebirth and the responsibilities that had come with them, but Hallam took them seriously. That was something she couldn't help but respect. "Fine. Ask Aerin to come get me and then you'll be free to do what you need to do."

She felt him sway closer to her, but he somehow held back from touching her. "You're staying with me."

Interesting. He might not want her as his mate, but there were forces at work that were pulling them together. Maybe she *was* better off with him for the time being. At least for now he had a certain degree of control over his actions. If they separated, he might revert into the mad animalistic being he'd been when she'd first met him.

Plus, she couldn't help but think she might be acting a bit selfish in her fear. He had a job to do, one that was important and her presence only complicated. She'd never forgive herself if one of his patients died because he wasn't able to focus on them. "Fine. But as soon as you're done, I'd like to go back to the ship."

"As you wish." He wrapped his hand around her arm and guided her forcefully toward the door.

It was easier to relax and let him tug her along beside him as they moved down the halls toward their destination. Spending time with Hallam wasn't unpleasant, even if he was more than a little irritable. She couldn't imagine what his life had been like in the years since the war; hell, she couldn't imagine what his life had been like during the war. Humans had long ago stopped trying to kill one another on a political level when the planet nearly became inhabitable. People were too busy trying to survive rather than get upset about someone else's personal business or beliefs.

Hallam's pace was a bit faster than Ina was ready for when they turned a corner, and she didn't quite make it around. Her shoulder bumped into the wall and she stumbled. "Shit."

She gasped when he puller her into his arms for a moment before checking her over. "Are you hurt?"

"I'm fine. I just didn't see the corner."

It was strange not being able to see his face clearly, and yet know that he was upset with himself for his carelessness. "I did not take that into account."

"It's fine. I just bumped the corner. You don't need to be upset."

"I'm not upset." He flexed his grip on her shoulder, the tension in his body radiating from him. "I will be more cautious."

True to his word, Hallam slowed his pace and kept her close to his side for the rest of the journey. That helped Ina relax and let her take in more of her surroundings. The air in this part of the building was warmer and smelled slightly of antiseptic. There were more computer monitoring sounds as well. Beeps and clicks echoed from various parts of the room Hallam led her into, and she could make out the vaguest impression of what she assumed were beds along the wall as they passed.

Hallam stopped and moved her hand so she could feel the edge of a chair. "Sit here and rest while I tend to my patients."

"Sure." There really wasn't much else she could say or do, and the last thing she wanted was to get in the way of someone's medical care. But after a few minutes of sitting in silence, Ina's nerves kicked in, making her chest tighten as an unexpected wave of anxiety hit her. God, things were moving too fast for even her to keep up and adjust to, and having long stretches of quiet weren't currently the best for her brain.

"The Grus male had injuries that were accidently caused by a cyborg." Hallam's voice wasn't too far away from her, and hearing his even tone helped her relax. "I'm preparing his body to be sent back to Grus Prime for his family to mourn."

"What's Grus Prime?"

"The station that orbits Zarlan, the planet you're currently on." There were some noises, something that sounded like a vacuum and a bag being sealed. "May he find the peace I didn't."

It shouldn't break her heart to hear him sound so dejected, but it did. "I hope you someday find the same."

Hallam let out a soft grunt. "The next patient I have is cyborg. I'll be communicating with him via our cybernetic link. After that, we can return to the others."

"Okay." And after that, she'd have to figure out what her next steps would be here on the planet.

Rather than sit there and do nothing, Ina stared at a shape in the room and did her best to focus her vision on it in the hope of improving her sight. She was starting to be able to see outlines, but even after several minutes of intense concentration, she didn't feel as though she'd made any progress. Yes, things would get better for her, but she hated having to wait.

A loud beep filled the room and she jumped from the suddenness of the noise. "God, what was that?"

"Communication from Grus Prime." From the sound of Hallam's voice, he wasn't pleased. "Yes, Commander Aidric. What can I do for you?"

"I received your notification about the death of our technician." Ina shivered at the cold tone from the man speaking. No wonder Hallam didn't like the Grus who lived in the station if this was how they were treated. "We'll be sending a shuttle down to retrieve him."

"Did you consider my request?" There was an odd note in Hallam's voice that Ina couldn't quite figure out. "The cyborg in question is currently waiting judgement in the prison."

"You know it's impossible for me to grant him clemency. Other Fallen will see it as an excuse to do whatever they want to the Grus with expectation of retaliation."

"This man's death was his fault. He used my Fallen brother as a means to an end. It was a purely selfish act." Even Ina who barely knew him and couldn't see, wasn't blind to Hallam's anger and frustration as it bubbled over.

Ina got to her feet and carefully made her way toward where she believed Hallam stood. Ignoring her fear and uncertainty, she reached for him and smiled when she felt the solid warmth of his back against her hand. "You did everything you could to help him."

"Ah." Aidric's voice was now coming from directly in front of her. "I should have realized your mate was there."

She felt Hallam tense under her hand. "My name is Ina."

"A pleasure to meet you." Aidric sighed. "How is Rykal making out with the Kraken? Have they been successful unloading the stasis tubes?"

"We will be checking in on them after I've seen to my patients." Hallam leaned back against Ina's hand, as though he were drawing strength from her touch.

"Have Rykal send me an update as soon as he can. I've been keeping the High Council at bay, but they grow more demanding by the hour."

"Maybe you could distract them by asking to grant a cyborg lenience?" She made sure to smile and cock her eyebrow, hoping she'd get her point across to the alien commander. "Just a thought."

She heard Aidric snort. "I'll take it under advisement."

"Thank you." She grinned.

"Thank you, Commander. We'll check on them now." She felt Hallam reach forward and the call was disconnected. "That was unnecessary."

"Or it might have worked. They won't learn to see you differently if you don't encourage them to try. Worst case, nothing changes, and the cyborg is killed. But if you're successful, then it means you've helped save another life."

She could tell he wanted to argue with her, but they were interrupted by another notification from the computer.

"Hallam?" Rykal's voice. "We need you and Ina back in the loading bay. Now."

"What's wrong?" Hallam turned and wrapped his hand around her arm, pulling her against him.

"We've removed ten of the stasis tubes from the ship. They're starting to shut down. The women are dying."

CHAPTER EIGHT

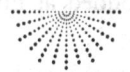

It had been a long time since Hallam had felt anything other than anger; and yet in the past few hours his emotions had flown from possessive desire, to annoyance and pride. Now, it was fear that drove him quickly down the hallway back to the transportation tube and the docking bay full of dying patients of alien physiology.

To make matters worse, Ina had gone silent.

He knew she was scared for her fellow humans, knowing how much they'd all given up coming out into the vastness of space. It could very easily have been her in one of those tubes, still sleeping while her body was being shut down. The thought of Ina being in there turned Hallam's stomach and drove him forward faster.

The moment the door to the loading bay opened, he was hit by the chaos of the situation. Aerin was directing their technicians to computer terminals, while Rykal and Lena were working on a tube that was shouting alarm claxons.

Rykal looked up the second Hallam entered. *It looks like we're not going to have a choice when it comes to which tube is opened next.*

"What's happening?" Ina ran out of his grasp and immediately into a medical tool tray that was off to the side. "Fuck!"

"Let me guide you to a chair." He could feel her frustration as if it were his own. "I'll keep you informed of what's happening."

Bring her over to Lena. She might be able to help. Rykal grabbed a chair and moved it beside his mate, who he whispered something to. Lena looked up and nodded at him. "Ina, I need your help over here!"

"Thank God." Ina's mutter was barely audible, even to his cybernetic hearing.

Hallam helped her over to her friend, but the moment he tried to walk away from her the possessive rage threatened to well up again. With each step from her side, he had to fight back the desire to go back to her, to push all others away, keeping her all to himself. It took effort for him to march to the closest terminal and type in his confirmation code to see what was happening. The details flicked past him, but he was having difficulty focusing.

It becomes easier once you've marked her, Rykal said through the cybernetic link. *The pain lessens, the urge to destroy everything in your path so you can get back to her. Your connection strengthens, deepens.*

Hallam couldn't imagine anything more powerful that what he currently felt toward her. *That will destroy me.*

It will make you better. Each of us becomes more than we were with our mates by our side. You'll see.

We need to determine what's happening with these stasis tubes. Taking a moment to collect himself, Hallam pushed past his primal side and looked once again at the readings coming from the stasis tube. "The female inside is showing reduced, but stable life signs. If we don't regulate the power surges coming into the tube, we'll have to bring her fully out of stasis or risk her dying."

Lena let out a frustrated shout. "I've got two more tubes surging."

Ina was up, out of her seat and standing by Lena's side. "Just because I can't see doesn't mean I can't be helpful. What are the readings?"

"It's bouncing between six thousand and fifteen thousand watts. The units aren't designed to handle that kind of surge." Lena stepped around Ina to get to the stasis tube. Her face pinched in a frown as she pressed a sequence of buttons. "This one's going to overload."

Hallam saw the life signs of the tube's occupant flicker and drop briefly before they came back to normal. "She needs to be removed before that happens."

"We can't pull all the women from stasis." Rykal looked over at him and narrowed his gaze. *We need to strictly control those of us who are mated to these women until they've adjusted.*

We might not have a choice in the matter.

Figure something out. If all the Fallen's leaders become violent because of an outside factor, the Grus high council will see this as an opportunity to clamp down on all of our people, saying we're not in control. Or worse. They'll decommission us all.

Hallam knew Rykal was right. "We need to find a way to stabilize the tubes."

Ina slammed her hands on the computer console. "It's got to be incompatibility with the power inputs. Our physiologies might be similar, but our technologies clearly aren't."

"Okay, we can do this." Lena looked over at Rykal. "You and Ina can try and figure out how to make the power work between our systems and I'll work with Hallam and Aerin to stabilize Tara's life signs."

Hallam thought he had everything under control, until Rykal took a single step toward Ina. The roar that came from him felt otherworldly as he flew at Rykal. His fist connected with Rykal's jaw, which caught him off guard and sent them both tumbling to the floor. Hallam was instantly aware of shouting and hands grabbing at his body to pull him from Rykal, who hadn't done anything to defend himself. But when there was a tiny bit of separation between them, Rykal lunged forward and pressed Hallam to the floor.

It was then that Hallam began to calm, Rykal scowling in his face. *I've given you space and forgiveness to this point. I understand your struggle. But if you don't get yourself under control, I will put you down myself.*

Hallam closed his eyes and focused on his breathing, trying to quell the rage. "It's too strong."

"No, it's not. You faced worse on the battleground with the Sholle. I won't touch her. I won't do anything to her that I wouldn't want another do to my mate. She's yours and you're hers, but now is not the time to assert your dominance. You have a life to save, so *fracking* save it!"

Ina squatted down beside him placed a hand on his shoulder. "Hallam?"

The concern in her voice was painful for him to hear. "I'm sorry."

"Help me back to the terminal."

Rykal let him go and Hallam was able to slowly get back to his feet. He ignored the confused looks from his staff, and the concerned look from Aerin. All he could focus on was Ina and doing what needed to be done to save the human woman inside the failing tube. Her touch immediately calmed him, making it easier to concentrate on what needed to be done. "The terminal is here. I need to check the tube itself."

"Good." Ina smiled at him. She wrapped her fingers around the edge of the terminal. "If we can't figure out our power issue, we might have to wake her up in a hurry. You'll need to be ready to help her if that's the case."

Hallam gave himself to the count of three to get himself under control. He took a deep breath and straightened, forcing his mind to the place of calm where he'd gone in the past during war time. Ina was here and no one would touch her. She needed him to be strong, to be in control of his actions so everyone would come out the other side of this alive. Locking his attention on the stasis tube, he looked for any fluctuations in the patient's vitals and kept an eye on the stasis tube power signals.

"There's an odd reading coming off this unit." He ran a scan, trying to pinpoint what might be causing it. "It's acting like a beacon."

"That's what the Sholle picked up through subspace." Rykal joined him, their altercation already forgotten. "Show me."

Hallam brought the signal up on the screen. "The stasis tubes aren't sophisticated technology. They shouldn't have the capability of sending a signal at all, let alone one that's penetrating into deep space."

Rykal leaned in closer to examine it "It's as though the signal from the units are harmonizing with something else that's boosting their natural state."

"That's possible." Ina shook her head. "I mean we only have the elements found on Earth and Mars. It's possible that something exists out here that acts as a natural amplifier. Stranger things have happened."

"I thought the whole point of bringing the Kraken here was because this building is dampening the signal, preventing it from getting out." Lena slapped the side of the stasis tube. "I need to know if my passengers are going to be okay, or if we're about to unleash the horny cyborg apocalypse when we have to wake everyone up at the same time."

Ina cocked her head, and Hallam could feel her working through the problem. "What if the signal and our power issue are actually two sides of the same problem?"

That got everyone's attention. Lena came beside her. "What do you mean?"

"The stasis tubes were fine until we got here, right? We've been traveling through deep space for decades without any hint of a problem, or any attraction from other lifeforms.

"That's right. We flew past everyone unnoticed. We didn't have a single malfunction, which is surprising as hell."

Ina nodded. "There's something here that's amplifying the signal. It might be the same reason why Rykal became aware of you when the ship entered this sector. It could also be the reason why now that the signal is basically trapped in this facility the stasis tubes are starting to short. They're being bombarded in some sort of weird feedback loop."

Hallam wasn't an engineer, but he didn't need to be one in order to understand what Ina was implying. "We need to find the source of the feedback and block it before all the stasis tubes shut down."

"I need Ina's help to do this." Rykal turned to Hallam. *Brother, I need to be near your mate. She's the best chance we have at finding the source of this problem, but she's still blind. I'll need to guide her.*

He knew what Rykal was saying, even understood how important this was. Still, Hallam didn't know if he was strong enough to keep his emotions in check, to give up control and put Ina in someone else's hands so she could make this better. He looked over at where she stood and was surprised to see her looking back at him.

There was something in her expression that said *trust me, I can do this.* But more than that, there was the realization that *he* needed to let her do this. That he needed to relinquish the control he'd so desperately tried to cling to since his rebirth had been forced upon him. This was Ina's problem to solve, hers and Rykal's. Hallam only needed to do his part, to help his patient if she needed it, and let the others do their jobs.

He nodded to Ina, hoping she could see him and turned his attention back to the stasis tube. *Do what you need to do. I won't get in the way.*

Rykal didn't wait a second longer and moved to stand beside Ina. "What do you think might be causing the feedback?"

"It has to be a substance that we don't have on Earth. Something that has some sort of reflective properties that are dense enough to bounce back our signals. A reflective substance, like a polished mirror, or glass. I can't fucking see well enough yet to be able to figure that part out."

Hallam didn't need to be connected to Ina's emotions to know how frustrated she was. But unlike himself, she was able to push past her frustrations and refocus. "Let's try it this way. Lena, can you link the base computer to the one on the Kraken?"

"Yup, just give me a minute."

"Rykal, if you can run a scan on the loading bay and compare the metals and minerals that are present here that are not listed on the Kraken's database, then we might be able to narrow down who our culprit might be."

Hallam would have listened more to her plan, but the alarm on yet another stasis tube sounded off. Aerin raced over to him and they shared a look. They were going to lose this tube in the next few minutes if they didn't act now. Not bothering to ask for permission, Hallam looked over the controls for the tube and initiated what he hoped was the activation sequence.

"What the hell are you doing?" Lena shouted at him from the ship.

"We need to wake her up now, or she's going to die." He reached out to Rykal, knowing he'd fill Lena in. *This tube is shutting down. If we don't pull her out of stasis right now, she won't make it.*

Do what you need to do to save her. We'll worry about the consequences later.

Hallam looked up at Aerin. "She might go into distress if we have to cut short the wake cycle. Do you have readings on the human physiology?"

"Yes. I took scans of Ina and Lena the moment they landed. I also saw the full cycle when they woke Ina up. Based on these readings we're not going to have time." Aerin looked over her shoulder where the others stood. "I can reprogram some nanobots to help jumpstart the patient's systems. It might help."

"Do it." Hallam turned his attention to the tube. "I'm going to open this now and pull her out."

The lock on the stasis tube was still engaged and wouldn't open until the cycle was complete. There appeared to be no way for him to initiate an emergency open, which meant he was going to have to physically force the lock apart. Using his enhanced eyes, he scanned the unit for any points of failure to exploit, finding one near the seam off to the right of the locking mechanism. Forcing it open would cause a blowback of gasses and fluids that wouldn't have drained; the noise would be powerful.

"I'm opening the stasis tube. This will be loud."

Hallam pulled his fist back and slammed it into the side of the tube, denting the metal and causing a small break in the seam. He punched it again and again until there was enough of a buckle that he was able to grasp the edge of the lid with both hands. Using the entirety of the strength held in his cybernetic arms, he pulled up. His arms shook from the strain and for a moment he didn't think he had the power to pull the metal apart. The loud groan of the lock straining to hold itself together increased, encouraging Hallam to keep going.

"You've almost got it!" Aerin was beside him, a nanobot injector in her hands. "That's it!"

The boom of the gasses exploding from the stasis tube slammed into Hallam the second the metal gave way. The force sent the cover flying, to slam into one of the computer terminals behind it. Hallam was prepared for the blast and only stumbled back a few steps.

He recovered and bolted back to his patient's side. "Help me get these tubes off her. They won't be able to retract normally."

They worked quickly to free the still sleeping woman as her vital signs began to fluctuate and drop. The computer alarm was joined by the sound of a second stasis tube going into a warning cycle. He looked over to Ina surprised to see her leaned over the terminal typing. "What's the status of blocking the feedback?"

"I've almost got it!" She pushed Rykal out of the way and moved over to another terminal. "Five minutes."

A third stasis tube warning alarm sounded as Hallam pressed the injector to the side of the woman's neck. "I'm not sure we have that long."

He pulled her free from the stasis tube and carried her over to the emergency bed in the back of the loading bay. *Aerin, bring a stimulant. The nanobots won't be fast enough to save her.*

Coming. She grabbed another injector and raced over. *This should work.*

I hope so. He pressed the second injector against the woman's neck, tossing it onto the medical tray. "Come on. Wake up."

Her skin looked sickly and lacked the warmth that both Ina and Lena shared. Her breathing was shallow, and her body trembled continuously from shock. Hallam ignored the rest of the alarms, knowing if he couldn't save this woman the chances of the others dying increased exponentially.

Aerin let out a frustrated groan. "She's not going to make it."

"Give me another stimulant shot."

"That might kill her."

"Then we're no worse off then we are right now." He held out his hand. "Quick."

Aerin prepared the injector and tossed it to him. Hallam didn't hesitate to press the injector to her neck. It took another five seconds before the woman gasped and her eyes flew open. She immediately began to thrash on the table, and it took them both to hold her down.

"Calm down. It will be okay."

The woman's eyes widened, and she screamed. "Help me! Someone help!"

Aerin made comforting noises, but it didn't seem to help. *She wouldn't be able to understand us yet.* "Lena!"

. . .

LENA JOINED THEM, quickly and gently placing her hands on the woman's shoulder. "Tara, Tara, it's okay. You're going to be okay. You're safe here. We're all safe."

Hallam backed away when the woman's vital signs stabilized and let Lena and Aerin do what they needed to help her. The rush from saving her life, from the intensity of the last few minutes had blocked everything else from him. It was only then that he realized the other alarms on the remaining stasis tubes had stopped and Ina and Rykal were leaning back against the wall.

Ina.

In those few moments, he'd also forgotten about his mate, about the overwhelming urge to possess and be with her. The urge was still there, but it was smaller now, tucked away in the back of his brain where the itching once resided. He started to come over to her, when she looked up and jolted.

"What's wrong?" He took another few steps closer, uncertain of what the emotions were that he felt coming from her. "Are you hurt?"

She shook her head, as she bit down on her bottom lip.

"Then what's happening?"

Rykal moved away when Hallam got close, giving them some privacy. Hallam cupped her face and looked into her eyes. It was then all the pieces fell into place. "You can see again. You can see me clearly."

She nodded, smiled and stepped into his arms.

CHAPTER NINE

Ina didn't have time to process the emotions churning inside her when she realized that she could see again. She'd been trying to tell Rykal how to run a comparison scan using the Kraken's systems when she pushed him away and did it herself. She was halfway through the scan when she realized what was happening, but then more alarms sounded, and any chance she had to think about the implications fled.

When they discovered the element that was causing the interference – something Rykal called *Netium* – she was able to adjust for it and stabilize the systems. There was nothing more she could fix, which left her with a few tense moments to stare at Hallam and his frantic attempts to save the woman in the stasis tube.

"She's not going to make it." Lena's breath caught in her throat, adding a quiver to her words. "Shit."

"Have faith. Hallam is one of the best doctors we have on the planet." Rykal squeezed his mate's shoulder. "If anyone can save her, he can."

Ina could feel Hallam's determination from halfway across

the room. She might as well have been plugged directly into his brain, she was so tuned in to his emotional state. There was no lack of confidence, no concerns that he didn't have the skills to save her. But what she did feel was a trickle of fear that despite all his abilities, they'd still fail, and someone would be without their mate.

Ina gasped when something surged inside Hallam, so powerful it could have been a physical blast against her chest. Aerin tossed something over to him which Hallam pressed against the woman's neck. In one moment, there'd been little signs of life, and in the next she was gasping and calling out for help.

Lena moved quickly to the woman's side, no doubt to offer the same reassurance that she'd given Ina when she'd been pulled out of stasis. But Ina was no longer interested in Lena, the woman, or even the Kraken's systems that had threatened to expose them all. The only thing she could see, could feel, was Hallam.

He looked up at her and as their eyes met, she felt his shock and pleasure when he knew she was finally able to see him. Ina moved around the side of the computer console and slowly walked over to where he stood. She took the time to memorize all the features about him that she'd been unable to see only a short time before. He stood only a little shorter than Rykal, but his hair was far longer, nearly down to his shoulders. It was black but had a bit of a blue tinge to it that seemed to accent his olive skin. But it was his eyes that took Ina's breath away. They were green and they glowed bright enough that she was able to see them from a distance. The closer she got, the more intense she found them, especially with his gaze locked fully onto her.

She stopped only a few feet away from him and smiled. "Hello." Her voice sounded breathy and she hated that it made her sound as though she were ready to fall into bed with him.

Even though that was not far from the truth.

"You've regained your vision." He didn't return her smile, but she could feel his relief. "It took longer than it should have with the nanobots."

"They had a lot of damage to repair." Now that the emergency had passed and she was healed, Ina didn't know what to say. "Is your patient going to be okay?"

Hallam nodded. "She'll need to adjust to her new world, but Lena seems capable of helping."

"That's good." Ina clasped her hands in front of her. "I think as more of us wake, it will be easier to wrap our heads around what's happening. Around what our new lives are going to be like."

"There will no doubt be an adjustment period for you all."

Something that Ina would have to deal with herself.

"Hallam?" Lena called over from where she stood with the woman. "Aerin is going to inject Tara with the nanobots unless you have any concerns."

He looked back at them, before nodding. "I want to make sure everything is okay with her, then you and I can pick up where we left off."

There was heat behind his words, a sexual promise of what would come next. Ina was somehow both thrilled and terrified at the prospect of spending the rest of her life with a man this intense. "Yeah, sure. You do what you need to. I'm not going anywhere."

She watched as he tended to his patient, which gave her time to think. This really was going to be for the rest of her life. There was no going back to Earth and the life she'd walked away from. Not that staying here would be a hardship, nor being with Hallam a problem, but everything suddenly felt *big*. She'd regained her vision, they had a new home with new people to get to know. She had a mate who despite all logic and reason she cared for after only knowing him for a few hours.

That shouldn't be possible. In Ina's experience, there was no such thing as love at first sight, or destiny. Shit, she hadn't even seen Hallam until a few moments ago, and yet she was standing here staring at him as though he was the most precious thing to her in the universe. Her life had always been about plans and paths, logic and reason. It's what made her a good engineer.

The thought of her surrendering to a force that she didn't believe in felt like a betrayal to her ideals.

Rykal came to stand beside her, no doubt watching Lena the same way she was watching Hallam. "You're a talented engineer. I'm sure we'll be able to use your skills once you've had time to learn our systems."

"Thank you." Ina breathed through the surge of adrenaline that still lingered through her. "I'll have a lot to learn."

Rykal looked down at her. She felt as though his glowing crystal blue eyes could see right into her soul. "You're handling this situation incredibly well. While I don't know your race well, if a Grus woman was in your situation, I can't imagine many of them would handle matters with the same level of grace that you've showed."

"That's because I'm silently freaking out on the inside." She let out a strained chuckled. "I know in my heart that Hallam and I are meant to be together, but my brain is pushing back against it. I've been awake for *hours*. Not days, or weeks. Nowhere long enough to even have a serious conversation with him about who he is, what his life is like, what kind of future he'd want to share. How is it possible that I feel as though he is the most precious thing in the world to me?"

"I don't know." Rykal shook his head. "I knew before I laid eyes on Lena that she was meant for me. That something in the universe had facilitated her arrival, a gift meant just for me. We haven't been together long, but I know it's exactly right. That we will both be happy for the rest of our days. Knowing that there are mates for my brothers, that the same connections and feelings that I share with Lena are waiting for them, makes all of the torment that we've collectively endured to this point worth it."

"But how – "

Rykal turned toward her. "The how and the why doesn't matter as long as you're happy. Life has given us a gift. One that we best not squander."

He left Ina standing there and went to Lena, who was now smiling down at Tara. Hallam stood close by, and she knew he wanted to be there as a support for the others, but that he wanted even more to be with her. That was at least something she could help him with. "Hallam?"

His gaze snapped immediately to her. "Do you need help?"

"I think I might need to lie down. My head isn't quite right." It wasn't exactly a lie. She had so many thoughts and feelings swirling around inside her just then, Ina was certain she'd get washed away by it all. "Unless you're needed, could you show me where the room is?" She almost said *our room* but couldn't quite get the words to come out.

Rykal shrugged. "Aerin is here if we have a problem. You two should have some time alone."

Relief washed through Ina as Hallam walked away from the others and held out his hand for her to take. "I'd like to examine your eyes as well. I want to make sure the nanobots have done their job properly."

Not that they needed the excuse, but it felt good to have a logical reason to spend time together. *He's your mate. You don't need to pretend any longer.*

Ina fell into an easy walk beside Hallam, marveling at how large his cybernetic hand was wrapped around her fingers. "Now that I can see you, I'm finding it hard to reconcile the image I had of you in my head with the reality."

"Is that a problem? What I look like?"

"No, not at all. It's just…" She held up their joined hands and looked at them. "You felt warm and real. I knew you were a cyborg because I was told that, but I guess it hadn't fully registered in my head. Seeing your cybernetics drives that reality home. I can't imagine the pain you must have been in to have warranted this amount of cybernetic replacement."

Hallam kept his gaze forward as they continued to walk. "I was inexperienced when it came to war."

Ina's chest tightened when the weight of his words descended on her. "I don't think anyone is truly ready for war."

"The Grus certainly weren't. Our high council had wanted to negotiate with the Sholle, the creatures who'd attacked our planet to strip it of our resources. Little did they know that they would have been better off trying to talk to a star. The Sholle did not care for us, our lives. Only for what resources they could pull from the soil and the air. We were little more than fodder thrown in front of the full force of their army. A vain attempt to slow them down long enough for someone to come up with a plan to stop them."

"And that was the man who used the dead and turned them into cyborgs?"

"Aidric." Hallam stiffened for a moment. "I'd been angry at him since the moment I'd opened my eyes after my rebirth. I'd never asked to be a part of war, of killing. I was a medic who wanted to become a doctor. I wanted to save lives, not take them. That choice was ripped from me, much as my arms and leg had been when I was caught in the explosion."

Her heart ached for him. "I'm so sorry you had to go through that."

"At the time, I believed it to be the end of my life. But now that I'm here with you, I can't help but wonder if there was something larger at work. That the only way I could get to you was to go through that pain."

"No. Don't say that." God, the thought of his suffering even slightly being connected to her, turned her stomach.

Hallam slowed his pace as he gave her hand a gentle squeeze.

"I say this now with a clear head. If that was the price I had to pay, I would pay it ten times over."

Ina swallowed past the sudden tightness of her throat, unable to say anything in response.

The twists and turns of the path they took through the corridors felt familiar, even if she'd never seen the gray crumbling walls with her own eyes before now. She knew that the door they had stopped in front of led to the room she'd previously been in, the bed that they'd shared a short time before. This was little more than four walls, but Ina knew she could make it a safe spot for them both. A place where they wouldn't need to fear the outside world, to worry about war and the repercussions of what might come from the Kraken's arrival in the sector.

This place was just for her and Hallam. A place where they could figure out what it meant for them to be mates, to see what path they were now on together. Ina pressed the button to open the door and stepped inside. There was little of Hallam's personality housed here, but perhaps that's because he too didn't know who he was.

Life had an odd way of throwing you for a loop, smashing your expectations, before making it difficult to put the pieces back together. Sometimes life even changed the puzzle on you, so you didn't know what the picture was supposed to be. But once you found the edges, made a line that you could work from, then things could slowly fall back into place.

Ina was that edge for Hallam. She knew that he'd been struggling silently with the weight of his war wounds far longer than he should have. The Grus used their dead to save their race but gave little thought of how to care for them afterward. While their relationship defied all logic and reason, Ina knew it was the right thing to do. She could help him find himself, discover who he was now beyond a cyborg.

He'd been waiting for her to come to him.

And perhaps, she'd found a new purpose for her life.

Ina turned back to him and held out her hand. "I don't understand how or why I was drawn here to you, but I'm happy I was. Let's learn what comes next together."

He smiled – a small barely there one, but a smile nonetheless – stepped forward and took her hand.

CHAPTER TEN

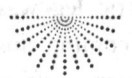

A shiver of desire raced through Ina's body as Hallam stepped past the threshold of the room and the door slid closed behind him. There was something wonderful about being away from the constraints of Earth's cultures. The expectations that surrounded sex, family and what relationships were supposed to be like, didn't apply here. The cyborgs accepted that the women from the Kraken were mated to them, that it didn't matter how short a time period they'd been together; they belonged to one another and fuck anyone who tried to get in their way.

While Ina's brain still might be rebelling at the thought of it, her body was completely on board. Her nipples were hard, and her pussy was wet knowing that in a few moments they would be stripped naked and holding one another on the bed behind her. She didn't have to justify her desires, didn't even need to make sense of them; Ina only needed for them to be and to accept Hallam's love and desire for what it was.

The soft glow from his cybernetics cast soft beams of light through the fabric of his uniform, and now that Ina was able to see it, she found it gave him a truly otherworld look. "Take your shirt off. Please?"

He cocked an eyebrow before doing as she'd asked. The damage to his body must have been extensive given how much of his torso had been replaced with enhancements. Both arms and part of his chest had been replaced, and she could even see the top of where his cybernetic leg was fused with his hip. Ina couldn't stop herself from coming close to him to reach out and run her fingers along the warm surface.

"When I couldn't see, I wasn't able to really tell which parts of you were real and which were machine."

"Aidric continued to make modifications to our systems over the initial few years after the war. I'd always assumed he was trying to find a way to make us more efficient killers. But there were aspects of his changes that were more…impractical. Like making our limbs warm."

"He was trying to give you a little bit of your life back."

"He was trying to assuage his guilt." Hallam reached up and ran a hand through her hair, his fingers getting caught in her curls. "I don't want to talk about him any longer."

Ina shivered. "Okay."

He fisted his fingers in her hair, and the strength of his touch pulled a soft gasp from her. He'd been so gentle with her that first time, and she couldn't help but wonder if that had been because she'd lacked sight, lacked the ability to defend herself. Now that she was able to see again, would sex with Hallam be different, be rawer than before?

God, she hoped so.

He tugged her head back exposing her neck to him. Ina didn't try to fight against it, instead letting her body melt against his hold. Hallam lowered his mouth to the junction of her shoulder and neck, the spot he'd bitten before and licked along the skin and fabric. "You're mine."

She moaned. "Yes."

"I'm going to mark you again so no other man will touch you." He moved his free hand to cup her breast, squeezing it hard. "I want to hear you scream with pleasure."

Shit, Ina knew there was going to be a whole lot of that if he kept doing what he was doing. Her legs began to quiver, and she had to fight against the urge to rip her clothing off so she could feel her skin pressed against his. Thankfully, whatever connection they had, Hallam was aware of her desires and started removing her clothing. It didn't take long for her to kick off her boots and push herself free of the offending material, to leave her blissfully naked.

Hallam's gaze traveled down her body, lingering on her breasts, her neck, the swell of her hips. His fingers followed the path as he touched random parts of her, flicking her nipples, teasing her sides, cupping her pussy so the pressure from his hand was firmly against her clit. Ina moaned and had to lean forward against him for fear of her legs giving out on her. Hallam didn't hesitate and scooped her into his arms, carrying her over to the bed.

As he laid her down, Ina stretched out wide, putting herself on display for him. She was growing addicted to the way his eyes would flare when he stared at her, the glow of his cybernetic eyes flashing visibly brighter as his arousal pulsed. He didn't look away from her body as he removed his remaining clothing, leaving them both finally naked. It was then that she was able to see not only all his cybernetic limbs, but the inside of his biological leg. There was a dark green patch that appeared swollen and flared out.

"What's that?" She sat up to get a better look.

"That's my *rondella*. It one of our sex organs." He put his hands back into her hair and tugged her face closer to his cock. "I had thought it dead after my rebirth, but your presence has brought it back to life. Brought me back to life."

"So, if I touch it, you're going to get aroused?" Oh, that was something she liked the sound of. "Lucky me that I'm able to see it now."

"I believe that I'm the lucky one." There was that small, wry smile of his. Ina couldn't help but wonder if Hallam had depths to his sense of humor that he hid from everyone, or if her presence woke that part of him as well.

That was a question to be answered on another day.

Right then, the only thing Ina cared about was Hallam's erect cock bobbing tantalizingly close to her mouth. She looked up and held Hallam's gaze as she moved forward and sucked the tip of his cock into her mouth. His nostrils flared, the only indication of his approval of the way she swirled her tongue around his tip. It was hard to hold back her grin, suddenly overwhelmed with joy and arousal, knowing that she was able to make him happy.

Ina wrapped her hand around his shaft and began to slide her fingers up and down the length of him as she sucked and licked his cock. Her eyes eventually drifted closed as she continued to work him over, loving the way she could feel his body tremble as she continued to arouse him. She shifted again, this time moving so she had access to his *rondella*, curious as to what would happen if she stroked it as well.

The first brush of her fingers along the obviously sensitive skin ripped a groan from Hallam. The hand in her hair tightened but didn't move to pull her away from any of his erogenous spots. Okay then, that was permission enough to keep going. Ina scraped her nails along his *rondella*, making swirls along the skin with one hand as she continued to fist his cock with the other. She took more and more of him into her mouth, until she was scared that she'd get dizzy from lack of oxygen. But she didn't want to stop, not when Hallam was moaning and moving in rhythm with her ministrations. His body vibrated and she could feel his arousal growing as her movements grew more frantic and purposeful.

His cock somehow hardened even more in her mouth, and for

a moment she thought he was going to come. Hallam even groaned and she felt his *rondella* pulse beneath her fingertips, but there was no other sign of his orgasm. He did step away from her, gasping. "I don't know how you're able to do that. It shouldn't be possible."

"What?"

"My pre-orgasm. It's the sort of thing that only Grus can experience. A necessary physical function of being able to procreate."

Ina sat back, giving her head a little shake. "You mean you're able to have children?"

"No, it shouldn't be possible." But based on the look on his face, he didn't appear to believe that.

Ina hadn't considered the possibility of children before now. It was never something she'd necessarily wanted for herself, especially given the condition of life for most people on Earth. It wasn't that she had any concerns about being a mom – she thought she'd be a pretty good one – but until this moment it hadn't seemed a likely scenario. "Is there anything we need to do to prevent conception?"

"I'm still not even sure if our two races are biologically compatible in that way. Your nanobots can be activated to prevent a pregnancy if we discover that's something you don't want."

"I haven't thought about it. Not really."

Hallam dropped to his knees and placed his hands on her legs. "Would it be something you might want. Someday?"

"Yes." The answer came from her quickly, but it was honest. "I'd never wanted to bring a child into life back on Earth. It had felt cruel. But here with you, yes. I think I'd love that if it were to happen."

Hallam's eyes slipped closed for a moment as he nodded. "Then we'll let the universe decide our fate."

"It hasn't led us astray so far." She smiled. "Come here."

Hallam didn't hesitate to climb on top of her, covering her fully with his body. His cock pressed hard against her pussy, and it only took a slight adjustment to allow him to push fully inside her. It felt amazing to be so full, to have his shaft stretch her pussy and hit all the hidden parts of her that she loved to feel touched. Her clit was hard, swollen from her arousal and Ina knew it would take very little to pull her orgasm out of her.

One moment Hallam was on top, and then the next he rolled them so she was riding him. Her breasts hung low and with him below her his hands were freed up to be able to touch and pinch her nipples. He leaned up and sucked one pink tip into his mouth, teasing the nub with his tongue.

"Yes," she said, little more than a sigh as she ground down hard on his cock. "More."

Her pussy clenched around him as she continued to ride him, now more than ever focused on chasing her pleasure. Hallam knew exactly where, when and how she needed to be touched, making her orgasm a foregone conclusion. She relaxed into the sensations and let the pleasure rise, crest to a point where she'd be overcome.

The first wave of her orgasm started off small, a ripple of delight that heated her nerves and blasted away any lingering darkness. The second wave was far stronger and pulled a shout from her before stealing what remained of her breath. Her pussy squeezed around his cock and Hallam's fingers dug into her hip and side as she rode out her orgasm. The second she was done, he flipped them once again, regaining the dominant position. He looked down into her eyes, forcing her to focus through the haze of pleasure on him.

"Mine." His smile wasn't subtle, nor was his happiness.

Hallam thrust into her hard and fast as he lowered his face to her neck. She felt his mouth on her skin, nipping and licking at the spot he'd bit earlier. He would do it again, this time so everyone would know that this mark was his, that she was his.

Ina didn't care, even took a perverse pleasure in knowing that she'd wear his mark. If she'd ever had any doubt that she belonged to Hallam and him to her, it was gone now.

It only took a few hours of being blind to see exactly what she needed from life.

When Hallam's body shivered and she felt his mouth clamp down on her neck, rather than tense and fight it, she relaxed into the pain. The surprise came when that pain morphed into a pleasure so bright and strong that a second equally powerful orgasm slammed into her. She cried, riding the sensations until she was no longer able to think. The only thing that existed was Hallam and the feelings he elicited inside her. He thrust harder and she was suddenly aware of him coming, a scent filled the air as his come filled her body. She was bathing in everything about him, knowing him on a level that she'd never experienced with another being.

Finally, blessedly, they both stopped at the same time.

Hallam's breathing came out in short, sharp gasps and he wrapped his body around her, pulling her into a deep embrace. She'd never felt so protected or loved in her entire life. Resting her ear against his heart, she listened to the steady beat and let it lull her to sleep. When she woke some time later, she was surprised to find that they hadn't moved, but a blanket now covered her body.

"Did I snore?" She placed a kiss to his chest, firmly on the cybernetic plate.

"If snoring is the loud noise that came from your mouth, then yes. I was growing worried that I'd broken you."

She chuckled. "Not broken. Just bad genetics."

"It was endearing." He ran his fingers through her hair. "I have developed a tremendous affection for you. Something that I wouldn't have imagined possible given how briefly we have known one another."

Ina smiled against his chest. "I think I might love you too."

"It's...strange to have such emotions this quickly." He hummed low in his chest. "It's strange for me to have any emotions beyond anger. They had been removed from my rebirth."

"This is good, right?"

"Most definitely." He reached down and tipped her chin up so she had to look him in the eyes. "I love you, Ina. I'm so happy the universe brought you into my life. For the first time since my rebirth I feel whole."

Yes, that was it exactly. She'd had a part of her missing for so long, she's assumed that there was something wrong with her. All along, she'd been missing her mate. "I love you too."

Time didn't count when it came to matters of the heart. Ina knew that this was exactly where she wanted to be, and that Hallam was who she wanted to be with. Everything else, they'd figure out as they went along.

EPILOGUE

Hallam stepped into the security area of the prison and waited for the scan to be completed. He'd been surprised when he'd received Aidric's communication to join him here, but the brief yet urgent wording made it such that he couldn't say no. Ina had only smiled and pushed him out of bed when he'd begun to grumble about leaving her.

"Just because I'm around doesn't mean you're allowed to shirk your responsibilities."

They'd only been together a few days now and so much had happened in that short period of time it was difficult for him to process the implications of it all. Everything felt right with Ina in his life, calmer in a way he was certain he'd never felt even before his rebirth. The fact that he'd held so much anger deeply inside him for so long and was now free of it felt as though a weight had been forever lifted from him.

The prison security scan finished, and the all clear signal was given. The blast doors opened, revealing Aidric standing in the middle of the smaller antechamber. The Grus commander looked every bit as neat and collected as he ever did, but there was something off about him. Perhaps Hallam wasn't used to seeing the man in person and not over a communication screen. Or perhaps there was something going on that he was unaware of.

"Commander." He nodded respectively at Aidric. "I was surprised to receive your request."

Aidric's soft blue gaze raked over Hallam's face. "I see you've finalized your bond with your mate. That's good."

Hallam was only slightly surprised at the acknowledgment. "Ina has brought light to my life. I didn't know you'd come down to the planet. Is Rykal aware?"

Aidric looked away. "I'm not obligated to tell my brother of my movements."

Interesting. "But you are obligated to inform the leader of the Fallen that a dignitary is here."

Aidric snorted. "I'm no dignitary."

If he was on the planet and Rykal wasn't aware, that meant he was trying to do something off the record. "What can I do to help?"

"I came to meet with Zee regarding your cyborg patient and his decommissioning."

Hallam felt his eyes go wide. "I wasn't expecting you to put yourself out that way."

"I couldn't exactly make these sorts of arrangements over the coms." Aidric lifted his chin slightly. "Word of this couldn't get back to the high council. It wouldn't benefit anyone."

"No, it wouldn't." No, if it became public knowledge that a cyborg who'd taken the life of a Grus – accidently or not – could live, chaos would ensue. "Why do you need me here?"

Aidric's entire demeanor changed. His body stiffened and the muscle in his jaw jumped. "Come with me."

Hallam followed Aidric through the corridors, past the security monitors and hidden weapons ports. He knew that in the event of a breakout, this hallway would become a death trap to any creature who dared step food inside. They didn't speak as Hallam became more tense the longer the silence stretched on.

Turning a corner, they entered a small office where Zee, the warden of the Zarlan maximum security prison stood. His dark olive skin nearly shone in the low light of the room. His bald head highlighted the cybernetic plate that comprised a part of his skull.

Zee had died in battle, not from a wound given to him by the Sholle, but from a blaster shot from a Grus soldier who'd betrayed him. Hallam nodded at him in greeting. "I can tell from the look on your face that we have a problem."

"We do." Zee's deep voice held unmistakable contempt.

"After we'd come to an arrangement regarding your patient," Aidric said as he sat at the chair by the door, "we were notified of a disturbance in solitary confinement."

Hallam narrowed his gaze. "Who?"

"Rennick." Zee spat the name as though it was a poison on his tongue.

Hallam couldn't imagine what it was like for Zee needing to keep the man who'd ended his life alive and cared for in his rebirth. He wasn't certain it was a task he'd be able to complete. "What's wrong with him?"

Aidric thumped his head against the wall behind him. "He has an itching in the back of his brain."

Shit. "The human we just woke from stasis."

Aidric nodded. "She's the mate of a murderer."

ACKNOWLEDGMENTS

Thank you everyone for reading, the first four novellas in the Cyborg Protectors series! I hope you enjoyed spending time with the cyborgs and their mates. These stories have brought me a lot of joy to write, and I'm so excited that more of their stories are coming to you in the near future. The next four novellas in the series are currently available in e-book and on KU and will soon be available in print format.

Cyborg Protector Series
  Book 1 – Consumed by the Cyborg
  Book 2 – Mated to the Cyborg
  Book 3 – Saved by the Cyborg
  Book 4 – Healed by the Cyborg
  Book 5 – Chained to the Cyborg
  Book 6 – Freed by the Cyborg
  Book 7 – Exposed by the Cyborg
  Book 8 – Redeemed by the Cyborg

ABOUT THE AUTHOR

Alyse Anders is the author of the Cyborg Protector series of erotic sci-fi novellas. When she's not sitting in front of her computer with her imagination stuck in a far away nebula, she's at home with her husband and two dogs, usually eating far too much chocolate for her own good. Check out more of Alyse's books on Amazon, KU or her website www.alyseanders.com.

CPSIA information can be obtained
at www.ICGtesting.com
Printed in the USA
BVHW071555170920
589008BV00004B/247

9 781777 038274